Sometime after catching his first shad and before tasting his first beer he'd tasted the softness of Libby Delacourte's mouth. And later, much later, in a sweltering vortex of heat and need and pubescent longing, he'd stepped across the line separating childhood from adolescence and pulled her along with him, leaving the former behind forever.

Russ Hennessey had loved her. It was as simple as that. He'd loved her from the time she was seven years old, and she'd repaid his devotion by leaving town with Eric Richards, without so much as a word of explanation or even a goodbye. She'd carried the guilt of her behavior around for years, imagining a dozen different scenarios by which she could absolve herself. It appeared her time was nearly at hand.

JEANETTE BAKER

Chesapeake Tide

MIRA®

ISBN 0-7783-2049-9

CHESAPEAKE TIDE

Copyright © 2004 by Jeanette Baker.

www.MIRABooks.com

Printed in U.S.A.

ACKNOWLEDGMENTS

I'd like to thank Peter Riley for his expertise on the subjects of PCBs and water pollution, Dorothy Farrell, my mother-in-law, for her help with the title *Chesapeake Tide* and, of course, my husband, Stephen Farrell, for his attention to detail.

One

Elizabeth Jane Delacourte had married down. It had taken her some time to admit it. Seventeen years, to be exact. But now that she had, there was no getting around it, no polite way of excusing the obvious or mincing words, even if she had wanted to sugarcoat the truth.

Her epiphany came upon her suddenly, two months after her divorce was final. She woke one day in the bedroom of her lakeside Southern California condominium and looked around at the trappings of her life: the beige walls and the beige carpet; the sterile pretentiousness of her green faux-leather couch and chairs, Eric's choice, not hers; the Formica bar separating the dining area from the kitchen nook; the sliding glass door and aluminum window frames; the wood-veneer countertops and cabinets; the solarium entry; the photos of Chloe at various stages of her life; and the king-size bed that now slept one. She realized what she should have accepted long before. She'd made a mistake.

Not that she hadn't been warned. The Beauchamps, her mother's people, dark-haired, golden-skinned, thin-lipped, temperamental, exotic and venomous as tropical lizards, hailed from the Louisiana Delta, where voodoo was still considered a religion. They'd passed down their powers of observation to Libby's mother, Nola Ruth—powers she'd brought with her to Marshyhope Creek, Maryland, all those years ago. She'd taken one long look at the golden beauty and Colgate smile of the young actor who'd taken up residence in Marshyhope Creek for the summer, and pronounced him unsuitable to grace her table, much less call on her only daughter. Libby's father, a personal-injury attorney who could never quite meet his wife's expectations because of his penchant for accepting nonpaying clients, rarely sided with his wife. This time he did.

But Libby, seduced by the lights of Hollywood, a northern accent and a brilliant white-capped smile, defied them both. She called up the rebellious streak that made its frequent and regular appearance at defining points of her life, turned her back on Marshyhope Creek and the people who loved her, and eloped. Before the honeymoon was over her lust had dried up and she found herself tied to a boy too immature, too self-absorbed and too shallow to assume the role of husband at any time in the present or near future.

Libby did not consider herself a martyr, nor was she lacking in intelligence. What then had kept her three thousand miles away from her home, mired in the trappings of a loveless marriage? Again, the answer came to her on the very heels of her question. It was pride. All the Delacourtes had their share of pride, and Libby, with her Beauchamp genes from her mother, had a double dose.

It was Eric who finally ended it. "Things just aren't the same," he'd told her. She'd stared at him, wondering what he referred to, considering that he'd spent no more than a total of thirty days in a row in her presence for the whole seventeen years of their marriage. She kept silent, however, for fear he might change his mind and that she might, in a moment of remorse, allow him to come back.

She sighed, looked at the clock, turned off the alarm, pounded the pillow and burrowed down into the covers. She had another fifteen minutes before it was time to wake Chloe for school, another fifteen minutes to mull over the direction of her life.

What she really wanted, if she was perfectly honest, was to relegate her soon-to-be ex-husband to the postage-stamp part of her brain that deserved to be lobotomized and move on as if she'd never known him. She would have done it, too, quite easily, if it weren't for Chloe, difficult, frustrating, sixteen-year-old Chloe, her only child, the feminine image of her beautiful, absentee father who had recently decided to reinstate himself in his daughter's life.

Libby's stomach rumbled. She rested her hand on her waist and squeezed a full inch of flesh between her thumb and first finger. The significance of that inch came upon her slowly. Panicking, she threw the covers aside, jumped up, stepped out of her pajamas and positioned herself sideways in front of the full-length mirror. Once again she pinched the flesh of her stomach, this time rolling the offending inch between her fingers. She sucked in her stomach, and pinched again. Better. Only a half inch this time. Keeping her muscles tight she walked into the bathroom and stepped on the scale. Immediately, the audio voice responded, "One hundred twenty-six pounds."

It was Eric's scale and she intended to get rid of it this very day. Only a man would devise a scale that pronounced a woman's weight out loud to the world. What woman in her right mind would want that kind of deeply personal information broadcast so that anyone in the vicinity of her entire fourteen-hundred-square-foot condominium could hear it?

"That does it," she fumed, stepping off the offending machine. "I've had it. Time to get serious. No more Starbucks caramel Frappuccinos. No more bagels and cream cheese from the deli and no more carbs after five o'clock at night."

She turned on the water in the sink, found her toothbrush, squeezed a hint of Extra Whitening toothpaste on the bristles and marched into Chloe's room. "It's seven o'clock," she said firmly, and waited.

Chloe didn't budge. Libby sat on the side of her daughter's bed and pulled the comforter aside with her free hand. "You told me to wake you half an hour earlier than usual."

Chloe's voice, muffled and thick with sleep, drifted out from behind her hair. "I changed my mind."

"It's too late for that," said her mother.

"Why?"

"Because you've been to Saturday school three times this month for tardies. You're running out of Saturdays. You'll be thrown out of summer school."

"Five more minutes," said Chloe.

Libby swallowed her toothpaste. "Sorry. Get up now."

No answer.

Libby's voice sweetened and lowered. The Delta-flavored accent she couldn't completely eradicate even after seventeen years in the golden state came back to her. "Do you know what they tell parents to do with children who are habitually late and won't get out of bed?"

"What?"

"Dump cold water over them and be sure the sheets get nice and wet."

Chloe sat up. Her eyes were sleep puffy. Silver hair framed her face like a halo. "You wouldn't," she said witheringly.

"Probably not," her mother agreed. "But I will ground you. You'll come straight home every day. No more after-school theater and no more dance class until you go a whole quarter without another tardy."

"Dad wouldn't let you do that to me," Chloe said smugly.

Libby's eyes flashed. "Try me."

Chloe shrugged a tanned shoulder and fixed slanted blue eyes on her mother. "Whatever."

"Are you getting up?"

"As soon as you leave."

Libby frowned.

Chloe sighed and threw the covers aside. "I'm naked. Do you mind leaving my bedroom so I can get up?"

"Of course not," Libby said, averting her eyes and hurrying to leave. She stopped at the door. "Why would you sleep naked?"

"You bought me T-shirt sheets. I can't feel them with pajamas and, besides, I was hot. This is California, not Siberia."

Libby left the room without answering. There was nothing more to say. Chloe's reasons were solid. There was nothing wrong with sleeping in the nude. Libby had done it herself, many times, but she hadn't been alone. Why was she disturbed that her sixteen-year-old daughter would choose to sleep without a stitch on? She would have to think about it, analyze it, resolve it. Libby was a great analyzer. She would isolate her feeling and diagnose the problem. Then she would dissect it, bit by bit, until it was stripped clean, bluntly exposed, the solution clear.

Forty minutes later she was still in the middle of the process when Chloe, fully clothed in her usual black, joined her in the kitchen.

She stared pointedly at her mother's grapefruit and black coffee. "Are you on another diet?"

"Good morning to you, too," Libby said brightly. "As a matter of fact, I am."

"Why?"

"I've gained six pounds."

Chloe dumped an indecent amount of Lucky Charms into her bowl and began picking out the marshmallow bits and popping them into her mouth. "Since when?"

Libby thought back to when she'd last been one hundred and twenty pounds. "I'm not sure. Three months, maybe four."

"You don't look any fatter."

"Thank you."

Chloe shrugged. "Don't thank me. It's the truth. You're

always obsessing over your weight, but your clothes fit and you always wear the same size." She licked her fingers. "Do you know what I think?"

"Please, enlighten me."

"I think you have an eating disorder."

Libby nearly choked on a mouthful of grapefruit. "You're joking."

Chloe shook her head. "We learned about them in school. You have all the symptoms." She ticked them off. "Obsession with weight, always thinking you're fat when you're not, starving yourself with weird diets that never make you look any different, checking labels on everything, feeling guilty when you eat something fattening in public. Face it, Mom. You're a classic case."

Libby's first reaction was to deny and her next was to retaliate. She was instantly ashamed of both. *Sixteen years old,* she reminded herself. *She's sixteen years old. You're above squaring off with your sixteen-year-old daughter.* She opted for maturity, swallowed and smiled. "That's very interesting. I'll keep your diagnosis in mind. Meanwhile, I'll watch what I eat for a while just to make sure those six pounds don't turn into ten."

"Whatever lifts your skirts," Chloe said.

Libby's eyes flashed pure fire. Her voice was soft and dangerous and very southern. "What did you say?"

Chloe yawned. "You heard me."

"Yes, but I was hoping I'd heard wrong. Wherever did you pick up that piece of vulgarity?"

"Daddy."

"I don't believe you. Your father is immature, lazy and selfish, but never vulgar."

Chloe stood, leaving her chair pulled out, and shouldered her backpack. "I'll relay the compliment. By the way, I'll be home late. I have a theater-club meeting and Daddy's picking me up for dinner."

"It's a school night," Libby reminded her. "Be sure he has you home early."

"How about eleven o'clock?"

"Nice try."

"What if I have all my homework done?"

Libby considered the request, mentally willing herself to be objective, something she had difficulty doing when it came to Eric. "Only if your homework's done. Otherwise it's nine o'clock and not a minute later."

"I don't know why you have to be this way," Chloe countered. "You never used to be unreasonable. It all started when Daddy came home for good."

Libby stood and began clearing the table. "I disagree. It's an age problem. Fortunately, it has time limits. Come here and kiss me goodbye or I won't be able to make it through my day."

Chloe groaned, reluctantly pecked her mother's cheek and walked out, slamming the door behind her.

Libby sighed, rinsed the dishes and stacked them in the dishwasher. A growing desire for independence was only a part of Chloe's recent rebellion. Most of their conflicts arose over Eric. Now that he'd decided to return to the West Coast permanently, Chloe was obsessed with him and with the perceived glamour of his lifestyle, neither of which Libby approved.

She picked up Chloe's box of Lucky Charms and absentmindedly reached in for a handful. Sanity returned before the bits of marshmallow and puffed wheat reached her mouth. Hastily she dumped the offensive particles into the garbage disposal and secured the dishwasher door. "I am *not* a classic case," she said, leaving the kitchen to collect her jacket and briefcase. She deliberately ignored her reflection in the full-length hall mirror and walked into the garage.

Libby, honest with herself more than she wasn't, felt the sting of Chloe's pronouncement. Not that she believed she had an eating disorder, but wasn't there something wrong when a thirty-seven-year-old woman was never satisfied with her appearance, when she kept checking her reflection in store windows and pulling out her mirror to reapply lipstick twice every half hour? When had she become so insecure over her looks? The question was a rhetorical one and she already had the answer. Elizabeth Jane Delacourte, golden girl, homecoming queen of Marshyhope Creek's lone high school, had thrown it all away for a man, and not just any man. She'd changed the direction of her life for Eric Richards, who, before the ink was dry on their marriage certificate, suggested, strictly for her benefit of course, that she was unsophisticated, frumpy and lacking in relevant conversation.

At first she'd believed him, and later, even when she knew better, even when she no longer cared what Eric thought of her, occasionally the old wound would throb. It was throbbing now that Chloe, her precious child, thought that her father, who'd shown virtually no interest in her until three months ago, walked on water.

The three lanes of the 101 Freeway North to Ventura were jammed with the usual rush hour traffic. Libby tapped her thumbs nervously on the steering wheel of her Toyota Corolla and blew a strand of hair off her forehead. It was unusually hot for July. California weather wasn't normally unbearable until August and September, but how could anyone predict the temperature in a state without seasons?

Her meeting was scheduled for eight-thirty and she was late. Like mother, like daughter. A new BMW cut her off. She slammed on her brakes and fumed silently. What was she doing living in this place where people ordered Coca Cola martinis and lined up with sleeping bags for the premier of a *Stars Wars* film, where the air quality on the best of days was only fair, where drinking water from the tap was a health risk, where the normal wait for a seat in a restaurant was at least two hours, where deluded mothers tossed aside their children's youth, paid thousands of dollars for headshots, drove countless miles to parade their sons and daughters before casting directors in the pathetic and vicarious pursuit of a three-second commercial blip.

Libby wanted out, but where would she go and, more to the point, *how* could she go now that Eric was taken with the idea of being a parent?

She turned into the parking lot of the Juvenile Court Building, pulled out her parking pass and pushed it into the receptacle. The gate lifted. She found her usual spot, grabbed her briefcase and raced inside.

Nora McCoy, assistant district attorney, had been frowning for quite some time. Libby could tell by the depth of the depressions on either side of her mouth. Nora wasn't happy, and revealing the contents of Libby's report to these warring parents wouldn't improve her mood.

"Sorry," Libby mouthed as she slid into the empty seat at the end of the conference table. She nodded at the two attorneys and their clients seated on either side.

Nora began the meeting with her usual introductions. "Mr. Irvine and Ms. Benedict, this is Elizabeth Delacourte, our expert on analyzing DNA samples. Libby, you already know both attorneys. Since we're pressed for time, I suggest that Ms. Delacourte present the results of the tests." She hesitated and cleared her throat. "May I say, before we begin, that there is a great deal more to parenting than a similar genotype. The child in question is six years old. Whatever happens here today will benefit no one. Mr. Irvine, you will still be responsible for child support and, Ms. Benedict, you are still required by law to allow visitation." She looked first at the grim-faced man and then at the woman who was not aging well. "Do I make myself clear?"

"Yes," said the parents simultaneously.

"Will you accept the ruling in this case?"

This time the man said, "Yes." The woman merely nodded. She would not meet Nora McCoy's eyes.

"Very well. Shall we proceed?"

Libby opened her briefcase, passed out six copies of her report and came right to the point. "This won't mean anything to you unless I interpret the numbers. Please, bear with me for a moment. Basically, there are eight areas we test when paternity is questioned. Let's start by looking at line one hundred. That sample of blood came from your son, Jeremy. Line two hundred is a sample from Mr. Irvine. We call these controls. Everything is measured according to these two lines. The numbers in the boxes are called alleles. These are found in different places on the DNA molecule. Related individuals have different intensities of the identical number, a lighter and darker six, for example. Unrelated individuals have four distinct numbers at one or more locations."

Libby drew a deep breath. This wasn't her typical case. She knew of no way to soften her conclusion. "In nearly every box, the alleles show four different numbers. Jeremy and Mr. Irvine are not biologically related."

A strangled sob rose from the man's throat. He covered his eyes. For long minutes the only sound in the room was the ticking of the clock on the wall. Finally, he lifted his head. "I knew it," he said. "I've always known it." He looked at his ex-wife, a doughy woman with orange hair, round sad eyes and thirty-five extra pounds around her middle, a woman well past the age of mothering a six-year-old. "How could you?"

Although no one was more than three feet away, collectively they strained to listen. "I wanted a baby," she whispered. "I was forty-two. My time was nearly up. Nothing was happening with us."

"Damn you," he said bitterly. "Who is Jeremy's father?"

The woman's voice was flat, deliberate, as if nothing mattered. "I don't know. I went to a sperm bank."

The man's eyebrows lifted. "You did what?"

"You heard me." She started to cry. "I was artificially inseminated."

Nora McCoy stood. "This matter, while relevant to the two of you, has no place here. As far as the court is concerned, Mr. Irvine is Jeremy's father. He is still responsible for child support and he is six months in arrears. The consequences for failure to pay are salary garnishment or jail. I'll leave the four of you here to resolve this matter." She collected her papers. "Libby, please join me in my office."

Without a word, Libby followed her out the door and down the long hall into a small room with a single desk, two chairs and a narrow window. "Dear God." She leaned against the wall and closed her eyes. "That was awful."

Nora poured two cups of coffee. "I've seen worse. It's all in a day's work around here."

Libby picked up the cup, wished it held something stronger than coffee, and drained it. "I can't take this anymore. This isn't what I want. I'm a biologist. I'm tired of being the voice of doom to people too selfish and immature to live up to their responsibilities."

"Be fair, Libby. It isn't always like this."

"Yes, it is. The circumstances are different but someone is always disappointed." She shuddered. "What could she have been thinking?"

"Who?"

"The mother."

"You heard her. She wanted a baby and it wasn't happening. She was desperate. Forty-two-year-old women have trouble getting pregnant, especially with indifferent husbands. She did what she had to do.

"We've all had high school biology, Nora. Any educated person would know that Jeremy couldn't have come from both of those people, one maybe, but not both. There are specific rules of genetics for which there are no exceptions and brown eyes aren't possible with her green and his blue.''

Nora McCoy grinned. ''Not all of us paid attention the way you did.''

Libby's cell phone rang. ''Excuse me,'' she said. ''I should take this.''

Nora waved. ''Take your time. I'll give you some privacy and see if anything's happened in the conference room.''

Libby settled into a chair, removed her earring and glanced briefly at the number in the window of her phone. Suddenly, everything stopped. Ignoring the persistent ringer playing ''Scotland the Brave,'' she stared at the number, her fingers unable to perform even the simple function of pressing the receive button. The song played itself through once and then stopped. Libby did not answer her phone. The number remained on her screen along with the message, *one missed call.* She waited another minute and pressed first her message button and then her password. There was nothing. With shaking fingers she pressed her call-back number.

''Hello.''

''Hello, Daddy.''

''Libba Jane?'' That voice, one she hadn't heard more than a dozen times in the last seventeen years, froze her into an alert stillness.

''Libba Jane,'' he said again. ''Is that you?''

''Yes.'' *How long had it been? A year, two years?* How much time had passed since she'd heard that familiar voice, soft on vowels, liquid of consonants? She'd lost track, preferring to forget the years of forbidding silence with only an occasional obligatory phone call.

''It's been a long time, honey.''

''A very long time.''

She could hear the tremor in his voice. ''It's your mama, Libba. She's had a stroke. It looks bad. She wants you home. She wants to see Chloe once again, before—'' He left his sentence hanging.

"Dear God."

"You need to forgive us, Libba Jane. We never thought you'd stay away for good. I'm sorry. We were wrong. Please, come home."

Home. Libby closed her eyes and the smells came back to her. The fishy, brackish odor of the Tidewater; sweet peaches ripening under an unforgiving sun; loamy, dank marshland; vanilla and sugar floating from the door of Curries Ice Cream Shop; old leather and dust from her father's library; lavender and magnolia, lemon wax, new grass. Today was a sign. The phone call was a sign. She was going home.

She blinked back tears. "I'll come."

"Thank God," her father said.

Two

Chloe's slight body, framed in the doorway of her room, was as rigid as a deer rifle. "I'm not going," she said.

Libby, busy with packing, didn't answer.

Chloe tried another approach. "I can't go. It's almost time for summer school midterms. I'll flunk everything."

"No, you won't. People have emergencies. We'll work it out."

"I can stay with Dad."

Libby turned toward her daughter, hands on her hips. "Your grandmother is gravely ill. I'm her only daughter. You're the only grandchild she'll ever have. Shame on you. This isn't about you. You have no choice. You're going."

"How long do we have to stay?"

"I don't know."

"If it's more than two weeks, can I come home?"

"I don't know."

"What *do* you know?"

Libby's cheeks flamed. "I know my mother nearly died. I know that I have a spoiled, self-absorbed daughter. I know I have an ex-husband who, at every defining moment of my life, has let me down. Shall I go on?"

"You're not supposed to do that, you know."

"What?"

Chloe was enjoying this. Her mother took the bait just as she always did. "Put Dad down in front of me. It's bad for my self-concept because he's part of me, just like you are."

She watched Libby struggle with her temper, hoping her dark side would win. Even though it was unpleasant to sit through one of her lectures, it was worth it. She was always so penitent later on. On more than one occasion her mother's remorse had led to a new pair of shoes or a CD from Tower Records.

Libby wet her lips. "You aren't your father, Chloe. Obviously, he and I don't see eye to eye on most things. If we did, we wouldn't have divorced. I don't see you as an extension of him at all. You are your own person, and whatever difficulties you and I have are ours alone. They have nothing to do with him."

This wasn't going the way Chloe had planned. There was nothing left but brutal honesty. "Mom, I can't go to Maryland with you. My life is here. I have an important part in the school play. My friends are here. You've described Marshyhope Creek to me. I wouldn't fit in. I'm not the cheerleader-homecoming-queen type. I don't care about sports. I don't care about school spirit. I like living here. I'm not a Southerner. Please don't make me go."

Libby sat down on the bed. "I'm asking for a month, Chloe, six weeks tops. That's it. Surely that isn't too much. I've been here for seventeen years without a break. I'd like to go home to visit. I'd like to see my mother again. It may be the last time. Can you give me that?"

"That's another thing." Chloe sat down beside her mother. "It's been years since we've visited your parents. I don't even know them, not the way I know Dad's. Why not? You always change the subject when I ask you about them."

"It's complicated," Libby began. How much was too much to tell a sixteen-year-old? She decided on the truth. "They didn't want me to get married. They said it wouldn't last. I wanted to prove them wrong." Her laugh was completely devoid of humor. "They were right, of course, but I couldn't admit it. That's why I never went home. I suppose it all comes down to pride. I didn't want them to know they were right.''

Chloe's nose wrinkled. ''If you want my opinion, you didn't have much of a relationship with your parents if you couldn't admit you'd made a mistake.''

''I thought I had one with my mother,'' Libby said slowly. ''My dad was always away working on one cause or another. He never seemed to have time for a family. I resented that.''

''My dad wasn't around much, either,'' Chloe reflected, ''but now that he is, I want to make up for lost time.''

Libby slid her arm around Chloe's shoulders. ''I won't stand in your way. Give me a little time. Please?''

''Why can't you go alone?''

''I'm proud of you. You're my one accomplishment. I want to show you off. Please humor me.''

''Six weeks is tops. If I hate it, I'm coming home,'' Chloe warned her.

Libby held out her hand. ''It's a deal.''

Reluctantly, Chloe took it. ''Dad isn't going to like this.''

''I'm sure you'll be able to handle him,'' her mother said coolly.

In the end, it was Libby who was left with the responsibility of managing her ex-husband. He showed up at her door the next morning, without the courtesy of a warning phone call, taking up time she couldn't spare.

''I could dispute this, you know,'' he said, flicking a speck of lint from the sleeve of his cashmere sweater.

Libby folded her arms and leaned against the doorjamb. ''You could, but you won't.''

''You seem very sure of yourself.''

Libby ignored his comment and asked the question she'd wanted to ask for some time. ''Tell me, Eric, why you've suddenly become so interested in your daughter. For the last fourteen years I can count on one hand the times you've been home more than two weeks in a row.''

He didn't deny it. ''I was working. Actors have to go where the work is. Besides, people change, Libby. I've never been fond of babies. Now that she's older, we have more in common.''

''She's not supposed to be your friend. She's your daughter. Whether you have anything in common with her or not is beside the point.''

Eric sighed. ''I didn't come here to argue with you.''

''Why did you come?''

''May I come inside?''

''I'm in the middle of things right now. I'd like to settle this quickly.''

''You're not going to make this easy, are you?''

''Should I?''

''I'm sorry it turned out this way, Libby. I really am. But you're just as much to blame as I am. You could have walked at any time these last seventeen years. Why didn't you?''

''I could ask you the same question.''

He shrugged and shoved his hands into his pockets. ''I don't know. I suppose it was too much effort. It didn't matter. There wasn't anyone else I was serious about.''

''In other words, having a wife and child was a convenient excuse.''

''I suppose so. What do you want me to do? That's all water under the bridge. I can't go back and change anything. I'm sorry if I wasted your life.''

''Speak for yourself,'' she shot back. ''My life is just beginning.''

''Libby,'' he appealed to her. ''Chloe doesn't want to go. I think it's selfish of you to force her.''

Libby felt the familiar rage that came and went with her ex-husband's scattered logic rise up in her chest. She counted to ten and waited until she was in control of herself. "What do you suggest?" she asked calmly.

"I think you should think of Chloe and stay here."

"My mother had a stroke, Eric. She may not make it. Are you implying that if you were faced with similar circumstances you would ignore your mother's request?"

"My mother hasn't absented herself from my life for the last seventeen years."

She hated him. There was no other emotion strong enough to describe her feeling. *Relax, Libby,* she told herself. *If you lose your temper, he wins.* She thought a minute. "I have a suggestion."

He looked wary. "What is it?"

"I'll keep Chloe in Marshyhope Creek for two weeks. That should be long enough for her to get to know her grandparents. After that, if I feel the need to stay longer, I'll send her home. We have joint custody. You can take care of her."

"For how long?" He was less than enthusiastic.

Libby suppressed a chuckle. "I'm thinking of permanently relocating. I've never cared for California. Besides, Chloe and I are in a difficult place right now, the usual mother-daughter thing. She needs her father, and since you have so much in common, I'm sure she would love to live with you. You can send her to me for summers and vacations."

His mouth dropped. "You're not serious?"

What had she ever seen in him? "Are you saying you don't think it's a good idea?"

"I can't have her live with me."

"Why not?"

"The circumstances aren't right." His voice crept up. "I'm gone a lot. I haven't arranged my life to accommodate a child."

"She's not a child, she's a teenager."

"That's not the point. She's a minor. She needs a schedule and regular meals and bedtimes. What do I know about that?''

Libby's eyebrows lifted. ''You're surprising me, Eric. I had no idea you were even aware that raising a child requires sacrifices.''

He stared at her, his eyes narrowing. ''You're playing with me. You never intended to give her to me, did you?''

''I considered it,'' she lied. ''However, your arguments make sense. If you really can't take her, I suggest you hold this trip up to Chloe as a good idea. She isn't happy about it and you're not helping.''

He ran his hand through his perfectly groomed hair. ''I see your point.''

''Thank you.'' She turned away.

''You've changed, Libby,'' he said softly. ''You've lost your sweetness.''

''It didn't get me very far, did it?'' she returned. ''Goodbye, Eric.''

Eric, waiting in the school parking lot for his daughter, would have missed her if she hadn't called out and flagged him down. Her appearance shocked him. ''Chloe, for God's sake, what have you done to your hair?''

''Colored it.'' She tossed her pack onto the floor of his Corvette and climbed in beside her father. ''I don't want to go to Marshyhope Creek.''

''Who colored it?''

''I did. This trip will ruin everything. Besides, Mom's making noises about staying for a long time. I don't want to live in the South.''

''You need a professional for such a drastic color change. Why did you choose black? You have beautiful hair. It's just like—''

Chloe arched an eyebrow. ''Yours?''

''Yes, as a matter of fact. What's wrong with that?''

''It isn't black, Dad, at least not all of it.'' She held up a piece of hair. "These are streaks. Can we get together on the same subject? I want to stay here with you."

He signaled and maneuvered into the line of traffic. "Hold on, Chloe. I need to concentrate."

She simmered in self-righteous anger and stared out the side window. They were heading west and the glare was directly in her eyes. She closed them. Life wasn't fair. Children were chattel, no better than pets, at the mercy of their parents' every whim, just like in the nineteenth century. If only she were two years older. She could get a job and live on her own. She folded her arms and relaxed against the headrest. Supporting herself wasn't the answer. She'd done enough shopping in Beverly Hills and on Wilshire Boulevard to know that minimum wage wouldn't cut it. What she really wanted was for her father to step up to the plate and offer to have her live with him.

"Dad," she began experimentally. "I think it's great that you're living close by."

He smiled.

Encouraged, she continued. "Isn't it terrific that we can see each other whenever we want to?"

"You bet."

"It's too bad that Mom wants to go back to Maryland just when you and I have started to really get to know each other."

He nodded.

"I wish it was possible for me to stay here. Don't you?"

He fiddled with the radio. "Yes, I do, Chloe."

She pounced. "Maybe there's a way."

"A way for what?"

"To have me stay here."

He turned to her, a frown marring his forehead. "What are you talking about?"

"You weren't listening to me," she accused him.

"Of course I was."

"Tell me what we were talking about."

"You said you didn't want to go with your mother to Marshyhope Creek."

"Well?"

"Well, what, Chloe? You can't always have what you want. This trip is important to your mother. She wants you to see your grandparents. It's the right thing to do."

"I can't believe you're taking her side," Chloe argued. "I don't want to know my grandparents. They haven't wanted to know me until now. Don't you think it's more important for me to know my own father?"

"We already know each other."

"We haven't spent more than three months together in my entire life. You've always been away on some shoot. Do you think that's enough?"

"You're exaggerating, and if I haven't been around, it's because I was working. You and your mother seem to forget that." He tugged at the knot of the buttery-soft sweater tied just so around his neck. "We'll have plenty of time when you get back. Take it on the chin, Chloe. Nothing lasts forever. Do this favor for your mother. You won't be sorry."

Chloe stared at him, at the perfect profile, the long eyelashes, the carefully put-together clothes, and wondered, not for the first time, whether it was really a benefit to have such incredible-looking people for parents. She was bound to be at a disadvantage. The odds were against her even coming close to such physical beauty. Anyone meeting Libby and Eric would automatically assume their offspring would share the same physical attributes. Not that Chloe thought there was anything wrong with her looks. However, she was a realist, and *spectacular* wasn't an adjective that was going to be applied to her appearance anytime soon. Fortunately, she wasn't hung up on beauty. There were more important things at hand, like not burying herself in a Southern town too small to warrant a dot on the map. "You don't want me," she said at last, resorting to emotional blackmail.

"This isn't about doing what's right for Mom. You don't want me to live with you."

"That isn't true, Chloe." His voice was sharp with guilt and exasperation. "I came back to Los Angeles to be with you. If I didn't want you I wouldn't have driven through this traffic nightmare to pick you up and take you home with me. Try not to be so dramatic."

"I wonder where I got it," she muttered.

"Your mother has her heart set on going to see her parents. She's had a very hard time of it since they cut her off. Libby is a small-town girl. She always was. Living here has been a strain. She's done as well as can be expected, but she's never fit in. Surely you can give her a brief visit."

"What if it isn't a visit?"

"We'll tackle that hurdle when we come to it. My guess is that if you're miserable, she'll be miserable. She won't stay if you're unhappy."

"Why can't I stay with you?"

He sighed. "Christ, Chloe, you're relentless."

"Answer the question."

"I'm not set up to take care of you. You'd have to transfer schools. I'm not home every night. I may have been an absentee father, but even I know it isn't good to leave teenagers home alone."

"I can stay by myself," said Chloe sulkily.

"Of course you can," her father agreed, "now and then."

"Will you send for me if Mom decides to stay in Maryland?"

"She won't."

"If she does?"

"God, Chloe, all right. You win. I'll send for you."

"Promise."

"I promise."

Satisfied, Chloe sat back in her seat and closed her eyes again. Her heart constricted whenever she thought of her father. Despite the trappings of the *good* life, she sensed a vulnerability in him, as if something was missing. She wanted to protect him. It was selfish of her mother to take her away. He needed someone to take care of him. He needed Chloe. The sun had gone down during their argument. "I want to eat at Spagos."

Eric laughed. "You're a spoiled brat," he said. "I can't believe your mother allows this kind of behavior."

"She doesn't. And I'm not spoiled. Spoiled brats don't appreciate the gifts they're given. I do. I've only eaten there once, with you. I want to go again."

He picked up his cell phone and shook his head. "You're a smart girl, Chloe, too smart. I'm no match for you. I'll see if I can get a reservation."

Three

Nola Ruth Delacourte reclined on a daybed pulled out on the porch of her big white house on the outskirts of Marshyhope Creek and looked across at the water, a finger of the Chesapeake. On the other side of the inlet, migrant workers picked peaches in Marshall Hadley's grove. It had been a dry spring, drier than most she'd seen in her sixty-five years, and the summer promised to be dry as well. By eight o'clock that morning a relentless wet heat had settled over the land like a steam bath from which there was no respite. She squinted her eyes and smiled into the steamy morning. The workers, gathered together from other farms to help shuck the grove, were cooling themselves, bathing in the murky water. The sight of dark, bare-skinned bodies, shiny and water slick, reminded her of earlier, lustier days when she was young and hot-blooded and the nights held out promises of magic and romance and music.

Sometimes, her faded hearing came back and her ears, too damaged to really listen to the conversations around her, picked up the old familiar strains of the blues. There was BoBo Jones with his sax and Johnny Fontana on the trumpet and Moss Daggett banging his spoons. The music was sweet and sharp and so achingly poignant it could charm the clothes right off a woman's back. Those were years worth remembering, when she had her youth and her looks and her hearing, the absolute power of a young woman in full bloom with all of life ahead. Where had the time gone?

Where had *she* gone? Who was that old woman looking back at her from the mirror? Life wasn't fair. She didn't feel any different, not until the stroke had suddenly pulled her into a dervish of helpless dependency, making even the smallest tasks insurmountable challenges.

Lordy, Lordy, where was Libba Jane? Where was her precious, spirited, exquisite daughter? How had such an absurd argument come between them and grown until there was no going around it and seventeen years had blinked by? How could something as insignificant as a man have parted them? Somehow, their words had gotten away from them. Passions were high and things that shouldn't have been said were said. Still, Nola Ruth was completely unprepared for the finality of their break. Libba had always been so sensible, with one exception. But she wouldn't think of that now. It was water under the bridge. Libba was coming home with her child and without Eric Richards. Except for seventeen empty years, Nola Ruth couldn't have planned it better.

"Nola Ruth." Her husband's voice cut through her thoughts. "Can I get you anything? Iced tea or lemonade, maybe?"

She shook her head and didn't look at him, hoping he would fade back into the dim hallway from where he'd come. Coleson Delacourte, as unresponsive to his wife's moods as he'd been forty years ago, walked out on to the porch and sat down beside her.

"The doctor said you should use your voice as much as possible, Nola. Your speech will improve faster."

"My speech is fine," she snapped, angry that he'd brought up a sensitive subject. She abhorred weakness, more so in herself than in anyone around her.

Cole bypassed her anger. "I want to talk about Libba and Chloe."

Nola Ruth looked at him and waited.

"There will be some adjusting to having a child in the house. It won't be the same."

"I know that."

"We've only had Libba," her husband continued. "Kids are different today. Chloe is California born and raised. She's not going to settle in right away. I don't think anyone should mention staying here permanently."

"Are you censoring my speech, Coleson?"

Coleson Delacourte looked at his wife, shriveled and broken, old before her time, but still beautiful. Nola would be beautiful if she lived to be a hundred. It was in her bones and in her eyes and in the lean, exotic length of her. She was first-lady material. He'd told her that long ago. It had pleased her. There was a time, long ago, when she had been easily pleased. Not anymore. "That's exactly what I'm doing, Nola Ruth," he said softly.

She did not look away. "You never cared before," she said. "Why now?"

"You're wrong," he said gently. "I cared a great deal."

Nola Ruth looked down and fidgeted with the fringe of her linen wrap. "I won't say anything, not unless Libba brings it up first."

"Thank you."

She hoped he'd go now that he'd said what he came for, but he didn't. "Do you remember the first time I brought you home?"

"Why are you bringing that up now?" she asked, impatient, as usual, with his resurrecting the past.

"You were so young and so lovely."

"Do you have any idea how that makes me feel, now that I'm not?" she demanded.

"Everyone ages, Nola Ruth," he said patiently. "No need to be sensitive because you aren't twenty-five anymore. You're still the loveliest woman I've ever known."

"I'm not sensitive about my age, Coleson, or my looks. It's my condition I find hard to tolerate."

"The doctors say you're doing well."

She didn't look at him. "That's encouraging. I wonder

how they'd feel if they were in my place, unable to perform even the smallest act of independence."

Coleson Delacourte, a spare, fit man looking much younger than his years, shrugged his shoulders. "You're one feisty woman, Nola Ruth."

She didn't answer him. Cole was a good man, a philanthropist. The word *no* wasn't in his vocabulary. Once, forty years ago, she'd loved that about him. When had it changed? When had the sensitivity she'd admired become weakness in her eyes? She couldn't pinpoint a specific moment. Perhaps it happened gradually, when she was no longer grateful, when she realized that he was content to putter at the law, to take those cases that no one else would take, to set aside his fees more often than not, to allow their daughter, their only child, to attend the local public school and then, later, live at home and attend a state university when it was most important for her future to go elsewhere, when all the right people went elsewhere.

Everything Cole did, he did in the name of principle and balancing the scales. He was a civil rights advocate well before it was politically correct, well before Thurgood Marshall and *Brown v. Board of Education of Topeka* turned everything below the Mason-Dixon Line upside down. In his own way, he was a hero. Nola Ruth had heard him described in exactly those terms. She had no use for heroes. She wanted nothing to do with a martyr who sacrificed his family in the name of righteousness. Because of him Libba had left the Tidewater and gone where no self-respecting Southern woman would think of going, to Hollywood, and with an actor, no less, a self-absorbed, shallow shell of a boy-man who lived in the imagination of the moment pretending to be someone other than himself, traits that did not lend themselves to his settling into being a serious marriage partner.

Cole sat beside her, relaxed, back curved, elbows on his knees, one hand under his chin, lean, flat-bellied, with all his original hair. He wasn't a man given to excesses. He rarely drank, never smoked and ate only to fill the emptiness in his stomach. He was as different from Eric Richards as a man could be. Women were supposed to marry men like their fathers. Nola Ruth would have liked to see Libba marry someone like Cole, only more ambitious. She would have liked her daughter to be appreciated, even treasured.

"Do you still blame me for her leaving us?" he asked.

To be kind or to be truthful, that was the question. She decided on honesty. "Not directly."

"What does that mean?"

"You didn't send her out the door, Cole. She brought Eric home. She was attracted to him. You were as unhappy about it as I was. We pushed her away with our disapproval. I let her go because I wanted her to come home on her own. I didn't want history to repeat itself. Neither of us can help what we are."

He looked surprised. "Thank you. I didn't expect that."

She shrugged, a ragged painful lifting of one shoulder. "She's coming home. That's all that's important."

Coleson Delacourte struggled within himself. She could see it in the folding skin between his eyebrows, in the tense line of his jaw and the rigid set of his shoulders. "She's a thirty-seven-year-old single mother with a Ph.D. in biochemistry. What in the hell will she do with herself in Marshyhope Creek?" he asked at last.

Nola Ruth frowned. "What is that supposed to mean?"

"Who will she talk to? I can't think of a single woman her age in this town who's done what she has."

"Women are different, Coleson. She'll do fine. This is Libba's home. She'll find her place."

A shadow darkened the blinding brightness of the walkway, diverting their attention. A small, cocoa-skinned woman carrying a basket hobbled toward them.

Nola Ruth stiffened. "It's Drusilla Washington trying to pawn off more of her vegetables." She gripped her husband's arm. "Send her on her way, Coleson. I don't want her to see me like this. We don't need anything from her."

Cole frowned. "What's gotten into you, Nola? She's a harmless old woman. I'll send her around the back. Maybe Serena needs something for dinner."

Nola Ruth closed her eyes and turned her head away. Her grip on her husband's sleeve relaxed. She pretended the woman wasn't there.

"Good evenin', Mr. Delacourte, Miz Delacourte." The old woman nodded her head and offered up the basket. "I grew me a fine crop of sweet potato plants, tasty as they come. Serena might like to stir some into a pie or two if you're thinking of company."

Nola Ruth willed her hands to stay motionless. There was no point in asking how she knew Libba was coming home. Drusilla always knew everybody's business.

Cole rose, lifted the towel and looked into the basket. "They look good, Drusilla. Go on around to the kitchen and tell Serena to buy up the whole bunch."

The black woman grunted and smiled. Her gums were black and one front tooth was missing. "You won't be sorry, Mr. Delacourte." She turned and shuffled toward the back of the house. "Verna Lee says hello."

"Tell her I'll be in for some more of that tea. It helps me sleep like a baby."

"I'll do that, sir. She got some healing potion for you, too, Miz Delacourte. I'll bring it next time I come."

Nola Ruth waited until she was sure the woman was out of sight before shuddering. "She's dreadful. As if I'd even consider that voodoo nonsense."

"Verna Lee doesn't have anything to do with voodoo. Her specialty is alternative medicine. You know that."

"I know nothing about any of that and I intend to keep it that way."

Her husband shook his head. "I keep telling myself that

this edge you've cultivated is due to the stroke. God help me if it isn't. God help us all. I hate to say this, Nola Ruth.''

She braced herself.

"You've become a very difficult woman."

Her eyes widened and then she laughed. "Oh, Coleson, that didn't even wound me. Surely you can do better than that.''

"I'm a lawyer, Nola Ruth," he reminded her. "I can do much better than that, but I choose not to.''

"Always the gentleman, aren't you?''

"Be grateful.''

She looked at him curiously. Coleson was rarely sarcastic. "Since when have you taken to giving Verna Lee your business?''

He lifted her hand and laced his fingers through hers, but he didn't look at her. "I've always felt a certain responsibility for Verna Lee Fontaine. She hasn't had an easy time of it. She deserved better.''

Nola Ruth lifted a hand to her throat. The air was too thin, as if she were pulling it into her lungs through a narrow straw. "I'm tired, Coleson," she managed. "I think I'd like to sleep now. When will Libba and Chloe be here?''

He looked at his watch. "Their plane landed in Richmond two hours ago. Libba had to rent a car. I'd say they should be here in about three or four hours. I've asked Serena to hold supper." He kissed the back of her hand. "Get some rest, Nola Ruth. I'll wake you if they're early.''

She nodded and closed her eyes, shutting out her porch, the workers in the peach grove, her husband's voice and the memories it evoked, everything but the thought of her daughter driving up the long road leading to the circular driveway. Seventeen years would have changed her, but how?

Nola Ruth allowed her imagination to wander and conjured up a thirty-seven-year-old woman with her daughter's coffee-colored hair and dark eyes, her oval face, slender bones and shapely, beautiful legs. Libba would still be slim. She was half Beauchamp and all the Beauchamps looked malnourished as children, turning into adults with lean, attractive bodies. Not even seventeen years could change that. Her hair would be different, though, shorter, more coiffed. She was an adult, after all. Perhaps her skin would be different as well. It didn't rain in California and the summers were hot and dry. Perhaps she would have crow's feet or even wrinkles. Perhaps she would be suntanned with bleached hair, a tattoo and several holes in each of her ears.

Nola Ruth chuckled at the absurdity of her thoughts. Libba Jane would've had to change a great deal to come home sporting a tattoo. Still, it wasn't impossible. How odd to be so ignorant about her only daughter. Once they had been so close. She wanted that closeness again. Nola Ruth had become very aware of the limited time she had left. She was quite willing to give most of it away if it meant she could have her daughter by her side again.

She pursed her lips and unsuccessfully tried to blow a cool stream of air up to where a few wisps of hair rested on her forehead. Lord, it was warm, the warmest summer she could remember.

Libby Delacourte came back to Marshyhope Creek on a day so hot the asphalt blistered and curled like pigskin in a barbecue pit. By noon, drinking water flowed hot from the taps and shadowed doors showed inky black against the blinding whitewash of peeling storefronts. Cicadas and hummingbirds, searching for relief, dove down into the cool green stranglehold of southern pine and dogs lay like the dead in the dripping shade of hickory hardwood trees. Heat rose, fans hummed, images shimmered like gasoline fumes, and still the mercury climbed until even the tepid swimming hole near Marshall Hadley's peach grove brought no respite to the migrant workers camping on its banks.

Those who saw her return and who'd been around long

enough remembered the way she'd left all those years before, seated in the front seat of a Chevy four-by-four, her arm wrapped possessively around a startlingly handsome boy. Those who thrived on detail and gossip reported that the boy had been busy with the wheel, steering with one hand while the other dangled out the window, fingers clamped around a half-empty beer can minus even the pretense of a concealing brown bag. A cigarette hung from the corner of his mouth and Janis Joplin's classic lyrics, decrying freedom, blared from the radio at a decibel level outlawed long ago by the peace-loving citizens of Marshyhope Creek.

This time Libby was driving and a child sat beside her, a young girl with pale hair tipped with black, black clothes and a sulky pout to her mouth.

Libby and her child, squinting against the sun's glare, had crossed the Potomac by ferry, driven at reasonable speeds across the three-mile span between Kent and Annapolis Islands, bought fresh corn and peaches from a dusky-skinned, carmine-lipped hawker near the brush-lined shoals of the Nanticoke River and reached the Creek by three o'clock that afternoon, more than two hours ahead of schedule.

Libby had planned it that way. She wanted time to look around, to settle in, to feel the familiar rhythms again. She turned off the road, ignored a sputtering Chloe and climbed out of the car to walk across a wooden bridge with a dual view of the bay and the town. The wood of the railing was smooth under her palms and the hot afternoon sun beat down on her unprotected head. It was foolish to be out without a hat in the heat of a Maryland summer, but she'd been too long in a place where the seasons all blended together, indistinguishable except for a few inches of annual rainfall that turned the gray-beige of the hills into green for a few, too brief weeks of the year.

The suffocating blast of humidity renewed her spirit. She was home. The tree-lined shore of the bay, bordered by a twisting ribbon of water, appeared metallic-blue in the sunlight, gray and coolly serene in the shadows. The sight of green trees and blue water and sun-washed sand was a welcome relief to her country-starved eyes. Here there was room for violent storms and clouds and brisk, cheek-stinging winds. Libby drank in the gentle, low-lying landscape of the woodlands, fields and marshlands, the timeless meeting place of eagle, heron, duck and osprey, with the grateful appreciation of a lost sinner who meets his savior after a long and difficult journey.

Chloe had followed her. "Why are we stopping?" she demanded.

Libby leaned back against the railing and pointed toward Marshyhope Creek. "Look over there. Nothing's changed in all these years. See that building holding up the boarding with the screen hanging on a hinge and the pale blue shutters? That's Horace's Mercantile and Dry Goods. The building beside it is Clayton Dulaine's diner and filling station." The faded orange Open For Business sign was the same one Libby remembered. "Those white columns over there belong to City Hall, where the courthouse, jail and police station are." Libby pointed to the north. "There's the library and the Catholic Church where I was baptized and had my first communion."

"It looks like something out of a movie," said Chloe.

Libby nodded. "They were all designed by the same antebellum architect. That white building used to be Doc Balieu's infirmary. The pharmacy is close by. I wonder if he's still practicing."

"What's that?" Chloe pointed to a brick building sitting on a lush piece of green grass taken up by a slide and jungle gym.

"That," Libby said, "is the school where forty-some heat-drugged kindergarten-through-eighth-grade students are, right this minute, looking out the long windows into the summer sunshine and wishing summer school was over.''

''I can relate,'' replied Chloe.

Libby pushed back her sunglasses for the full experience. As always, the residential district was divided by the creek. Shacks with aluminum roofs and run-down tenements on one side and tall, gracious, white-pillared homes set back on enormous green lawns on the other. Standing off by itself, belonging to neither side, just out of sight behind a cluster of pine and sand dunes and set back on a full acre of beautifully manicured lawn, would be Hennessey House.

Libby smiled. ''See that house, the white one with the wrap-around porch?''

Chloe nodded.

''That's my old boyfriend's house.''

''You had an old boyfriend?'' Despite herself, Chloe was curious.

Libby nodded. ''That house has incredible memories for me—in the kitchen around the wide oak table, outside on the porch and in the tree house that Russ and his brother built all by themselves. Everything that was ever important happened to me there.''

''Like what?''

Libby decided on the partial truth. ''Russ dared me to eat my first raw oyster.''

''What else?''

''I had my first beer and smoked my first and last cigarette.'' She'd also lost her virginity upstairs in the big, old-fashioned bedroom, but she wasn't about to reveal that to Chloe or the fact that she'd adored the Hennessey twins, Russ and Mitch, indiscriminately for as long as she could remember, first one and then the other. She'd sit around the old pine table in the kitchen and soak up the sharp-tongued love administered in equal doses of suffocating hugs and long-handled spoon slaps by Cora, the family matriarch.

Chloe ran across the bridge and down the embankment.

Shedding her shoes, she dipped her toes in the marsh water. "Careful," Libby called down to her. "There are leeches in the water."

Chloe nodded, acknowledging her mother's voice, but she continued to dabble her feet.

Libby opened her mouth and then closed it before saying anything more. It wouldn't kill Chloe to come up against some unpleasant Maryland consequences. Shrugging, she returned to her musings.

The family that was so much a part of her youth was all gone now. Generations of black-haired, tight-jawed Hennesseys had wrestled on the lawn, drunk hard lemonade on the peeling steps of the wraparound porch, coupled and given birth in the cavernous big-house bedrooms. For as long as Libby could remember, Hennessey hospitality meant bourbon straight up, iced tea and peach pie for all those born within the confines of the small, picturesque community of French and Irish immigrants perched on the western side of the bay. No one ever bothered to knock. At any time of day or night neighbors would call through the screen door, stamp the sandy soil from their shoes and pull up a chair in front of the scrubbed pine table in the kitchen, prepared to wile away a goodly portion of the day. For the Hennesseys, who thrived on company, the inconvenience of unexpected visitors traipsing through the hallway on the way to the kitchen was a small price to pay for their uncontested position in the community.

By the time high school rolled around, Libby had developed a serious crush on Russ and remained uncharacteristically constant for four years until Eric Richards came to town. Russ graduated from some college out west and Mitch took over the fishing fleet and died a few years later. Libby lost touch after that. She'd heard that Russ married Tracy Wentworth, a girl from town, and they'd had a child, but the marriage didn't last. Not many did these days, she reflected, not even in Marshyhope Creek.

Twisting a strand of dark hair and tucking it into the knot at the back of her head, she took one last lingering glance at the view, committing it to memory before pulling herself away. *Get a grip,* she told herself. *It's time to go home.*

She smiled at Chloe. "You're awfully quiet."

"I'm trying to imagine you with a boyfriend."

"Why is that so hard to imagine?"

Chloe shook her head. "You're my mother. It's hard to think of you as young."

"Well, I was." She took her daughter's hand. "Come on. It's time to go."

Four

Libby followed the road for several miles along the creek. At the fork, she turned the car into a carriage path that ambled in twisted, weed-filled profusion to the spacious green lawns surrounding her parents' home. A driveway of hard-packed earth canopied by ancient oaks led to a three-storied colonial of deep porches and white pillars that, even after seventeen years of semi-banishment, Libby called home.

It was the kind of view that postcards are made of. No one who walked that gracious, leaf-strewn path and lingered at the base of the enormous oak to inhale the scent of mimosa and listen to the drone of bees could look up at the big white house, framed by acres of green lawns and gold sky and blue water, without experiencing that catch of breath, that tingling of the blood, that slight acceleration of pulse that envy inevitably brings. Libby was no exception.

Thirty-seven years ago Nola Ruth Delacourte had given birth to her only child in the large second-story bedroom she shared with her husband. For Libby, the iron-rich earth of her birthplace would always be home. Only here, in the house where she'd slept nearly every night until she'd married, could she be renewed. In the brick kitchen, with its hanging copper pots, she found the peace of mind that eluded her elsewhere, while stuffing herself on peaches and pecans and Serena's homemade cobbler topped with vanilla ice cream. In the cool, dark library, in the gated pasture, in her mother's sunny drawing room and old-fashioned parlor were the roots of a heritage as graceful, as elegant and refined, and as necessary to Libby as California had been raw and crude and vital and exciting.

There was a time when the blood-stirring energy of the golden state had cast its spell over her. Loud and flamboyant, it pulsed with an energy that seemed unpretentious, alive, completely foreign to anything Libby had ever known. But the magic ended abruptly, leaving her aching for home.

Libby parked some distance from the house, unbuckled her seat belt and nodded at an unusually silent Chloe. Together, and yet apart, they walked up the long circular driveway. "My God," the girl breathed, "it looks like something out of *Gone With the Wind*. I can't believe I didn't remember this."

An old woman was asleep on the porch. She looked familiar and yet—Libby hesitated. The woman opened her eyes slowly.

Libby gasped and stared at her mother. "Mama?"

Nola Ruth smiled with one side of her mouth and held out her arms. "Libba Jane?" she said, carefully forming the words. "Is it you?"

Libby nodded, struggling to hold back her tears. Carefully, she sat down beside her mother and drew her into her arms.

"Baby. My baby," Nola Ruth crooned, stroking her daughter's silky hair. "So pretty. Still so pretty."

After a minute, Libba sat back and looked at her mother. "God, Mama. You must have had a terrible time. I'm so sorry."

The unaffected side of Nola Ruth's mouth turned up in a smile. "I'm better now." She looked up at Chloe and held out her hand. "Come here, child. Let me look at you."

Chloe approached her grandmother, careful not to touch the outstretched hand, trying not to shrink back. One side of the woman's face was pretty, nearly perfect, like her mother's, sculpted by the same fine sharp bones, the round dark eye framed by thick lush eyelashes. The other side drooped grotesquely, pulled down to such a degree that the red rim of the eye was painfully evident.

Nola Ruth looked her fill at her daughter's child, taking in the girl's fair hair with those dreadful black streaks, the heart-shaped face, the defiant chin, the startling Siamese-cat-blue eyes, the fearsome slimness of her long, thin legs and the clothing that looked as if it had come from a poor-quality thrift shop. The child was a hybrid, combining the best of the Delacourtes and Eric Richards, not a pretty child, definitely not pretty, but with the promise of something more than prettiness to come. "You're a lovely thing," she said softly. "Do you know that?"

Chloe flushed. *Thank you* was the usual reply, but somehow it didn't fit here. The woman had simply stated a fact instead of offering up a compliment.

"Have you anything to say for yourself, child?"

"I'm Chloe."

Nola Ruth nodded. Her eyes twinkled. "I thought so."

"I wanted you to know."

"Thank you." She couldn't look away. The girl was so self-possessed, so earnest.

Chloe shifted uncomfortably and Nola Ruth collected herself. "You'll want to see Coleson." She reached for the bell on the small table by her side and shook it.

Footsteps sounded in the hall and a black woman of indeterminate age stepped out on to the porch. She looked at Libby and her face broke into a smile. She lifted her hands to her cheeks. "Thank the Lord. Libba Jane, you're home."

Libby stood and reached for the woman to hug her close. "Serena, you never change."

The black woman stepped back, keeping both hands on Libby's arms, and searched her face. "Neither have you. You're still as pretty as a billboard poster."

Libby motioned toward Chloe. "This is Chloe, my daughter."

Serena nodded politely. "Pleased to meet you, Miss Chloe. I baked a chocolate cake for you. It was your mama's favorite."

Chloe smiled her first genuine smile of the day. "Call me Chloe. I love chocolate cake. It was very nice of you to think of me."

Serena's eyebrows lifted. She looked at Libby. "You've done a fine job, Miss Libba."

Nola Ruth spoke up. "Serena, will you tell Mr. Delacourte that Libba Jane and Chloe have arrived? I think we'll give everyone a chance to settle in before you serve supper."

"It'll be my pleasure, Miz Delacourte. He's out back in the gazebo, just waitin' to hear." She hurried away.

Libby turned to her mother. "I expected you to be much worse after Daddy's phone call. Are you really better, Mama?"

Nola Ruth shrugged. "I never did care for hospitals. My mama said to avoid them, that people go there to die. I couldn't get any rest with all those nurses poking me and waking me to check my temperature and my blood pressure. I'm much better now that I'm home."

Cole Delacourte came running around the corner of the house, his shirt unbuttoned and flapping in the breeze. "Chloe Megan Richards," he shouted, "come and hug your granddaddy."

Instinctively, Chloe responded to his joyful command. She laughed and danced down the steps, skipping across the lawn to meet him. He lifted her in his arms and swung her around and around until they collapsed in a tangled heap of arms and legs and laughter.

Libby's eyes filled. "I should never have stayed away so long," she said.

Nola Ruth wiped the disapproval from her face and

smiled indulgently. "Sometimes we don't know what to appreciate until it's gone."

Libby shrugged. "Or sometimes we realize we never needed it at all."

Her mother didn't ask what she meant. Nola Ruth didn't believe in prying. She knew that everything she wanted to know would come out eventually. It always did. Patience was all that was required.

Grandfather and granddaughter, arms clasped, walked back to the porch. Libby smiled and walked into her father's arms. "Hi, Daddy." Still holding his hand, she stepped back. "So, what do you think of the grown-up Chloe?"

"My goodness." Cole took both of Chloe's hands in his. "This gorgeous young woman can't possibly be my granddaughter." His eyes twinkled. "Are you the one who locked herself in my bathroom when you were three years old?"

"Mom!" Chloe turned on her mother. "Did I really do that?"

Libby laughed. "You had an independent personality very early."

"I was three. That has nothing to do with now."

"You're still independent."

Chloe loved the look of this tall, lean man with a webbing of wrinkles around his fine blue eyes. "Don't worry, Granddad," she assured him. "I won't be locking myself in any more bathrooms."

"I'm relieved to hear it." Her grandfather winked at her. "But I wasn't especially worried." He looked at his wife. "Shall I carry you into the back? If we eat outside, we can watch the sun set over the bay."

"I have a wheelchair, Coleson. There's no need to be so chivalrous."

Ignoring her protests, he scooped her up into his arms. "I enjoy being chivalrous. Libba, if you'll open the door, we'll be on our way."

For a fraction of a second, Libby waited to see her

mother's reaction. When there was no more than a slight pursing of her lips, she hurried to open the door. A blast of cold air propelled her backward. "You've installed air-conditioning."

"We have it," said her father, "when your mother allows us to turn it on." He stepped in front of her and continued down the hall. "It should have been done long ago."

"An idiotic notion," her mother called back over his shoulder. "This house has stood for nearly two hundred years without it. We've become soft people, Libba Jane, not nearly as strong as our ancestors."

Libby motioned Chloe into the house. "After you."

Chloe sighed and preceded her mother down the long hallway. "Why would I want to look at a bay?" she whispered furiously. "I have the entire Pacific Ocean at home."

"This isn't just a bay," answered Libby. "It's the Chesapeake Bay, the protein factory of the East, if not the entire country. It's beautiful and humbling and, just now, in terrible danger."

Chloe was interested. "Why?"

"Pollution from farms and factories to the north have killed huge numbers of fish and blue crabs. Chemicals have destroyed hatcheries and spawning areas. Limits have been set for fishing and crabbing and harvests are down. But it will be a generation before the bay returns to its previous prosperity."

"How do you know all this?"

Libby shrugged. "Everyone who lives here knows it. It's all we talk about, our only debate. Sides are taken and lines drawn. There's no faster way to begin a fight than to take a stand and state an opinion."

"Nice place you've brought us to, Mom. I can't wait to get clubbed to death some dark night because I'm a tree-hugger."

Her sarcasm barely registered with Libby. She looked around curiously, noting the changes, the refurbished windows and new upholstery, the fresh paint and updated window hangings. For the most part the house looked the same, only better, old-fashioned, rich and warm with colonial colors uniquely different in every room, harvest gold, robin's-egg blue, Indian red, reflecting the tastes of seven generations of Delacourte ancestors.

She opened the back door and gazed out at the wide expanse of water, the Chesapeake at sunset. The smell of it assaulted her senses and stopped her short. She breathed deeply and clung to the pillar on the back porch. Had she forgotten that it smelled this way, brackish and metallic, pungent, a mixture of fish and salt and pine and dirt, teeming with underwater life? Or maybe she'd never noticed because she'd grown up on its shores and known nothing else?

Chloe passed her and looked back curiously but didn't stop. Libby drank in the view; the rich green grass sloping gently downward to the bay; blue water, glassy beneath the setting sun; a lone trawler, silhouetted against a copper-penny sky; a single blue heron circling in the distance; the white gazebo and lawn chairs; her father depositing her mother in one of them, her daughter flopping down at their feet as if she'd done so a thousand times.

Emotions surged through her body, overwhelming, threatening, more than frightening. Libby sat down on the porch and rested her head against the pillar. Her stomach lifted and the sky spun drunkenly.

"Libba Jane," her father's voice called to her. "Come along, honey. Have some lemonade."

The command steadied her, turned her thoughts toward her father. He'd changed, become confident, assertive, more present than she remembered. She'd always adored him, but her memory was that of a remote, soft-spoken, apologetic man, content to leave the raising of his child to his wife. She walked across the lawn, accepted the sweating glass of lemonade and sat down in an Adirondack chair. "This is beautiful," she said softly. "I'd forgotten."

Cole Delacourte nodded. "I can't think of another view that compares with this except for Hennessey House."

"Where is that?" Chloe asked.

"Across the water, set back a ways from town," said her grandfather. "It was closed up for a while, but Russ Hennessey's had it opened up again. He's coming back home to run his daddy's business."

Libby's cheeks burned. "I thought he moved away years ago."

Nola Ruth spoke up. "He's coming back. Beau Hennessey left the business to both boys. After Mitch died a few months ago, Effie Blair kept on working the office. She said that Russ was moving back. Working a fleet of trawlers is a young man's job."

Cole shook his head. "Mitch's death was a tragedy. He was all set to marry Sue Ellen Cavendish when he was diagnosed with leukemia. He went quickly, thank God."

"Leukemia?" Libby frowned. "That's unusual, isn't it, for a man his age?"

"The townspeople here have had their share of illnesses," said Cole, "but I don't know that it's unusual."

"Has anyone else in the area come down with leukemia?" asked Libby.

"As a matter of fact, I think we've had several cases. No one we know personally, except for Mitch. Why do you ask?"

"Leukemia is found in adults who've had exposure to radiation or chemicals. Is anyone investigating the cause?"

"There's been some rumor in town. The Environmental Protection Agency has opened an office. I never put much credence in blaming the water, although that's what some folks are saying. We've had problems with overfishing for years. More than. likely the federal presence is here to enforce commercial fishing limits."

"It's possible. The EPA has more than one role."

"As I was saying," Nola Ruth interrupted impatiently,

"Russ Hennessey is coming back to town and he has his work cut out for him."

"Why is that?" Libby was surprised. "Russ is a born fisherman." There was much more she could have said. She could have added that before he was twelve he could maneuver a trawler in seas that would make a lesser man lose his lunch, and by sixteen he could find the best netting spots on the bay without using a loran. Before he was eighteen years old he could out-harvest and out-shuck every fisherman on the water.

But she said none of those things. Her interest would be too obvious and there would be questions she didn't care to answer. But the memories were strong and private and deeply personal. Russ Hennessey was as close to a legend on the water as an ordinary mortal could be. He'd hand-crafted his own fishing lines and fought his first shad at six years old. He'd worked as a deckhand on his daddy's trawlers, pulling up bucket after bucket of soft-shelled crabs, glistening wet and cobalt-blue as they squirmed on the dock in the shimmering heat of summer afternoons. And somewhere, after his first shad and before his first beer, not too long before, he'd tasted the softness of Libby Delacourte's mouth. And later, much later, in a sweltering vortex of heat and need and pubescent longing, he'd stepped across the line separating childhood from adolescence and pulled her along with him, leaving the former behind forever.

Russ Hennessey had loved her. It was as simple as that. He'd loved her from the time she was seven years old, and she'd repaid his devotion by leaving town with Eric Richards, without so much as a word of explanation or even a goodbye. She'd carried the guilt of her behavior around for years, imagining a dozen different scenarios by which she could absolve herself. It appeared that her time was nearly at hand.

"I never did like that girl he married," Nola Ruth said, stringing out the words with her Louisiana drawl. "You remember her, Libba. She was a schoolmate of yours, the Wentworth girl.'' She appealed to her husband. ''What was her first name, Cole?''

''Tracy.''

''That's it. Cheap thing.'' Nola Ruth fanned herself. ''They had a child, a daughter, but Cora Hennessey had her doubts.''

Libby drained the last of her lemonade. ''About what?''

''Never mind,'' answered her mother. She nodded at Chloe. ''Little pitchers—''

Chloe rolled her eyes and stared at the bay.

Her grandfather laughed. ''What she means is Russ and his wife tried for years to have a child. When they finally gave up, Tracy announced she was pregnant.''

''It happens that way sometimes,'' said Libby.

Nola Ruth stared at her husband over her daughter's head. Their eyes met and he shook his head slowly. Only Chloe noticed and wondered at the unspoken message that passed between them.

Five

Verna Lee Fontaine hummed as she wiped down the counters of her health food/coffee shop. The herbs she'd hung from the ceiling in the back room were dried and ready to grind, and she'd decided to keep them in containers beneath the glass counter where people could see them. Occasionally, she would break into song, her rich, throaty alto filling the empty spaces in the room and rattling the prisms dangling from the tree branch that served as a jewelry stand.

Her grandmother hobbled in from Verna's house in the back and lingered in the doorway, smiling at the picture the younger woman made. She was tall and lush, with full breasts, narrow hips and long, lovely legs that just now were exposed through the slit of the calf-length, flowered skirt she'd knotted around her waist. She had golden eyes, a small pert nose and a thick mass of tawny ringlets twisted on top of her head and secured with a chopstick. Only the caramel color of her skin and the fullness of her lips revealed her African heritage. Verna Lee was approaching forty-two, but no one looking at that vivid, expressive face would have marked her as a day over twenty-five.

Drusilla sighed. Watching Verna Lee flit effortlessly from door to windows to stairs and back to the door again was a reminder of her own age and its limitations. There was something about Verna Lee that drew the eye, something raw and primitive and vital. She shook away her woolgathering and remembered her errand. She had a message to deliver. "Mornin', Verna Lee," she called out.

Verna Lee stopped singing and smiled. "Good morning, Grammy. I didn't hear you come in."

"You was singin'."

"Yes." She twisted a ringlet around her forefinger. "Have you eaten breakfast?"

"Hours ago."

"Good." She crossed the room and kissed the old woman's weathered cheek. "I didn't want to make you any, anyway."

"I could use some coffee."

"Why don't you make some for the two of us? Put in some of that New Orleans chicory I brought back with me. It'll take out the bitterness."

"My coffee ain't bitter."

"You only think it isn't. Sometimes it is."

Drusilla grumbled as she made her way to the kitchen. Verna Lee watched her grandmother with an anxious wrinkle between her brows. "Is your arthritis bothering you?" she called after her. "I wish you wouldn't insist on living all by yourself. I have plenty of room."

"No, it ain't botherin' me."

"Why are you limping?"

"I walked to the market yesterday and stopped by the Delacourtes on the way back."

Verna Lee's lips tightened. "What for?"

"I had sweet potatoes left to sell. Mr. Delacourte always buys 'em from me."

"Did he buy them this time?"

"Every last one."

"I hope they were a bad batch."

Drusilla finished measuring out the coffee and put the water on to boil. "Shame on you, Verna Lee. Mr. Delacourte's been good to me. He even asked after you. He wants more of your sleepy tea."

Verna Lee returned to her counters. "He knows where to find it."

"That's what I told him." She tilted her head. "Libba Jane's comin' home."

"So?"

"I just thought you'd want to know."

"Libba Jane Delacourte was always too curious for her own good. Sometimes, I thought—" She shook her head. "Never mind."

"She's bringin' her child with her, a girl."

Verna Lee's hands moved in slow circles **on the glass.** "That's nice. It will give Nola Ruth someone else to persecute."

Drusilla poured two cups of thick, chicory-rich coffee and walked back into the shop. "You're in a sour mood today, child." She handed her a cup. "Here. Maybe some coffee will help."

Relenting, Verna Lee pulled up a stool, accepted the peace offering and sat down, crossing her spectacular legs. "What's she like?" she asked, despising herself for her interest.

"Who?"

"Libba's daughter."

"Don't know. I heard the news from Serena."

"I wonder why she's coming home after all this time?" mused Verna Lee.

"Nola Ruth nearly died," Drusilla reminded her.

Verna Lee's hand tightened around her cup. "That's right. I remember now, not that Mrs. Delacourte and I run in the same social circles."

"Should you?" her grandmother asked pointedly.

Verna Lee released her breath. "No. Of course not. I don't know what's the matter with me today."

"Full moon?" suggest Drusilla.

"Possibly." Verna Lee's eyes had a dreamy quality. "I

wonder if Libba Delacourte is as gorgeous as she was in high school.''

"Don't waste any time over it. You'll see her soon enough."

"I doubt she'll ever set foot in this shop."

"Maybe she will and maybe she won't."

"She won't be here for long, anyway. No one in her right mind would trade California for Marshyhope Creek."

Her grandmother didn't mention that Verna Lee had done exactly that. She simply nodded. "Libba was a nice little gal, all dark eyes and dark hair and a smile that lit up the world." She glanced at her granddaughter. "Just like you. Nola Ruth went into a decline when she left with that boy."

"Where is *that* boy?" Verna Lee asked.

Drusilla shrugged. "Ask her when you see her."

"I just might do that."

"No reason why you shouldn't. You had the same schoolin'."

"No one knows that."

"That's your fault, Verna Lee. You always were a smart one. No one would be surprised to find out you came home with an education."

Verna Lee left the room and came back with the coffeepot. She refilled their cups. "Things are fine the way they are, Grammy. I love this shop. It's a whole lot better than being a wage slave and haggling over hours and raises and pension plans. It suits me. I've never deliberately kept the fact that I have a degree from anyone. Because no one expects a black woman from Marshyhope Creek to have a college degree, it just doesn't come up."

The old woman eyed her shrewdly. "If you say so."

Verna Lee smiled over the rim of her coffee cup. "So, do you have any other gossip to tell me?"

"Russell Hennessey's comin' home to run his daddy's fishing fleet."

The younger woman's eyes widened. "Well, well, well,"

she said softly. "Libba and Russ home at the same time. It won't be dull in Marshyhope Creek this summer."

Russell Tremayne Hennessey pulled his Ford Explorer over to the side of the road, removed his sunglasses and stared across the gold-tipped waters of the Chesapeake. The sun sat on the bay like melted copper. Trawlers and single-manned boats would all be docked by now, leaving what they hadn't caught to the brown pelicans and giant blue herons and an occasional migratory loon on its way to the colder, cleaner ponds of Maine. As a child, Russ had dreamed of birds and what it would be like to feel that lifting, soaring, tightening-of-the-stomach sensation at the surge of an updraft, to experience the power of wind beneath spread wings and know that the world was miles below.

He wondered, not for the first time, how he could have left. Seventeen years ago it seemed reasonable to put the pain and disappointment behind him and move on. But now, in retrospect, he'd been a fool. The pain had abated in its own time, and the memories had followed him on that mad, diabolic flight out of Marshyhope Creek, away from the light-struck, water-bright bays of Maryland, west through the smoky Blue Ridge Mountains and the red-earthed flat-lands of Virginia, north across the Mason-Dixon Line into the rolling green farmlands of Pennsylvania, breaching for the first time in his life the boundaries where no self-respecting Southerner would willingly exile himself. How he'd come to believe the flight syndrome was the only way to deal with the downward trajectory of his life was a mystery.

As close as he could tell, it had all started when Libba Delacourte ran off with a boy too wet behind the ears to know what to do with his hanging body parts. Her defection had shocked Russ. Mitch had told him, albeit reluctantly and by mail and after all other topics had exhausted themselves, that Libba had run off with a Yankee and then, rubbing his nose in it even deeper, married him.

Russ had gone into such a decline that he no longer attended classes, was put on probation and subsequently kicked out of the Citadel. That led to a stint in the army as a private, a return to Marshyhope Creek, a bad marriage, another flight as far and as fast as his wherewithal would take him, another attempt at college, successful this time, and a career he'd tired of, given up and sold out in order to come home. It was a crapshoot, giving up a successful architectural company, starting over at his age, but the way he saw it, he had no other option. He'd come for Tess, his love, his only child, his fifteen-year-old daughter, whose recent behavior had forced his ex-wife to break down and ask for his help.

Russ acknowledged that he'd been a disappointment as a father. He hadn't wanted a child, not at first, and not with Tracy. The idea of having a child with Tracy Wentworth left him shuddering. She was dangerous, spoiled and self-absorbed, and she had no concept whatsoever of child-rearing. As long as Tess was obedient, dressed well and disappeared when her mother was occupied, all was well. But now that Tess was growing up, now that she had opinions and preferences and a will of her own, Tracy couldn't cope. Russ had sued for custody, but Judge Wentworth, Tracy's father, had influence.

Not only had Russ been denied custody, he hadn't even been awarded normal visitation privileges. Throwing up his hands, he'd left town, preferring to see his daughter on rare occasions when Tracy needed a break, rather than haggle over alternate holidays and weekends. It wasn't his first mistake. He realized that now. Tess needed something solid in her life. She needed a role model, someone other than her frazzled, hysterical mother, a woman who had no interests, served no useful purpose and had difficulty concentrating on a serious conversation.

Russ turned off the engine, climbed out of the car and walked down the bank to the water. The Chesapeake—America's giant protein factory, environmentalists had called it in earlier, richer days. It was no longer true. Commercial harvests of American shad had almost disappeared in the Virginia and Maryland portions of the Chesapeake. Valleys of underwater greenery, life support for dozens of species of fish and fowl, simply vanished. Pollution and commercial fishing were cited as the primary causes. The environmentalist's answer was to remove the fishing pressure and allow the spawning stocks to rebuild, a harbinger of death for the watermen of the bay.

He hoped the fishing lobbies had enough power to hold them off. If not, he was doomed before he ever took over the Hennessey Blue Crab and Fishing Fleet.

Cupping his hands, he bent down and dipped them into the sun-warmed water, then tasted it. Nostalgia flooded through him. He'd swallowed his first mouthful of salt-tinged bay water when he was only three years old. Clutching Mitch's hand, he'd waded in up to his waist under the anxious gaze of his mother and the approving one of his father, and lost his balance. He'd been under for a full ten seconds before he was pulled, waterlogged and gasping, up on the beach. Four years later, he'd pulled in his first shad. Libba was there by then. She'd been there when he'd captained his first trawler, nursed his first hangover, brought down the largest harvest of the summer and beat his daddy's shucking record. She'd been there for every first he'd ever had, first date, first dance, first kiss, first—

He stood abruptly and walked back to the car. That kind of thinking served no purpose. The pain had dissipated long ago, leaving nothing more than a slight regret. He'd moved on. Better to leave it at that.

A single car with a yellow decal signaling a Hertz rental hugged the road ahead of him, moving at the speed limit. Obviously, the driver was a woman. Deciding against passing, he resigned himself to a tedious three miles or so until the road forked into two lanes near town. He fiddled with the radio, reduced his speed and settled into a reasonable following distance when the car turned down a private road. Russ stared after it curiously. He knew that road better than anyone except for the three people who called it home. Who would be calling at dinner hour, especially now that Nola Ruth was bedridden? He was intrigued enough to think about calling at the Delacourtes' himself. But sanity returned before he could act on his thoughts. He'd never been a favorite of Nola Ruth's and he wanted to see what was left of the Hennessey Blue Crab and Fishing Fleet before the sun went down.

Russ parked on a side street, turned off the engine and opened the car door. The blast of humidity permeated his skin. The Chesapeake in July. Crossing the railroad tracks, he climbed over the dunes and down to the dock where the headquarters of the Hennessey Blue Crab and Fishing Fleet had stood for more than a century. The condition of the building reflected hard times. The same splintered planks and railing, the cheap aluminum door and shingled roof that he remembered from childhood greeted him. Cracked white paint peeled in an uneven pattern and the single window was still whitewashed shut from the penance duty of countless Hennessey heirs.

He stopped at the door, inhaled deeply and pushed it open without knocking. A gray-haired woman sat behind a meticulously kept desk. She did not immediately look up. Russ quelled his impatience. He wasn't going anywhere. When she finally deigned to notice him, her eyes widened and a smile of unmitigated joy lit her face.

"Russ Hennessey?" Her voice rose and cracked. She pushed back her chair and walked around the desk to throw her arms around his neck. "Land sakes, child. As I live and breathe. Is it really you?"

Russ grinned and kissed the woman's cheek. "In the flesh. How are you, Effie?"

"Tickled pink. It's about time you came back. This ol' place hasn't been the same without you."

"I'm not sure I can make it work, Effie. This was never my thing."

Her smile faded. "That's not the way I remember it. You're a born waterman, Russ. The best I've seen. Haven't you sowed enough wild oats for ten lifetimes? I would have thought all these years away—"

"C'mon, Effie," he chided her. "You know I always meant to leave. This was Mitch's baby."

"C'mon yourself, Russ Hennessey. I know nothing of the sort. This is your home. This is where you belong. People are depending on you. Their livelihoods are at stake. Billy Dupree's been taking a skeleton crew out on two boats, but it isn't enough. These men need you."

The sun-dark line of his jaw hardened. A dozen emotions flickered behind his eyes before they emptied and became unreadable again. "Nice of you not to put any pressure on me, Effie," he drawled.

She laughed. "I know you better than you know yourself, sugar. You're gonna stay and give it all you've got. The boy I remember won't let us down."

"I'd like to get a handle on all the new rules and regulations before I decide anything permanently."

Effie's eyes twinkled mysteriously. "There might be a bonus in it for you."

He went along with it. "Go on."

"Libba Delacourte's come home to be with her mama while she's recovering."

Russ shook his head. "You never give up, do you, Effie?"

"Don't talk that way to me, Russell Hennessey. I wasn't born yesterday. I remember the way it was with the two of you."

"You got it right, Effie. The qualifying word is *was*. Libba Jane and I are ancient history. For Christ's sake, we both married other people."

"She's divorced, just like you."

"That doesn't mean anything. Everybody's divorced."

"I'm not."

"Lord, Effie—" He stopped. "Never mind. It doesn't matter." He looked at his watch. "Isn't it past closing time?"

"I thought you might want to start right in and look at the books."

"I do. But you don't have to stay."

"I wanted to be sure you could get inside."

She was offended. He'd make it up to her, but not tonight. "I appreciate it, Effie. It was mighty nice of you. But it's late. Herb'll be waiting for his dinner. We'll take this up in the morning."

She looked at the clock. "My gracious, it is late." She picked up her purse. "Everything is labeled in the files. If you can't find something, call me at home and don't mess anything up."

"Yes, ma'am. I didn't see a car. Are you walking home?"

"Yes."

He opened the door. "I'll drive you."

"You been gone too long if you don't know how silly that sounds. Marshyhope Creek isn't any bigger than a football field. There's more energy goes into getting into that big car of yours and pulling on the seat belt then there is walking down the street to my house. Save the chivalry for Libba. I already got me a man."

He grinned. "I'll keep that in mind."

"You do that." She hesitated.

"Spit it out, Effie."

"The thing is, I've been meaning to retire for some years now. I won't leave you in the lurch or anything, but I can't be here full-time now that you're back. Herb wants to do some traveling. We're looking at Florida.''

Russ's heart sank. Effie had been with Hennessey Blue Crab and Fishing for as long as he could remember. Her hopeful expression stopped the words in his throat. Somehow he would manage. "Don't worry about it, Effie," he said gently. "Take your Florida vacation. You deserve it.''

Two hours and a dozen files later Russ still couldn't concentrate. The small office hummed from the noise of the wall-mounted air conditioner. Cold air blasted him from behind. His last meal was seven hours ago and his stomach roiled with emptiness, guilt and a new emotion he couldn't place, something that was more than tension but not quite anxiety. At some point he would have to fill the hole in his stomach and then call his ex-wife to tell her he was home again. He would eat first because after their conversation he was fairly sure he wouldn't feel like eating again that night. But it wasn't lack of food, nor was it the thought of talking to Tracy, that prevented him from interpreting the profit-and-loss statement Effie had so carefully filled in. It was her news that hobbled him and kept the numbers two-stepping in front of his eyes. *Libba was home.*

There had never been a time when Russ didn't know Elizabeth Jane Delacourte. Everyone who lived on the northern side of Marshyhope Creek in that exclusive community of green lawns and white homes and pedigrees predating the Revolutionary War knew one another. But the first time he really saw her was when she entered Miss Warren's second-grade class in the middle of the school year. She had contracted pneumonia as a toddler and her anxious mother insisted on teaching her at home. By the age of seven, she'd bloodied her knees and fallen out of trees so often that her father insisted his only daughter was well enough to attend the local public school.

Standing there skinny and scared, dark hair pulled back

in a lopsided bow, eyes dark and enormous in her pale pixie face, scabby knees showing beneath her crisp, plaid jumper, she showed a promise of something more. She'd searched the room for a friendly face, those expressive eyes sending a mixture of fear and hope, until they'd stopped at him. He grinned. She smiled. His breath caught. Few things would remain in his memory with the same crystalline clarity as that first time he saw Libba smile.

At first glance she was nothing out of the ordinary. Dark-eyed, dark-haired girls with the sculpted bones, ivory skin and square jaws of their French ancestors were a common-enough sight in Marshyhope Creek. But when Libba smiled, that was something else entirely. There wasn't a man, woman or child whose breathing didn't alter for a good minute or two while staring into that vibrant face, wondering what it was about her that held the casual observer spellbound. Taken individually, her features were pleasant enough to spark a passing interest, but not so unusual as to inspire that liquid, bone-weakening jolt of awareness that comes only occasionally in a lifetime to the very few and the very lucky.

Russ had always known that no one but Libba could bring the glory of that wild, fire-leaping heat to his blood. No one since had come close to touching his heart. There was a time when he was sure she felt the same. Hell, he would have staked his life on it, poor judge of character that he was. And yet, two months after he'd left for college, after she'd promised to love him forever, Libba Delacourte had run off with a passing stranger.

He was over it, of course, over her, over the anger and the hurt, even over the desire for retribution. If he stretched it a bit, he could even find it in his heart to be grateful to her. If it weren't for Libby's defection, he would never have joined the army, never seen the world, never broadened his horizons, so to speak. He wouldn't have Tess because he wouldn't have married Tracy. He wouldn't have wasted years of his life in a disastrous marriage. Maybe he was being too charitable. Maybe Libba Jane did have something coming to her after all.

Six

Chloe stared at the ceiling of her bedroom, unwilling to expend the energy necessary for a morning stretch. She'd been awake for nearly twenty minutes. It was still not even eight o'clock in the morning and it was already hot. Her grandmother had a cardinal rule for running the air conditioner. *Don't,* unless the thermometer read one hundred degrees in the shade. For the first time in her life, Chloe understood the meaning of the word *hot.* She'd used the term before, even believed she'd meant it before, but she hadn't really. *Hot* had nothing to do with California, not even in September when the temperature rose to the mid-nineties in the Valley. Given what she now knew, she would define what she'd previously known at home in Ventura County as comfortably warm. *Hot* had nothing to do with the gentle, temperate rays of a California sun. *Hot* was something completely different. *Hot* meant *this place* where she had been banished. *Hot* meant Marshyhope Creek and the mind-drugging, steam-bath, mosquito-biting heat of a Maryland summer.

Nothing helped, not the four tepid showers she'd taken every day for the three days she'd been here, not the inadequate air conditioner that never quite made it to her second-story bedroom, not the fans humming in every corner of the house, not even the ice cubes melting on her chest. The heat slowed her body. Her movements were slothlike, her mind scrambled. She had no appetite. She couldn't sleep. She hated this place and everyone in it, with two exceptions, her grandfather and Serena.

After finally dragging herself out of bed, she headed down to breakfast. While serving the meal, Serena came up with the suggestion that Chloe be sent to the hardware store in town to purchase two molleys to fit over the screws to be drilled into the lathe-and-plaster walls of her grandmother's sitting room, their purpose to hold pictures of Chloe as a baby. Her mother had brought them from home and Nola Ruth wanted them hung immediately. No one had objected to the errand and no one had volunteered to drive her. The last place on earth Chloe wanted to be was in a hardware store in a hick town in the middle of nowhere. But she said nothing. Rules were different here in Marshyhope Creek. At home she would have complained and wheedled her mother for a ride. Here, the thought had occurred to her, but she knew better than to waste her time.

Dressed in her skimpiest top, the spaghetti-strapped one that bared her belly, and a pair of cutoff, rolled-up denim shorts, Chloe stepped out on the porch. Her grandfather sat on the bottom step holding up a bicycle that had seen better days.

"Hi," she said cautiously.

"Hi, yourself." He grinned at her and nodded at the bike. "This'll help you get there."

"That's okay, Granddad. I don't mind walking."

"It's three miles into town, Chloe. After ten minutes in this heat, you'll be grateful. I oiled the chain and checked out the brakes."

He was so sweet and so enthusiastic. Chloe didn't have the heart to tell him she wouldn't be caught dead riding a bike. She'd find a bush to park it under and no one would be the wiser. "Thanks, Granddad," she said.

"You know how to ride a bike, don't you, sugar?"

"Yes." She gripped the handlebars and swung her leg

over the crossbar. "Don't worry about me. I might take some time to look around."

"It's about time you thought of getting a driver's license."

"That was on the agenda before we came here."

"I see." Cole reached into his pocket and pulled out a ten dollar bill. "Here's a little something to tide you over."

"I don't need any money, Granddad."

"Take it, just in case. You never know. A little extra cash can be mighty handy in a pinch."

Reluctantly, Chloe pocketed the money. "Thanks," she said again. "It's really nice of you."

"My pleasure. Run along now. It's a straight ride to Main Street. You won't get lost."

Conscious of her grandfather's eyes on her back, Chloe pedaled down the long driveway and out onto the dirt service road. Only when she reached the highway leading into town did she brake and slide off the seat. Holding on to the handlebars she began to look for a place to stow the bike. She chose a clump of brush set back from the road. By the time she'd dragged the bike down the embankment, hidden it in the bushes and climbed back up, she was breathing heavily. Sweat trickled down her forehead, the insides of her thighs and between her breasts. God, she hated this place.

Keeping to the side of the road, Chloe lingered in the shady spots, wishing she'd brought a water bottle. How long was three miles, anyway? She was quite sure she'd never covered such a distance on foot in her life. What were they thinking, Serena and her family, to send her on a mission like this? It was more than inconvenient, it was dangerous. Any old pervert could come by and kidnap her. Her father would flip out if he knew the chances Libby was taking with his daughter's life.

She was sure she'd missed the turn into town. Her top was drenched, her toes had blisters and her hair hung in lank wisps around her face. She'd made a mistake about the bike. Anything was better than this, anything at all. Dismissing every warning she'd ever heard about riding with strangers, she turned at the sound of a car engine and stuck out her thumb.

An old pickup, so rusty and banged-up its color was no longer discernible, passed by, leaving her in a cloud of dust. Discouraged, Chloe gritted her teeth and started down the road again. She was an idiot to have come with her mother. She should have thrown a temper tantrum, refused to eat, held her breath. Hell was no worse than Marshyhope Creek.

A sound came from the other direction. Another car? Chloe shaded her eyes, squinting against the glare. The same truck was coming toward her, slowly. A trickle of fear slid down her spine. She looked around. There was nowhere to go. She couldn't outrun a truck or a man. Lifting her chin, she waited. The truck made a U-turn and stopped beside her. Chloe released her breath. The driver was a boy, near her age with straight black hair, dark, hooded eyes and a face so sharp and severe and beautiful it could have graced the cover of a magazine. He leaned across the seat and opened the door. "Need a ride?"

Chloe climbed into the truck and pulled the door shut. "Thanks."

He nodded.

"I'm going to the hardware store in Marshyhope Creek," she volunteered

With one hand on the wheel, he pulled a cigarette from his pocket, stuck it in the corner of his mouth and pushed in the lighter on the dashboard. "Who are you?"

"Chloe Richards."

"You're new here."

It was a statement, not a question.

"I'm not staying," she said quickly. "My grandparents live here. My mom came to visit because my grandmother had a stroke."

He bent his head to light the end of a cigarette, drew in and exhaled. Her heart flipped.

"Cole Delacourte's your granddaddy."

"How did you know?"

"Nola Ruth's the only lady I know in Marshyhope Creek who had a stroke."

"Who are you?" Chloe countered.

"Bailey Jones." He pulled out on to the road. "Where ya from?"

"California."

"Hollywood?"

"No, but close enough. Hollywood isn't all that great." She looked around. "I guess if you lived here all your life, it might seem great."

He grinned and Chloe's eyes widened.

"It might at that," he said.

"Where do you live?" she asked.

"Outside town."

"Do you go to school?"

Again he grinned. "Now and then."

Chloe's heart pounded. "How old are you?"

"Eighteen."

She relaxed. Eighteen she could handle. "I really appreciate the ride."

He glanced down at her shoes. "You wouldn't get very far in those. I'm surprised they let you out dressed like that."

Chloe flushed. "What's wrong with the way I'm dressed?"

He shrugged. "It's twelve noon, hotter'n a fry station, and you don't have anything on. You'd likely have passed out from heat stroke if I hadn't stopped."

"So, this is an act of mercy."

"What did you expect? I'm not into cradle robbing, if that's what you're thinking."

"I wasn't thinking anything of the sort," Chloe snapped.

She couldn't help adding, "You're not all that much older than me."

"How old are you?"

"None of your business."

"Fair enough." The cigarette hung from the corner of his mouth. A breeze blew his hair back from his forehead. He tapped the steering wheel and whistled in time to the music coming from the radio, a song Chloe had never heard of. He didn't look at all offended.

She stared out the window, cheeks burning.

"Didn't anybody ever tell you not to hitch rides with strangers?" he said when the song was over. "I coulda been an ax murderer or a rapist."

Chloe snorted. "Please. I'm from Los Angeles. I'd know a rapist if I saw one. You're definitely not the type."

He raised one eyebrow. "What type am I?"

"The dumb, naive type. My friends and I would eat you for breakfast."

"Whatever you're into, I guess," he said amiably. "You could be wrong."

"Not a chance. You already made your first impression."

"So, I'm stuck with dumb and naive?"

Chloe almost smiled but caught herself in time. "That's right."

"I don't understand the part about eating me for breakfast. Is that some California joke?"

"It means you aren't up to speed. No one who is anyone would associate with you."

"I get it." He chuckled. "Maybe Marshyhope Creek and California aren't all that different."

Chloe frowned. "What does that mean?"

He pulled over to the side of the road. "It means you get out here."

Her mouth fell open. "You're dumping me, in the middle of nowhere?"

"Relax, Chloe. Marshyhope Creek's about fifty yards

from here, just around the bend. The hardware store's two blocks away.''

''Why can't you drop me off there?''

He stared out the window for a bit and then looked directly at her.

Chloe Richards felt her heart race. She was quite sure she had never seen anyone so beautiful in her life.

''You won't have a prayer of fitting in if you're seen with me.''

''Why not?''

He threw the cigarette out the window. ''Let's just say I'm not acceptable company.''

''What's wrong with you?''

''I don't fit the mold.''

''What's the mold?''

He frowned. ''You sure do ask a lot of questions.''

''Well, what is it?''

''Jocks are the mold. Jocks and guys in ROTC heading for the Citadel or Annapolis and girls who like 'em.''

''I won't fit the mold, either. I'm not into sports. I'm going to be an actress. But it doesn't matter, anyway. I already told you I'm not staying, so drive on.''

He shook his head. ''Either way, this is where we part company.''

''Maybe you don't want to be seen with me, dressed the way I am with nothing on,'' she challenged him.

He laughed. ''That's it. Now, get out of my truck.''

Chloe opened the door and slid out. She leaned into the open window. ''No wonder you're not acceptable company. It isn't because you're not a jock, Bailey Jones. It's because you're rude.''

His teeth were very white and she had never seen eyes so dark in her life.

''Bye, Chloe Richards. It's been nice meeting you.''

''Yeah, sure. Stop by any old time.''

He lifted his hand in a farewell salute. She stepped back,

away from the truck, a slim straight little figure, rigid with injured pride and indignation.

Taft's Hardware sat on a corner, a square building with a flat roof and wooden doors that were securely closed. A wheelbarrow, garden supplies, brooms, shovels and packaged seeds cluttered the entrance. Chloe pulled at the door. It wouldn't budge. Then she saw the sign. Closed for Lunch. Come Back at 1:00. Now what? How could a store be closed in the middle of the day? Stores had salespeople who lunched in shifts. She'd never heard of a store that was closed in the middle of a weekday. Why had they sent her on this errand at lunchtime? One more reason to hate Marshyhope Creek.

The sun beat down relentlessly. She was hot, sweaty and beginning to feel sick. Her stomach rumbled. Defeated, she walked down the street, empty of anything alive in the sweltering noonday heat. It never occurred to her to go home without accomplishing her errand. She had her pride, and there was something about Cole Delacourte that made her seek his approval.

Across the street, a door opened. Music drifted into the air. Drawn to the soothing sound and to the tall woman energetically sweeping the front sidewalk, Chloe made her way to the other side of the road. "Hello," she said politely.

The woman stopped sweeping. "Hello, yourself." Her smile was lovely. "I've never seen you before."

Chloe shook her head. "I'm visiting my grandparents. I'm waiting for the hardware store to open."

"It's mighty hot out here. Would you like to wait inside?"

Chloe sighed with relief. "Yes."

"I've got some iced herbal tea or maybe you'd like a smoothie?"

"A smoothie? You have smoothies in Marshyhope Creek?" Chloe had died and gone to heaven.

Verna Lee laughed and pointed to the window of her shop. "Perks has everything, coffee, tea, herbs, health foods, books, cards, whatever you're looking for." She held out her hand. "I'm Verna Lee Fontaine."

Chloe took it. "Chloe Richards."

"Who are your grandparents?"

"The Delacourtes."

Something flickered behind Verna Lee's eyes. "Really? You don't look like a Delacourte. Your hair's beautiful."

Chloe nodded. "Thanks. I look like my dad."

Verna Lee opened the door. "Come on in and sit down."

Chloe followed her inside and looked around appreciatively. The decor was pure eclectic with deep couches, low tables and bookshelves filled with interesting titles. Two glass cases offered various dried leaves and twigs, all neatly labeled. Colorful china and crockery sat on the shelves and the tables, along with candles, beads and incense of every imaginable scent and color. "I like this," said Chloe reverently, grateful for the cool air blowing from the vents. She sat down on one of the couches.

"Thank you. Where are you from?"

"California."

"Ah, California."

"Have you been there?"

Verna Lee nodded. "I went to school in San Francisco."

Chloe's blue eyes slanted in surprise. "Why did you come back here?"

"My grandmother is old. There was no one else to take care of her. She needed me."

Dubious, Chloe nodded. Selflessness to such a degree that one would sacrifice San Francisco for Marshyhope Creek was beyond her.

Verna Lee moved efficiently, as if the heat and humidity had no effect on her. She set two sweating glasses of ice cubes and golden liquid on the table in front of Chloe.

"Taste that and tell me if you like it. I'll join you if you don't mind."

Chloe sipped it tentatively. "It's delicious," she said. "You put sugar in it."

Verna Lee shook her head. "It's naturally sweetened with cinnamon and spices. My own recipe. You should feel better in a minute."

"I feel better already."

Verna Lee sat down beside Chloe and crossed her legs. "Tell me about yourself, Chloe Richards. How long will you be here?"

"I'm not sure. My mother said two weeks, but it may be longer. We thought my grandmother was dying, but she's nowhere near that. Not that I want her to be," she said hastily. "It's just that now everything is up in the air and I had things going on at home."

"Occasionally, life throws us a loop." Verna Lee touched Chloe's leg briefly, gently. "Sometimes, in the end, it works out for the best."

Chloe changed the subject. "Do you know someone named Bailey Jones?"

Verna Lee's smile faded. "I do."

"What's wrong with him?"

"Nothing," said Verna Lee stiffly. "Bailey hasn't had an easy time of it and folks around here have long memories."

"He gave me a lift into town," Chloe explained, "but he made me get out before anyone saw us. He said it wouldn't be a good thing to be seen with him."

Verna Lee sighed. "Bailey Jones doesn't fit the mold of a good ol' boy. He's his mama's only son and sole support. Lizzie Jones is half Cherokee Indian, one of the few left around here. Some say she's got a drop of African blood as well. Whatever the case, she's in poor health. They live in a trailer on the other side of the marsh. No one knows who Bailey's father is. The boy's got more than his share of pride. That's his only flaw. Otherwise, he's a hardworking kid who deserves a break. It isn't pleasant being on the outside looking in.''

''Are you saying I should try being his friend?''

''How are you at swimming against the tide and taking on lost causes?''

Chloe lifted her chin and smiled. ''I like a good challenge.''

Verna Lee lifted her glass in a toast. ''Go for it, girl.''

Seven

Russ Hennessey flicked the end of his last cigarette into the ashtray and ran his hands through his hair. Pushing back his chair, he extinguished the office lights, locked the door and stepped out on to the dock. He was through for the day and it wasn't yet time to pick up Tess. It would be too much to hope that the regular Friday evening poker game at Taft's Hardware was still in existence.

Against his better judgment, he headed in the direction of Main Street. Sure enough, the door of the hardware store was invitingly ajar and the voices inside were rowdy, male and somewhere on the harmless side of tipsy.

Russ stepped inside and grinned down at four familiar faces. "Where can a man find a good poker game in this hick town?"

Two hours later Fletcher Sloane threw down his cards, turned his head and spat a six-foot stream of tobacco juice out on to the street. "Jesus Christ. Where'd you learn to play poker, Hennessey? I lost nearly half my paycheck tonight. Shelby'll kill me."

Russ laughed. "Stop pretending you're henpecked. You always were a lousy player, Fletch. Stop torturing yourself and find some other way of passing the time."

The other men, Luke Chartier, Gus O'Bannion and Horace Taft, slapped their thighs and chuckled. Fletcher couldn't keep it going. He folded too fast and Russ always won. Their rivalry was good-natured and of long standing. No one ever lost more than a twenty and a case of Coors. It was their tradition to meet every Friday for a friendly game of poker. Taft would close up shop early and whoever was in town would turn up for the game.

Luke Chartier brought the subject up first. "Clifford Jackson's back in town."

Russ leaned back in his chair and lit his first cigarette of the night. Tess was after him to quit, but it was going to be harder than he thought. "So?"

A customer wearing the sweat-stained overalls of a farmer wandered into the dry goods store.

"I'm closed," Horace shouted. "Can't you see the sign?"

"The door was open. I need a linchpin for my tractor."

"You ain't gonna do no plowin' tonight," said Horace. "Come back first thing in the morning and I'll see what I can do."

The man grumbled and turned to go.

"Close the door behind you," Horace ordered. "We're in the middle of a card game here."

"Actually, we're finished," Russ reminded him.

Chartier resurrected his initial subject. "Are you still hiring for the fleet, even with Jackson in town?"

Russ frowned. Had they always been so suspicious of government agencies or had the restrictions of the last few years changed them? "What's Jackson got to do with my hiring practices?"

"He's EPA," said Gus O'Bannion. "Don't do no good for us to sign on if we're gonna battle the EPA."

"Cliff will go by the book as long as we do. I'm not planning on bucking the system. Why is the EPA here, anyway?"

The men looked at one another. Horace spoke first. "Some people, tree-hugger types, think the bay water's got chemicals or something in it. Some of the fish and crabs have turned up bad.''

"Any truth to that?" Russ asked.

"There's always some truth to rumor," replied Gus. "Nothing serious as far as I'm concerned." He frowned. "What if Cliff closes you down?"

Russ blew out a blue-tinted swirl of smoke. "Why should he? I won't be doing anything illegal. More than likely the government's sent their boy down to pacify those who have questions. That way they can claim they're working on the problem."

Fletcher Sloane shook his head. "They got all kinds of rules and regulations about when and where we can fish. It ain't a free country anymore."

"Let me worry about that."

"You always did have a soft spot for ol' Cliff Jackson," Gus said. "Who'da thought he'd end up a big shot in Washington?"

"Cliff always was bright and he had talent," Russ reminded him. "He's worked hard to get where he is."

Horace wiped the sweat off his gleaming forehead. "Christ, it's hot. I hope you're still sayin' that in three months, Russ. Mitch and your daddy had a hard time with the bastards."

"I'll be all right." He stood and stretched. "I'm calling it a night."

"Hell, Russ, it's only eight o'clock," Fletcher complained. "I got to recoup my losses. Shelby won't let me in the door."

Russ grinned. "My advice to you, my friend, is to stop right now and go home to your wife. You lost twenty bucks. Suck it up. Buy Shelby some flowers and take her for a walk around Main Street."

Gus O'Bannion chuckled. "So speaks a man who signed divorce papers before the ink was dry on his marriage certificate."

"Russ never wanted to marry Tracy Wentworth in the first place," observed Horace. "Forgettin' the marriage license on their weddin' day was the first sign."

Russ ignored the ribbing, pocketed his winnings and made his way toward the door.

"Hey, Russ, what's the hurry?"

"I'm supposed to pick up my daughter. Tracy will figure out something else for her to do if I show up late. It's a pattern with her."

"Jesus." Fletcher shook his head. "He ain't even married to her anymore and she's still got him jumping through hoops."

Russ stubbed out the remains of his cigarette, finger-combed his hair and threw his now-dry piece of chewing gum out the window. Tracy could smell beer on a man's breath from clear across a room, twelve hours after he'd had one. He wanted nothing to provoke her into refusing this rare visit with his child. *His child.* The jury was still out on that one. Reserved, self-absorbed and devoid of any resemblance to him at all, Tess was still his daughter and he loved her desperately. An entire weekend with her was rare. Tracy usually had her scheduled so tightly he couldn't get in more than a few hours. That would change. Somehow he would make it change now that he was home for good.

With a hollow in the pit of his stomach, he approached Judge Wentworth's white-pillared colonial mansion set on a spectacular finger of land jutting out into the bay. Tracy had never seen the point of living on her own with Tess, not when she had an elegantly appointed suite with all expenses paid.

Tracy answered the door herself, another rare occurrence. "You're late," she said pointedly.

He refused to take the bait. "I'm sorry. I got held up."

"Tess has a mighty bad sunburn. I don't want her down at the dock."

"She won't be down at the dock," Russ mimicked her dutifully.

Tracy handed him a bottle of pills. "This is her medication. She takes it two times a day."

Russ took the bottle. "What's it for?"

"Depression."

Russ's brows knitted. "Depression? What's this all about?"

"Tess has—" she paused delicately "—problems."

"Problems? Hell, Tracy. She's fifteen years old. What kind of problems can a teenager have that would require antidepressants?"

"She has an absentee father, for one thing. Girls get their self-concept from their father's opinion of them."

"Well then hers must be pretty good because I'm crazy about her."

Tracy rolled her eyes and, once again, Russ wondered what he'd ever seen in her. Quite possibly he'd been interested because her pale, delicate looks were the antithesis of Libba's warmth. She was different in other ways as well and the comparison wasn't a favorable one. He hadn't seen it at first, mostly because there was no one quite like Libba. The quivery brightness that Libba Delacourte brought into a room was missing from every other female he'd ever known. But she'd chosen someone else and Russ had to marry somebody. Tracy had been available and interested. It was his worst mistake. He'd known it well before the wedding day. His mother had warned him. "She's not for you, Russ," she said. "That woman is flighty and selfish. She'll bring nothing to you. She's a taker."

In the end he'd balked at leaving a church full of wedding guests, limiting his feeble protest to forgetting the marriage license. There was a flurry, a twenty-minute wait while Mitch, his brother and best man, retrieved the license and the wedding commenced not too far off schedule. There was something to be said for Freudian slips, however. Everything had deteriorated from the day he'd said "I do." By the time their first anniversary rolled around, he had to be drunk to even climb into bed with her and get it up. He wasn't proud of it, but he hadn't been faithful and Tracy knew it. Neither of them ever discussed divorce. He hadn't the guts. The Hennesseys were Irish Catholic. Not a one had ever been divorced.

Surprisingly, Tracy had turned up pregnant. How, he had no idea. As far as he knew Tracy took care of their birth control, not that three minutes once a month, the average frequency and duration of their sex life, required much in the way of birth control. Somehow, however, she'd conceived and Tess was born. If he'd bothered to think about it, his daughter's brown eyes might have raised some questions in his mind. But in the end it hadn't mattered. The moment he held Tess in his arms for the first time, he was caught. That feeling hadn't changed in fifteen years.

"Are you going to cooperate and make sure that Tess takes her medication?" Tracy demanded.

Russ gritted his teeth and mentally counted to ten. "Yes," he said softly.

Tracy turned away. "Tess, your father's here." She did not invite him inside.

Tess walked slowly down the spiral staircase and across the foyer to stand before him. "Hi, Daddy," she said listlessly.

His heart lurched. "Hi, sweetheart. How are you?"

She shrugged. "Okay, I guess."

He picked up her overnight bag. "I'll have her back on Sunday night."

Tess's eyes widened and she looked at her mother.

"She has a party tomorrow evening," Tracy announced. "You'll have to bring her home before six."

"Before five," Tess said quickly. "I have to get ready."

Russ felt the familiar rage course through him. "I haven't

seen you in three months, Tess. Surely you can miss the party this time.''

''I can't, Daddy,'' she wailed. ''I really can't. It's Celia Merritt's party and if I don't go everyone will talk about me. She wasn't going to invite me in the first place, but Dixie Ryan got sick and can't go.''

Her logic escaped him. ''Why would you want to go to a party where you're not wanted?''

''You wouldn't understand, Russ,'' explained Tracy. ''Girls are different. It's hard to fit in and harder to stay in. It would be foolish for Tess to pass up an opportunity like this.''

''What opportunity?'' His voice was cold now and furious. ''Merritt owns a diner. He barely got through high school.''

''Nevertheless, his daughter is powerful. Tess has to live here in this town. It's important to keep the right connections.'' Tracy crossed her arms tightly against her chest. ''Now, if you're going to be difficult and refuse to bring Tess back on time, she won't be able to go with you.''

Rage consumed his brain. He could barely see. ''Tess, honey.'' He fought to control his anger. ''Do you want to come with me or not?''

''I do, Daddy, I really do.'' She looked at him hopefully. ''But maybe this isn't the best weekend. Maybe you could pick me up the weekend after next.''

''What's wrong with *next* weekend?''

''Skylar Taft is having a sleepover. Her party is even more important than Celia's.''

He set down her overnight bag, reached out and hugged her. ''All right, sweetheart,'' he said gently. ''We'll get together the weekend after next.'' Without a word to Tracy, he turned and walked back to his car.

Libby forced her eyes open and stared at the ceiling. One more minute, she promised herself. I'll stay in bed just one more minute and then get up. Exercise wasn't practical in the heat of midday and Marshyhope Creek had yet to become progressive enough for a gym. Either she had to rise at dawn or forgo exercise completely. Six extra pounds wouldn't disappear by themselves. The French desserts Serena had been feeding her for a week didn't help, either.

Groaning, Libby threw aside her sheet, the only bedcover she could tolerate in summer, and stumbled to the bathroom. She splashed water on her face, brushed her teeth, dragged her hair back into a ponytail and pulled on her shorts and tank top. Carrying her socks and tennis shoes in her arms, she tiptoed downstairs. It was a few minutes past six. No one would be awake yet.

She chose the meandering river path for her run. Already, the water shone a silvery blue under the spreading rays of morning sun. The woods, nesting grounds for cranes and ospreys, rang with birdcalls. Trawlers heading south to the island fishing grounds churned their way from the calm waters of the bay to the rougher ones of the Atlantic. Dewdrops bubbled on grass and shrubs and the cicada's tick-ticking had given way to the singsong chirping of crickets.

After the first half mile, Libby came alive. Pain and breathlessness disappeared and the ground fell away from the soles of her tennis shoes. She felt the beating of her heart, the blood in her temples, the bunching of her muscles, the sweat beading her brow, flowing down her back and between her breasts. The flush of well-being began in her brain and spread down from her chest to her stomach, her arms and legs. She passed the harbor, the peach grove and Blue Crab Beach, where she and Russ would swim naked, catch crabs, roast fish in the sand, drink beer and make love behind the rocks on that last summer he was home.

She was honing in on the docks now. Two trawlers, decks empty of watermen, their engines silent, were tied to their moorings. A movement caught her eye. A man, dark-haired and tall, with lean, ropy muscles, climbed from the cabin to stand on the deck, his profile to her. He wore faded jeans that conformed to every movement of hard, straight leg muscle, and a denim shirt rolled to the elbow. A cigarette was clamped in his teeth.

Libby slowed to a walk. No one would mistake him. The man was born to the breed. She'd seen him first. It gave her a slight advantage. Mustering her courage, she approached the trawler. He was writing something on a tablet, completely preoccupied with his task.

"Hi, Russ," she said softly.

He turned quickly. Black hair fell across his forehead and slate-blue eyes smoldered down at her. A variety of emotions played across his face, shock, pleasure, wariness. "Well, well, well," he drawled, blowing a blue-tinted curl of smoke in her direction. "If it ain't Miz Libba Jane Delacourte in the flesh." He drew out the word *Miz* until the very word itself sounded like an insult. "How are you, Libba Jane?"

"I'm doing well. How about you?"

He nodded. "Staggerin' blindly, as usual."

"Are you back for good?"

"I think so." His blue eyes were narrow, his mouth hard. "And you?"

"I'm not sure yet," she said honestly. "I need a job and I have a daughter who's California-spoiled. Before I can make any permanent plans, I've got to convince her that Marshyhope Creek has potential."

He whistled. "Times sure have changed, haven't they? Can you imagine our parents asking us if it was okay to move?"

His criticism stung. "That really doesn't apply. Moving wasn't even a possibility. Our families have lived here for generations."

Russ hopped down to stand beside her. "Don't get your feathers ruffled, Libba Jane. Your mother's family isn't from

Marshyhope Creek and every one of your daddy's brothers and sisters relocated elsewhere.''

She changed the subject. "I heard you were out West somewhere.''

He nodded. "That's right.''

"Why did you come back?''

"You do get right to the point, don't you? Same as always.''

"What did you expect?''

He stroked his chin, looked up at the sky and pretended to think about her question. "Well, the thing is, I don't know what to expect. There was a time when I knew you as well as I knew myself, or at least I thought I did. But that's long gone. So, as far as I'm concerned, you're a mystery to me, Libba Jane. When it comes to you, I'm startin' fresh.''

Libby swallowed. She deserved the sarcasm and the subtle tongue-lashing. There was nothing left to do but grovel. "I know it's late to try to make amends, but I'm sorry, Russ. I have no excuse for what I did to you. It was thoughtless and cruel. I hope you'll forgive me.''

He stared at her. "Did you practice that for long?''

Her lips twitched and then she laughed out loud. "I started when my daddy told me you'd come back to take over the business.''

"You're a terrible actress.''

"Thank God for that. At least you'll know when I'm telling the truth.''

He held out his hand and grinned. "Apology accepted.''

She took it and smiled. "I heard you're divorced. I'm sorry.''

"Thanks, but that's the best part. It was a mistake from the beginning except for Tess.''

"Tess?''

"My daughter,'' he explained. "She's fifteen going on twenty.''

Libby groaned. "I know what you mean. Wait until you meet Chloe."

Russ tested the name. "Chloe. I like it. When will that be?"

"Whenever you like. She's adrift right now because she doesn't know anyone her own age. That'll change when school starts."

"Careful, Libba Jane," he warned her. "You sound like you're settlin' in."

"Truthfully, I'd like to. I never did care for California. I'm glad to be home, but that's only the half of it. I need a job and I need to reach some kind of agreement with Chloe and her father."

"What happened there?" he asked casually.

Libby shrugged. "Like you, I made a mistake. I was too young to know what I wanted."

He studied her face. "You look exactly the same."

"Thanks," she said lightly.

"It isn't a compliment, Libba. Some things just are." He changed the subject. "I'm sorry about your mama."

"Thanks," she said again. "She's much better than I expected." She looked at her watch. "I've got to be going. Nice talking to you, Russ."

"I'll be seein' you around. Stop in any old time. I'm back at Hennessey House. You know the way."

She picked up her pace, aware of his gaze on her back, conscious of her six extra pounds, willing her pounding heart and wobbly legs to respond normally. Did she want to see him again? Her pulse accelerated. He wasn't quite the same as she remembered. He looked like the old Russ Hennessey, but there was something more there, a sophistication, an absence of bravado, an honesty that appealed to her. He wasn't as model-beautiful as Eric, but to Libby he was better-looking in a rugged, masculine, take-charge kind of way. Russ Hennessey was the kind of man who would always be in control. Seventeen years ago his protective, alpha-male tendencies had rankled the young Libby Hennessey and she'd chosen a different kind of man, a man who believed a woman should shoulder her own burdens and half of his. Now she was of a different mind. It would be a tremendous relief to have someone take care of her once in a while.

There were a million questions she wanted to ask. Tracy Wentworth was one of them. She knew Russ would marry someone, but she never imagined it would be Tracy. The Tracy she remembered refused to swim in the bay for fear of ruining her mascara and wetting her hair. In school she'd been excused from physical education because her milky skin couldn't tolerate the sun. She was always leaving class to take some sort of prescribed medication for her delicate constitution. Personally, Libby thought she was a classic hypochondriac. She'd gone out with Mitch for a while and Libby had tolerated her in the spirit of maintaining a friendship with Russ's brother, but Tracy's cloying manners and pretentious attitude toward anyone who lived on the wrong side of the creek made it difficult. Libby was relieved when Mitch broke off the relationship and surprised to learn from Shelby Sloane that Russ had taken up with Tracy less than a year after Libby had left for California. It was almost insulting. Russell Hennessey had been a catch. He deserved someone infinitely more worthy than Tracy Wentworth. To his credit, the marriage had been a brief one. But there was a child. Libby sighed. A child meant forever, no matter how one wished it otherwise.

Eight

Drusilla Washington shook the dirt from the plant in her hand and frowned. These budding sweet potatoes with their stunted stems and oddly shaped leaves were the least appetizing she'd ever harvested. Odd that they were so small when the ones she'd picked the other day were perfect. Hopefully, these plants weren't typical. Otherwise, if the crop continued to grow poorly and if there weren't more pregnancies in the migrant worker's camp she wouldn't be able to add to her nest egg this winter. She knew Verna Lee would take care of her, even take her in, if Drusilla was of a mind. The girl had a strong sense of family. But Drusilla had her pride and she liked her independence. She would stave off the day when she could no longer do for herself as long as possible.

She thought of the woman who had come to her the day before. The girl was young and very near her time. Her husband had promised Drusilla a healthy portion of his day's earnings for assisting at the birth. She could buy a week's worth of groceries with the money, maybe even a luxury or two she normally didn't allow herself, like a pound or two of soft-shelled blue crab or a good ham with a bone in the middle. Her stomach growled. She folded her blanket and took down her umbrella. She would stop by the woman's shack just to be sure the herbs she'd given her yesterday were working their magic.

* * *

A low moan and the anxious black face of the young husband answered her knock. "She be at it since early mornin'," he croaked, rubbing his hands nervously on his overalls. "If I don' git to de fields, I won' be gittin' my wages."

"You run along," said Drusilla. "She don't need you now."

With a nervous half smile, he took one last look at the woman moaning on the stained mattress and hurried out the door.

Drusilla found a bucket and walked to the outdoor pump. "Don' you be frettin' now," she told the girl when she returned. "Ol' Drusilla goin' take care o' you. It won' be long now."

She looked around. The sharecropper's shack was a temporary dwelling, clean but pitifully stark, designed to house the tide of migrant labor for as long as the harvest lasted. Pulling a handful of clean rags from the shelf, Drusilla sat down on the mattress and lifted the girl's gown to examine her. She was more than halfway there.

"There, there, chil'," she crooned as the girl cried out against the next contraction. "You doin' jes fine."

Three hours later the child had still not come. The mattress was drenched with blood and sweat and the young woman had long since passed out from the pain. Drusilla's round face was shiny and giant wet circles stained the underarms of her dress. She was worried. Something was very wrong. Frowning, she thought back to her mentor, Minnie Hobbs. Only once had Minnie allowed her to turn a breeched baby. It was long ago. If only Drusilla could remember. For the space of time it takes to hear a heartbeat, she thought of calling Verna Lee, Verna with her college education and her knowledge of herbs. Just as quickly she disregarded it. Verna would insist that the woman go to a hospital, something the young family could never afford.

Her eyes lit on the large cooler that served as an icebox. Moving quickly, Drusilla opened the lid and found what she was hoping for. Breaking off a fistful of lard from the block, she warmed it on the hot plate in the corner before smearing it over her hands and up her arms clear to the elbow. Positioning herself on the mattress, she spread the woman's legs and reached into the birth canal with both hands and waited for the next contraction. It came quickly. Grimacing against the bone-crunching pain, she slowly, with painstaking care, pulled the infant free.

For a full minute she stared in horror at the creature she'd delivered. The baby's face, arms and legs were normal, but beyond that, Drusilla knew that in all her years as a midwife she had never seen anything quite like the tiny female lying in her lap. The infant was horribly deformed, with soft, purple, fleshy masses attached to her chest and abdomen that moved and pulsed like living things. A soft, mewling cry brought Drusilla to her senses. "Dear Jesus," she whispered. "Dear Jesus."

The woman on the mattress stirred but did not waken.

Drusilla looked at the torn body of the new mother. Then she looked down at the tiny monster she'd delivered. Life was hard enough for a young couple without this. It didn't take a prophet to see the future. If the child lived, the father would stay loyal for a while, averting his gaze from this thing he'd created, avoiding his wife in the superstitious fear that the two of them together would create another like the first. He would stay away for longer and longer periods of time, seeking work in nearby counties until finally it was easier to keep on going, to never return, to put this life and this woman and this child behind him forever.

The infant coughed and cried briefly. Drusilla made her decision. Quickly she stood and tied off the cord, wrapping the afterbirth in a towel-size rag. Then she swaddled the infant tightly in the brand-new receiving blanket she'd found on top of the dresser and sat down in a chair by the door. Crooning softly, she let the words soothe her troubled soul.

"Hush little baby, don't you cry,
Drusilla's gonna sing you a lullaby."

Her fingers found the pulse fluttering in the baby's throat
and squeezed firmly. Her eyes filled. She lost the words and
hummed the next few lines. The child was still.

"Hush little baby, don't say a word,
Drusilla's gonna buy you a mockingbird."

She looked down once more. Above the swaddled blanket, the baby's head was perfect, full and well shaped, the
skin fudge-colored, the lashes long. Dr. Balieu would need
to file a report. He wouldn't notice the faint purple bruises
on the baby's throat, not when he saw the rest of her. She
looked perfectly content as if she were sleeping, not dead
at all. Looking at that precious face, Drusilla nearly forgot
the atrocity beneath the blanket.

"Dear Lord," she whispered, "forgive me, but life is
hard enough for us colored folks. We don' need no more
than we already got."

The woman on the mattress woke and lifted her head.
"Where's my baby?" she croaked.

Drusilla tightened the blanket around the child and
crossed the room to the bed. "Don't fret too much. She be
with God."

With a low moan the woman turned her face to the wall.
Silent tears slid down her cheeks to mingle with the blood
and stains on the now foul mattress.

Later, as Drusilla walked home in the drugging heat of a
summer evening, she wondered if she'd taken on too much.
The young husband, who wasn't more than nineteen, had
shown an unusual maturity. His first concern had been for
his wife, and the words of comfort that she heard him speak
were exactly right. He'd insisted on paying Drusilla the
agreed-upon fee despite her assurances that she never

charged for stillbirths. Maybe the two of them could have managed the child after all.

When Drusilla tried to speak of her reservations to Dr. Balieu, he hushed her before she could explain.

"I don't want to hear another word about it, Drusilla. Sometimes babies die. These people don't lead the healthiest of lives. The poor child was dreadfully deformed. In my mind, dying early was the best that could happen to the infant."

Still, the doubt lingered, and for the first time in years, she stopped by St. Jude's on the way home to light a candle and make an offering, the exact amount that the bereft father had pressed into her hand two hours before. She justified her visit with the knowledge handed down to all voodoo priestesses, that Christianity had its roots in the religion of the Dark Continent. She wouldn't tell Verna Lee. The girl didn't always see things the same way as Drusilla, especially when it came to midwifery. She thought her grandmother was too old. But who would service the migrant workers and other poor folks who didn't have insurance cards for big fancy hospitals? Those years in San Francisco had given Verna Lee a different perspective. She didn't always know her place. A black woman should know her place. Drusilla's head hurt. She rubbed her temple. The doctor said it would be all right. No need for Verna to know anything at all.

Libby had noticed the shop the first time she made the trip into town. It was so *California*. Even the name, Perks, would have fit into the Santa Monica/Venice Boulevard scene. She turned the knob and pushed open the door. The jingle of bells greeted her. A large black man, whom Libby recognized immediately, stood at the counter deep in conversation with the woman behind the counter, Verna Lee Fontaine. Both turned at the sound of the bells.

Cliff Jackson's face lit up. "Libba Jane Delacourte. I

heard you were back. Where have you been keeping yourself?"

"At home with my mother." She shook his hand and nodded at the woman. "How are you, Verna Lee? Your shop is wonderful."

The woman was obviously sincere. Verna Lee Fontaine lifted the corners of her mouth in a brief smile. "Thanks. What can I do for you, Libba Jane?"

"Iced tea would be nice."

"I'm fresh out, but I'll brew some if you don't mind waiting."

"Take your time."

Verna disappeared behind the swinging doors that led to the kitchen.

Libby smiled at Cliff. "How have you been, Cliff?"

"I'm doing well, thank you. I heard about your mama. I'm sorry."

"Thanks. Actually, she's much better than I thought." She changed the subject. "I didn't realize you were back in this neck of the woods. I heard you're working for the EPA."

He eased his big linebacker's body into a low chair. "I'm here for the summer setting up an office. There've been a few problems around this area of the bay."

"What kind of problems?"

"Pollution, possibly even the subterranean wells, although I doubt it."

Libby's intuition kicked in. "PCBs?"

Cliff hesitated. "I'm not sure yet. I haven't got anything that amounts to much. As far as I can tell the test results show sludge with residual toxic metals."

"What kind?"

Cliff shrugged. "Nothing specific. Mercury, lead, some chromium. Could be paint or plastics."

"Are the PCBs high?"

"Not serious enough to terminate the fishing industry, but

enough to cause an unusually high amount of asthmatic bronchitis, and skin conditions among the sharecroppers.''

"What about the contaminants?'' Contaminants blocked testosterone and created alarming amounts of estrogen in animals dependent on the estuaries. But she doubted that Clifford Jackson or anyone else at the Environmental Protection Agency would willingly admit that connection.

"High enough. PCBs were banned along with DDT in the seventies, but chemicals still pollute hundreds of our waterways.''

"What about the human implication?''

"Those are still theoretical, however—'' Cliff shrugged. "No one wants to believe lower sperm counts and increased levels of prostate and testicular cancer in men and breast cancer and endometriosis in women could be the result of chemicals currently sprayed on crops, gardens and lawns all over the United States.''

"In other words, the most toxic chemicals known to man can be found on the shelves of local hardware stores. Does Dr. Balieu think the contaminants are in the fish?''

"That old quack? He could eat bad fish three times a day and never put two and two together.''

"Maybe not. But he's the only doctor we've got,'' she said quickly. "Any rise in cancer rates, primarily liver or kidney?''

Cliff shook his head. "Not that I could find out. But there is something unusual in the oxidation levels around the creek.''

Libby felt her palms sweat, a sure sign of internal agitation. No one would come forward to substantiate it, but the link was there and it wasn't DDT or any other toxic pesticide found in manufacturing or farm runoff. Biological oxygen demand was always evident in areas where stored radioactive nuclear waste had leaked into the groundwater. Her dissertation was based on it. She'd seen the results in alligators in the Florida Everglades, herons from British Columbia and bald eagles from the Great Lakes regions. Nearly twenty years after the drums were buried, descendents of wildlife exposed to uranium were born apparently healthy, but upon closer inspection carried two sets of sex organs. Female gulls in California were sharing nests for lack of male mates, terns in New Bedford Harbor had bizarre sex organs and twisted beaks. The long-term effect on humans was horrifying to think about. *Slow down, Libby,* she told herself. *BOD doesn't always mean nuclear spillage.* "Have you heard about the unusual rate of leukemia?" she asked casually.

"That's why I'm here. Could be the runoff from farms along the Susquehanna." Clifford stroked his chin. "Although a high biological oxygen demand isn't all that dangerous. Sometimes it's beneficial."

"What about shellfish in local waters?"

"The supply is down. But that could be due to overfishing. We just don't know."

Libby's mouth was dry. "Are you working on it?"

Cliff sighed. "I can't do everything, Libba. I need manpower. Right now there isn't any to spare."

Libby took the plunge. "I'm available."

"What about your credentials? Got any?"

"I'll admit to a few."

"Do you need a job, Libba Jane?"

"I'd like a job and this is my field. I'd like to come home for good."

"Are you staying?"

"I think so."

"I need more than that."

"You said you needed help for the summer. I can give you that and a few months more for sure. I can't promise full-time. I came home to be with my family. But a few hours a day would work for me. As for staying permanently, I'm not absolutely sure I can do that. I have a daughter. If she settles into school here, we'll stay. If not, I'll take her back to California.''

''This job isn't a popular cause around here. Close as we are to our nation's capital, there's still a states' rights mentality here on the peninsula side of Maryland. Folks don't like squealing on one of their own.'' Cliff didn't like it himself. He'd grown up on these waters. There wasn't a man within fifty miles of the Cove that he hadn't sworn and fished, arm-wrestled and slept off a drunk with. An investigation could lead to a fishing blackout. ''Can you do that, Libba? Do you have any experience with people spittin' on your shoes or in your face when you tell 'em they can't go to work in the mornin' to feed their families?''

''So far, no.''

He nodded. ''Fair enough. Come on in day after tomorrow and we'll talk.''

Verna Lee returned with a pitcher of tea, two sweating glasses and a flask filled with a clear liquid. ''Help yourself,'' she said. ''I've got a few things to do in the back. Holler if anyone comes through the door.''

Deciding against the sugar water, Libby picked up her glass and sat down across from Cliff. ''Are you worried?'' she asked bluntly.

His smile was grim. ''I'll tell you that when you're officially on the payroll.''

''I'll be in day after tomorrow.''

''Don't disappoint me.''

She drained her glass and looked around. ''Verna Lee's done well for herself.''

Cliff looked around. ''It's a nice little place.''

''My daughter thinks so, too.''

''How old is she?''

''Chloe's sixteen.''

''Good Lord.''

Libby laughed. ''Exactly.''

"This promises to be an interesting summer," Cliff observed. "All kinds of people are coming home."

"If you're warning me that Russ Hennessey is planning on taking over his daddy's fishing fleet, don't bother. I already know."

"That one could be difficult for you, Libba. I don't need a conflict of interest here."

"Don't be ridiculous, Cliff. That was a long time ago. We married other people."

"And look how that turned out."

Libby raised her eyebrows. "Since you're so well informed, how did it turn out?"

"It doesn't take a genius to figure it out when you both come home divorced."

"I'll be leaving now," she said politely. "Give Verna Lee my regards."

"Will I be seeing you day after tomorrow?"

"You can count on it."

Clifford Jackson, his forehead wrinkled in concentration, stared at the door for a long time. He liked Libba. He'd always liked her and respected her, too. He felt the same way about Russ. Hell, he'd known Russ Hennessey most of his life. There was a streak in him that some would call soft. Clifford knew better. Whatever it was that drove Russell Hennessey had nothing to do with softness. He was smart. He liked to read and he was a whiz at numbers. Every once in a while his conscience showed up as a dangerous penchant for the underdog in a town where redneck mentality was as homespun as cotton candy at a carnival.

Cliff had first witnessed it in the second grade at Lafayette Grammar School. He'd been one of six black students in a classroom filled with the offspring of illiterate crackers from the soybean fields and the affluent few from the socially correct side of Marshyhope Creek. Russ had been one of the latter. From the sidelines, Cliff had watched the kickball and foursquare games of the white boys with interest and more than a little longing. It was Russ who suggested that he play. Even in 1974, black children did not assume their welcome. Clifford's mother had warned him expressly of the dangers of overstepping his place. It was Russ who'd noticed him first, hanging back, pretending not to show his need.

At first, Cliff believed it was the promise of his height and shoulders that attracted Russ's attention. Later, much later, he realized that Russ was a law unto himself. He flouted convention whenever possible, and nothing lit the fires of his temper more than inequity, whether it was on the docks, in the classroom or on the football field. Russ Hennessey didn't care about the color of a man's skin any more than he cared who his father was or on what side of Marshyhope Creek he was born. He'd worked the trawlers with shrimpers and dockhands, black and white, since he was seven years old. According to Russ, the measure of a man was the effort of his hustle. He'd decided early on, when Clifford stopped a fly ball in the outfield with a dive that bloodied his nose and broke his finger, that Cliff Jackson measured up just fine. And because it was Russ who passed judgment, everyone else accepted it as well.

Verna Lee walked out of the kitchen. "What was that all about?"

Cliff shrugged. "You heard as much as I did. She's got the right credentials. Lord knows she'd be accepted around here. One of their own, so to speak." He grinned. "You could say a ripe peach just fell into my lap."

"You might be taking on more than you can handle."

"So, what else is new?"

"Sometimes it doesn't pay to rehash the past, Clifford. You dig too deep and everything around the hole starts to crack."

"Tell me something I don't know."

"Libba Jane's daughter doesn't concern herself with appearances and she won't be happy when her mama tells her they aren't going home. Your new employee may not last.''

''I'll take my chances.''

''I always thought yours was an unlikely friendship.''

''Whose?''

''Yours and Libba Jane's.''

Cliff shook his head. ''Libba and I knew each other, but Russ was my friend. We lost touch for years until I took the job with the EPA. I was looking for an architect to remodel the house I'd bought in Georgetown and his name came up. Apparently he and his partner had a high-profile firm specializing in unique designs. Russ didn't disappoint me. Why he sold out is a mystery to me. He had to be making money hand over fist.''

''It doesn't surprise me at all,'' Verna Lee said. ''Russ always was a homebody. His daddy's company wasn't big enough for both boys and Russ always was odd man out.''

''Why was that?''

Verna Lee shook her head. ''Who knows why a parent prefers one child over the other? Jealousy, maybe, or else old Beau Hennessey knew that Mitch wouldn't make it anywhere else? All I know is that if there's anyone who belongs in Marshyhope Creek, it's Russ. His roots go back two centuries and he loves the place.''

Cliff thought back to their occasional conversations and remembered Russ's answer when asked of his future plans. He'd shrug and grin, replying that he'd finish school, settle down in the Cove, marry Libba and raise another generation of Hennesseys to terrorize the peaceable citizens of Marshyhope Creek.

Libba Delacourte. Now, there was one fine woman. Not that he would verbalize that sentiment in front of Verna Lee. He didn't consider himself particularly intuitive, but even he could feel the animosity between the two women when they were together.

Still, even now, seventeen years after high school, thinking of her made Clifford smile. There had been no one sweeter, smarter or prettier than Libba Jane Delacourte. It wouldn't have mattered even if they had been the same race. For as long as Cliff could remember everyone knew that Libba belonged to Russ. She'd soothed his temper, forgiven his wildness and balanced his quicksilver moods with nothing more than a quiet whisper. Everyone with eyes could see how she felt about Russ Hennessey and that was her problem.

Bright, ambitious, elegant, the town's golden girl was meant for much more than a two-bit town full of rednecks. Libba had been as antsy to leave the stranglehold of Marshyhope Creek as a rat stuck too long in a coffee can. Cliff knew it, her teachers knew it, her parents wanted it and Russ suspected it, but her dreams didn't threaten his until the day he watched her rendition of Julia in Chekhov's *A Doll's House*. Cliff remembered the way the drama class sat that day, mesmerized, allowing her voice to wash over them, humbled by her talent, touched by her symbolism, shaken by the combination of words and thoughts that had taken root in her mind.

The rest of that day, Russ had been strangely quiet. By Monday of the following week he was himself again, but Libba was different. There was a glow to her, a guarded sensuality that wasn't there before, and her behavior toward Russ was definitely more proprietary. Clifford had known what it meant right away. Coming from a different world, he wasn't as particular about matters of the flesh as were those who lived on the *right* side of Marshyhope Creek. Russ had staked his claim and that claim was Libba Delacourte. At the time, Cliff had deemed it a senseless gesture. He would have sworn on his daddy's gravestone that Libba and Russ were paired up permanently. It was as plain as the red in her cheeks when she looked at him. Who would've ever thought the girl who loved literature would turn into a scientist?

"I never could figure out why Libba ran off like that," he mused.

Verna Lee snorted. "Libba Jane had Hollywood on her mind. She wanted to be an actress. She would have taken off with anyone who promised her a stab at it even if he didn't have all that hair and white teeth."

Cliff was losing interest in the conversation. Verna Lee was having her usual effect on him. His gaze lingered on her golden skin, her sultry mouth, her wild tawny hair and settled on her long, long legs. "Why are we talkin' about this?" he asked.

She laughed and moved toward him. "I'm open for another two hours, Cliff. Come back later."

"You're a tease, Verna Lee."

"Sometimes," she admitted. "And sometimes I give you everything you want. That's the reason you keep coming back."

She was wrong, but he didn't contradict her. He didn't know what he wanted from Verna Lee Fontaine, but it was more than sex. "Not everything," he said, leaving the implication open, waiting to see where she'd take it.

"Don't, Cliff."

"Why not?"

Verna Lee ground a fist into her waist. She looked like an Aldo Luongo painting, one long golden leg exposed by the slit in her turquoise sarong, tawny curls spilling over bare shoulders. Her voice was soft, regretful and thoroughly serious. "Let's just say I've had enough of upwardly mobile black men trying their hardest to pull themselves up the corporate ladder. I've been that way before. I won't make the same mistake again."

"Maybe you picked the wrong man."

"No doubt of that."

"Why not give it another try?"

"Are you willing to give it all up and buy me out of half my store?"

"Not a chance."

She nodded. "You have your answer."

Nine

Russ removed the pencil tucked behind his ear, made an adjustment to the weekly report, entered the numbers on the adding machine and frowned at the result. To say that the books were in bad shape would be an understatement. The late Mitch Hennessey had no head for business. The most Russ could hope for was to break even. More than likely he would operate at a loss, dipping into his own retirement savings. For how long was the million-dollar question. He left the thought hanging. Billy Dupree, baseball cap in hand, stood in the doorway of the office.

Russ grinned. It was time to teach these dinosaurs how to fish. "Where've you been?" he asked Dupree. "I thought you'd never get here."

Billy pulled a toothpick from his mouth. "We're all waitin' on you, Hennessey. Two trawlers and their crews. You still know how to crab, or am I doin' all the work? Could be that fancy degree of yours made you soft."

Russ grinned. "Up yours, Dupree." Shrugging a faded gray sweatshirt over his head, he preceded Billy out the door.

They climbed into a long, narrow workboat. Russ pulled up the throttle to full speed, signaled two other boats to follow, and headed toward Irish Creek, steering the thirty-five-foot workboat through the heat and shrouded stillness of water and woodland. Two hours later, he slowed down to a two-knot crawl and began laying out his first trotline with the ease of a master. When two were in place, he began the harvest. At a regular, almost mechanical pace, he pulled his bait up from the depths and passed it over the roller, allowing it to submerge in the water behind them. A crab clung tightly to each piece of brine-pickled eel. Like clockwork, before the crab broke water, he slipped a net under it, superficially glancing to see if it met legal size requirements, five inches across the back shell. Sure enough, almost every bait had a crab attached, hanging on with powerful claws and chewing on eel. Using a long-handled net, he plucked them off the line and tossed them into baskets.

"You were right, Hennessey. I never would have thought to look on this side of the water," Billy said, nearly four hours later. "There's a powerful lot of crabs in this creek. Most of 'em over six inches. This size'll fetch top prices at the wharf."

Russ lit a cigarette and leaned against the bait tank. "Hell, I'm just warmin' up. Stick with me, Dupree, and see if your take isn't twice the size you're used to."

Billy lifted his hand in a mock salute. "Aye, aye, Captain. Lead the way. You won't find me complaining."

When the baskets were filled to the brim, the men pulled up the nets and turned their boats toward Marshyhope Creek. Russ was tired and muscles he'd forgotten he owned, ached. He rubbed the back of his neck and stared out across the bay. Splayed across the horizon like a penny on the railroad tracks, the sun's rays had turned the channel into a river of gold. Pilings and an occasional trawler stood silhouetted against a blazing sky. Behind them, a purple dusk dogged the boat's wake. Ahead, a copper-splashed path beckoned. Summer on the Chesapeake, the promise of heaven, or as close to it as a man had a right to see. For years, Russ had taken it for granted. He never would again. "What are the chances you can unload the catch today?" he asked.

Billy maneuvered the boat close to the mooring and

waited while Russ jumped out on the dock. ''I'll call ahead to make sure,'' he said, ''but I don't think you'll have any arguments about fresh crab whatever the time of day. I'll inspect the catch tonight, check to be sure they pass muster and see you tomorrow.''

The call came before dawn the following morning. Russ fumbled for the telephone through a sleep-induced fog. ''Holy shit, Dupree,'' he snarled when he heard the waterman's voice. ''It's four o'clock in the morning.''

Dupree's words were terse, angry. ''There's something I gotta tell you.''

''Now?''

''This can't wait. I'll meet you at the dock. If I'm wrong, I'll buy you a beer. Hell, I'll buy you ten beers.''

Russ stared at the phone, groaned and climbed out of bed.

Less than twenty minutes later, the two men faced each other on the dock. ''This better be good, Dupree,'' Russ said.

The waterman pulled his cap down low over his eyes. ''*Good* is hardly the word I'd use.''

Russ controlled his temper. Billy, a brawny independent young Frenchman, wise in the ways of his ancestors, would not be hurried. ''Are we going somewhere?''

''Shad Landing and we're going alone.''

Russ's eyes narrowed. ''Shad Landing's closed to trawlers. It's illegal to fish there. The quickest way to close us down is to operate in illegal fishing grounds.''

''We won't be taking no trawler, and whatever the government says, it's still the best place to pick up a cross sampling of crabs.''

''All right. Let's get to it.''

''You're the boss.''

Russ kept his thoughts to himself as he watched the waterman expertly maneuver the craft through the shoals, back across the bay and into outlaw waters. Billy pulled in his trotlines and unhooked the crabs, tossing them into baskets.

Russ set his teeth. Crabbing off of Shad Landing was strictly prohibited. They would be arrested on the spot if anyone reported them. Still, Billy had worked the waters of the Chesapeake islands with his father since he was four years old. If anyone knew what he was doing, it was Dupree.

Without a word, Billy turned the boat and motored back to the docks. He jumped from the boat to the pier and secured the lines, all without a word of explanation. Then he picked up the basket. "Come with me. I want you to see this."

Twenty minutes later, Billy had the crabs laid out execution style so their underbellies were exposed. Russ stared in shock. From stunted claws and suspicious-looking lumps to oozing abscesses, every one, without exception, was horribly mutated. "What in the hell is going on here?"

"I don't know." Billy took off his cap and wiped his brow with the back of his hand. "At least thirty percent of yesterday's catch looks like this, too, I think."

"What do you mean, *you think?*"

Dupree wet his lips. "I buried the diseased ones, otherwise I wouldn't have dragged you out this morning to show you what they look like. I was hoping Shad Landing would be different."

"You're not telling me anything."

"I sold off most of the catch without inspecting 'em."

Russ felt like he was choking. "You did what?"

"I'd sold about a quarter of 'em without even looking at 'em. It's the way things are done now. The wholesalers and restaurants come by and order, then the flunkies come in and pile the crabs into buckets. No one looks at them until the cook drops 'em into boiling water." Sweat rolled down his forehead. "You're gonna be getting some calls on this. I was hoping Shad Landing would be different. There's no way we can sell 'em."

"You got that right. Put these on ice," Russ ordered. "Call the lab in Salisbury and tell them to send someone out here. Meanwhile, I'll call the distributors and tell them we can't deliver our orders until this is straightened out.''

''Have you thought about what it's gonna do to us, Mr. Hennessey? Even if we spread out the crews on the shrimp boats, we'll have to lay off the crab skippers.''

Russ rubbed his temples and swore. All this before six in the morning. ''We have no choice. These animals could be poisoned. I can't be responsible for that.''

Russ crushed his cigarette under the heel of his shoe, then he sat down behind the desk and switched on the lamp. Posted on the wall was the phone list—mostly on-call numbers of the local seafood distributors. He started at the top with Angelle. Offering as little explanation as possible, he moved down the list, smoothing the waters, promising future orders, wondering how long it would be before every supplier on the shore knew he'd supplied stunted crabs to the Cove and if the honest business practices he prided himself on were ashes on the wind.

He was on the *D*s, methodically checking off names, his speech so rehearsed it sounded genuine, when he came to an unfamiliar name. Nothing much changed in Frenchman's Cove. Family businesses were generations old. *Diedrich.* An odd name on this side of the bay. He pulled the file, opened it and skimmed the page. It was his brother's medical record. John Diedrich was Mitch's oncologist.

Russ frowned and began to read more carefully, paying particular attention to the dates, leafing backward until he came to the beginning. His hands shook when he closed the file, turned off the light and walked to the window.

He stared out at the darkening sky. It would rain tonight. Mitch had never liked rain, not like he had, not like Libba, either. Strange that she should come to mind at defining moments of his life. Maybe it wasn't so strange. She'd been there for all of them. The three of them were inseparable.

Mitch, Russ and Libba Jane, people would say, almost as if the three names were one word.

Mitch had been a sun-worshipper, refusing to wear a hat on the boats even when his freckled Irish complexion had burned to a painful red. Russ, blessed from birth with an extra dose of melanin that darkened his skin to a bronze glow, had teased him, calling him Rudolph and Pinkie and every other cruel, ego-shriveling name brothers forced to compete almost from the hour of their birth often do.

He thought of Mitch as he'd last seen him, bitter, edgy, hard-drinking, desperate for a cure for a disease that had none. Mitch, his brother, his nemesis, his shadow, his womb-mate, riddled with and battling cancer for *five* years until he'd succumbed six months ago. Russ blinked away the moisture gathering at the corners of his eyes. Why hadn't anyone told him sooner? Why had Mitch downplayed his illness? They were brothers, dammit, twin brothers. Whatever their differences, they were family, flesh and blood. Who had decided that Russ, the oldest, would be the one to leave, the banished brother, excluded from the family legacy? The answer was a rhetorical one and *banishment* was too strong a word. He had never seen eye to eye with his father, and unlike Mitch, he had a good head for the books. It was logical that he should be the one to go on to college, make his way doing something else. Hennessey Blue Crab and Fishing couldn't pay the bills for more than two families. Even that was stretching it. Still, Mitch was his brother. If he had known, he would have come home sooner, when it could have made a difference.

It was after nine when Russ climbed into his Blazer. He pressed down on the clutch and shifted into first gear. The day had been long and he was tired, but he didn't want to go home. *Home.* When had Hennessey House last been home? The answer was immediate. When he'd lived there with his parents and Mitch. Now his family was gone, with the exception of Tess, and her mother kept her under lock and key at the judge's big white house outside of town. No, he wouldn't see Tess tonight. He wasn't in the mood. He needed a drink and a smoke.

Leaving the town limits, Russ followed the back road toward Frenchman's Bend and Cybil's Diner. Pulling into the gravel parking lot, he rolled to a stop. Strains of Reba McEntire drifted through the night. He turned off the engine. Leaving the keys in the ignition, he walked inside. It was darker than a tar pit at midnight. Russ leaned against the doorjamb, waiting for his eyes to adjust to the gloom.

Cybil's Diner wasn't really a diner, it was a bar. The name was a holdover from the prohibition era when liquor was traded, gambled, sold and consumed in the back room behind the eating area. Eventually the wall had been knocked out, a pool table installed, and the last patron who remembered ordering food from Cybil died of old age. The fact that it was the only bar between Frenchman's Cove and Marshyhope Creek and every man in town, professional and blue collar, frequented its sagging, vinyl-covered booths and bar stools, kept it from becoming seedy.

Russ walked in and hesitated briefly, allowing his eyes to adjust to the gloom. It was a blinding ninety degrees of wet humidity outside in the evening heat, but here in the bar the shadowy darkness was the same at noon as it was at midnight. He looked around and experienced a rush of nostalgia. The same uneven, cleat-gouged floor, the hazy tobacco-filled air, the hard click of cue against ball, the occasional shout of laughter from a hard drinker who'd tipped one too many.

Some things were different, of course, a testimony to the passage of time. The gray-green, black-and-white RCA featuring Walter Cronkite had been replaced by Peter Jennings on a color Toshiba. The big news was the Middle East, not Vietnam. A We Accept Personal Checks and Credit Cards sign sat on the bar, and there were women in the room. Women who wore their skirts long and their hair short, women with monogrammed T-shirts and painted toenails peeking out from silver-and-beige mules, women who sipped pink-and-green drinks with umbrella-studded fruit. Russ missed the old days of peanuts and beer. He didn't recognize anyone, but it was still early.

Something soft and deliciously curved pressed against him. "What'll you have, stranger?"

Russ looked down at the inviting female rubbing her breasts against his arm. "Beer." His voice was huskier than usual. He cleared his throat. "Whatever's on tap."

"You got it," she purred. "Don't go away, now. My break's in ten minutes and I want to spend every little bit of it with you."

"I'll be here," Russ promised.

True to her word, exactly ten minutes later the barmaid slid under his arm, leaned against him and stuck her tongue in his ear. "Wanna dance?" she asked breathlessly.

Russ, experiencing a similar change in his breathing pattern, decided that dancing was better than what she obviously had in mind. He swung her out into the middle of the floor and pulled her into his arms.

"I'm Rosalind," she said before plastering herself against him. "Who are you?"

"Russ."

"You must be new in town. I'da noticed if you'd been in before."

Russ was recovering his equilibrium. "It's been a while."

"Where you from?"

"Marshyhope Creek."

"That's right around the corner," she protested. "How come you never been here before?"

Russ grinned, a flash of white in the dark room. "I have, honey. But it was long before your time."

She pouted and tossed her long, bottle-blond perm. "You're not that much older than me. Besides, I like older men. They're better in bed."

Russ, who'd guessed her age to be just past jailbait, didn't contradict her. Let her think what she wanted. The little lady had drop-dead curves and a voice like honey, but he wasn't planning on harvesting her crop. He made a point of staying away from schoolgirls. He preferred women nearer his own age. But that didn't mean he couldn't enjoy the dance.

Insinuating his leg between both of hers, he tightened his arms and dipped her backward. The music changed. Willie Nelson's You Were Always On My Mind blurred the edges of his resolve. He pulled her close again and pressed her head against his shoulder. Locked together, they barely moved until the song ended. Someone dropped another quarter into the jukebox.

Russ's eyes adjusted to the gloom. Two women walked in and sat down in a corner booth. The dark-haired one turned and looked directly at him. He winced and then realized her eyes probably hadn't adjusted to the dimness and she couldn't see well enough to recognize him. What was Libba doing in a hole like this?

"My break's over, handsome." The blonde laved his ear. "If you're still here at closing time, I promise it'll be worth it."

She was cute, but he knew he'd regret it. "It's not that you aren't tempting," he said gently, "but I'm afraid not."

She sighed. "Why is it all the good ones are already taken?"

He tweaked a curl. "Don't give up."

"I won't," she promised. "It's my ticket outta here."

Russ walked off the floor and took a seat at the end of the bar. The night promised to be interesting.

Libby sipped whipped cream off the top of her Irish coffee. She was definitely uncomfortable. The diner had never appealed to her. She wished Shelby had chosen another place to catch up on old times.

"Libba Hennessey, are you hearin' a word I said?" Shelby Sloane asked indignantly.

Libby smiled. Shelby had been her oldest friend. They'd known each other since birth and hung out with the same crowd in high school, but it wasn't until after graduation that their friendship deepened. Libby believed, although Shelby denied it, that they'd both been in competition for Russ. After he left town, Libby needed a friend and Shelby stepped in to fill the gap. Flame-haired, blue-eyed, reed-thin and gorgeous, two parts loyal to one part crazy, she spoke her mind and was a self-proclaimed gossip. Still, she was the only one from her high school crowd that Libby still considered a friend. Years could pass, but when they reconnected it was as if they had seen each other the day before. "Why don't we go someplace else?" Libby suggested.

"Good Lord, Libba Jane. This is the only place in town that has a liquor license. I'm askin' if you think Fletcher's cheatin' on me. I think that deserves a drink."

Libby sighed impatiently. "Fletcher is not cheating on you, Shelby. He's crazy about you. Just because a man joins a baseball league does not mean he's tired of you. If you're really worried, why don't you watch him play?"

Shelby's long manicured fingernails clicked against the tabletop. "I hate baseball. Fletcher knows I hate baseball. If I went down there to the field, he'd know somethin' was up. He'd probably think I was checkin' up on him."

"Well?" Libby said pointedly.

"For Pete's sake, Libba Jane. I can't have him think I'm jealous. It gives a man a terrible advantage."

"You've been married for fifteen years. Don't tell me you're still keeping score. Give the guy a break, Shelby. He'd be flattered."

Shelby's perfectly shaped eyebrows quirked. "You really think so?"

"I do."

"Okay, I'll do it." She lifted the bottle of Moosehead to

her lips. "Won't ol' Fletch be surprised when I show up tomorrow night?"

"Care to dance?"

Libby glanced up from the scuffed cowboy boots, past the patched jeans to a sun-lined face and thinning brown hair. "No thanks," she said, smiling gently.

"I would." Shelby slid out of the booth and stood before him, hands on her hips. "Care to take second best?"

The man grinned and his eyes moved boldly up the length of her tanned legs, revealed by the short denim skirt. "You're a pretty thing. I feel lower than a snake's belly that I didn't ask you first."

Shelby shrugged her shoulders. "It doesn't bother me. I'm used to it, at least when I'm with Libba. Do you want to dance or not?"

He slipped his arm around her waist and maneuvered her to the middle of the floor where several other couples were already circling.

Libby sighed and began searching through her purse for her car keys. Shelby didn't normally throw herself at strangers. She had quite a reputation in high school, but marriage and two children had quieted her down substantially. She must be seriously upset with Fletcher. Her fingers connected with the end of her key chain at the same time she remembered that Shelby had driven. There was nothing to do but wait until her friend grew tired of her dancing partner. Tucking her purse into the corner of the booth, she slid out of the seat and headed toward the ladies' room.

It was black as pitch in the hall. She pushed open the door and waited until the blond waitress came out of the stall. The girl was too young to have been in school with her. Without speaking, she left the room. Libby washed and dried her hands, smoothed her hair and walked out into the darkness. Someone came out of the men's room at the same time. There was barely enough space in the hall for one person, never mind two. Libby waited for the man to pass. He didn't move.

Assuming the initiative, she stepped into the hall only to have a firm hand grasp her arm and pull her back around. "Leave me alone," she demanded furiously.

"Take it easy," said Russ. "It's only me. What in the hell are you doing in a place like this?"

Libby blinked. "Russ, is that you? I came with Shelby."

"That's what I thought. Well, then, what you need is the full experience." He started down the hall to the bar, pulling her after him. Strains of Johnny Cash filled her ears.

"Let's dance," Russ said.

"No." Libba twisted her arm in an effort to loosen his grip. It didn't work. "Will you let me go?"

"Not a chance." He nodded toward Shelby. "Your friend'll be out there all night. May as well take advantage of the time."

"I don't want to dance with you, Russ Hennessey," she hissed. "I've spent the last seventeen years doing what I didn't want to, but it's over. You better understand that now."

"Give over, Libba. I know what you've spent the last seventeen years doing, and it so happens that I need your help and your experience. Now, I don't like to beg or threaten, but it does seem as if you owe me one or two. How about it, Libba Jane?"

Libby's eyes widened. "What are you talking about?"

He pulled her into his arms. Instinctively, as if it had never forgotten, her body fit against his, filling up the spaces just like old times. Her feet moved to the music.

"I know you're a biologist. What I don't know is what kind?"

"My speciality is genetic mutations. Why?"

"I don't think I need the genetic part, but mutation is definitely up my alley."

The box spewed forth Reba McEntire's husky lyrics.

"Please, tell me what this is all about."

"It's the crabs," he said. "They're horribly deformed, every one of them. It's like the water is poisoned." His breath was harsh against her ear. "Then I found Mitch's file. Testicular cancer, environmentally acquired. I thought he had leukemia."

Libby pulled away. "Now, wait a minute, Russ. You're jumping to conclusions. That diagnosis doesn't mean what you think it does. We're all susceptible to environmental hazards. Whether we come down with something or not depends on the health of our immune system. Besides, leukemia is sometimes environmentally acquired, too."

"What about the crabs?"

"I don't know."

"Will you come and see them?"

"Of course I will." She hesitated. "Does anyone else know about this?"

"I sent Billy Dupree to the lab with some samples."

Libby sighed with relief. He wasn't planning to hide anything.

"I never really got over you."

Her mind, sorting out the possibilities, didn't register the words.

"Was there anything specific about the mutations?" she asked. "Was it mostly eyes or torsos or legs?"

"Did you hear what I said?" he demanded.

"Sorry. What was it again?"

"I never got over you."

Her breath caught. She forced a laugh. "Yes, you did. You not only got over me, you married Tracy Wentworth within a year."

She smelled wonderful, like apricots. Libba had always reminded him of fruit, warm, lush, peach-colored fruit. Her skin in the summer was incredible, rich and golden, her lips and cheeks coral-colored. "That was a mistake," he said flatly.

"Obviously. But that doesn't mean you didn't think it was right in the beginning."

"I married her to spite you."

"You're drunk."

"I never drink enough to get drunk."

"Really? That's new."

"When did you turn so bitchy?"

"Watch it, Russ. Just because I'm not agreeing with you for a change is no reason to insult me. I've apologized once. I won't grovel forever."

"You called me a drunk."

"I said you *were* drunk. I didn't call you a drunk. The two are quite different."

"I don't see it."

She'd had enough. The words, the song, dancing with Russ. She couldn't stand it any longer. Breaking out of his hold, she stalked across the floor to where Shelby and her cowboy were locked in an intimate clinch. "If you don't drive me home right now, I'll never go anywhere with you again."

Shelby blinked in surprise. One look at Libba's expression convinced her. "Sorry, Vaughn." She smiled regretfully at her partner. "I gotta get goin'."

"Too bad," the cowboy mumbled. "I was havin' a real good time."

"Me, too," she called back, and then ran after Libby.

Shelby was worried. Libba had burst into tears the minute she'd turned on the ignition and didn't stop until they'd pulled into the driveway of her family home. Libba never cried and certainly not the way she had tonight, dry, retching, wounded sobs that spoke of desperation and lonely highways and country roads leading nowhere and, most of all, loss, aching, permanent loss, the kind Shelby would never have believed that Coleson Delacourte's elegant, sophisticated daughter could possibly have known.

"Can I help you, Libba Jane?" she asked tentatively.

Libby shook her head.

"It can't be that bad, honey. You'll see, everything will look better tomorrow."

"I've made such a mess of things, Shelby. I'm thirty-seven years old, alone, living with my parents, nothing to show for my life, and all because of a stupid mistake. What kind of example am I for Chloe?"

Shelby thought a minute. "That's just plain dumb thinkin', Libba Jane," she said after a bit. "What about all your education? What about Chloe? If it weren't for that little mistake, who I'm assuming is your ex-husband, you'd probably be married to Russ Hennessey, have ten kids and a whole lot of resentment because he stifled your gifts. Besides, we all make mistakes. Most people marry wrong the first time. Why do you think we all watch *Oprah?*"

Libby blinked at her friend. "Do you really think so?"

"I know so. You lit outta town for a reason, Libba Jane. Think about that. At least you married an outsider. Think about poor Russ and Tracy. They have to look at each other all the time. That could be damn awkward."

"I never thought of that," Libby admitted.

"Well, start thinking about it and be grateful. You're in the prime of your life, Libba Jane. You still have your looks and your figure. You're smart and educated. If you want to start where you left off, you should be nicer to Russ."

"That's ridiculous, Shelby. I don't want to start where I left off. What good would that do?"

Shelby twisted a red curl around her painted fingernail. "Somebody, I can't remember who, said something about protesting too much."

"His name was Shakespeare," Libby said dryly.

"Whatever. I always thought there was something in that."

Libby pulled the door handle and climbed out of the car. "Good night, Shelby."

"Good night, darlin'. Keep your chin up. Women our age shouldn't make a habit of cryin'."

Stifling a gurgle of laughter, Libby watched her friend drive away.

Ten

Libby turned to inspect herself in the mirror, smoothed the skirt of her cream-colored linen suit and picked off a non-existent piece of lint. It wasn't an official interview, but she decided to dress as if it was. She'd pulled her hair back in a twist, brushed her lids and cheeks with peach blush, applied gel to her lips and critically examined herself in the mirror. Six extra pounds or not, this was as good as she got.

Chloe's voice, sharp and demanding, came from the doorway. "Where are you going?"

Libby quailed. All her instincts recoiled at the thought of lying to her child. On the other hand, the truth would wreak havoc with her plans. Chloe would become hysterical and Libby would have to forgo her meeting with Cliff, or she would leave Chloe to her own tantrum and be accused of neglect. She decided on the middle ground. "I'll tell you later, when I know for sure." She changed the subject. "What plans do you have for the day?"

"I'm going with Granddad into Salisbury. I begged him to take me. Otherwise I'd do what I always do. Read to Grandma, listen to her lecture on the fine points of being a lady, eat lunch, help Serena in the kitchen and lie out on the sundeck for a full five minutes before my skin blisters."

"Sounds good," Libby said, hearing none of it. She hooked her purse over her shoulder, pecked her daughter's cheek before easing past her and ran down the stairs.

Her father opened the door for her. "You're in a hurry."

"I have an appointment."

"Is it a secret?"

"Bless you, Daddy. I'll tell you everything when I get home."

"When will that be?" he called after her.

"Lunch. I'll be home for lunch."

"It'll be a hot one," he warned. "It's not even eight o'clock and the temperature's over eighty."

Cliff Jackson believed in casual. He wore a pair of cargo shorts and a T-shirt that read Save the Whales. The office was equally as casual. The walls were covered with travel posters of beautiful people, smiling mammals and clean, white-sand beaches. Track lighting hung from the ceiling and a desk with a banker's lamp faced the window. There was a single stool and one comfortable chair behind the desk. Plants in colorful pots leaned toward the sun. A detailed map of the bay covered an entire wall, and the smell of rich coffee swirled through the air. Libba sniffed appreciatively.

"Mornin', Libba Jane." He nodded toward the coffeepot. "Coffee?"

"I'd love some. How are you, Cliff?"

He looked her over. "Not up to my usual, but then I never was a morning person. You're serious about coming to work with me?"

"I have a few questions."

He looked surprised. "Fire away."

"How long will this job last?"

"There may not be enough work here in Marshyhope Creek to sustain a permanent office. How does Washington, D.C., sound to you?"

Libby shook her head. "I came home for a reason. I don't want to live in a big city and I don't want to uproot Chloe again. She's starting high school."

Cliff drummed his fingers on the table. "Do you want a guarantee?"

"Yes."

"Two years," he said. "I can give you two years part-time and then you can renegotiate if you're not happy. With your credentials, you won't starve."

She pulled an envelope from her purse. "I brought a résumé."

He took it from her. "I'll keep it for the files. I've already checked up on you. You've been mighty busy since you left town."

"Speak for yourself."

He grinned. "When do you want to start?"

She looked around. "Today, but I'll need some furniture."

He shook his head. "The thing is, Libba Jane, you'll be here on your own for a good part of the time. I'll be in D.C. most of every week."

She laughed. "You're joking."

He shook his head.

Her smile disappeared. "I'm flattered by your confidence in me, Cliff, but do you really think that's wise? It's going to take some time for me to figure everything out."

"You'll have a computer, e-mail, a fax machine, a telephone and all the files. There's nothing here you haven't seen before. You'll be fine."

Libby shook her head. "I don't think so. This will be a new area for me. I've got the knowledge but not much experience. I've worked for the D.A.'s office for the last four years. Environmental hazards are a different ball game. I'm going to need some help."

"I checked out your credentials. You interned in Catalina and in the Newport wetlands. You're not as inexperienced as you think and you'll have all the help you need. I'll be a phone call away."

"What if I need more than that?"

"I'll catch the shuttle or drive down. We're only a few hours apart."

She groaned. "This is the other side of the world and you know it."

"This isn't a big operation, Libba. Your being here works out for the agency. If you hadn't shown up, I'd be relocated back to the capitol, anyway, and the problems here would be prioritized. This is personal for me. I'd like to see this job finished. This is where I grew up. My family is here."

"What's so important that you have to go back now and not next month when I'll feel more confident about what I'm doing?"

"There's a vote coming up in the Senate. It concerns opening up a wildlife reserve in Alaska to oil drilling. I need to get up there, work out some petroleum projection figures and determine just how many barrels of oil that reserve has. If it's big, you'll see oil rigs dotting the landscape from Ketchikan to Juneau."

She stared at him. "Good God."

"Can I count on you?"

Thoughts, thick and complicated, flitted through her mind. She could take a leave from the D.A.'s office. She would beg Chloe for understanding. Her parents already wanted her to stay. There would be no problem there. The question was, *Did she want the job? Or did she want to go back to California and read DNA tests for unfit, unwilling parents?* "I'll take it," she said recklessly. "But you have to promise that you'll come if I need you."

"I'll be around periodically. I've a small interest here in Marshyhope Creek myself."

"Verna Lee?"

He laughed, his smile white as bleached bone in his dark face. "How did you guess?"

She shook her head. "Just a hunch."

He stood. "Since you're set on starting today, take my chair. I'll pass over the open files and we can talk about them." He looked at her pencil-slim skirt and matching jacket. "If comfort is important to you, I'd drop the fancy outfits. They aren't practical for mucking out shrimp boats and collecting water samples. Besides, you're not in California anymore. It's hotter'n a fry station at lunch hour."

She hesitated, her mind on something else.

"Is something bothering you, Libba Jane?"

"Russ Hennessey sent some mutated blue crabs to the lab. Have you heard anything about that?"

Cliff frowned. "When?"

"Yesterday, I think. I said I'd look at them."

"Go ahead. See what you can find out. We'll tackle the files tomorrow."

"I'll go home to change. Chloe thinks we're going back to California. I have to break the news that I've taken a job. She won't be pleased. I only hope she doesn't slit her wrists."

He looked startled. "Jesus. Is it that bad?"

"Not quite. She'll probably want to slit my wrists."

He shook his head. "Good luck. Call me if you find out anything. Otherwise, I'll see you tomorrow."

Nola Ruth despised the tendency toward casualness that seemed to have taken over the world. Lunch at home meant white tablecloths and linen napkins. Once, when Libba was a child, it also meant formal attire. Now Coleson wore tan slacks and a golf shirt while Chloe had on her usual uniform of cutoff shorts and a tank top. Nola Ruth prided herself on being properly dressed, in silk and pearls, her hair and makeup immaculate. She surveyed her daughter's attire and breathed a sigh of relief. Thank goodness Libba Jane hadn't succumbed to the sloppy chic of modern young people today. She looked beautiful with her coffee-dark hair pulled back in a severe style that flattered only those fortunate enough to have good skin and the right bones. Nola Ruth approved of her clothing, too—creamy linen and pearl earrings with only the faintest touch of makeup. Libba always did have beautiful skin, ivory in color, completely poreless. And those eyes, liquid dark, with lashes like feathers. Nola Ruth sighed. She could have had anyone. How could she have thrown herself away on Eric Richards?

Chloe picked up her fork and speared a cucumber from her salad plate. Nola Ruth frowned, folded her hands and bowed her head. The child couldn't help her lack of religious training. "Coleson, please say grace before Chloe expires of hunger."

Chloe flushed, set down her fork and crossed herself.

"Thank you, Lord, for the food and the company. Amen." Cole Delacourte smiled kindly at his granddaughter. "Was that quick enough for you, Chloe?"

"It's just that I'm not used to praying," Chloe explained. "We never do at home."

Nola Ruth addressed her granddaughter. "We don't blame you for your lack of religious education, darling. Your mother was very remiss. I'm sure she sees the error of her ways."

"There is more than one way to live a spiritual life, Mama," Libby said, then changed the subject. "This chicken salad is delicious. I think Serena uses rosemary. Do you like it, Chloe?"

"Uh-huh."

"Answer yes or no, darling," Nola Ruth said. "Uh-huh isn't polite."

Coleson's rare temper flared. "For Pete's sake, Nola Ruth, let the child eat. You don't need to educate her. She's fine the way she is."

"Of course she is," Nola Ruth smiled sweetly. "I'm sorry if I've offended you, Chloe. I didn't mean to."

"I'm not offended, Grandma." She looked at her mother. "Where did you go this morning?"

"I'll tell you after lunch."

"Tell us now," Coleson said. "Unless it's a secret."

"No, it's no secret," Libby said slowly. "There's an environmental problem here in Marshyhope Creek." She looked pointedly at her daughter. "I'd like to talk to you about it after dinner, Chloe."

"Why can't you talk now?"

"It affects you as well as me," Libby explained.

"Tell me now."

"It can wait."

Chloe set her fork down. "I'm not hungry," she said. "May I be excused?"

"For heaven's sake, Chloe," her mother exploded. "You just don't know when to stop. I'd like to talk to you about this sensibly, but if you're going to pull your I'll starve myself routine, I'll tell you now. I'm going to work for the Environmental Protection Agency."

Chloe's face was very white.

Libby hurried on. "It's not exactly permanent."

"What does that mean?" her father asked.

Nola Ruth watched her daughter draw a deep breath.

"I don't know. It could be a few months, maybe more, depending on how long it takes."

"No," Chloe cried out.

"It's a wonderful opportunity, Chloe," Libby said quickly. "You'll see. I've always wanted to work in my field. When school starts you'll make friends and everything will be fine."

Nola Ruth glowed. "It's a wonderful opportunity. How fortunate that things are turning out the way they are."

"You promised," Chloe whispered. "You said I could go home. You said six weeks, tops."

"We haven't been here for six weeks, Chloe."

"You just said we could be here for months."

Libby fell silent, shamed by the burning accusation in her daughter's eyes. "I'm sorry, Chloe, but this is important to me."

"You're not sorry. If you were really sorry, you'd take it back."

Libby's lips tightened. "What I meant is that I'm sorry you're so disappointed. It won't be as bad as you think."

Chloe was standing now, rigid defiance stiffening her slight body. "It won't be bad at all because I'm going home. I'm calling Dad. He promised that I could come home. He'll come and get me if you don't send me back."

"Chloe, please," Libby pleaded. "Stop this. You can't go back to California. Your home is with me."

"Who decided on that one?" Chloe shouted. "I don't remember being asked who I wanted to live with."

Nola Ruth opened her mouth. "*Whom*, darling, not *who*."

Almost immediately her husband's foot pressed down on hers warningly.

"Chloe, you're behaving badly," her mother said. "Sit down and let's discuss this rationally."

"I'm not discussing anything with someone who breaks her promises. You're a liar."

Nola Ruth gasped. Her husband's hand clamped down on her arm.

Tears rolled down Chloe's cheeks. "Dad will come and get me. You'll see. I'm calling him now." She ran from the room.

Nola Ruth turned on Cole. "What is the matter with you?" she demanded.

Cole resumed eating his lunch. "You were about to say something you would eventually regret. I stopped you. Chloe doesn't need us to disapprove of her. It would hurt her to admit she would rather go home than stay here. I didn't want to put her through that."

"Are you saying that you approve of that child's behavior?"

"*That child* is our granddaughter. She's angry, hurt and scared. Her entire life has been disrupted. If what she says is true, I don't blame her." He looked at his daughter.

"Look at me, Libba Jane," he ordered. "Did you in fact promise Chloe that she could go back to California if you decided to stay?"

Tears welled up in Libby's eyes. She nodded.

"What were you thinking?"

"She wouldn't come with me. I thought she'd change her mind once we got here."

"For pity's sake, Libba Jane," her mother interrupted. "Chloe is a little girl, a very spoiled little girl. That's your fault. She actually believes she has the same rights and privileges as an adult. Children aren't consulted as to where their parents decide to live. They aren't capable of making those decisions. I can't believe what I heard here today."

"Chloe's smart," Cole said, "and insightful. I can see why you made the mistakes you did." He sighed. "It's not all your doing, honey. From what I can tell you were a single mother for the most part, too busy with earning a living and acquiring an education to build friendships. It's no wonder you turned to Chloe. Now you've got to live with what you've created."

"She can't go home," Libby said woodenly.

"It might not be a bad idea to allow her to live part of the year with her father," Cole said gently. "It's not an unusual arrangement for a teenager."

Libby pressed her fingertips against her eyelids, willing the tears back. "You don't understand, Daddy. Eric won't take her. He doesn't want her. Oh, he'll act the part of the adoring father now and then, but he won't have her living with him. He's not capable of doing for anyone else."

"Well, it's settled, then. Chloe stays here with us." Nola Ruth leaned her head back against the high chair and smiled. "Don't tell me that you aren't delighted, Cole. You've always wanted Libba to come home."

"That was never the issue," Cole replied dryly.

Libby was beyond misery. She wanted to explain, but the hurt was too personal, too deep. She'd learned long ago that vulnerability was not something Nola Ruth Delacourte appreciated. Her mother flourished when life ran smoothly. Keeping up appearances was as necessary to her as sugar in her coffee and jelly on her toast. *Keep the late-night confidences for the confessional,* she'd told her daughter. Libby had never forgotten. She'd learned her lessons early and well. If an invitation to a party never came, she said nothing. If a secret valentine didn't reciprocate, no one ever knew. If someone hurt her feelings or called her a name or tripped her at school, she breathed hard, lift her chin and shrugged it off. But Chloe was a horse of a different color. She'd been raised very differently, and at this very moment, her father was most likely breaking her heart.

Libby crumpled her napkin and left it beside her plate. "Excuse me," she said. "I need to find Chloe."

Her father nodded. Her mother was uncharacteristically silent.

She found Chloe in the study, a masculine room with deep leather sofas, shelves of thick books, hunter-green accents and the faint smell of cigars. The child sat curled up in a corner couch, the phone tucked between her chin and shoulder. Her hands shook and her words, monosyllabic and muted, were thick with tears.

Libby waited, unseen, just inside the door until Chloe hung up the phone and buried her face in her arms.

"Chloe," Libby said brokenly, "please, listen. Give me a minute."

Chloe shook her head. "Go away."

"It won't be that bad. You'll see." Libby approached the couch and reached out a hand to touch the narrow, tanned shoulder.

Chloe jumped up, wild-eyed. "Don't touch me. I hate you. I'll hate you forever. I'm leaving this place as soon as I can, and when I do, I'm never speaking to you again. I'll never call you or visit you or see you." Saliva and mucus ran down her face. Libby pulled a tissue from a box on an end table and handed it to her. Angrily, Chloe rejected it, wiped her nose on the back of her hand and then on her shorts and ran out of the room, down the long hallway, through the kitchen and out the back door.

She continued running along the road, past the peach grove and the bee farms, past the fruit vendors and the fishing holes. Ignoring the waves of heat swimming up from the pavement, she tripped, rolled down the embankment, lurched to her feet, waded across the creek, climbed the other side and ran into the cool, green woods. She ran until she could no longer summon her breath, until the parched rawness in her throat screamed for water, until the dizziness blurred her vision and shards of pain exploded behind her eyes, until chills and nausea brought her to her knees and she crawled, gasping and sick, into the shelter of a tree brilliant with white bark and silver leaves. Leaning her head weakly against the trunk, she cried until her swollen eyes could no longer open. Then she fell asleep.

She lay unconscious, oblivious to the changing afternoon, the darkening clouds, the shifting wind, the rustle of leaves, the cry of a loon and the approaching footsteps. It wasn't until she heard a human voice, amused and faintly familiar, that her awareness returned.

"Hey, sleeping beauty," the voice said. "Remember me?"

Chloe rolled over, forced open her swollen eyelids and met Bailey Jones's dark and curious gaze.

Eleven

Chloe rolled over on her stomach, her humiliation complete. "Go away."

"You look like you could use a friend."

"Oh, really," she said bitterly. "Now you want to be my friend. You weren't so eager the other day."

"That was different."

The boy squatted down beside her, balancing on the balls of his feet. Through the space between the crook of her elbow, she ventured a glance at him. He was completely still and comfortable against the backdrop of the woods. Somehow she knew he would wait her out no matter how long it took. If only her eyes weren't so swollen.

"Why was it different?" she asked.

"That was about me. This isn't."

Chloe rolled over and sat up. She had nothing to lose. "My mother is staying here and I have to stay with her. My dad doesn't want me."

Bailey nodded but did not look surprised. He said nothing.

There was something about him, the dark eyes, the intensity of his pose, that encouraged confidences. Chloe kept talking. "My mother promised that we'd go home. I wouldn't have come with her if I thought she was staying."

"What about your dad?"

Her lip quivered. "He promised, too. Both of them lied to me."

Again he nodded.

"I hate them," Chloe sobbed, dropping her head in her hands. "I can't stay here. I just can't."

"I suppose you've never broken a promise," said Bailey.

"No, I haven't, at least not an important one," she amended. "Have you?"

He thought a minute. "Not that I recall, but then I don't promise much. You never know when life changes."

Suddenly, she wanted very much to know what he was thinking. "What'll I do?"

He shrugged "Nothing to do. Living with Cole Delacourte in that big old house with your mama can't be all that bad. You'll do all right."

It wasn't what she wanted to hear. "That's easy for you to say. No one's making you stay in a place you hate. You don't even go to school when you don't want to."

He stared at her. "Do you always do that?"

"What?"

"Come out and say things like they're God's truth when you don't know what in the hell you're talking about?"

Chloe's blue eyes glared back at him. "I think I hate you, too."

Bailey laughed. "You don't know me well enough to hate me." He stretched out his hand. "Dry your eyes and come on home with me. I'll feed you."

Chloe hesitated. She was both attracted to and repelled by this strange boy with his quicksilver moods, his matter-of-fact acceptance of his place in the world and his beautiful, beautiful face. "Are you a decent cook?"

"Better'n most," he admitted. "I'm not sure you'll like what's on the menu, but if you're hungry enough, you'll eat anything, I guess."

The woods were dim and cool and darkly shadowed. All at once Chloe was worried about the time. "I should call my grandfather. He'll be worried about me."

"There's no phone where we're going." He stood completely still, waiting for her answer.

Chloe stood and dusted pine needles off the back of her shorts. "Who else lives with you?"

"Just Mama and me."

"Where's your dad?"

Bailey took off ahead of her. "Don't know," he answered. "He left before I was born."

"Do you have brothers or sisters?"

"No," he said again. "I'm the only one."

Chloe ran to catch up with him. "Like me," she said.

She watched the corners of his mouth turn up. "Like you," he said softly. "That's about the only way we're alike."

"Verna Lee said we should be friends," she said conversationally.

Bailey shoved his hands into his pockets. "How do you know Verna Lee?"

"She gave me iced tea when the hardware store was closed. I like her."

Bailey nodded.

"Do you think she's beautiful?" Chloe asked.

He frowned. "I never thought much about it."

"I do," confided Chloe. "She's the most beautiful woman I've ever seen."

"You must have seen quite a few living in California."

Chloe tilted her head. "California has lots of beautiful people, but most of them are plastic."

"Plastic people?"

"You know, artificial. They have plastic surgery and colored hair. Verna Lee is naturally beautiful, like my mother."

Bailey reached out to tug a strand of Chloe's silvery hair with its black tips. "What about this? Is it real, or do you dye it?"

"Most of it is real. The black isn't."

"You don't look much like your mama."

"No." Chloe's voice was hollow. "I look like my dad, sort of."

"What does that mean?"

"I'm blond and blue-eyed like he is, but that's about it. He's an actor," she said, as if that explained everything. "I'm not as good-looking as either of my parents."

Again, she'd called up in him that brief, flashing smile. "You look all right, Chloe" was all he said.

She hadn't been fishing for a compliment, but it pleased her, small concession that it was. Chloe stopped talking and looked around. "How far is it to your house?"

"It's not a house." He pointed straight ahead. "We're nearly there."

She strained her eyes. At the end of the path was a trailer, as old and rusted as the truck beside it. The door was open and a delicious, meaty smell floated toward them. Smoke curled up from a firepit outside. Laundry hung from a line anchored between two trees. A picnic table was spread with a tablecloth and two place settings. Outside the trailer, on a wooden bench, sat a woman with long black hair and a faded but clean cotton dress that had seen better days. She did not get up when the two of them approached. Her stare was vacant, the dark eyes empty of life. All at once Chloe saw that she was blind.

"Mama," Bailey said gently. "I've brought someone home. Her name is Chloe Richards."

"Richards." The woman rolled her tongue around the name, testing it. "I don't know anyone named Richards."

"Chloe is from California. She's Cole Delacourte's granddaughter."

The woman's forehead wrinkled as if she was deep in thought. "Come here, child."

Chloe looked at Bailey. He nodded. She stepped forward.

The woman lifted her hands, long and thin and elegant, to Chloe's face. Gently, she examined it, tracing her bones, outlining her lips, the forehead, the fullness of her cheeks.

"My, you're a pretty thing," she said in her husky drawl. "You must be Libba Jane's daughter."

Chloe found her voice. "Yes."

"I'm Lizzie Jones. You're welcome here, child."

"Thank you." Her stomach growled.

The woman laughed. "We're having stew. It's not much, but it'll fill the hole in your stomach."

Suddenly, all Chloe wanted to do was sit around the table and share a meal with this sad, pretty woman and her beautiful son. "I'll set the rest of the table," she volunteered.

"I'll find another plate," Bailey said, and disappeared into the trailer.

"Bailey doesn't bring friends home very often," said his mother. "You must be special."

"I don't know about that," replied Chloe. "I think he feels sorry for me."

"Why is that?"

"I want to go home to California," Chloe said honestly. "My mother said we were coming for a visit and now she's found a job here."

Lizzie Jones listened intently as if what Chloe said was of utmost importance. "Have you taken a dislike to Marshyhope Creek?" she asked.

"It's not that." Chloe sat down beside her. The woman's eyes followed as if she could see. "I have friends at home, a whole life and things I want to do. My dad is there, too."

"I'm so sorry, Chloe," the woman said, and Chloe believed her. "I think Bailey would rather be somewhere else, too."

"Why can't you move?"

"Where would we go?" Lizzie asked. "I can't work. We own the land here. It isn't much, but we survive. I suppose he'd be gone if it wasn't for me. I wish—"

Her son's cheerful whistle stopped her. "Never mind." She rested her long brown hand on Chloe's knee. "It might not be as bad as you think, living here. Your mama grew up in this town. She'll help you find your way."

Bailey hopped down from the trailer, his arms full. "You made biscuits," he said approvingly. "That means you're feeling better."

"I do feel better. The nap helped."

The words came out before she could stop them. "Is something wrong with you, Mrs. Jones?"

A shadow crossed the woman's face. "Just an ache in my bones, is all." She smiled. "Doesn't that stew smell good? Bailey's a wonderful cook."

Chloe's eyes widened. "Bailey made the stew?"

"He cooks all our meals," she said proudly.

Chloe watched him ladle the rich brown meat, vegetables and gravy into bowls and set them on the table. "Can I help you, Bailey?"

"It's done. All we need to do is sit."

His mother stood and walked directly to the table. Carefully, she stepped over the bench and sat down. "Sit beside me, Chloe," she said.

Chloe took her place. Remembering her mistake at lunch, she waited before picking up the spoon. Lizzie held out her hands palms up. Bailey took one hand and with the other reached for Chloe's. Lizzie began to pray. "Lord, bless this food and this house and all the people in it. Thank you for bringing Chloe to us today and help her to return often. Amen."

Chloe's cheeks burned. These were nice people. Her grandparents were nice people. It wasn't their fault that she was here. They didn't deserve her anger. She deeply regretted her outburst earlier in the day.

"So, Bailey," she said around a mouthful of biscuit and delicious stew. The meat was different, stringy with a strong flavor. She liked it. "Tell me about the high school here."

He finished chewing before he spoke. His manners, she decided, were decent.

"What do you want to know?"

"Is there a drama department?"

"The school puts on a play every year, so I suppose there's one. It isn't my thing."

"What is?"

"Painting," he said, "as in art."

"Really?"

He nodded, swigged down the rest of his milk and refilled his glass.

"Do you have anything you can show me?"

He hesitated.

"Go on, Bailey," his mother said softly. "I'll get the dishes. Show Chloe what you've done."

"Do you know anything about art, Chloe?"

"No," she said honestly. "But I've been to lots of museums. My dad knows a lot about art, I think. I just know what I like. It's different every time," she explained. "But when something hits me, I know I like it. I'm sort of an Impressionist person. I like the French painters."

He looked at her, surprised and pleased. "You know a lot more than ninety-nine percent of the people in Marshyhope Creek." He stood. "Come on. I'll show you what I've done. Some of the paintings aren't finished yet, but you'll get the idea."

Together, they walked to a shed in the back of the trailer. Inside, Bailey pulled a chain that dangled from the ceiling. Light flooded the room. Canvases of every size were stacked against one another on the floor. He pulled out two of them, levered them against the wall and stood back. "So," he said, "what do you think?"

Chloe didn't know much about painting, but she knew when something was very good. The canvases exploded with light and color. The room lit up. Her blood warmed and her nerve endings drummed with energy. She recognized the peach grove immediately and the black sharecroppers in various stages of their chores. The scenes were rich and seductive and filled with joy and pain. "What else do you have?" she whispered.

He flipped through the stacked canvases and pulled out another. Chloe gasped. He'd captured an outdoor flea market, carts alive with jewel-like colors, black vendors with ropy muscles, white teeth and red bandannas, so real she could hear their shouts and smell their wares.

She gazed at the scene, drinking in the warmth and texture, and then she looked at the boy beside her, proud and defiant at the same time. "You have an amazing talent, Bailey Jones. Do you know that?"

He shrugged. "Sometimes, I think maybe I do. Sometimes, it doesn't matter." He searched through his paintings one last time and pulled out a portrait.

Chloe recognized Lizzie Jones immediately, but a different Lizzie than the one she'd shared a meal with. The woman in the picture was riddled with pain. "What's the matter with her?"

"She's blind, just woke up one day and couldn't see. She has something wrong with her blood. She's dying," he said matter-of-factly.

"What about drugs?"

"Prescriptions cost money. We don't have any."

Chloe remembered her one visit to the emergency room and the street people waiting to be seen. Her mother had explained that certain hospitals were obligated to help the poor regardless of whether or not they could pay. "Can you get welfare?" she asked.

He shook his head. "Not permanently," he said, "and not if you own anything. This land is ours. She won't sell it, not even to help herself."

"I'm sorry, Bailey."

He threw back his head. "Don't worry about us. We get along all right."

"You'll get along more than all right if you keep on with this painting. Have you ever tried to sell any of these?"

"I've thought of it."

"People do that in Los Angeles. They set up their paintings on a street corner and sell them. They aren't half as good as these."

He smiled. "I'll try it sometime."

Chloe hesitated.

"What's wrong?"

"I don't want to leave. Really, I don't. But my family will be worried about me."

"I'll drive you home."

She thanked Lizzie for the meal and waited in the truck while Bailey helped his mother into the trailer. Chloe hadn't been invited inside. Bailey Jones had his share of pride.

He climbed in beside her and turned the key. The engine rattled to life.

They were silent most of the way back home. Bailey stopped at the end of the road leading to the Delacourte house.

Chloe looked at him. "Aren't you going to drive me in?"

"Do you want me to?"

"Yes."

Resigned, he turned down the road and into the long driveway, stopping in front of the house.

Cole Delacourte was smoking a cigar on the porch. He walked up to the car and held out his hand. "How are you, Bailey?"

"Fine, sir."

"I see that you found my granddaughter."

"I'd say she found me. But she's safe and fed. My mama enjoyed her company."

"I'm glad to hear it. Her mama's worried." He nodded at Chloe. "You better run inside, sugar, and tell the women you're still in the land of the living. They were imagining all sorts of foolish things and there was nothing I could do to convince them otherwise."

Chloe opened the door and stepped out. "Thanks, Bailey. I had a nice time. I hope I'll see you soon."

"Bye, Chloe. You know where to find me."

She drew a deep breath, straightened her shoulders and braced herself to face her mother.

Twelve

Libby sat across from her daughter in her parents' comfortable living room of cream-colored couches, colorful pillows and mahogany furniture, willing herself to remain calm, reasonable, sane, when what she really wanted to do was hurl vases, pace the floor and, if she dared to be honest, smack the surly expression from Chloe's mutinous little face. "Let me see if I understand you," she said carefully. "You ran off into the woods, fell asleep for hours, woke up to find a strange boy hovering over you and then you went home with him to eat dinner." She drummed her fingers on the coffee table. "Do I have the facts correct?"

Chloe nodded.

Libby saw red. "Do you have any idea how stupidly you've behaved?"

"It wasn't like that at all," Chloe argued. "You're turning it around."

"How am I turning it around?" Libby couldn't keep the sarcasm from her voice.

"I already knew Bailey," Chloe explained. "I met him the other day. He gave me a ride into town."

"He did what?" Libby couldn't believe her ears. Had all her warnings about accepting rides from strangers fallen on deaf ears? Had she failed completely as a mother? "Are you saying you got into a car with a stranger?" Her voice cracked. "Chloe, how could you?"

"I don't know." Chloe hung her head. "It didn't seem that bad at the time and it turned out all right."

Cole Delacourte walked into the room in time to hear Chloe's confession. "Bailey Jones isn't a bad sort. Chloe won't come to any harm with him."

"That isn't the point," cried Libby. "She didn't know anything about him. She could have been killed or kidnapped."

"This isn't Los Angeles," her father reminded her. "Although I'm sure such things happen in small towns, it hasn't happened here. Bailey is Lizzie Jones's son."

"Is that supposed to make me feel better?"

Chloe lifted her head. "What's wrong with Lizzie Jones? I like her."

Libby's eyes met her father's. How did one explain a woman like Lizzie Jones to a teenager?

"Lizzie had a hard time of it when she was young," Cole said slowly. "She survived in the only way she could. It destroyed her reputation. I always wondered why she never left Marshyhope Creek."

"They own the land," Chloe said. "It's all they have."

Coleson nodded. "That must be it."

"Bailey is an artist," Chloe offered. "I saw his paintings. He's really good."

Libby sat down beside Chloe. "I want you to promise me you won't go there again."

Chloe stared at her mother. "Why not? If I have to live in this place, at least I should be able to choose my own friends."

"You won't have any friends if you associate with Lizzie Jones."

"I'm associating with Bailey."

"It's the same thing."

"Verna Lee said I should be his friend."

"I have no idea what Verna Lee's motives are, but she's

not your mother and she doesn't have your interests at heart. I want you to stay away from Bailey Jones and his mother.''

"You haven't given me one good reason,'' Chloe argued.

"Chloe,'' her mother said helplessly. "This is a small town. It isn't Los Angeles. I want you to be accepted. You can't behave the way you did at home.''

"I can't believe you're doing this,'' Chloe said bitterly. "You weren't like this before. I don't want to live here if I can't pick my own friends.''

Again, Libby looked at her father for help.

He shrugged. "She's got a point,'' he said. "Maybe Chloe can change things around here.''

"Like you did?'' Libby burst out. "You've been trying to change the world for forty years and nothing's happened.''

"A great deal has happened, Libba Jane,'' he said gently. "Maybe, in your eyes, fresh from California, it doesn't look like things are different, but they are. Chloe might bring even more change. Her ways may be accepted merely because she's not a native. What's the worst that can happen?''

"She could be completely ostracized.''

"The Delacourtes stand for something in this town. She'll be all right.'' He smiled at Chloe. "Why don't you say good-night to your grandma and go up to bed.''

Chloe kissed his cheek on the way out. "Thanks, Granddad,'' she whispered before leaving the room.

Libby clenched her hands, stood and walked across the room to stare out the window, a slim figure in white shorts and a sleeveless blouse tied in a knot around her waist. She looked no older than her daughter. "I would rather not have Chloe be a martyr, Daddy. I want her to be happy. Why can't somebody else pave the way?''

"You can't control everything, Libba,'' her father said slowly. "Chloe's bright. She understands more than you think. What's important to you isn't necessarily important to her. You brought her here. She had no choice in the matter. Now it's time to step back and allow her to make her own way.''

She turned around and appealed to her father. ''Was it this hard for you?''

''What?''

''Raising me?''

He laughed. ''Hell, no. You were about as perfect a child as anyone could hope for. I wasn't and neither was your mama. We wondered if we had a changeling. For years we waited for the other shoe to fall.''

''And then it did,'' she finished for him.

Coleson Delacourte grimaced. ''I always wondered what you saw in Eric Richards. Later, I realized it could have been anyone. You wanted out.'' He fixed his piercing blue gaze on his daughter. ''What I never did figure out was why. It seemed as if you had the world by the tail. What was it that made you so hopping eager to leave?''

Warmth stole into her cheeks. Libby didn't color like most people, a bright uncomfortable red that began somewhere around the chest and moved upward, leaving no one in doubt that the person suffered from miserable embarrassment. Libby's blush was a warm, delicate apricot, a subtle dusting of the apples of her cheeks and the tip of her nose. It became her. She shook her head. ''I don't even remember now.''

''I always wondered if it had anything to do with the Hennessey boy.''

She brushed off his implied question. ''It doesn't matter. I'm back.''

He hesitated. There was more to be said, but perhaps not now, not yet. ''So you are. We're very grateful.''

She walked past him, kissing his cheek on the way out. ''I have a big day tomorrow, Daddy. Good night.''

''Good night, Libba Jane. Look in on your mama before you turn in.''

"I will."

Libby walked to the end of the long hallway and hesitated outside of her mother's room. It was Chloe's voice she heard. Peering inside she saw her daughter seated on a stool beside her mother's chair.

"I'll do that, Grandma," Chloe said. She took a small bottle from Nola Ruth's hand and unscrewed the lid. "It smells good."

"It's the best night cream I've found. It's kept my skin soft all these years. You won't need more than a dab."

Chloe dipped her finger into the pot and gently patted the cream around her grandmother's good eye and cheek. "You have beautiful skin," Chloe agreed. "It's like Mom's."

"You have lovely skin, too, Chloe," Nola Ruth observed. "It's golden, like the Beauchamps'. You get that from me. Watch out that you don't get too much sun, though. Even olive skin can burn."

"I know." Chloe dipped her finger into the pot again and reached for the disfigured side of her grandmother's face.

Nola Ruth shrank back. "Never mind about that."

Chloe ignored her. Softly, her fingers brushed her grandmother's cheek and orbital bone. "Doesn't that feel good?" she asked.

Nola Ruth nodded.

"You want both cheeks to be soft and smooth, don't you?"

The woman stared at her granddaughter. "Doesn't it disgust you?" she asked bluntly.

"What?"

"My eye droops and my cheek sags. It's ugly."

Chloe continued to pat her grandmother's cheek. Then she leaned over and kissed it. "Nothing about you is ugly, Grandma," she said gently. "Don't be so hard on yourself."

Nola Ruth's eyes brimmed with tears. She squeezed Chloe's hand. "I don't deserve you, young lady," she said, "but I'm so glad you're here."

Libby backed away, careful to tread lightly and not disturb the scene in the bedroom. Trust Chloe to break through her grandmother's armor and set the situation straight.

Morning dawned, clear and hot. From Libby's bedroom window, the Chesapeake flowed molten in the wake of a brilliant sun. Still exhausted after a restless night, she dragged herself to the bathroom, splashed water on her face, brushed her teeth and pulled on faded cutoffs and a cotton shirt. She didn't bother with makeup. Brushing back her hair, she reached for her visor, slipped into her deck shoes and walked downstairs. The house was silent. The smell of sweet fritters and coffee wafted through the hallway. Fumbling for her car keys, Libby ignored the kitchen and its tempting aromas. The engine of her mother's Volvo turned over and in less than three minutes she'd reached the dock and the offices of the Hennessey Blue Crab and Fishing Fleet. Fortified with a twice-rehearsed speech, Libby walked to the door and turned the knob. It was locked. She frowned and turned back to the gravel parking lot. The Volvo was the only car in sight.

Where was Russ Hennessey? It was after six. If she didn't find him soon it would be too late to take a boat out on the water. Libby climbed behind the wheel again and drove back through town. A Chevy Blazer was parked in front of Perks. Coffee sounded very good. Libby pulled into a parking space, left the car unlocked and walked into the shop. Once again she was interrupting. Verna Lee and Russ were holding a conversation across the counter. Neither one turned around.

She waited a full ten seconds and decided she had been ignored long enough. "Good morning," she said.

Both of them turned. "Good morning, Libba Jane," said Verna Lee.

Russ merely nodded his head.

"Am I wrong, or did you leave a message at my office about getting an early start?" she asked, addressing him.

He held two cups in his hands and lifted one of them. "We did. I thought you could use some coffee. This is for you."

She took it. "I took you at your word when you meant early."

"I'm flattered."

"Don't be. It isn't personal."

Russ grinned. "I'm all yours."

Libby smiled at Verna Lee. "Thanks for the coffee." She looked at Russ. "Shall we?"

"After you. See you later, Verna Lee."

Verna Lee waved. "Nice to have you back, Russ. Bye, Libba Jane."

Russ opened Libby's car door. "I'll meet you back at the dock."

Libby looked at him. "Sometimes I think I rub Verna Lee the wrong way."

"I didn't notice anything. Why?"

Libby shrugged. "Never mind. We weren't ever really friends. She was too far ahead of us in school. I always admired her, though. She was so exotic and confident." She laughed. "I'm just being overly sensitive."

A smile hovered at the corners of his mouth. "You've changed. When did you ever care if someone disapproved of you?"

"I'm thirty-seven," she reminded him. "It makes a difference."

His eyes rested briefly on her shoulder-length dark hair pulled back into a youthful ponytail before moving down to inspect the slim lines of her legs barely covered by faded, sun-washed shorts. "You're really honing in on middle age," he said, keeping his face straight. "I wouldn't have known you."

"Like I said," Libby replied, refusing to banter with him,

"I've changed." She closed the door and rolled down the window. "If we aren't out in the water in ten minutes you won't have anything to show me."

"See you at the dock in five minutes."

Libby pulled out onto the road without looking back. She could feel the familiar coil of irritation begin in her stomach. She didn't know why she was bothered, only that she was. Whether it was Verna Lee or the fact that Russ was so cavalier about this morning that he didn't notice the time, she hadn't figured out yet. Maybe it was Chloe's defiant independence and her father's supporting that defiance. Libby prided herself on her ability to analyze a given situation, isolate the problem and come up with a solution. The most difficult part, the part that prevented her from sleeping and left her feeling as if she had a hole in her stomach, was pinpointing exactly what was bothering her. She needed more than the five minutes it would take to drive back to the dock to figure it out. Until she had more time, she would chew bicarbonate for the twist in her stomach and try her best not to appear inept at her first day on the job.

Libby hopped from the pier to the deck of the boat without help and positioned herself so that she was safely away from all moving parts.

Russ started the engine and maneuvered away from the dock. Between sips of coffee he studied her surreptitiously. She didn't look her age, although she had that aura women have after they turn thirty-five. No one would make the mistake of believing she was ten years younger, but she still looked good, damn good, with an ageless kind of appeal a woman on the green side of thirty just didn't have. Libba fit the profile. She was slim and fit, with thick hair and clear, tight skin. The sun lines around her eyes were barely visible in the early light of morning. Physically, she had aged well. He hadn't expected less. She'd always been a looker.

Somewhere between Verna Lee's shop and the dock,

she'd put on lipstick. He noticed it right away. Not that she needed lipstick. She had the kind of face that looked good the minute she rolled out of bed in the morning. He wondered how she'd grown up so unaware of the effect her physical appearance had on men between the ages of fourteen and seventy. Most likely it was Nola Ruth's doing. She was so afraid her daughter would lose her virginity before her wedding night, forever ruining her marriage prospects, that she'd created the opposite effect, a woman who was insecure about her own physical attributes.

Libba was a Delacourte on her father's side, a Beauchamp on her mother's. She came from a long line of Mediterranean women known for their warm temperaments, long memories, and a loose and easy grace that spoke of innocence and seduction in the same breath. Nola Ruth had raised her daughter in the legacy of her ancestors, women who concealed an icy intelligence beneath the fine-boned beauty of porcelain teacups. Formal, graceful, hospitable women with steely spines who, five generations before, had seen their land razed, their homes torched and their men emasculated without losing the serene dignity that characterized southern females of a certain class. Libba Delacourte was a lady. There was no mistaking the real thing. His own mother, granddaughter of Irish immigrants who'd made good, had seemed less than she was when Libba walked into the room.

He liked the idea that Libba would dress up for him, even if it was only lipstick and earrings. Deep in his soul, Russ Hennessey harbored a craving for beauty and elegance. Instinctively he'd known, even as a boy, that possessing Libba would go a long way toward satisfying that craving. When he sat down to dinner in Coleson Delacourte's eighteenth-century dining room so many years ago with its intricately wrought wood, carved chimney and silver serving dishes, where books lined the shelves and hand-blown decanters glowed under muted light from crystal chandeliers, when the lawyer nodded approvingly at something he'd said, when he looked across the mahogany table at Libba's austerely beautiful face, he felt revitalized, born anew. This world of propriety and refinement, of cultivated taste and understated elegance, where ideas, politics and philosophy were discussed as naturally and casually as his father discussed fish counts and the price of diesel, was a world as foreign, as tantalizing, and far more desirable than any he could have dreamed up in his imagination.

Elizabeth Jane Delacourte was the Madonna of Marshyhope Creek, the town's golden girl, completely loved, unconditionally accepted, the acknowledged center around which the limited social life of the Cove revolved. Because he had always been secretly afraid of losing her, Russ had staked his claim early, in the only way he knew how. He'd taken her virginity. Somehow he knew that despite the sexual revolution sweeping through the sixties, a girl like Libba wouldn't give herself to a man unless she was committed. He made her love him and, in so doing, tied himself to her as tightly and irrevocably as the cinch knots in his father's fishnets.

Those were the years Libba glowed from within with a flame-lit, shimmering brightness that gave Russ the swaggering confidence that earned him his reputation on the tidewater. The memory of that brightness had wreaked havoc on his mind, his love life and, eventually, his marriage. He'd fallen once, early and hard. For Russ it was Libba or no one. She was the reason he'd left Marshyhope Creek, the reason he'd married so suddenly and disastrously. Now he was home again and so was Libba. The possibilities were interesting. This time Russ was in no hurry. He'd learned through painful experience that the inevitable would happen one way or another. Rushing relationships led to ties that strangled, to pity that turned to contempt and to hefty child support payments and a terrifying loss of control. He wouldn't make the same mistake twice.

When he was well out into the bay he checked the co-ordinates on the Loran, set the speed control and lit a cigarette.

Libby spoke for the first time since they'd left the mooring. "You really should give those up. How long has it been? Twenty years?"

Russ blew out a stream of smoke. "Just about."

"They'll kill you."

"They could."

"It's a fact, Russ."

"Well, now, let's explore that for a minute. My daddy fell off a trawler in one of his daily binges, and if I heard correctly, his liver was so swollen it looked like a twenty-pound bowling ball." He stopped to suck in another lungful of smoke. "As for Mitch," he continued, "he was thirty pounds overweight, kept a stash of whiskey in his desk at the dock and looked twenty years older than me even before he came down with cancer. As far as I can tell, I'm the healthiest Hennessey my family produced."

Libby sighed. "Ordinarily, I'd agree with you. But under the circumstances—" She stopped.

"What circumstances?"

She could barely hear him over the hum of the motor. "Let's look at the crabs first and then I'll tell you what I think."

"Fair enough."

Russ kicked up the speed and Libby laughed with delight. Skimming over the water, the spray cool on her face, was almost like flying. Too soon, Russ cut the engine speed and moved into the vicinity of the trotlines.

Libby frowned. "I hope you're not considering doing any fishing here, Russ. If I've read the coordinates right, this isn't legal."

"Yeah, and now I know why. I hope you have a strong stomach," he said grimly, hooking the first line and pulling it up over the side. "I brought you here because I want you to see exactly where this is happening. Maybe you'll notice something in the area we've missed, something we might have in common with the Great Lakes or the Hudson. Those areas are all contaminated with runoff from farm waste. If we knew—''

Libby took one look at the pulsing, mutated mass that couldn't possibly be a Maryland blue crab and thought of the ramifications on the human population of the bay. Suddenly she felt a lightness in her head that meant an abrupt departure of blood from her brain. She pressed the back of her hand against her mouth and gagged.

Russ dropped the line back into the water, slipped one arm around her waist and steadied her. He focused on the flare of her nostrils and the tiny pores in her skin. A slight beading of perspiration dampened her forehead. She smelled like perfume, the expensive kind. "Easy does it, Libba Jane," he cautioned. "We've just started. They're all like that. You're not much good to me if you're swooning on the deck.''

''Dear God,'' she groaned. ''This is terrible.''

''My sentiments exactly.''

She pulled herself together and stepped away from him. ''What could have happened to them?''

''You're the expert. You tell me.''

She didn't want to tell him, not yet when she wasn't sure. ''I have an idea, Russ,'' she began, ''but I can't say for sure, not until we get the lab reports back. Let's pull as many of these in as we can and ship them to Salisbury.''

His mouth settled into grim frown lines. ''You were about to tell me something earlier. What is it?''

''I don't want to speculate about something as serious as this. Please, be patient.''

''The lab in Salisbury has our samples, but they're not telling me anything.'' His voice was strained. ''I want to know what you know, or at least what you suspect. A lot of people are depending on me and we're out of business until this is cleaned up.''

Libba's eyes were very dark in the pale cream of her face. His argument made sense. He would be the injured party if the bay was closed to commercial fishing. ''According to the reports Cliff left me, the water samples show high amounts of toxins,'' she replied. ''Certain toxins—mercury, lead, et cetera—have been linked to skin diseases, birth defects, deformities in animals and cancer in humans. The worst would be to learn that it's invaded our natural water supply. Lake Michigan trout are inedible because of their chemical content. Eel fishing in the St. Lawrence has been terminated for the same reason. PCB-infested rice killed sixteen people in Japan. In this country, the FDA has the power to seize any fish it believes to be contaminated.''

''In other words, this isn't just a temporary setback. This is death to the entire industry on the Chesapeake.''

''It's also possible, although not probable, that toxins have invaded our subterranean wells. That's a longshot and I haven't run any tests of my own,'' she warned him. ''This is supposed to be a part-time job for me.''

Russ ignored her disclaimer and focused on the issue at hand. ''What in the hell are you talking about?''

''Those who live outside of town and drink well water could be at an extremely high risk for cancer and birth defects.''

Suddenly he felt cold. ''That's all of us. We all live on the outskirts of town.''

Libba nodded.

''What kind of cancer?''

He knew the answer before she confirmed it. The print on Mitch's medical file was burned into his memory.

Her voice was no more than a whisper. ''Leukemia, testicular and ovarian cancers.''

Thirteen

"What do you mean, you'll tell me later?" Cole Delacourte fixed his courtroom stare on his daughter. "You show up, white-faced, in the middle of dinner, and say you're not hungry. The least you can do is tell us where you've been."

"I'm not refusing, Daddy." Libby worked to keep her voice even. "I said I'd explain later."

"Stop badgering her, Coleson." Nola Ruth threw a warning glance at her granddaughter, summoned a twisted smile and pointed at the plate of piled-high crabs. "Have one, Libba Jane. You're much too thin. You know what they say, excessive dieting destroys the skin."

"I'm not on a diet, Mama. I'm watching my weight."

"Well, whatever. Have a crab. No, not that one." She pushed her daughter's fork toward a meatier serving. "This one."

In the hall, the phone rang.

Serena, ageless, mahogany-skinned, glided into the room. "Dr. Balieu's on the phone for you, sir."

"Thank you, Serena." Coleson wiped his mouth, excused himself and left the room.

Libby picked at her food, wondering how, after this morning, she could possibly force a bite of crab into her mouth. She watched as her daughter cleaned her plate and reached for another crab. Quickly, she picked up her water glass and just as quickly set it down again. Was there anything served on the bay that wasn't cooked, steamed or boiled? Mentally she chastised herself. There was nothing wrong with the crabs or the water that Serena had placed on their table.

Chloe glanced at her mother's face and frowned. "Are you feeling okay, Mom? You don't look very good."

"I'm fine." She smiled brightly. "I have a surprise for you."

Chloe groaned. "The last time you said that, we moved."

"It's nothing like that," Libby assured her.

"What is it?"

"You've been invited to a party."

"That's impossible," Chloe said flatly. "I don't know anybody."

"Whose party is it?" asked Nola Ruth.

"Cecil Taft's daughter, Skylar. She's turning sixteen. She's invited several girls, Tess Hennessey among them, to a slumber party. When Tess learned that Chloe was new in town, she asked if she could bring her along to the party and Skylar agreed. Isn't that nice?"

"How do they know about me?" asked Chloe. "I've never heard of either one of them."

"Russ Hennessey is an old friend of mine," Libby said. "I told him you were bored and lonely because of our move and he told me about his daughter. He called her, explained your circumstances, and she invited you to go with her to Skylar's party." Libby appealed to her daughter. "What do you think?"

"I think you're insane," Chloe replied. "I'm not going to a slumber party where I don't know anyone. Do you have any idea how pathetic you've made me sound?"

Libby's mouth dropped. "Chloe, don't be ridiculous. It isn't like that at all."

"It sounds like it."

Libby appealed to her mother. "Mama, help me, please."

Nola Ruth fixed her dark eyes on the lovely, Nordic beauty of her granddaughter's face. "She's right, Chloe.

Normally, I'd agree with you, but because you're Libba Jane's daughter, it won't be taken the wrong way.''

Chloe's brow wrinkled. ''Why not?''

Nola Ruth's mouth turned up and she shrugged. ''It's always been that way. All your mama ever had to do was show up. It didn't have anything to do with anybody else. Some would call it an aura. Personally, I think it's just plain luck. Once a reputation is established, it's hard to change it, good or bad.''

Libby stared at her mother. ''What on earth are you talking about?''

''You know it's true, Libba,'' her mother chided her. ''It's the reason you came home. People who have the gumption to up and leave Marshyhope Creek for the big city don't usually itch to come back.''

Libby's face burned. She was very conscious of Chloe's regard. She could feel her sixteen-year-old mind working, measuring, digesting her grandmother's words. Libby wet her lips. ''I had a wonderful childhood,'' she admitted, wondering why she felt so attacked, so compelled to defend herself. ''I can't think of anyone I know who grew up here and didn't.''

''There are plenty who didn't.''

''Who?'' Against her will, the question popped out. She had no desire to continue the conversation.

''Lizzie Jones for one, and Bailey.''

''Who else?''

''Verna Lee Fontaine,'' her mother continued, ''and Russ Hennessey, to name a few.''

Chloe was immediately interested. ''I know Verna Lee.''

''What was so terrible about Verna Lee's life?'' Libby demanded. She didn't want to talk about Russ.

''A young girl like that, pretty and smart, raised by that dreadful old woman.'' Nola Ruth shivered.

Libby frowned. ''You never did care for Drusilla. Why is that, Mama? She's a harmless old lady.''

"Harmless?" Nola Ruth's knotted hands twisted the cloth napkin in her lap. "I suppose she could seem so, to some."

Libby's curiosity had been whetted. She wanted the conversation to continue, but she was very conscious of Chloe seated on the other side of the table, drinking in every word. This heart-to-heart with her mother would have been unheard of seventeen years ago. Nola Ruth Delacourte was a private person who believed in preserving one's dignity. "Keep it to yourself, Libba Jane," she always said. "The world has a way of punishing those who disclose too much."

Serena walked into the room carrying a silver coffee pot. She poured coffee for Libby and Nola Ruth, a rich dark brew heavy with chicory. Then she began clearing the dinner plates. "Mr. Delacourte said he was finishing up some work in the study and to go ahead and have your coffee without him."

Chloe pushed her chair away from the table. "I'm going for a walk."

"What about the party?"

"What about it?"

Libby summoned hidden reserves of patience. "Are you going?"

"Do I have a choice?"

"Of course you do."

"Then, no. I'm not going."

"Chloe," her mother pleaded. "You might like it. Don't condemn something you haven't even tried."

Chloe folded her arms against her chest. "You said I had a choice. If you didn't mean it, just tell me I have to go."

Libby wanted to strangle her. How could this lovely child with her silvery angel's hair and bluer-than-blue eyes inspire such a rage in her? Libby's voice was sharp-edged, cold. "All right. Suit yourself. Don't go."

"Thank you," Chloe said, smiling sweetly.

"Don't go far," her mother called after her, "and take my cell phone."

Chloe didn't answer.

Libby sighed and sank back in her chair.

Nola Ruth sipped her coffee, offering no comment. That would have been unusual enough in itself to draw a question from Libby, but she was too preoccupied with thoughts of Chloe. "What do you do, Mama, when everything seems more than you can bear?"

"You have no idea what a woman can bear, Libba Jane," her mother said dryly. "The idea that you think you're at rock bottom amuses me."

The verbal slap took Libby aback, but only for a moment. She wasn't a child and she refused to be intimidated. Her mother had alluded to secrets and she wanted a part of them. "I'm not at rock bottom. That's a relative judgment that no one can make for anyone else. I'm curious, Mama. What do you do when times are hard?"

Her mother's dark eyes flickered. "I pray."

"You aren't even religious. I thought you didn't believe in God."

"Being religious has nothing to do with it. When you need to pray, there's always a god."

"Isn't that a bit too convenient?"

"That's the beauty of it."

"What matters, Mama? In the end, what really matters?"

Nola Ruth pulled back her lips in an attempted smile. "You matter, Libba Jane. You and Chloe. Our children matter. That's all."

Suddenly the urge to bare the truth became overwhelming. "I know you lied to me," Libby began. "Your parents died well after I left Marshyhope Creek. When Eric and I drove through New Orleans, I was curious. I wanted to know about them. I found out they were living exactly where you said you'd grown up."

Nola Ruth nodded but she didn't seem bothered to have her deception uncovered. "Did you stop in to see them?"

Libby shook her head. "I wasn't thinking of family just then. It wasn't until later, after Chloe was born, that I contacted them. Your mother invited me to visit. I never did."

Her mother's eyes were deliberately vacant, veiled against her.

"Does Daddy know?"

"Shame on you, Libba Jane, to think I would keep anything from your father. Of course he knows. He knows everything. It's time you did, as well."

"I don't understand."

Nola Ruth leaned back in her chair, leaving the coffee to grow cold. "It isn't a pretty story, but it's mine. I want you to know because it's your right. I handled things the way that was good for me. I don't know whether or not the same way will be good for you and it certainly won't be for Chloe. You'll have to decide."

"I'm listening."

"Pour yourself a cup of coffee, Libba. It's good New Orleans coffee. This story will take a while and it isn't one I'm proud of. I won't blame you if you hold it against me. I will blame you if you don't do as I ask."

Libby poured her coffee, recognizing the command for what it was, a moment needed for an old woman to regroup, to settle herself, to meet her dragons face-to-face. She prepared herself to work at paying attention, to force herself to appear interested, to endure the ramblings of a woman whose brain wasn't what it had been. What, after all, could Nola Ruth Delacourte, the quintessential lady, the charming hostess, have done that was dreadful or memorable or even worth recalling? Libby could not have anticipated the nature of the story that came from her mother's memories. The words, spilling from the older woman's mouth, came quickly, sometimes unintelligibly—fascinating words, repelling words, in the soft, liquid tones of the Louisiana Delta, in third person, as if the series of events had happened to someone else.

Magnolia Ruth Delacourte had lived in Marshyhope Creek for forty-one years, but she was not a native. The Beauchamps hailed from farther south, from a city with older, richer, deeper traditions, a city whose ethnic roots were as established as the heavy wet air and spicy smells; the floating duckweed coating whiskey-colored bayou waters like melted chocolate; the wrought-iron balconies weeping Spanish moss; the yeasty smell of beignets and chicory; the filthy, colorful, authentic neighborhoods; the raw oysters, crawfish pie and gumbo; the étouffées and jambalayas; the ragtime, Cajun and jazz; the floods, the sweat, the soft, still wonder of bayou nights; the red beans and rice that could only reach consistency when cooked at the low altitudes of the French Quarter; and, beneath it all, Catholicism, entrenched and traditional, like a greedy parasite on the rim of a Baptist South.

Resting in its below-sea-level nest, shielded by levees, swept by rains in winter and summer, bearing the residue of silt from a thousand northern tributaries, New Orleans perched at the mouth of the Mississippi River, an aging voodoo priestess, familiar, covetous, mysterious, enticing, sweetly addicting in her sultry power.

This was Nola's city. It had shaped her character as inevitably as the wind and rain, the cold winters and hot, heat-stunning summers of a deeper south had shaped Anton Devereaux's. Two people with simmering passions. A girl on the verge of womanhood, molded by conflicting influences, a decadent city, an ancient religion and a heritage of aristocratic privilege and shameful self-indulgence. A young man, square-jawed, hot-blooded and hardheaded as the iron-rich Piedmont soil.

They met on a summer night in 1962. Nola, daughter of

a scion of New Orleans society, had escaped the confines of the annual debutante ball. For months now, she'd sensed that the world was changing and she was restless. She wanted to change with it. The soft music, yellowed linen muted with age, gleaming silver, crystal chandeliers, young ladies dressed in white, and young men from the finest families in the city held no allure for her.

Nola was seventeen, a smoldering dark-eyed beauty with exquisite features and magnificent proportions. In that Creole city populated by French, Spanish, West Indians, French Huguenots and Native Americans, she could have been any or all of those ethnicities. Men of every race and color turned around for a second look at her and were entranced. Nola did not look seventeen. She had never looked seventeen. The night of her fourteenth birthday she went to bed a child and awoke looking like she would look for most of her life, beautiful, alluring, ageless.

Anton Devereaux was passing out leaflets for a civil rights rally. What he saw when he glanced up at the dark-haired, honey-skinned girl in the breathtaking white dress was something he hadn't the ability to express in words. He knew only that he wanted her more than he'd ever wanted anything before. She was beautiful, her accent proclaimed her a Southerner, and the crucifix on the slender chain around her neck told him she was a Catholic. The last was the only problem he could foresee. She had skin the color of cream-drenched coffee, black hair and dark, dark eyes. He'd seen lighter-skinned black women. It never occurred to him that she could be white. By the time he found out, the damage had been done.

Disregarding the stammering protests of the New Orleans schoolmate who was his host, he followed her down the street with but one thing on his mind, to acquire Nola Ruth Beauchamp for his own. Anton was one of a new breed of black men on his way up in the world, men who refused to stand when there were available seats in the rows labeled

Whites Only, men who made it their business to read and
write, to speak their passions and vote, men whose political
clout and bravado would bring forth a new kind of South, a
new kind of Democratic Party. What he lacked in finesse and
experience, he made up with strength and conviction. If he
drank more than his share he was honest and direct. If he
gambled, he never cheated. If he came home more often than
not with a blackened eye and split lip, no man could say he
ran from a fight. His family was an honorable one.

Two generations before, a Devereaux left the West Indies
with five pounds in his pocket to sign on as a cabin boy on
a boat fishing for cod out of Boston Harbor. Gradually, he
earned enough to migrate down to the warmer waters of the
Chesapeake and open up a dry goods store. Every generation since had kept the business strong.

Anton was a beneficiary of the Civil Rights movement,
the first in his line to aspire to a college degree. At Yale
University he found himself caught up in the fire of the day.
Malcolm X, Angela Davis and Huey McBride were his heroes. He had no use for the peaceful Martin Luther King.

Anton was obsessed with quality. In Nola Ruth, with her
boarding school education, her love of French philosophers,
her graceful diplomacy, her aspiring artistic talent, the fluent, musical way she had of switching from English to
French to German, he believed he'd found his ideal mate.
That her designer gown and diamond-studded shoes cost
more than six months' profit from his father's business
meant nothing to him at all.

At first it rankled that she refused to introduce him to her
family. But his mind was on the movement and his body
filled with fire for the beautiful girl who was his lover.
"Later," he told himself. "They'll accept me later, with my
Yale degree and my place in the world. After all, she has
to marry somebody, and who better than a young educated
black man on his way up?"

As for Nola Ruth, she watched the tall, rugged young man

with the square jaw, wide shoulders, broad workman's hands, coffee-colored skin and yellow eyes walk toward her, and something dark, elemental and forbidden slumbering deep within her leaped to life. She smiled and held out her hand, accepting the leaflet he handed her.

Forty-some years later, Nola Ruth still felt cold sweat gather between her breasts when she recalled the events of the weeks that followed. Anton's courtship was swift, intense and forbidden. She told no one, but her mother suspected she was meeting someone. Of course, she had no idea who it was. Nola Ruth could still recall her mother's thin, disapproving lips warning her to be careful, that a gently bred girl must be beware of her reputation.

But Nola Ruth, born in that city of sin, ignored her warnings. She was deliciously shocked the first time Anton's hot tongue entered her mouth and his hand closed over her breast. More times than she could count in those first weeks, he took her to staggering climax, first in the roomy back seat of the Studebaker provided by his nervous New Orleans host, then in the Beauchamp summerhouse, on their veranda swing, in the sitting room always late at night after the servants had retired, and finally beneath the sweating, lavender-scented sheets of the bedroom Nola Ruth had occupied from her earliest memory, the bedroom backed up to the master suite where her parents slept in serene ignorance.

Anton lacked refinement, but he was intelligent. He understood the rules of the rising black upper middle class and he intended to abide by them. Marriage was his intent, but he wasn't completely sure of Nola Ruth. She was acquiescent and generous when it came to lovemaking. He had never experienced so willing and sensitive a bed partner. But there was something removed about her, as if only her body participated while her mind looked on from somewhere else outside of herself. It was this otherworldly quality that attracted him, and at the same time kept him on edge, slightly insecure, never quite knowing where he stood.

Only during sex, at the crest of her climax, with her head thrown back, her eyes closed, her breathing labored, was he completely confident that she belonged to him. He used her incredible physical appetite to his advantage. Withdrawing himself completely, he teased her with the tip of his erection. "Marry me, Nola," he murmured. "Marry me, tonight."

"Please, don't stop," she gasped, arching her back to bring him back inside of her.

He was twenty-one years old, at the peak of his sexual potency. Sweat poured down his chest. Deliberately, with great effort, he held himself away. "Come away with me, now," he begged.

Nola Ruth bit her lip. Anything to end this torture. "Yes," she moaned. "Yes, yes, yes." With all her strength, she palmed his muscle-corded buttocks and pulled him deeply into her.

Pressing his face between her breasts, he groaned and drove and pumped until he was empty.

Nola Ruth never forgot the events that followed their trip across the Louisiana state line into Nicholson, Mississippi, nor would she forget the ride back home with her father the next afternoon. It was something the Beauchamp family never spoke of, but Nola recalled it more clearly than any family photograph lovingly detailed in the family album.

Anton and she spent what was left of that night driving the back roads, not connecting with the main highway until Pearl River, breakfasting with truck drivers at an all-night doughnut shop. Nola Ruth ate in the car, afraid to be seen. She refused to underestimate her father. Anton roused the justice of the peace at eight o'clock. Blood tests were unnecessary in Nicholson. Swallowing to control her panic, Nola stared at the Adam's apple in the man's throat as she mechanically responded to his questions. How had she come to this?

She had never intended to marry Anton Devereaux, only

to seduce him. He was a magnificent young animal, lean, hungry-eyed, predatory, forbidden, a perfect specimen for mating. She loved him, but he was completely unsuitable. Marriage was an institution to be entered into with deliberation and calm, a unity of compatible background, education, family, religion, wealth and race, a symbiotic understanding of one's role in life. She hadn't counted on the incredible skin-to-skin closeness, the mind-stealing wanting of him, the sensations of strength, slick hard steel and hair-roughened muscle, the magic of hot nights and movement and rising tension, the quivering, peaking desire and finally, the sheer joy of shattering climax. It was enough, almost. The sick, jealous rage at the thought of his hands on another woman's body was her Rubicon. Nola Ruth knew it wasn't the sort of love that would last forever, but she reached for it, taking whatever time she had.

In the end, she might have listened to her better judgment, but he caught her at a bad moment. She would have died to reach that climax. She'd read about women like her, addicts of the flesh, the nymphomaniacs of ancient Greece. For a long time after Anton, she stayed away from men until she met Coleson, warm, dear, wonderful Coleson, who comforted her, loved her, made her feel treasured and secure, helped her to realize it wasn't sex she was addicted to, but the intoxicating heat and presence of Anton Devereaux and the exhilarating rush that came from indulging in the forbidden.

The elopement was absurd and doomed to fail, but the hours that followed were exercises in sensory hedonism, worth everything that came later. Reflecting back, Nola Ruth marveled at the marvelous stroke of fate that had brought Anton Devereaux to New Orleans that summer. Without him, she would never have known passion. Gauging her own marriage and those of her contemporaries, she realized that most women, unless they were willing to risk the shame of discovery, went to their graves never knowing the true meaning of the word.

Her father found them that very day. His influence was great, even in Mississippi. Anton was thrown in jail on charges of kidnapping, statutory rape and misogyny. He was twenty-one to Nola's seventeen. He was black and she white. There was simply no response to the terrifying power, the icy coldness of the four men in blue police uniforms who read the charges. She would never forget the shocked horror on Anton's face when they accused him of abducting and raping a *white* woman.

She waited for news of him for more than two months, but there was nothing. He'd simply disappeared.

If she had been braver, with the steady confidence of Coleson Delacourte or even the foolhardy, throat-closing courage of her daughter, it would have ended differently. She would not have been dispatched to her aunt Eugenie in Marshyhope Creek, where she'd lived behind closed curtains for six months. She would not have given birth in a back bedroom with clenched teeth, cold metal between her legs and tears running down her cheeks. She would not have given up her child into the hands of a colored midwife, yellow-skinned, gold-toothed Drusilla Washington. She would not have risen from that bed believing, for half a lifetime, that nothing more than Anton Devereaux's seed had been cut from her body.

But Nola Ruth was not brave and perhaps it was for the best. If the events had turned out differently, she would never have married Coleson. There would be no Libba and no Chloe. It was a strange thing to realize, this late in life, that her greatest joy lay in anticipation of the time with her daughter and granddaughter.

She never returned to New Orleans, never communicated with her parents and never saw Anton Devereaux again. Her penance was seeing the child, hers and Anton's, nearly every day, although this part she kept from Libba. It tore at her heart and ate away at the pleasure she should have taken in her husband and the daughter they had together.

Libby stared at her mother, eyes wide with horrified comprehension. "My God, Mama. I don't know what to say. Are you saying you have another child, a black child out in the world somewhere?" Her voice cracked. "How could you do that? You, of all people."

"I told you how."

"I don't believe it. I *can't* believe it."

Nola Ruth sighed. "My darling, that's irrelevant."

Libby shook her head "I don't want to hear this. It isn't fair. Why are you telling me? Why now?"

"I had a very close call, Libba Jane. I won't last forever. I want you to know how it was. I want to do the right thing." She leaned forward and gripped her daughter's hand. "When the time comes, I want both of my children to share in what I have to leave them. Promise me you'll do this, Libba. Promise me now."

"Of course I promise. If it makes you feel better, why don't you leave a will?"

"I can't do that."

"Why not?"

"I couldn't bear the humiliation."

"You'll be dead," Libby said bluntly.

"It would all have been for nothing. Can't you see that?"

The question loomed between them. Finally, not wanting to know but not able to help herself, Libby voiced it. "Have you kept in touch with this person?"

"I'll tell you, Libba Jane, but not now, not yet. I need to hold on to something."

"You said you didn't keep anything from Daddy. Surely he doesn't know this."

"He knows."

Libby stared at her mother, imagining her as she must have been, younger, lovelier, with the same rebellious spirit as her own and Chloe's, only magnified a hundred times more. She stood and nearly fell over. Her legs and back ached with tension. "I think I'll go upstairs," she said slowly. "Good night, Mama."

"Aren't you going to kiss me, Libba Jane?"

Libby hesitated. She was angry, but she wasn't clear why. She felt raw and betrayed and not at all like bestowing a gesture of affection on the one responsible for those feelings. Forcing herself, she brushed a brief kiss on her mother's cheek.

Nola Ruth accepted the salute. "Sleep well," she said, and pretended not to watch her daughter leave the room. They'd all left her, Coleson and Libba Jane and Chloe, forgetting that she couldn't move. It would be Serena who lifted her into her chair and wheeled her to the downstairs bedroom that was hers alone. Cole didn't sleep there with her. In the beginning, he'd tried to, but she wouldn't have him. She refused to have him feel sorry for her. Pity turned so quickly to contempt. She couldn't bear for Cole to hold her in contempt.

She rang the bell and in a moment Serena was by her side. "You here all by yourself, Miz Delacourte? What are they thinking of leaving you alone like this?"

Nola Ruth dismissed their neglect. "It doesn't matter." And it didn't. She wanted to be alone. Her reverie had stirred the memories. Libba knew enough now. Any more wouldn't be prudent. But there were more tantalizing tidbits from the past and she wanted to finish them. Deliberately, she removed her mind from the present, remaining passive while Serena's cool hands settled her into her chair and wheeled her down the long hall, across the Persian carpet and into her bedroom. "I'll sit awhile, Serena," she said.

The black woman nodded and positioned the wheelchair by the window. "Shall I check you in an hour or so?"

Nola Ruth nodded. "Sooner, I think. I just had coffee."

Serena found Nola's cell phone, punched in a number and

left it on the small table within reach. She patted her own pocket. ''Press the button if you need anything.''

Nola didn't answer. She was far away again. Anton Devereaux had exacted his revenge. He'd stolen her passion and her spirit, the luminous, quivery brightness that set her apart. Desire she'd felt again, but never the heady, reckless, mind-stealing heat that came over when he ran his hand down her spine.

There had been one startling encounter at the Fourth of July picnic after she'd married Cole. It was a stifling, heat-baked afternoon in the town square. Clothing clung to sweat-soaked skin. Flies swarmed around tepid lemonade glasses. Hats wilted and drooped. Noses burned and conversation lagged. Nola Ruth threw her hat on the grass and languidly waved her accordion-folded napkin. A white halter dress flattered the deep gold skin of her back. Heat didn't bother her. Summers in New Orleans were far worse than in Maryland. Cole had gone for another beer. She could see him from her seat under the trees, deep in conversation with a neighbor. A breeze from the bay cooled her bare shoulders and lifted her hat, carrying it several feet from where she sat. Before she could move, a lean, masculine form retrieved it. ''I believe this is yours,'' the man said.

He wasn't Anton, but she knew the type, or rather, she felt his pull. The magic, the desperate sexual addiction she'd felt for her first love, had begun just this way, a smoldering glance, a brushing of skin, a casual question that wasn't casual at all. Nola reached for her hat with her left hand. She didn't miss his gold wedding ring.

Before either of them could speak, Cole had returned. ''Beau, I'd like you to meet my bride, Nola Ruth Delacourte. Nola, this is Beau Hennessey.''

''Nice to meet you,'' she said breathlessly.

''You look familiar,'' Beau said.

Nola's heart stopped. ''Really?''

Beau nodded but didn't elaborate.

Nola lifted a hand to her forehead. "I'm a little dizzy, Cole. Would you mind if I went home?"

"Of course." Coleson slipped his arm around her waist. "I knew this heat would be too much for you."

Beau called after them. "If you think it's hot here, you should visit the Louisiana Delta. Nice seeing you, Nola Ruth."

After that, she didn't see much of Beau. She had no idea if she'd met him years ago in New Orleans, but she lived in fear of finding out and avoided him as **much as** possible. She ran into his wife, Cora, occasionally, **but the two** families didn't socialize. She'd sent a gift when Cora's twins were born and received one of similar value when Libba made her appearance six months later, but that was all, until Libba entered grammar school.

Retribution. That was the way Nola Ruth justified her daughter's attachment to Beau Hennessey's son, an angry God doling out justice for the sins of her youth, the confessions missed, the novenas ignored, the penances not taken.

Serena came back into the room. "Are you ready now, Miz Nola Ruth?"

"Yes." She smiled with half of her face. "I've seen enough of this day. How about you, Serena?"

The black woman groaned. "I've been on my feet for sixteen hours today. I'll be ready for my bed quicker'n you can say St. Joseph."

Two hours later, Nola Ruth gave up on sleep and allowed Russ Hennessey to return to her thoughts. He was an appealing child, she admitted, with the freckled cheeks and sharply hewn features of his Irish wood-sprite mother and the blue eyes and lean-hipped, athletic grace of his father. It was more than his startling good looks that attracted Libba. Russ had the easy confidence, the absence of fear, the innate charisma that heroes are made of. From the time he was a small child, people noticed when he entered a room. On the dock, in the boats, on the football field, he stood out like newly minted silver in a stack of copper pennies. No woman, especially a book-loving, romantic, only child like Libba, could have withstood his appeal.

From their earliest acquaintance, Nola Ruth could feel their tension. It stretched between them like a tightly wound string. The worry of it kept her awake at night. Libba was brilliant and beautiful, sensitive and refined, a child of warmth and light and laughter. There were no hidden, dark-blooded stirrings to mar the perfection of her character. Nola Ruth wanted more for her than Marshyhope Creek, and she was desperately afraid that Russ Hennessey stood squarely, immovably in the way.

In the end she'd underestimated her daughter. Libba was twenty, two years into college and home for the summer when she succumbed to the inevitable, a breath of fresh air, an unfamiliar face, a casual, free-spirited liberalism that could only have come from outside the confines of Marshyhope Creek. It was difficult for Nola to admit, but she'd made a dreadful mistake. In her efforts to spare Libba from passion and despair, she'd discouraged Russ Hennessey's suit. He would have been a much better choice for Libba. At least he would have kept her at home. Perhaps he still would. She no longer knew. The truth was she really didn't recognize Libba Jane. The wide, melting, light-touched smile that characterized her daughter's face had disappeared. In its place was a dignified remoteness, a pleasant, correct expression that bothered Nola Ruth every time she looked at her. And Libba was thin. She'd always been thin, but not like this, not so the bones of her face stood out, giving her an exotic, hollow-cheeked quality. Nola remembered the curvaceous, long-legged beauty of her teenaged child and shivered.

Could it really be coincidence that sent Russ back to Marshyhope Creek at exactly the same time as Libba? The news of his arrival had thrown Nola Ruth into a state of self-absorption. She remembered the way her husband had looked at her oddly when she motioned Serena to pour coffee into his cup at the breakfast table. Cole was an herbal tea drinker who hadn't touched caffeine since the Kennedy years.

When the gardener announced that the ferns Nola had ordered for the greenhouse had come and the driver needed to be paid, she stared blankly at the man as if she'd never spent hours painstakingly designing and ordering the flora of her custom-built hothouse. Cole, who hadn't seen his checkbook since the day he married, left the room to deal with the driver. When he returned, it was to find Nola Ruth still aimlessly stirring the sugar she'd poured into her coffee more than ten minutes before.

"Are you all right, Nola?" he'd asked, eyeing the half-empty sugar bowl. Nola Ruth, ever figure-conscious, allowed herself jelly on toast or sugar in her coffee, never both.

She looked her husband in the eye. "How long have you known Russ Hennessey was back?"

He'd smiled and covered her hand with his own. "Beau Hennessey was my client. I knew the terms of his will. It was only a matter of time before Russ came home. He took a little longer than I expected, but he had to settle other matters. He's a Hennessey. I don't think he wanted his father's life, but his family loyalty is strong. He's the only one left. It's up to him to keep the company going. I imagine he wasn't too happy about settling into the same town where his ex-wife lives." He left the coffee, found another cup on the sideboard and poured hot water over his tea bag. "Why do you ask?"

"He and Libba Jane were seeing quite a bit of each other before she left with Eric."

Cole chuckled. "That was a long time ago, Nola. They both married other people. Surely whatever they had between them is over."

Nola Ruth had slipped back into her reverie without bothering to answer him. Men were such fools, even brilliant, thoughtful ones like Coleson. Because Cole was a man of exceptional character, he judged all others by himself. As if it were unheard of for a woman to still be in love with a man simply because she had married someone else.

Fourteen

The rich coffee smell emanating from Perks drew Libby inside. Two teenage girls sat at a table drinking smoothies. A man hunkered over the counter reading a newspaper, holding a ceramic mug. A woman with a baby on her hip talked with Verna Lee at the cash register. Libby lined up behind her.

Verna Lee looked over the woman's shoulder. "May I help you, Libba Jane?"

"I'll have a cup of your coffee of the day to go, please."

"I don't serve my coffee in paper cups," Verna Lee said. "It's bad for the environment. I would have thought that would matter to you, with your new job and all."

Libby's cheeks flamed. There was no mistaking the woman's tone and she wasn't going to let it go unchallenged. "I don't know what side of the bed you got up on this morning, Verna Lee, but I'll have that coffee in the same kind of cup you gave Russ Hennessey the other day."

Verna Lee filled a bright orange mug and handed it to Libby. "Feel free to take it with you. I know where to find you."

Libby dropped two dollar bills on the counter, hooked her fingers through the handle of the mug and left the shop with her coffee. She was steaming. For pity's sake, what ailed the woman? She hadn't said more than a sentence to Verna Lee Fontaine in her entire life. Why the woman should have taken such a dislike to her she had no idea, and more to the point, it wasn't worth finding out. She had more to worry about than Verna Lee's odd fits of temper. She'd spent a restless night. Her mother's confession had rattled her. It was as if the mother she'd grown up with had disappeared, leaving this stranger in her place. Then there was Chloe and her unwillingness to try to settle into a life here.

She unlocked the office door and glanced over at the blinking light on the fax machine. The lab reports on the stunted crabs should be back by now. Pulling the paper from the cradle, she turned on the desk lamp, settled into the chair and began to read. At the end of the page, she breathed a sigh of relief. The news wasn't good but it wasn't terrible, either. Fishing in the Cove was prohibited, but shad and crabs near Smith Island remained unaffected. Water samples were clean. She frowned. Would Russ think it was good news? Blue Crab spawning grounds at Smith Island were nearly fifty miles away, a good two hours by boat. She checked her watch. It was nearly eight o'clock in the morning. More than likely she would find him at the dock.

He wasn't alone. Libby heard the heated exchange even before she saw the woman. Tracy Wentworth was still small and blond with delicate features, a Marilyn Monroe voice and skin that was already showing her age. The woman greeted her warily.

"So," Tracy began, "you're here permanently."

Libby smiled noncommittally. "We'll see. It depends on a number of things, Chloe for one."

"Tess is looking forward to meeting her," Tracy said politely.

"Thanks for inviting her, but she won't be attending the party."

Tracy frowned. "Why not? Tess went to a considerable amount of trouble to get her invited."

"I think that's the problem. Chloe doesn't want to go where she isn't wanted."

"Isn't wanted?" Tracy's eyebrows flew up. "How does she know she isn't wanted?"

Loyalty to Chloe kept Libby from agreeing with Tracy. "She appreciates the invitation, but she'd rather make friends on her own." Her eyes met Russ's. "Thanks for trying to help, both of you."

Tracy shrugged. "It sounds like you have a handful for a daughter, Libba Jane. Thank goodness Tess has never given me a moment's trouble." She glanced at Russ, who was staring at her with narrowed eyes. "I think we're finished here. I trust that little matter we discussed won't be brought up again."

"Don't count on it," Russ said bluntly.

Tracy's cheeks pinkened. "Be careful, Russ." She nodded at Libby. "Nice seeing you again, Libba Jane."

"You, too, Tracy."

Libby sat across from Russ and waited until she heard the sound of a car engine. She tilted her head. "Good morning."

"It was at first," he acknowledged.

"Does she come around often?"

"More than I'd like."

"Why not tell her to stop?"

"She has full custody of my daughter."

"How did that happen?"

"Her daddy's the judge."

"What about a change of venue?"

"This is Marshyhope Creek, Libba. You've been gone a long time."

She considered his answer and realized how far she'd come. Small southern towns administered their own form of justice. The legal system in California would never allow a judge to rule over his own daughter's divorce proceedings. "There must be something you can do. She's your daughter."

Russ didn't answer. He was tired of thinking about what

he could do about Tess and even more tired of Tracy. How he could have been sucked into marriage with her was beyond him. He felt as if it had happened to someone else in another lifetime. The weariness was weighing him down, preventing him from going about his life. He wanted to feel alive again, to take pleasure in good food, good wine, conversation, friendship, possibly even attempt a real relationship.

He glanced at Libba, his eyes lingering on her wine-dark hair and ivory skin, her mink-brown eyes with their flecks of gold and that mouth—she had the most incredible mouth. Libba's smile would stop people on the street. It took him down memory lane all over again.

She was staring at him, a worried look on her face. That face had haunted his dreams and been the object of every adolescent fantasy he'd ever had. He'd never once looked at Tracy Wentworth, never even noticed she was alive, when Libba was part of his life. If he stretched it a bit, he might be able to blame Libba for the current state of his life. He tapped his pencil on the wooden desk. Hell, she might even owe him something. What would it take to get her to pay up?

"You haven't said a word in five minutes," Libby said. "What are you thinking?"

He decided to go for it. "I'm thinking that it's about time we had our heart-to-heart."

"Excuse me?"

"You heard me."

"I did, but I have no idea what you're talking about."

"I spent the better part of five years trying to figure out why you dumped me. I figure you owe me an answer."

He saw the color rise in her cheeks. It pleased him that she was uncomfortable. He'd intended to make her uncomfortable.

"I didn't dump you, Russ. I fell in love with someone else."

He dropped the pencil, pushed his chair back and walked around the desk, leaning against it, arms crossed, expression formidable.

She backed away from him until she felt the wall against her back.

"I was under the impression you were in love with me," he said relentlessly. "Do you know *why* I was under that impression, Libba Jane?"

She swallowed, knowing what was coming next.

Slowly, he pushed away from the desk and walked toward her, coming closer and closer until he was near enough to breathe her air. She could smell him, tobacco and soap and a faint woodsy odor that she would forever associate with Russ and home. He was too present. It was hard to draw breath. She turned her head to avoid looking at him. His hands on either side of her held her captive.

"This is ridiculous, Russ." Her voice was low, controlled. "Let me go."

Black hair fell across his forehead. Blue eyes burned. "I asked you a question. Aren't you going to answer it?"

"No, I'm not."

"I hashed it over a million times. A girl like you, a nice girl, the kind a man waits for and treats with respect, doesn't drop her white cotton panties for just any guy. You held out for a long time, Libba Jane. Why, when everything was going right for us, did you jump ship?"

Trembling with anger, she looked directly at him, her eyes so dark the pupil and iris blended together. "I don't wear white cotton panties anymore and maybe you didn't know me as well as you think you did. You certainly didn't appreciate me."

"Say that again?"

She opened her mouth but the words wouldn't come. Every ounce of Southern hospitality drilled into her from birth melted away. Once again in the slow-dance cadence of her life, in yet another defining moment when she could have set things right, Libby Delacourte was rendered speechless. Her throat closed. Dear God, she prayed silently. Make him go away. Make this not be happening. She squinted through her lashes, hoping against hope for the impossible. No such miracle for the likes of her. She shrank back, making herself as small as possible. She knew what he wanted, but she would die before she gratified his ego. She refused to touch him. No power on earth would make her touch him. She would pass out first. She would just hold her breath until she turned blue and fell on the floor.

He bent his head, his breath stirring the strands of hair near her ear. "Tell me you missed me, Libba Jane. Tell me nobody ever fucked you like I did."

A million responses formed in her mind, but none of them the right one. Sweat beaded on her forehead and collected between her breasts. Minutes ticked by as the sick nausea of shock and shame and regret warred with an aching sorrow she had never quite come to terms with. Seventeen years had gone by and Russ Hennessey still believed he could charm her out of her skivvies with nothing more than a touch and a suggestive comment. She didn't need loving that badly. She would never need it that badly. A sound on the street steadied her. Visions of how their compromising position would appear to anyone who walked in spurred her to action. Suddenly, Libby was herself again. Her voice came out clear and cold, a tribute to her years with the Ventura Country District Attorney's Office. "In your dreams, Russ Hennessey. I didn't miss you. Not one bit. As a matter of fact, I forgot all about you the minute I wiped the dust of this town off my feet."

His laugh was humorless. "You're a liar and I'll prove it to you."

His head bent and his lips came down on hers, hard. She should have objected, pushed him away, delivered a scathing diatribe belittling his methods and walked out of the office. He wouldn't stop her. But she did none of those things. Instead, everything inside of her went still. Time rolled back. She was a girl again, wanting nothing more than to exist within the sphere of Russ Hennessey's presence. Her lips parted. He deepened the kiss and her arms encircled his neck. She heard a sound, gravelly and triumphant, escape from his throat.

Recalling the incident later, Libby didn't remember who pulled away first. But all at once it was over, with no explanation, no apology or awkwardness or hint of possible future encounters. It was simply over with Russ leaning back against his desk and Libby standing against the wall with puffy lips, as if the drumming desire, the searing want, had occurred between two different people.

"You're looking mighty fine today, Libba Jane," he said softly. "What brings you here this morning?"

She mentally pushed away the kiss. *Why had she come?* Sanity returned. "The lab report came back. Smith Island is still open for crabbing."

"What about the bay?"

"Prohibited until more tests can be run. I'm sorry."

He nodded. "I expected as much."

She bent her head. He watched the dark curtain of hair swing across her cheek. "Do you have any idea how long this will take?"

"I'm sorry, Russ," she said again. "I'm a novice here. I'll e-mail Cliff and get back to you."

"Thanks for stopping by."

"It's been—" she paused "—interesting."

He grinned, the mocking, white-toothed grin that once would have turned her knees to jelly. "You could say that."

She turned to go.

"Libba."

She paused at the door. "If I were you, I'd try to talk your daughter into accepting Skylar Taft's invitation. Apparently she's the one who counts around here. Without her approval, Chloe doesn't have a chance of fitting in."

Libby groaned. "Easier said than done. I've already told her she doesn't have to go. If I insist, she'll resent me more than she already does."

"Why is that?"

"Chloe's a daddy's girl," Libby explained. "Eric wasn't around much while she was growing up, so every encounter with him became special. Now that he's settled in Los Angeles, Chloe was looking forward to spending more time with him. Then I uprooted her to come here."

"Why did you come back?"

Libby shrugged and leaned against the door. "Lots of reasons. Mostly, I just didn't fit there. I was tired of the smog and the traffic, of waiting forever on a weekend night to eat in a restaurant. Sometimes I couldn't even get into a movie unless I stood in line for an hour ahead of time. It's hard to get ahead when everything is so expensive. It just got to be too much. Then my mother got sick. It seemed like the perfect excuse to come home."

She hadn't intended to reveal so much of herself, but his interest encouraged her confidences. It was comforting talking to someone from her past, someone who'd known her better than anyone, even if it was Russ.

"There aren't any movies in Marshyhope Creek," he reminded her.

"Salisbury is close enough. What about you? Why did you come back?"

"I'll tell you sometime."

"That's not fair."

"I'll tell you everything, over dinner."

"When?"

"Tonight."

Libby considered his offer. Did she want to involve herself with Russ Hennessey again? It was a question that needed more than a minute to mull over. Curiosity won out. "All right," she said. "I'll meet you."

"You don't want the natives to know you're slumming?"

"I don't want Chloe to know I have a date," she corrected him. "Eric and I haven't been divorced that long."

"Fair enough, although I wouldn't call it a date. I'll make reservations at the Sealark for eight."

"What would you call it?"

"A fact-finding mission."

She smiled. "I'll be there."

He watched her leave. His invitation was spur of the moment, surprising him, like the kiss. What it meant he hadn't figured out yet. If he was smart he'd be gun-shy around Libba Delacourte. She'd wiped her feet on him once already and here he was again, honing in on her like a carrier pigeon. The trouble was she turned him inside out. If he was to make any kind of life for himself, it was about time he figured out why.

Fifteen

Chloe's mouth worked as she struggled against tears. She'd expected Bailey to agree with her. He was supposed to be her friend. She sat on the floor of the shed he used as a studio watching while he painted over a canvas.

"Why are you doing that?" she asked.

"I have to reuse them. I can't afford to buy a new one every time."

She watched his hands, caught by their sure, capable movements, pleased with their brownness and the lean length of his fingers gripping the brush. "I don't want to go," she said sulkily.

"Then don't."

"But you think I should?"

"Yes."

"Why?"

He didn't answer at first, busy with whiting out colorful splashes of paint on the canvas. Finally, when it was completely covered, he set his brush to soak, turned to Chloe and ran his clean hand through his straight black hair. He sounded impatient. "How do you know what you don't like unless you try it?"

"I know I won't like sitting around with a bunch of gossipy girls."

"You don't know that at all," Bailey said. "Who knows, you could be about to meet your new best friend."

Chloe thought she'd already done so. It was lowering to

think that Bailey didn't value their friendship as much as she did. "What if I hate them?"

Bailey stared at her, noting the smooth line of her slender brown legs, the points of her collarbone where the tiny gold ankh rested against the pulse in her throat, her slanted bluer-than-blue eyes and the gold-dusted hair with their black tips floating around her head. He wondered how long it would be before she recognized her own power. "You won't have lost much," Bailey answered logically. "It's only one night and it's still summer, so you won't have to wait a week before you get another day off."

"That's true." Chloe was waffling. There was really no good reason to stay home from the party except for the fact that she wasn't comfortable hanging with a group of people she didn't know. But she wouldn't admit to being shy. It was a flaw, and while adults from her parents' generation might be okay with it, boys from hers were not. Confidence was far more attractive, and although she played a good game on the outside, her insides turned to mush at the thought of crashing a high school slumber party. Still, she didn't want Bailey to know she was afraid, especially since he didn't seem to be afraid of anything.

"I can always say I'm sick and come home."

"You could," he agreed, "but they'd probably see right through you and it would be worse than if you stuck it out and pretended to have a good time."

"Where did you get to be so smart?"

He shrugged and changed the subject. "It's a hot afternoon. Are you thirsty?"

Chloe nodded.

"Do you want a beer?"

She hesitated briefly and then decided on the truth. "I don't do alcohol."

His face stilled, closing against her. "Suit yourself."

"Maybe we could drive into town and see if Verna Lee has more of her spiced tea," she suggested.

"I guess we could."

Chloe beamed and scrambled to her feet, happy he was choosing to extend their time together. Bailey Jones intrigued her. Every time she saw him, he left her wanting to know more.

She climbed into his ancient truck. "I like Verna Lee."

He nodded, struck a match on the dashboard and bent his head to light a cigarette.

"Do you like her?"

He blew out a swirl of smoke and considered her question. "She's nice enough."

"She's real," Chloe said. "More real than anybody here, except maybe my grandfather."

Bailey frowned. "What's that supposed to mean?"

"Oh, I don't know." Chloe waved her hand in a general sweeping gesture. "Everybody here is syrupy. They pretend to be nice, but they don't mean it. I feel like they're judging everything about me, my clothes—" she fingered her spiky black tips "—my hair, the way I talk. Verna Lee is different. She says what she thinks."

Bailey was quiet for the length of time it took to reach the heart of Marshyhope Creek where Perks hugged one corner of the street and the hardware store the other. He pulled into a diagonal parking space and sat for a minute, finishing his cigarette. He ground out the butt and opened the door.

Chloe opened her side and slid out of the seat. She felt ill at ease. Their camaraderie was gone. It had slipped away somewhere between the highway and the city limits.

Verna Lee's welcome almost made up for Bailey's lassitude. "Hi, you two," she called out from one of the deep couches. She was alone, her only company a latte and a magazine. "It's been such a slow night. I was wondering if I should even bother to stay open. Now I'm glad I did."

Chloe nudged Bailey. "See what I mean?" she whispered.

He ignored her and spoke to Verna Lee. "We came for some of your spiced tea."

"I made up a batch today." She stood, a fluid, graceful straightening of her long, shapely legs, and moved around the counter to the refrigerator. "Mint or lemon?"

"Lemon," they said in unison.

Verna Lee carried the glasses toward the couch where she had been sitting. She motioned for Chloe and Bailey to join her. "Come on down here and sit for a bit."

She waited while they settled in. "I thought you two might find each other," she said.

Bailey said nothing, his black eyes unreadable. "Thanks for the herbs, Miss Verna Lee," he said softly. "Mama sleeps better with them."

Verna Lee's smile faded. "You need to find a way out of here, Bailey. Your mother needs treatment in a hospital. Alternative medicine can only do so much."

"I know," he said in a low voice. "But she won't leave the land."

"She doesn't have to sell it."

Bailey made a swift, flat motion with his hands. Even Chloe knew the subject was closed. The mood had grown ugly. She tried to turn it. "It looks like we're staying here, Verna Lee," she said quickly. "My mother has a job."

The black woman's eyes moved over Bailey one last time before resting on Chloe's face. "I heard. How do you feel about that?"

"I'm not actually staying permanently," Chloe replied. "It's just a temporary move for me. As soon as it's legal, I'm going back to L.A."

Verna Lee sipped her latte. "How long will that be?"

"A couple of years at the most, or until I can convince my dad to let me live with him."

"That's a long time," Verna Lee said slowly. "If I were you I might try to work myself out of a holding-pattern attitude. You might like it here and then you'll have two places where you'll feel at home.''

Chloe didn't know whether it was the tea or the company, but suddenly she felt comfortable explaining her position. ''I've been invited to a party and I don't know anyone. Bailey says I should go, but I'm not sure.''

''Why not?''

''What if it doesn't work out?''

''If you don't go, you'll never know.''

''But if I do go and it doesn't work out everyone will know. By staying home, it looks like it was me who decided.''

Bailey was staring at her as if she had half her clothes on. ''That's the dumbest thing I've ever heard.''

Chloe flushed.

Verna Lee shook her toffee-colored mane over her face. ''Tell me if I understand. You're afraid they won't like you, so you're going to reject them first.''

Chloe hung her head. ''When you put it like that, it sounds terrible.''

''It sounds safe, Chloe. Why do you think the worst of people before you've given them a chance?''

''I've seen kids from other places try to fit into a new school. It doesn't work.''

''Never?'' Verna Lee asked.

''If they're guys and good in sports, sometimes it's okay, but girls are a different story. My friends are awful to them.''

''What about you?'' Bailey asked. ''Are you awful, too?''

''Not directly,'' Chloe admitted, ''but I don't step in and defend anyone. If I did, I'd be dead, too.''

''I think you may find that things are a bit different around here,'' said Verna Lee.

Chloe raised her eyebrows and looked at Bailey. ''I don't think so. Bailey told me I shouldn't be seen with him if I wanted to fit in. Tell me how that's different.''

Bailey drained the last of his tea. ''They don't like me

because I'm dirt poor and because my mother won't sell her land. You're Coleson Delacourte's granddaughter and your mama was the town's golden girl until she ran off with your daddy. They'll be rolling out the red carpet and licking your feet no matter what you do.''

''Unless I show up in a truck driven by someone who's dirt poor and whose mama won't sell her land,'' she snapped back.

Verna Lee laughed. ''Come on, you two. Chloe, do whatever you want. It'll work out. Everything usually does.''

Bailey stood. ''We'll let you close up, Verna Lee. No sense in your staying open just to entertain us.''

''It's my pleasure. Stop by anytime.'' She waved his money away. ''Put that back in your pocket. Your money's no good here.''

''I can pay,'' he said tightly.

''I know you can, but I'm not going to charge my friends for staying to have a glass of tea with me.''

Their eyes met and held. Finally, Bailey sighed and stuffed the money back into his pocket.

''Say hello to your mama for me, Bailey. Tell her I'll be out to see her real soon.''

''I'll do that.''

Verna Lee hugged Chloe. ''Come back, now.''

''I will,'' Chloe promised.

Bailey dropped her off at the end of the long brick path leading to her grandparents' home. He'd been silent on the way back. When she opened the door to slide out of the truck, he broke his silence. ''I don't need anybody to fight my battles.''

Chloe's mouth dropped. In the time it took for their eyes to lock, her shock had turned to cold, furious anger. ''You're a jerk, Bailey Jones. No wonder no one likes you.''

He gunned his engine and drove on, and even though she stepped back away from the truck, he left her covered in a layer of fine, red dust.

* * *

Libby knocked on Chloe's bedroom door. There was no response. "Chloe," she called softly, "are you there?"

"I'm here."

"May I come in?"

Libby heard a sigh, the creak of bedsprings and then the door opened. "What do you want?"

"I wanted to tell you that I won't be home for dinner. I'm meeting a friend."

"So? Why tell me?"

Libby frowned. "You sound upset. Is something wrong?"

"No."

"Are you sure?"

Chloe's eyes flashed blue fire. "Nothing that a ticket home wouldn't cure."

Her mother shook her head and turned away. "You're impossible. Good night. If you're still up, I'll stop in later."

The door clicked shut. She heard the muttered words "Don't count on it" through the oak panel. Chloe had always been a challenge, but this defiance was new. Libby hoped it was a short stage. Her patience was running thin. For the second time in her life, she had to quell the urge to slap her child.

Russ was bereft of speech. He'd seen Libba in school clothes, in denim shorts and in and out of her underwear, but never in his life had he seen the adult Libba Hennessey dressed up. She stood there at the entrance to the bar looking like the girl he remembered, yet she wasn't really that girl at all. She had moved to a place that didn't include him. She reminded him of all that was decadent, rich and forbidden, New Orleans chicory and cream, rich coffee and heat-baked sidewalks, chocolate and powdered-sugar beignets.

He blinked his eyes, looked away, his senses filled with

her image, and looked back again. Her eyes, huge and dark, glowed against the honey-gold of her skin. Her hair, the same velvety shade as her eyes, was pulled severely back from her brow and clasped with a barrette behind her head, allowing the thick mass to float around her face and touch her shoulders. A strapless red dress hugged her waist and hips, the sleek material coming to a stop several inches above her knees. Her legs were long and graceful in pale hose and heeled pumps. He knew she'd smell like peach blossoms, a scent as simple, clean and sweet as Hadley's grove on the banks of the Chesapeake. She'd grown up without him, but he wasn't through yet. He rose and made his way through the cloth-covered tables to meet her.

She smiled and his heart hurt.

"I'm sorry I'm late. Have you been here long?"

"Ten minutes, no more." He nodded toward the table he'd left. "I'd like to eat in here. The view's better. Can we enjoy it for a few minutes or are you hungry now?"

"I can wait for a while."

He led her to a small table near the window and pulled out her chair. A bottle of sparkling wine sat in an ice bucket beside it. Libby noticed that it had yet to be poured. "Thanks for waiting," she said, and sat down. "It's a gorgeous night, just the way I like them."

Russ poured her a glass of wine. "You like hot, dry nights when you don't have to wear a sweater and your hair doesn't curl from the humidity."

Libby's eyes widened. "You're amazing. I can't believe you remembered that."

He nodded. "It would be even more amazing if I didn't. You were an original."

"Strange." Her forehead creased. "I didn't think of myself that way at all."

"Does anyone?"

She considered his question. "Maybe. Someone with confidence might. Chloe might."

"I have to meet your Chloe."

"There's plenty of time for that," Libby said hastily. She picked up her wineglass and focused on the view. Men made her nervous, especially good-looking, sweet-talking men with slate-blue eyes and wicked grins. She'd fallen in love with one and married another. That was enough for one lifetime. This time she was looking for something different. This time she would hold on to the advantage.

She knew what Russ wanted. It was as obvious as a cool drink of water from a tall, clean glass. It would be so easy to fall under the spell of his considerable charm, to let his sexual magnetism wipe out her inhibitions. But she'd already had experience loving Russell Tremayne Hennessey and she didn't want to go down that road again. Love had proved to be an overrated emotion. Tying herself up in knots over a man wasn't a mistake she intended to repeat. Dinner in a romantic restaurant with a view of the bay was as far as she would go. "Isn't the view incredible?" she asked.

His eyes never left her face. "Incredible."

He was too close. She shifted and sat back in her chair. The blood pulsed, alive in his throat. He was darkly tanned from the sun and the smell of him brought back memories. She inhaled the combined smells of sun and salt and wind and the sweet, weedy hint of tobacco—masculine smells. His hair, dark with glints of red, curled around his ears. Suddenly, she wanted to touch him. Reaching out, she twisted a curl around her fingers, barely grazing his jaw. The electric quality of the contact startled her. She drew back, shaken and self-conscious, wanting more yet desperately afraid of the wanting. Embarrassed, she said the first thing that came to mind. "Your hair's too long."

The Russ Hennessey of eighteen, or even twenty-eight, wouldn't have looked beyond the obvious. If the woman he wanted was hungry he would have obliged her. But Russ had learned something about women in the years between twenty-eight and thirty-seven, and he knew that this woman, no matter how raging her hormones, wasn't ready to wake up next to him in the morning. He smiled and ran his hand through his hair. ''I'll see about getting it cut.''

It took a moment for his words to register. She nodded shakily and felt the color rise to her cheeks.

Russ congratulated himself. Dinner at the Sealark was an inspiration. The view was the same spectacular one he had grown up with at Hennessey House for eighteen years and taken for granted. It was something he resolved never to do again. The Chesapeake at sunset was a canvas of incomparable beauty, the image of paradise untouched. From their table by the window, blue herons, gulls and brown pelicans circled in a pink-tinged sky, beating their way up from the great backwater. Farther below, floating on a calm current, Canada geese and green-necked mallards tolerated one another's presence with remarkable fraternity. The bay water, a benevolent sea of liquid amber, lapped gently on hunter-green shores. As they watched, the sky darkened, the sun dipped into the horizon and faint pinpoints of light appeared in the distance. The effortless splendor of nature humbled them—she, who had watched western sunsets equally as breathtaking for seventeen long years, and he, who'd waited nearly as long to see them again.

The food was superb, simple and expertly prepared. The service was excellent and Libba…Libba was breathtaking. There was no other word for it. Years later Russ knew he would not be able to recall the details of what she wore, but he would remember it was red and that the combination of red dress and dark hair and cream-colored skin had an effect on his senses that had nothing to do with broiled shrimp and a bottle of expensive wine.

Tonight, there was a sweetness about her that reminded Russ of the old Libba, the girl he'd grown up and fallen in love with, the woman he'd lost and cursed and wept over.

She'd dressed up for him. He knew it, just as surely as he'd known a golden sunset, dry wine and the restaurant where he'd taken her the night of his senior prom would sweeten her mood. Driving down the familiar dusty roads of the childhood they'd shared brought them together somehow, before circumstance and a stranger named Eric Richards had torn them apart.

"Tell me," she said, "what brought you back to Marshyhope Creek. Cliff told me you had a successful business designing homes for the rich and famous."

"Cliff exaggerated."

"By how much?"

"I had a business that paid the bills and left me a little to put aside," he said honestly. "It was creative and high stress. I traveled all over the world and allowed my child to grow up without me. By the way, Tracy lied."

"What?"

"When she said Tess had never given her a bit of trouble. She's having a hard time handling her right now. Apparently, Tess isn't fitting into the mold."

"Teenagers are like that."

Russ nodded. "Anyway, the money wasn't worth the price. When my partner wanted to retire, I sold out, made a tidy profit and here I am, doing what I always wanted to do in the first place. Hennessey Blue Crab and Fishing never could support more than one CEO and Mitch had the right of first refusal."

Libby frowned. "Why is that? You were the oldest."

"By about six minutes."

"That isn't an answer."

Russ looked out over the water. "Mitch was good at fishing."

"You were, too."

"But I was good at other things, too. Schooling came easily to me. Mitch had a hard time learning to read. He couldn't pass a math class on his own if he tried. But he could fish. It was a logical move to assume he would take over the business and I would go on to the Citadel, my daddy's dream.''

Libby wouldn't bring up the fact that Beau Hennessey was hardly an ideal father who did not believe in sparing the rod, not to Russ. It was a painful blot on their childhood, a memory best wiped out, never to be repeated. "So you're back. Coincidental, isn't it?''

''What is?''

''That we're back here together at the same time, almost at the same point in our lives.''

''What happened to your marriage?'' he asked.

Libby leaned her chin on her hand, wondering how much to explain. "We had different standards for personal integrity,'' she said at last. "That's all.''

''You had your daughter almost immediately. Is that why you stayed?''

''Yes, and no,'' she said slowly. "Eric was never around. He's a 'B' actor, meaning he works and makes a living, but just that. I was very busy with my education, working and taking care of Chloe. It was simply too much effort to initiate a divorce, especially since I was alone most of the time, anyway.''

''You're a beautiful woman, Libba Jane. Are you saying you were never tempted to make a life with someone else?''

She smiled at him. "Like I said, I was busy. There wasn't time for that.''

He left it alone. She was done with confessions and he wouldn't push it. The evening had lived up to his expectations. It was a start.

Libby felt anxious when he walked her to her car, and then, when he'd closed her door and watched her pull out of the parking lot, she felt reprieved and at the same time oddly disappointed. He'd made no attempt to touch her. She hadn't wanted him to. Her divorce was barely legal and Russ had ties, strong ties to Tracy Wentworth. Still…Libby pulled down the sun visor and glanced at her reflection in the small mirror. Coming home agreed with her. She looked good, better than she had in a long time. She frowned. Why hadn't he kissed her good-night?

Sixteen

Chloe sat on the frilly daybed, her feet tucked under her, an artificial smile pasted on her face. Tess Hennessey perched beside her, nervously dragging her fingers through her thin sandy hair. Skylar Taft lounged on one of the overstuffed chairs and Casey Dulaine on the other. Two girls whose names Chloe couldn't remember and who hadn't said a word between them the entire evening stretched out on the carpeted floor, pillows tucked under their arms.

Chloe would have been amused at the color scheme if only she hadn't been so bored. The entire room was decorated in various shades of pink—pink curtains, pink comforter, pink carpet, even the wallpaper was awful with pink flowers on a paler pink background. As if there wasn't enough already, Skylar's nightgown was pink with tiny pink rosebuds around the hem. Chloe's lip curled. She couldn't imagine anyone choosing to live in this juvenile cotton candy nightmare. Marshyhope Creek was light years behind the times.

Chloe decided that Skylar was the big cheese. She called the shots and dominated the conversation. "Have you been shopping for school clothes yet?" she asked her audience.

The two nameless girls nodded and offered nothing, as usual. Casey Dulaine, a plump redhead, waved her hand and shook her head. "Not yet, but Mama promised to take me to Annapolis next weekend."

"What about you, Tess?"

Tess Hennessey shook her head nervously. "I think I'll wait and see what everybody else is wearing."

Skylar nodded at this piece of wisdom while Chloe rolled her eyes. *Typical,* she thought.

"Will you be going to school with us, Chloe?" Skylar asked.

"I'm not sure."

Skylar leaned forward. Silky dark hair fell across her cheeks. "This is just a suggestion, but if I were you, I'd lose the black on your hair."

"Oh?" Chloe's eyes narrowed. "Yours is black."

Skylar ignored her. "It may be okay for California, but here it'll make you stand out. We don't go for two-toned hair around here."

"Maybe I'll start a new fashion," Chloe suggested.

All the girls except Tess tittered.

"Trust me," Skylar said. "It won't happen."

Chloe's smile thinned. "I'll keep your suggestion in mind."

"What about clothes?" Skylar persisted.

Chloe's hands closed into fists. "What about them?"

Skylar made a sweeping gesture with her hand to encompass her friends. "We can help you, if you want. There's nothing worse than giving everyone the wrong impression on the first day."

Chloe could imagine much worse, but she kept her mouth shut. There was no point in letting the natives in.

"Have you seen Bailey Jones lately?" Casey asked. "He's a hunk."

Skylar pulled out a cigarette case and lighter that anyone who had seen early Clark Gable movies would have recognized as a copy.

Chloe watched, fascinated, as Skylar flicked open the lighter and expertly lit her cigarette.

"Who cares?" Skylar said after she'd blown out a lungful

of smoke. "He's always been good to look at. That doesn't change what he is."

"What is he?" Chloe asked.

Skylar flicked the end of her cigarette with perfectly manicured fingers. "His mama is part Cherokee and part high yellow colored. No one knows who his daddy is. My guess is he doesn't, either."

Chloe's ears burned. "Why doesn't he know?"

"Because Lizzie Jones is a hooker."

Chloe looked at Tess. She appeared the most sensible of the bunch.

Tess nodded. "My mama says Lizzie's had so many men it'd be hard to pin down exactly which one fathered Bailey."

Sweet, sad Lizzie Jones. Chloe's stomach heaved. She fought back the gag reflex.

They stared at her, daring her to say something. This was it, the place where she should say something, anything, to stick up for Bailey, to show loyalty to her friend. She cleared her throat and opened her mouth.

A soft knock on the door distracted her. Quickly, Skylar ground out her cigarette, moved the ashtray under a low chair and waved the air in front of her face. "Perfume," she muttered, "hand me the perfume."

Casey reached across Tess, grabbed a bottle from the dresser and tossed it to Skylar, who sprayed bursts of fragrance around her head.

"Come in," Skylar called out.

A black woman poked her head into the room. "I laid out a spread for you in the dining room whenever you're ready."

Skylar stood. "Let's go," she said, a queen commanding her court.

Chloe was the last to follow. Halfway down the hall, she whispered to Tess. "I'm not feeling good. I need to find a bathroom."

Tess looked concerned. She pointed to a door at the end of the long corridor. "I hope you don't have to go home."

Home, that was it. "Tell Skylar not to wait for me," Chloe said. "My stomach really hurts. If it gets worse, I'll call someone to pick me up."

Tess nodded. "I'll tell her."

Gratefully, Chloe turned into the bathroom, locked the door and waited until there was only silence in the hallway. Then she slipped back into the bedroom for her backpack. Carrying her shoes, she tiptoed down the stairs and out the front door. Once she'd cleared the porch, she began to run until she reached the shelter of a copse of trees. Panting, she leaned against a huge oak to catch her breath and consider her options. She couldn't go home. She didn't want to answer her mother's questions. Bailey would be a logical person to call, but she was still mad at him. The only other person she knew in Marshyhope Creek was Verna Lee. Maybe she would let her stay awhile, at least until they were all asleep at home.

Chloe threw her backpack over the fence, pulled on her shoes and wiggled through the two rails. If only Bailey would drive by in his truck. She would tease him out of his mood. That is, if she could stop thinking about Lizzie. Not that Skylar Taft could be considered a reliable source of information, but Tess had corroborated her story. During the ten-minute ride with Tess on the way to Skylar's, Chloe had decided that although Tess Hennessey was afraid of her own shadow, she was harmless. She wouldn't spread rumors about Bailey's mother, not unless they were true and she was asked. Skylar was another story. Poor Bailey. Verna Lee was right. He needed to find a way out of Marshyhope Creek.

She slid her arms through the straps of her backpack and began trudging toward town and the descending sun. Twenty minutes later the heat and humidity had taken its toll. Chloe was thirsty and exhausted. She'd underestimated the distance. Her spirits were low. She had no idea if Verna Lee would take her in.

A car engine hummed in the distance. Too tired to even turn, Chloe kept walking, her eyes on the ground in front of her feet.

Russ Hennessey saw the slim, blond girl hugging the shoulder of the road, and drove on. He glanced into his rearview mirror, frowned and glanced again. Then he swore softly and pulled over. Setting his parking brake, he opened the door, stepped out and waited.

Chloe didn't look up until she was almost upon the Blazer. At first she didn't recognize Tess's father. When she did, her eyes rounded with fear. "H-hello," she stammered.

"Hello, yourself. Didn't I just drop you and Tess off about two hours ago?"

Chloe nodded mutely.

"What happened?"

She shrugged. "It wasn't working out."

"Why not?"

She shrugged again. Desperate circumstances called for desperate measures. "Would you mind driving me home?"

"Not at all." Russ reached for her backpack, walked to the passenger side of the car and opened the door.

Chloe hopped in and buckled the seat belt.

Russ swung out onto the road. "Tell me what happened, Chloe," he said. "I'm the one who suggested you be invited to this party. If anyone has done anything to you, I feel responsible."

"It's not your fault," Chloe assured him. "They're just not my kind of people, except for Tess," she said hurriedly. "She's very nice."

Russ laughed. "Tell me what you really think."

"No, really, she's the nicest of them all. It's just—"

"Just what?"

Chloe sighed. "Everything in Skylar's entire bedroom is pink, even the toilet seat."

Russ winced. "Ouch."

"She volunteered to help me pick out clothes for school."

"Who did?"

"Skylar Taft. As if I'd shop with someone whose idea of fashion comes from a Barbie doll catalog." Chloe could not have been more contemptuous.

Russ tried to remember what Tess had been wearing when he dropped the girls off at the Tafts'. "I guess pink is a popular color for little girls around here."

"They aren't little girls. They're teenagers."

"Point taken."

"I understand about the hair."

"The hair?"

"She said two-toned hair wouldn't go over here. I can see that." Chloe fingered the black tips. "I only did it to make my mother mad."

"Do you do that often?"

"What? Try to make my mother mad?"

"Yes."

Chloe thought for a minute. "More now than before."

"Why is that?"

"She's harder to live with than she used to be."

Once again, Russ laughed. He didn't know whether to be charmed or horrified by Libba's daughter. She was another original. Like mother, like daughter. "I remember a time when she wasn't so hard to live with."

Chloe stared at him. "How would you know? Did you ever live with her?"

"Not exactly. But I knew her better than anybody, except maybe Coleson and Nola Ruth."

"Or my dad."

Russ didn't contradict her.

Chloe persisted, intrigued by this picture of her mother. "Was she your girlfriend?"

He nodded. ''But before that she was my friend and my brother's friend and she was a good one.''

''Where is your brother now?''

''He died.''

''Was he a lot older than you?''

''He was my twin.''

''I'm sorry,'' Chloe whispered, stricken into silence.

''Thank you.'' He changed the subject. ''So, how do you like living in Marshyhope Creek?''

Chloe hesitated.

''Come on,'' Russ coaxed her. ''You can tell me the truth. My lips are sealed.''

''It really doesn't matter whether they are or not,'' Chloe said. ''Everyone knows how I feel. I hate it here. I want to go home. My dad is in L.A. and so are all my friends.''

''Your mom is here,'' Russ countered, ''and so are your grandparents. You can always make friends.'' He looked at her approvingly. ''I'll bet dollars to doughnuts that you're good at it when you want to be.''

Chloe looked surprised. ''Why would you say that?''

''You're interesting and you say what's on your mind. I like that. I bet other people do, too.''

''I don't know about that,'' Chloe said dubiously. ''I don't think Skylar Taft and her friends think I'm interesting.''

''Maybe you didn't want to be. Sometimes people sabotage themselves. They think a certain thing and then make it happen just to prove they're right.''

Chloe didn't answer him.

''On the other hand,'' Russ continued, ''Skylar Taft isn't the only game in town.''

''I've heard she's the one who counts.''

''Maybe you'll change all that.''

''Maybe I don't want to.''

Russ changed his tactics. ''What exactly is it that you don't like about living here?''

"Skylar Taft and her friends."

Russ knew from the source that Chloe's antipathy started long before today. "Is that all?"

"I guess so."

"So, let me get this right. If Skylar Taft didn't matter, you'd be happy as a clam staying here for good."

"Not exactly."

Russ grinned. "Now we're getting somewhere. What else is bothering you about this place?"

"Other than absolutely no culture, no movies, no mall, no museums, no plays, I can't imagine," she said sarcastically. "I want to be an actress. How can I do that living here? There's absolutely no motivation at all."

"The high school has a fair drama department, and Salisbury and Annapolis aren't all that far away."

"In Los Angeles, everything is right around the corner."

Russ conceded the point. "What else?" he asked.

"I miss my dad," she said softly. "I hardly saw him at all when I was little and now he lives in L.A. all the time. He would pick me up for lunch and I'd go over to his house after school. All that just stopped." Her voice shook. She looked out the window and willed the tears back, sniffing audibly. "My mother didn't care about that at all."

Russ's response to that pathetic little sniff shocked him. His heart hurt and he didn't trust himself to speak. Imagine having a daughter who wanted nothing more than to be with her father. He pulled out a tissue from a box on the seat and handed it to her. "I'll bet your mother wanted the kind of life for you that she had. It was a pretty good one."

"That's a dumb excuse," Chloe said miserably, wiping her nose. "We're not the same people. I didn't grow up here. Everyone knows you're not supposed to move kids in high school."

He'd give her points for logic. She was certainly a bright one. Not that it surprised him. He imagined that Libba's intelligence quotient was probably off the charts as well. He couldn't help comparing Chloe with Tess. The contrast was obvious. He pushed the thought aside, ashamed that his thoughts had traveled in such a direction. "You have a convincing argument," he said. "The question is, what can you do to make your situation tolerable?"

"I don't want to make it tolerable."

Russ chuckled, looked at her expression and wiped the smile from his face. "Sorry," he said.

Chloe stared out the window.

"You've got an advantage here, you know."

"How's that?"

"You're Libba's daughter. People in this town have long memories and she was a favorite. You're bound to benefit."

"I don't think Skylar Taft cares about my mother's popularity a century ago."

"No, but her mother does. She was one of those who wanted to hang around your mother, to bask in her glow, so to speak."

Chloe looked at him, suddenly curious. "What about Tess?"

"What about her?" Russ asked warily.

"Where does she fit into the Skylar Taft picture?"

Russ waited a full minute before answering, wondering whether he should couch the truth or just go for it. He decided she would find out, anyway. "I don't know, Chloe," he said honestly. "I wasn't around for a good part of Tess's life. I saw her periodically but not regularly, if you know what I mean."

Chloe nodded. "My dad was the same. Did you travel?"

"Yes."

"What do you do?"

"I designed houses."

She didn't miss the past tense. "Do you still do that?"

He shook his head. "Now I run a fishing fleet that's been in my family for generations."

Chloe wrinkled her nose. "I'd rather design houses. Do you miss it?"

He laughed. "Not as much as I miss other things." He turned down the brick drive that led to the Delacourtes'. "They won't be expecting you home."

She sighed. "I know. There'll be another showdown with my mother. Thanks for the ride."

"Do you want me to come inside with you?"

Chloe turned to him hopefully. "Would you?"

"Sure enough." He drove around the circular driveway and parked. "Shall we brave the lions?"

She laughed for the first time since climbing into the car. "It won't be that bad," she assured him. "My grandparents are really polite and my mom won't say anything while you're there." Chloe tilted her head thoughtfully. "I guess you know all that already. You probably know them better than I do."

He smiled down at her. "That was a long time ago."

"It's weird to think my mom had a boyfriend who wasn't my dad."

"I imagine it is." He followed Chloe up the porch steps.

She opened the door. "Here goes." She braced herself. "Hello, everybody," she called out. "I'm back. Is anybody home?"

For a moment there was only silence. Then, simultaneously, Coleson walked out of his study at the end of the hall and Libby peered over the balcony at the top of the stairs.

"Chloe?" her mother said. "Why are you home?" She saw Russ and her eyes widened. She ran down the stairs. "Has something happened?"

Russ waited for Chloe to answer. From their brief acquaintance, he was quite sure she could handle the situation. And he was curious. He wanted to see this interaction between mother and daughter. Chloe was nothing like Libba physically except for a certain leggy slimness, but they were similar in other ways. Watching the two of them, he knew he would have taken Chloe for a Delacourte even before she told him. They squared off, facing each other like two boxers in a ring.

"I decided to come home early," Chloe announced.

Cole Delacourte moved closer to the action.

"Why?" Libby asked.

Russ had to hand it to her. She wasn't hysterical, just surprised and obviously willing to allow her daughter the benefit of the doubt. His respect for her rose.

"I wasn't having a good time." Chloe was deliberately holding back.

Libby glanced at Russ and then back at Chloe. "I see you found Mr. Hennessey. Do you mind telling me how that came about?"

"I was walking home," Chloe explained, "and he came by. Since I already knew he was Tess's father, I thought it would be okay if he gave me a ride."

It wasn't, but Libby had no intention of verbalizing her disapproval in front of Russ. "Did something happen, Chloe?" her mother asked.

"Not directly. But I couldn't stay there. I was miserable. I'm not like them."

Libby sighed and Cole stepped in and spoke to his granddaughter. "Are you hungry, Chloe? We've eaten, but Serena can put something together for you."

Chloe nodded. She looked at her mother. "May I go now?"

"You may, but we'll finish this later. I have one more question, before you go. Did you tell anyone you were leaving or did you simply disappear?"

"Tess knows. I told her I didn't feel good. She promised to tell the Tafts."

"I'll call them and explain," Libby said.

"What will you say?"

"Exactly what you told me. You were feeling poorly and couldn't stay."

Chloe turned to Russ. "Thanks again for the ride, and for coming in with me. I guess I didn't need you after all."

Cole laughed, tucked his granddaughter's hand under his arm and led her out of the room.

Libby looked at Russ. "What's your version?"

He grinned. "She's a handful."

"Thanks a lot. You didn't answer my question."

"I found her walking along the road. It's a good seven miles from the Tafts' into town."

Libby frowned. "Why was she going into town?"

"To wait out the storm, I imagine."

Libby exploded. "What storm? This is ridiculous. It's not as if she hasn't been completely indulged her entire life. What's gotten into her?"

"Maybe that's the problem," Russ said slowly.

"I beg your pardon?"

"If everything's always gone her way, think of how she must feel now that it isn't."

Libby crossed her arms. "She's going to have to get used to it."

"Hey," he said softly. "Don't bury the messenger. I'm on your side. I also think she's a great kid. She's bright, she's got interests and more than her share of spunk. You've done a fine job, Libba."

Libby blinked, completely thrown. She wasn't good with compliments, professional ones, yes, personal ones, no. She tried to maintain her poise, tried not to melt or appear too pathetically grateful. "I—I don't know about that," she stammered.

"Just say *thank you*."

She smiled. "Thank you."

Seventeen

Libby shook her head. "I have work to do. I'm sorry, Shelby, but I'll have to pass on the country club today."

The term *country club* was a misnomer by any standard. There was no golf course, no tennis or racquetball courts, no exercise room. The facility, shared by the two towns of Marshyhope Creek and Frenchman's Cove, consisted of a low brick building shadowed by enormous oak trees. At the back of the building was a large sparkling pool, blue, clean and smelling of bleach. Women brought children to swim while they gossiped away long days beneath a blistering summer sun. Later, in early evening, their husbands stopped in at the bar, drinking themselves into comfortable stupors before returning home.

Shelby Sloane, on her way home from the open-air market, stood in the doorway of Libby's office. She shook out her red curls and thrust one hip forward. "Don't you dare disappoint me, Libba Jane Delacourte. I told everybody you'd be comin'. Besides, it's Saturday. No one works on Saturday."

Libby sighed and massaged her temples. She had the results of the lab report to record and she hadn't yet collected new water samples from Smith Island and Shad Landing. For two days in a row now the slides showed the water to be contaminant-free, which made no sense at all. If only she'd had time to acquire a little more experience before working on her own. Still, she could probably finish by eleven and meet Shelby at noon. She reminded herself that hers was a part-time position. "All right, Shelby. I'll give it a try. I'll meet you for lunch and a quick swim."

"I'll stop and pick you up. It's on the way."

"No," Libby said firmly. "I can't stay all afternoon. I'll meet you and then you won't feel pressured to leave early."

Shelby shrugged her tanned shoulder. "Have it your way. Don't be late. I won't order till you get there."

Shortly before noon, Libby stood in front of the long mirror in her bedroom, tugged the back of her bathing suit down over the cheeks of her bottom and surveyed her backside critically. She certainly didn't look like she had at twenty, but she didn't look half bad, either. Running in the mornings and refusing Serena's calorie-laden desserts helped. She pulled on a shift and deck shoes, found a towel in the linen closet and ran downstairs.

"Are you going somewhere, Libba Jane?" Her father leaned against the doorjamb. He was dressed casually in shorts, a golf shirt and tennis shoes.

"Daddy, I didn't realize you were home. Did you take the day off?"

"I don't go in as much as I did before, not since your mama's stroke."

Libby flushed guiltily. Her mother's confession weighed on her. Rather than think it through and deal with it, she'd pushed it aside, avoiding the topic and Nola Ruth. She'd spent virtually no time alone with her mother since she'd heard her story.

"Have you and your mother had a falling-out?"

"Not exactly," Libby hedged.

"What's the problem?"

Discussing *the problem* would take more time than she had. "I promised Shelby I'd meet her at the club," Libby said. "Can we talk about this later?"

"Of course." He turned away. "Don't wait too long.

Nola Ruth is fragile. You wouldn't want to do something you can't take back.''

It was a warning, no matter how she looked at it, a warning as only Coleson Delacourte could put it together—gently, carefully, kindly, but a warning all the same. There had never been any doubt in Libby's mind where his priorities lay. Nola Ruth had always been first with him. Libby found that fact easier to accept now that she had Chloe, but throughout her childhood it had caused her serious hurt. Now her mother was hurting. It couldn't have been easy for Nola Ruth to reveal what she had. Libby shuddered to think of making such a confession to her own daughter. It had taken a great deal of nerve and faith on her mother's part. Libby knew she was behaving badly. Avoiding her mother was childish. She would take care of it tonight.

After the short drive to the club, she pulled into the parking lot, such as it was, a packed-dirt area shaded by huge sycamore, oak and elm trees. A sporty red utility vehicle drove in after her and parked. A tall, long-legged woman stepped out.

Libby recognized her immediately. ''Hi, Verna Lee.''

The woman turned and waited for Libby to catch up. ''Hello, Libba Jane. Day off?''

''No. Just taking a break. I'm meeting Shelby for lunch. Would you like to join us?''

Verna Lee's yellow eyes narrowed slightly. She looked at Libby for a long moment and then she smiled. ''You've been gone a long time, Libba Jane, or you wouldn't ask such a ridiculous question.''

''Why not?''

Verna Lee pulled the scarf from around her head, freeing the long tawny-colored curls. ''I'll spell it out for you,'' she said. ''This is the *South*, not the kind of South they have in Atlanta or New Orleans or Savannah or Richmond. This is *country* South. That means I can no more sit down to lunch with you and Shelby than I can traipse across the room without a stitch on.''

''How ridiculous. I don't believe you. That kind of prejudice doesn't exist anymore. I would never have brought my daughter to such a place.''

Verna Lee's voice was low and fierce. ''Grow up, Libba. You took the job Cliff offered on impulse. You wanted to come home because things didn't work out for you in the big city. Did you spend any time researching what kind of place you were bringing your daughter to?''

Libby's face whitened. ''Why are you so bitter? Is it me you hate, or just the situation? And if what you say is true, why are you here?''

The black woman's face closed. ''I have my reasons.''

''You didn't answer my first question.''

''I don't hate you, Libba, and if I did, it wouldn't be personal.''

They had reached the door. Verna Lee pulled it open and walked in first, holding it for Libby.

''Why not join us, anyway, and shock everyone?'' Libby suggested.

''You don't give up, do you?''

''Not usually.''

A reluctant smile tugged at the corners of Verna Lee's mouth. ''I don't feel like taking on the world today, but I'll think about it.''

''Let me know.''

Libby found Shelby seated outside under an enormous umbrella, a gin and tonic in one hand, a cigarette in the other. She was striking in a black-and-white sundress that revealed her bronze shoulders and sculpted cleavage. Two women, one blond, one brunette, sat beside her.

Slowly, Libby approached the table. ''Hi,'' she said.

''Well, finally,'' Shelby greeted her. ''I thought you were gonna cancel.''

''Sorry. I got held up.''

"It must be such a drag to have to work," one of the women said.

Shelby held up her hand for the waitress. "Libba Jane likes to work. She's got one of those fancy degrees to prove it."

"My hat's off to you, Libba," the brunette said.

Libby stared at her curiously. The voice was familiar but the face was not. "Do I know you?" she asked.

"My God, Libba Jane. I'm Angie Ferguson. Have I changed that much?"

Libby's mouth dropped. Hastily, she attempted to recover. "Y-you look wonderful," she stammered. "Have you done something with your hair?"

Angie patted the helmet surrounding her face. "I color it now and then."

She'd also lost fifty pounds, but politeness kept Libby from mentioning it. "That must be it," she said.

The blonde spoke up. "You remember me, Libba. I know you do. We shared a locker all through senior year."

Libby nodded and sat down in the empty chair. "It's good to see you again, Beth Ann. How are you?"

"Busy. I'm divorced with three kids under ten. Buck pays me every month, though. He's a good daddy even if he was a lousy husband."

"Gin and tonics all around," Shelby said to the waitress, who'd materialized at her elbow.

Libby spoke up. "I'll have iced tea, please. I have to get back to work later this afternoon."

Shelby removed her sunglasses. "You gotta have priorities, Libba Jane. This is Saturday at the club with the girls. Work isn't part of it." Without pausing for breath, she turned to her friend. "I don't know why y'all are surprised that Buck didn't work out, Beth Ann. With a nickname like *hound dog* you shoulda known he wasn't gonna stay put."

"I thought I'd be the one to change him," Beth Ann said

dreamily. "We still get together now and then. Maybe he'll come back. I wouldn't say no."

Angie laughed. "If you don't mind his tomcattin' around."

Beth Ann tilted her head. "Actually, I don't. As long as I don't know about it, there's no problem."

Libby stared into her lap. Out of the corner of her eye she could see Verna Lee, spectacular in a red bikini, reading a magazine. She looked serene, cool and intelligent. Biting her tongue, Libby resigned herself to at least an hour of tedious conversation.

"What's Verna Lee doin' here?" Angie asked.

"Sunbathing," Shelby answered.

"That makes no sense," Beth Ann observed. "She's dark enough as it is. I still can't believe they allow those people in here. Nothin's the same as it used to be."

"She's beautiful," Libby said honestly.

Shelby nodded. "Libba's right. Verna Lee always did take the eye even now when she's almost long in the tooth."

"For heaven's sake, Shelby," Libby snapped, "she's five years older than we are."

"Nothin's the same as it was," said Beth Ann.

Libby desperately wanted to go home.

"I think you need a drink, Libba Jane," Shelby observed. "I've never seen you so jumpy in your life. You look like you'd rather be anywhere but here."

Either she was terribly obvious or Shelby's instincts had improved. "I'm sorry."

"Never mind that. Look who's here."

Libby started to turn around.

"No, don't look now." Shelby clutched her hand painfully.

Libby winced and stared straight ahead.

"Don't say a word, ladies. This one's mine."

Obeying Shelby's order, Libby focused on Verna Lee turning magazine pages on the other side of the pool.

A shadow fell across the table and Russ Hennessey's amused voice greeted them. "Ladies, what a pleasant surprise."

Shelby fluttered her eyelashes and leaned over to better display her cleavage. "Why, Russ Hennessey, as I live and breathe, aren't you the most gorgeous hunk? But then you always were." She pretended to pout. "I can't believe you've been in town for nearly a month and never once looked me up. I've been over to the office lots of times just to see you but you're not there. I know Libba Jane's seen you. I asked her to tell you to call me, but you never did, or she never did. I'm beginnin' to thing y'all are avoidin' me."

"It's nice to see you again, Shelby." Russ kissed her cheek and looked at Libby. "I didn't realize I had messages to call you."

"No one ever told me, either," Libba replied. "Shelby, I believe your nose is growing."

Missing the joke entirely, Shelby gasped and covered her button nose with a beautifully manicured hand. "Libba Delacourte, it's cruel of you to be pokin' fun at my nose."

"I think she's referring to a literary character who stretched the truth," Russ offered.

Libby stared at him. The Russ Hennessey she remembered had no interest or knowledge of literary references.

Shelby sighed with relief. "Thank goodness for that. It's bad enough havin' to watch every little thing that goes into my mouth without worryin' about my nose, too." She smiled and lowered her lashes. "You have no idea how difficult it is tryin' to keep yourself up when you're on the wrong side of thirty. Just ask Libba."

Russ took one look at Libby's outraged expression and laughed. "I don't think I'll do that."

"You remember Angie and Beth Ann." Shelby waved at them.

"Of course," Russ said smoothly. "How are you, ladies?"

"Will you join us, Russ?" Beth Ann asked.

"Actually, I'm just passing through. Thanks, anyway."

Libby watched him scan the pool area, nod his head and walk out through the club entrance.

Shelby sighed. "No wonder you never want anyone to see him, Libba Jane. He's too good to be true."

"What are you talking about?" Libby asked furiously. "Russ Hennessey is an *old* boyfriend. The operative word is *old*. What was all that about telling him to call you? You never said a word. You're acting like a cat in heat and that Scarlett O'Hara routine is ridiculous. What about your husband?"

Shelby waved her hand vaguely. "Fletcher's always around, but he hasn't been too attentive lately. He's got somethin' else on his mind. I think I'm gonna forget all that advice you gave me about staying married and go after Russ. Lord, Libba, he was gorgeous when we were kids, but who'd ever think a man could look like that in his late thirties?"

"Amen," agreed Angie.

"He's not any older than we are and we don't look all that bad, either," Libby returned.

"My looks take hours in front of a mirror. I bet he rolls outta bed like that when he wakes up in the morning." Shelby gave Libby a speculative look. "Not that you'd know what he looks like first thing in the mornin', or do you?"

"Of course not." Libby's hands clenched. "And I want you to stop being absurd. You can't flirt with Russ like you do everyone else. He doesn't know you anymore and Fletcher won't like it. Russ is his friend."

"He looks like he could handle Fletcher." Shelby shook her finger at Libby. "What bothers you more? That Fletch might hurt him or that the two of us might hit it off?"

"Don't be silly."

"If you don't want him, why can't I have him?" Shelby asked reasonably.

"Because you're married and because he doesn't want you. He didn't years ago and he doesn't now."

Shelby smiled. "You don't know everything, Libba Jane. I can be mighty persuasive when I try. That is, if you don't mind. After all, I don't want to horn in on what's yours."

"That's very considerate of you," Libby replied acidly. She took another look at her friend's face and gave up attempting to reason with her. "Do what you want, Shelby. You always do, anyway. Russ isn't mine anymore. You're not hurting me, but you are jeopardizing your marriage. Fletcher's a fine man. I just hope you come to your senses before any permanent damage is done."

Shelby placed a conciliatory hand on Libby's shoulder. "Don't be mad, Libba Jane. I'm just gonna have a little fun. You know I'm harmless."

Libby had lost her appetite and she certainly didn't need this. She downed her tea and stood. "So far, you've been harmless. I wish you'd listen to me. Don't do anything you'll regret. This is a small town and you of all people know what that means. Fletcher has to live here and so does Russ. I've got to get back to the office." She smiled woodenly at Beth Ann and Angie. "Nice to see you. Let's do this again when I have more time."

"Don't leave, Libba," Shelby begged. "I'm sorry. Lordy, you're touchy. I didn't mean to make you mad."

"You didn't make me mad. I have things to do." She gathered her belongings, met Verna Lee's amused glance from across the pool and walked away.

Libby turned on the ignition and twisted the air conditioning dial to full blast. With her mind on auto-pilot, she pulled out of the parking lot and instinctively headed west toward the Chesapeake.

She was thirty-seven years old. Seventeen years had passed, yet the idea of Shelby and Russ was still as painful as it had been when she'd run into Mitch at the dry goods store and he'd casually revealed what she'd been the last to know. Shelby and Russ. Russ and Shelby.

That was the summer Eric Richards had shown up in Marshyhope Creek. Eric with his blond good looks and his Hollywood smile. The rest was history. If only she could turn back time. She would handle it all so differently, or would she?

Sighing, she checked her rearview mirror, reduced her speed and turned the car in the direction of Marshyhope Creek. Regrets were pointless. She had work to do.

Eighteen

Libby sat outside on the porch swing slapping at the black-flies that bit her ankles. It was early evening. By midday the mercury had risen to a stifling ninety degrees and heat still hung oppressively over the Maryland side of the Chesapeake. Dinner had been difficult. Nola Ruth had been uncharacteristically silent and Chloe predictably sullen. Her father carried the conversation, teasing Chloe out of her mood and forcing answers from his preoccupied wife. Libby tried to match his mood, but she couldn't manage eye contact with her mother and in the end the effort had been too much and she'd retreated to the porch. Her leave from Ventura County would be over soon and Chloe would start school next week.

Her afternoon at the club, brief as it was, had unsettled her. No one had been unpleasant or unwelcoming, but if she never saw Beth Ann or Angie again, it would be too soon. The fact was she had nothing in common with any of them, Shelby included. Libby tucked a leg beneath her and pressed her bottom lip with her finger. How had her mother managed? She was an intelligent woman, educated, well read, with strong political opinions. Was she ever bored with the empty conversations around her or had her husband been enough?

She heard Chloe in the upstairs bedroom and smiled. It was odd hearing noises from the room that had been hers as a child. On her fifteenth birthday, Libby had graduated from the yellow room with the white canopy to the back of the house and the room with the mahogany four-poster. She hadn't regretted the move, but the yellow room had always been her favorite. It was perfect for a girl Chloe's age, young and bright, hopeful and feminine, a room designed as a refuge, a private retreat, a place for sleeping late on lazy mornings.

Libby smiled, remembering how hard it had been for Russ, an early riser, to wait until after nine to see her on a weekend morning. He'd been up before sunrise working his daddy's trawlers and was anxious to begin the pleasure part of his day. Phone calls were useless because her mother refused to wake her. Russ would drive to the end of the Delacourte's long, dirt-packed driveway, sneak behind the house and position himself below her room in the center of a lush flower bed. There, he bellowed as loudly as he could. "Wake up, Libba Jane, or I'm leaving without you. The day's half gone."

Libby would crack open the French doors and poke her dark, sleep-tousled head over the balcony. "It's the crack of dawn, Russ Hennessey. Go away and come back at a decent hour."

"Ten minutes," he had replied. "Ten minutes is all the time you've got." Inevitably, she would be down the stairs, sunny-faced and scrubbed, well within the allotted time. Libba had loved her sleep, but once, a long time ago, she had loved Russ more.

Cole Delacourte's voice interrupted her. "You're mighty quiet tonight, Libba Jane."

"Everyone's quiet tonight."

Cole pulled a cigar from his pocket, bit off the end and spit it into the shrubbery. "I'm not."

Libby laughed and made room for him on the swing. "No, Daddy. You always have something to say."

He sat beside her. "I hope that's a compliment."

"It is."

"How's the job coming?"

"All right, I guess. I'm not sure where the contaminants are leaking into the water or even *if* they're still leaking into the water, but I'm working on it."

"Does it have to be local? What about pesticides from the farms up north?"

Libby's forehead wrinkled. "Blue crab is a local shellfish. They don't migrate very far. My guess it's something here." She hesitated.

"Go on."

"Fish are one thing, it's people I'm worried about."

"Why?"

"We have a large concentration of leukemia for such a small area. That would indicate that contaminants have been here for quite some time. I'm not getting the whole picture. I wish I had my own lab here."

"Good Lord."

"Exactly."

"We don't drink much tap water," Cole said thoughtfully.

"We brush our teeth with it. We water our plants and cook with it."

"Should we buy a purifier?"

"We could, but it would be like locking the barn after the horse has already escaped. We need to find the source."

"Have you bitten off more than you can chew?"

Libby sighed. "That's an understatement. The truth is, I don't know where to begin."

Cole patted his daughter's knee. "You'll manage, honey. If there's anyone who can do it, you can."

"Cliff Jackson could do a much better job."

"He's not here and you are. Don't sell yourself short." Cole smiled. "You always were a tenacious little thing, butting straight into a challenge no matter how tough it was."

"I've changed."

"I don't think so."

It was cozy talking with her father, a man she had always admired but who had always seemed too preoccupied to carry on a conversation with his teenaged daughter. "Are you thinking of retiring, Daddy?"

He whistled. "That's a difficult question to answer. I suppose you could say I'm semiretired. I only take on those cases that really make sense to me."

Libby laughed. "You've always done that. It made Mama so mad. I can still remember the fights you had."

"I never fight with my family. I restrict my fighting to the courtroom," her father said mildly.

"Mama did enough for both of you."

Her father looked at her curiously. "Is that what you remember, Libba? Your mama and me fighting with each other?"

She shrugged. "It doesn't matter."

"I think it does. It might explain a lot of things."

"I didn't have a terrible childhood, if that's what you're getting at."

Cole Delacourte looked at his daughter's lovely profile, at her bare shoulders in the white halter top and the slim legs curled beneath her. With her hair pulled back into a ponytail she looked no older than she had seventeen years ago when she'd shocked the hell out of everyone and run away without so much as a by-your-leave. He'd always liked that phrase. A history buff, Coleson appreciated everything English, formal and old-fashioned. "What demons were you fighting, honey, and why did you come back?"

Libby's eyes were the warm brown of summer oak. She smiled. "I came back because you asked me. As for demons, I don't remember any in particular." She looked out across the bay and slapped away another blackfly nibbling at her ankle. She thought back to that summer and her dissatisfaction with the way her life was turning out. "I was edgy that summer and terribly bored. I felt sensitive all over, my skin, my mind.'' She shook it off. ''I'm not explaining very well, but everything was intensified and I couldn't get anything right. It was as if my nerves were exposed. Nothing made sense to me.'' She looked at her father. ''Have you ever felt that way?''

He nodded. ''The year I met your mama.''

Libby went completely still, willing him to continue, to finish the story her mother had begun.

Coleson Delacourte leaned his head back against the swing's cushion and closed his eyes. ''I often wonder if I would have done things differently, but then I think of Nola Ruth and the way she was and I know I wouldn't.''

''You loved her very much.''

Cole nodded. ''I still do.''

Libby hesitated.

Her father waited. The night was soft, the air thick with the smell of gardenia.

''Weren't you afraid of loving someone so much?''

''I considered myself lucky to be capable of such an emotion.''

''But didn't you wonder if she felt the same?''

''There's no wondering about it, Libba Jane. No one loves the same. Most relationships are sixty-forty. Ours is one of those. I'm the sixty, your mama's the forty. I knew that from the beginning.''

Libby shuddered. ''Doesn't that make you feel terribly insecure to know that your wife isn't giving as much as you are?''

''Not at all. Nola Ruth gives more than I do because it isn't as easy for her.''

She looked at her father. It was easier now that his eyes were closed and his body relaxed to examine him fully. ''Were you disappointed that I wasn't a boy?'' she asked out of the blue.

He smiled. ''Not for a single minute.''

"Mama told me a story," she hurried on. "She said you knew. Do you?"

He didn't pretend to misunderstand her. "All that was a long time ago, Libba Jane, before your mother was even eighteen years old. Imagine having to live down something your entire life because of a blip in time that happened before you were even a woman."

"It was a pretty big blip, Daddy."

"I suppose for a woman of her class and race, it was. The truth is, it happened more often than most of us realize. It's still happening, only the world has changed a bit, thank God."

"Don't say it didn't hurt you."

"Actually, it didn't. I felt sorry for Nola Ruth, sorrier than you can imagine that she went through such pain, but it wasn't about me. Our lives together, and with you, happened later. She was a different person."

Libby didn't dare ask which of the two people her mother had been was the one he preferred. She stared out into the inky sky with its thousands of stars and was comforted by the vast randomness of it all. Maybe the life and troubles of one small person didn't matter much in the scheme of things.

"Thanks, Daddy," she whispered.

Cole didn't answer her. He was somewhere else, far away, when the word *future* meant something entirely different than it did to a man approaching old age, a man with a grown daughter, a teenage granddaughter and a wife at the end of her years.

Abruptly he stood. There was something he needed to know, something that wouldn't wait. Only Nola Ruth had the answer. "Good night, Libba Jane." He bent down to kiss her cheek.

Libby looked up at him. Her eyes were liquid dark, almost black, as if the pupils had spilled their color into the irises. "I love you, Daddy," she whispered.

"I love you, too," he said automatically. It wasn't his daughter's love that he questioned.

He found his wife in the downstairs bedroom she now occupied. For the first time since her stroke, he hadn't bothered to knock. She was reading in bed. The unmarked side of her face was backlit by lamplight, as lovely to him as it had been when he first saw her.

She looked up and frowned. "Is something wrong?"

"Maybe," he said. "Maybe not."

Marking her place with her finger, she gave him her full attention. "What is it, Cole?"

Instead of his usual preferred spot, beside her on the bed, he took the chair near the window. "It occurs to me that I haven't asked you the obvious in a long time. I've just assumed it."

She waited.

He drew a deep breath.

Her laugh was indulgent, amused. "We've been married a long time, Cole. Surely you can ask me a question."

"Ah, but it's not the kind of question I usually ask."

"You're making me nervous."

"I wouldn't want to do that, Nola Ruth. Heaven forbid that I should make you uncomfortable in any way at all."

She stared at him. Coleson Delacourte wasn't a drinking man, but then perhaps the circumstances had never been serious enough.

He leaned forward. "Do you still love me, Nola Ruth?"

Her eyes widened. "Are you serious?"

"Completely."

"What an absurd question."

"Answer it, anyway."

Color rose in her cheeks and she fidgeted with the edge of the blanket. "This is ridiculous, Cole."

"Is that your answer?"

"What do you want me to say? Demanding a declaration of love isn't exactly conducive to a meaningful sentiment."

He stood and started for the door. "It appears I have my answer."

Nola Ruth's jaw dropped. "Cole," she cried out. "Come back and sit down."

"I don't think so."

"For pity's sake. Shall I beg? Is that what you want?"

He turned, his hand on the knob. "I want an answer, an honest, simple answer."

Her lips were dry. She wet them. "All right, Cole. I'll tell you. I do love you. I'll love you forever for a number of reasons, but mostly because in the nearly four decades we've been married, even in the heat of our worst arguments, you've never so much as hinted that I'm anything other than what I appear to be."

"That's enough, Nola Ruth," he said under his breath. "We don't need to discuss this, not now, not ever."

Coleson Delacourte was normally not an emotional man. His feelings were buried deeply beneath a veneer of cool reserve and hardheaded logic. In the courtroom he'd been compared to a barracuda, a lawyer with a killer instinct and a keen sense of his opponent's vulnerability. There had been other young lawyers in Washington beginning their careers at the same time, men fevered with excitement over the beginning of America's new era—men anxious to see their names in the history books and convinced that the South was the place and civil rights the issue of the future.

But Cole was different. Along with the fever and the instinct he brought with him to Washington an eye for detail, a nearly photographic memory and a courtroom presence that was helped by his cultured Southern accent, his lean six-foot frame and a pair of electric blue eyes that could wear down a witness's testimony on the stand without his ever raising his voice. The court became his arena, the media his friend. He never faltered, never disappointed, never wavered from furthering his ambition, until the day he drove home for a well-earned vacation. He had plans to sleep late, drink bourbon until he was dizzy, fish the fingers of the Chesapeake and roast his catch over coals on the white sand beaches of his boyhood, dressed in nothing more than a pair of tan swim trunks and a shirt without buttons.

Intent on his task and the twenty-pound test line that had suddenly gone taut, he didn't notice the girl with the golden skin and spectacular legs until she was nearly upon him. When he turned to look at her, for the first time in his life he lost the ability to speak.

Nola Ruth Beauchamp held out her hand. "Hello," she said in her slow, Southern, Delta-flavored voice. "I've never seen you here before."

Cole didn't remember his response. He only knew that nothing would ever be the same for him again.

Nineteen

Russ nodded at Libby warily. He was checking the instruments on one of his skipjacks while Fletcher Sloane loaded bait into the tank.

Fletcher grinned. "Well, well, well, if it ain't Libba Jane Delacourte. What brings you down to our neck of the woods so early in the mornin'?"

Libby smiled but her heart wasn't in it. "How are you, Fletcher? I could ask the same of you."

"Doin' well, thanks. I'm givin' ol' Russ here a hand. We watermen have to help one another out occasionally, don't we, Russ?"

Russ Hennessey grunted. He had a sixth sense when it came to Libba and it told him she wasn't bringing good news. "I'll be done here in a minute if you care to grab a cup of coffee."

She nodded. "Don't rush." She didn't tell him it might be his last run for some time. That would come later when she could break it to him alone.

His hair was still too long, she thought irrationally, but otherwise Shelby was right. There was nothing wrong with the rest of him. Russ Hennessey always did draw the eye. It was more than a combination of coloring and feature. He moved with a kind of boneless grace, as if he were utterly comfortable in his own skin, and he had a way of looking at a woman that made her believe she was the only one worth talking to in the entire room. He had a charming, effortless smile that exuded goodness and that he called up often, and he would do nearly anything for someone in trouble, whether he knew the person or not. Not a bad set of characteristics all in all.

He tossed the clipboard to Fletcher. "Take this back with you when you're done and give it to Billy. He has a few repairs to make."

Fletcher returned a mock salute and turned back to the bait tank.

Russ jumped from the boat to the dock and fell into step beside Libby. "What's on your mind?" he asked.

"Why is Fletch working for you?"

"His boats are grounded. One of his skippers disregarded the buoys and got a second citation. Fletcher's got a family to support. We all help one another when we can. You know that."

Libby remembered Shelby's lacquered nails and her brittle laugh. "Does Shelby know?"

Russ shook his head. "Shelby doesn't take bad news well."

"She's his wife. He should tell her."

"I agree, but then I'm not married to Shelby. Poor sucker."

"That's not very flattering."

"It's not my mission to stroke Shelby. Fletcher made his bed. Let him roll in it."

"Like you did?" Libby asked pointedly.

Russ thought a minute. "In a manner of speaking, yes. Except that I had the good sense to cut my losses and leave when the time came."

Libby stared at her feet, ashamed. "I'm sorry, Russ. That was uncalled for."

He nodded. "No problem. Now, about that cup of coffee."

Perks was busier than Libby had ever seen it. A young girl Libby didn't recognize served up coffee and muffins while Verna Lee manned the register. Russ and Libby took their places at the end of the line.

This time Verna Lee smiled at Libby. "How was your afternoon at the club?"

Libby rolled her eyes. "I left early."

"I noticed."

Russ looked from one to the other. "Did I miss something?"

"Just an inside joke," answered Verna Lee. "What will y'all have?"

"Coffee for me," Russ said, pulling out a handful of bills from his pocket. "And a latte for Libba."

"That has a ring to it," said the black woman. "Libba's latte. Maybe I'll name an espresso drink after her. How about it, Libba Jane? How would you feel about seeing your name on the menu?"

"I'd be honored."

Verna Lee laughed and turned to the next customer.

Russ nodded to an empty table. "Shall we stay here or do you want to talk in your office?"

"It's not good, Russ."

"Then it had better be your office."

They covered the distance from Perks to the EPA office without speaking. Inside, Libby pulled her chair from behind the desk and motioned for Russ to take the other one. "I wanted to tell you before it's official," she began. "There was an e-mail from Cliff this morning. A moratorium is being placed on commercial and recreational fishing for a hundred square miles of the Chesapeake. After Friday you won't be able to go out, not here. I'm sorry."

"What's happening?" he asked tightly.

"The official word is mercury levels are at an all-time high for fish this size and mutations due to PCBs have been found all throughout the bay."

"Is it the farms?"

Libby shrugged. "Partially, but we've always had farm

runoff. It's more than farm pesticides. I'm working on the specifics. I've contacted another lab where I can run independent tests. Right now, word has it that whatever's out there is enough to cause problems in the human population."

"What kind of problems?"

"I'm not entirely sure. Cliff isn't the communicator I'd like him to be. There's no point in speculation until the facts are all in."

He believed her. Not that it helped much, but he figured she wouldn't hold back if she had more information, not when it was this important to him. "It's not just me," he said slowly. "It's the men I've hired. Jobs aren't all that easy to come by in this economy. I have enough put away to last awhile, but a fishing moratorium means people here go hungry. That's all they know. You know as well as I do that welfare isn't something these men turn to, even in an emergency."

"You can lay them off."

His eyebrows lifted. "Excuse me?"

"If you lay them off, they can collect unemployment."

"That's not an alternative, Libba, not around here. You know that."

"It could be," she urged him. "At least for a while. It's better than nothing. And maybe by the time their benefits run out, the moratorium will be lifted."

He stared at her, a thousand thoughts running through his mind. "I could talk to them," he said, thinking aloud. "Maybe it would fly."

"Give it a try. It buys us some time."

Us. She said *us.* "Can we do dinner again," he asked abruptly, "this time with the girls?"

She looked surprised. "What brought that on?"

"I've met Chloe, but you've never met Tess. How about it?"

"Why would you want to put yourself through something like that?"

"What's that supposed to mean?"

Libby waved her hand. "Come on, Russ. Chloe isn't stupid and I'm sure Tess isn't, either. They're going to wonder why we're doing this. They're going to think something's going on with us."

"What's wrong with that?"

"Chloe's just getting used to my divorce. It hasn't been that long. I don't want her to think I'm bringing someone else into the picture."

"Why can't two old friends get together with their children?"

She held him with her gaze, forcing him to maintain eye contact. "Is that what it would be?"

He gave up. "It'll be whatever you want it to be, Libba. I've never been a slow learner and I'm no masochist. You've given me enough heartache for one lifetime. If you think I'm standin' in line for any more, you're wrong."

"Don't make more of us than we were," she said shortly.

He stood, his brows drawn together. "I can't believe you said that."

"We were twenty years old."

"What difference does that make?"

"*Heartache* is a strong term, don't you think?"

"Not for me."

She leaned across the desk, eyes wide and dark as old mahogany. "Are you deliberately trying to make me feel guilty?"

The old Russ, the boy she'd cut her teeth on seventeen years earlier, would have lashed out with something like, *if the shoe fits,* but Russ was no longer a boy. He inhaled deeply. "I'll tell you what. If I can get Chloe to *want* us both there, will you come?"

Her body relaxed. The tension left her face. "Are you a miracle worker, Russ?"

He grinned. "Not a miracle worker, but definitely an optimist."

"You're on."

He collected their empty coffee mugs. "I'll return these to Verna Lee. And then I've got work to do."

Libby didn't think for a minute that he would be successful at either task, but she'd bet her last nickel that convincing the watermen of Marshyhope Creek to accept what was tantamount to welfare wouldn't be as hard a sell as convincing Chloe to agree to an excursion with Russ and his daughter.

She finished up her report and e-mailed it to Cliff. Evidence of PCB contaminants was definitely greater in the shallow, saltier side of the bay. But it wasn't enough. There was a leak somewhere else and she needed manpower to flush it out. One person simply wasn't enough.

She called home to check on Chloe. Serena said she'd left with Bailey Jones nearly two hours ago. The two had carried fishing poles and a picnic lunch, neither of which allayed Libby's fears. She couldn't really prohibit Chloe from seeing Bailey. She just wished her daughter's preferences would have found a different direction. She needed a break and a tall, cool iced coffee.

Perks was empty now except for Verna Lee and the girl who was filling sugar jars.

"I came back for a refill, only cold this time," Libby said.

Verna Lee pulled out a pitcher from the refrigerator and filled a glass with amber liquid and ice cubes. "Here you are," she said, handing the glass to Libby.

Libby thanked her, sat down on a low sofa and picked up a copy of the local newspaper.

"Do you mind if I join you?" Verna Lee asked.

"Please." Libby moved to make room. "You've done a great job with this place."

"Thanks." Verna Lee sat down, crossed her legs and tucked her hair behind her ears. "What about you, Libba Jane? Are you here for good?"

"I think so. I took a leave of absence from my job in California, but that's nearly up. I have to go back or give final notice."

Verna Lee frowned. "It'll be hard on Cliff if you go home. I'm sure he's counting on you to stay awhile."

Libby nodded. "We've been over that. It really depends on Chloe and school."

"How so?"

"If she settles in, we're staying."

"I don't have any kids," Verna Lee said slowly, "but it seems like they have a way of settling in as long as you don't give them too many choices."

Verna Lee was interesting and intelligent. Why, then, was Libby offended when she offered her advice? "In other words, tell Chloe we're staying and she has to make it work."

Verna Lee nodded. "I'd use different language, obviously, but that's the gist of it."

"You don't know Chloe."

The woman's face closed. "I guess not."

Libby changed the subject. "Why didn't you ever marry?"

"How do you know I haven't?"

"All right. Have you?"

"Yes," said Verna Lee. "It was a long time ago and mercifully brief. We had no children, although I'm not sure that's a good thing."

"Where is he now?"

"Oh, Lord. I don't know. That was years ago and miles away." Verna Lee spooned sugar into her coffee and stirred slowly, her pinkie extended.

Libby laughed. "You do that exactly the way my mother does."

"Do what?"

"Hold your spoon while lifting your little finger."

Verna Lee's cheeks darkened. "Really. I wouldn't know. I've never met your mother."

Libby looked surprised. "Are you serious?"

"Yes."

"That's amazing. This town can't be any bigger than a football field and you've lived here for years."

Verna Lee corrected her. "I was born here. But I only came back a few years ago. I imagine there are quite a few people who've never met one another in Marshyhope Creek."

The door opened and a large man in a police uniform stepped inside. Libby recognized Earl White's shaved head immediately.

He nodded his head. "Ladies."

Verna Lee smiled. "Can I get you a cup of coffee or an iced tea, Earl?"

"Not today, Verna Lee." He looked around the brightly decorated shop. "Is your grandma around?"

Verna Lee's full, pouty mouth puckered. "I haven't seen her since yesterday afternoon. Is there a problem?"

"Have her give us a call down at the station. We have a few questions to ask her."

"What kind of questions?"

Earl spread his hands. "I really need to speak with Drusilla first."

"For heaven's sake, Earl. She's my grandmother. If she's in some kind of trouble, I want to know what's going on. Do you really think she wouldn't want me in on it?"

Earl White scratched his head. "Now, there're procedures, Verna Lee. I got to follow orders. That's all there is to it."

Libby cut in smoothly. "Of course you do, Earl. Is there anyone else we can talk to about this?"

"It's Drusilla we need, Libba Jane. She can clear the

whole thing up one way or another." He paused at the door on his way out. "You might think about hirin' a lawyer."

"Holy Christ." Verna Lee's hand was at her throat. "What has she gotten herself into?"

Libby walked around the counter to the phone. "I'll call my father."

"You don't have to do that," Verna Lee said sharply.

"Drusilla knows my father. She trusts him. Besides, is there another lawyer in Marshyhope Creek?"

Verna Lee shook her head. "This has to be a misunderstanding. She's seventy years old. What could she have done?"

Libby lifted the phone to her ear and punched in her home number. "We'll have to find her."

"Fat chance. She could be anywhere. She has a message machine at home. I'll just keep calling her until she answers."

Coleson Delacourte picked up the phone on the first ring. Quickly, Libby described the interchange with the police officer.

"Where is Drusilla now?" her father asked.

"No one seems to know."

"I'll see what I can do. Call me if she shows up."

"Thanks, Daddy." She handed the phone to Verna Lee.

The black woman dialed her grandmother's number and twisted the gauzy fabric of her skirt in her fingers. She bit her lip and shook her head. "No answer. I'll have to leave a message." After a minute, she spoke into the phone. "This is Verna Lee, Gran. Call me as soon as you get in."

She replaced the phone and looked at Libby. "What did your father say?"

"He wants you to call him when Drusilla contacts you."

Verna Lee paced the length of the shop and back again. "I should have paid more attention. She shows up every other day or so, but she's so damned independent. I've asked her to come live with me, but she won't hear of it.

She goes to those hovels the sharecroppers live in and God knows what she does there. She hasn't been herself in a long time. I thought it was nothing more than aging.''

"You don't know what it is. Let's wait and see.''

"You heard Earl. He said she needed a lawyer.''

Libby hesitated. "Am I in the way, Verna Lee, or do you want me to stay?''

"Please stay. I don't want to be alone right now.''

Libby found the Closed sign and positioned it in the window. Then she refilled Verna Lee's glass and sat down beside her. "So,'' she began conversationally, "tell me where you lived in California.''

"San Francisco,'' Verna Lee replied automatically. "I went to school at Berkeley, got a degree in art history, worked for an advertising company, made some money, came home and bought Perks. I always wanted to own my own business.''

"I don't blame you,'' Libby said admiringly, looking around at the painted walls and brightly colored prints.

"What about you, Libba Jane?''

"Me?'' Libby shrugged. "I don't know. I think I had visions of taking Hollywood by storm.''

"Cliff said you were good.''

"Cliff's reference point is Marshyhope Creek's high school drama club. I wasn't good, not at all. It took me about three weeks to figure that one out. After that I turned to something far more satisfying and much more likely to help me find employment.''

"Not making it in acting must have been hard for you.''

"Why do you say that?''

"Everything always came so easily.''

Libby's face reddened. "Not everything.''

"Is that why you came home, because you thought it would be the same?''

"I came home because my father called to say my mother was ill and because of Chloe.''

Verna Lee's eyebrows rose. "Chloe?"

Libby nodded. "I can't manage her alone and Eric wasn't much help. I had the misguided idea that children can't get into trouble here."

Verna Lee's rich laughter caught her off guard. "You can't be that naive."

Suddenly it was all too funny and Libby laughed with her. "Apparently so."

Libby didn't know when she first realized they weren't alone. It was more of a presence than anything she heard.

Verna Lee felt it, too. Together the two women turned in the direction of the kitchen. A small dark woman hovered in the doorway. Verna Lee breathed a sigh of relief. "Gran," she said, rushing to hug her. "We've been so worried. Where have you been?"

"I've been at home workin' in my garden. Where do you think I've been?" She nodded at Libby. "How are you, Libba Jane? It's good to see you."

"I'm fine, Drusilla."

Verna Lee took her grandmother's shoulders in her hands and shook her gently. "What's going on? Tell me what happened?"

"You're squeezin' me too hard." She tugged at the hands gripping her shoulders. "What's got into you, Verna Lee?"

Libby watched Verna Lee visibly control herself. Her grip gentled. Her voice calmed. "The police were here, Gran. They want to ask you some questions. Do you know anything about that?"

The old woman's expression didn't change a bit. "I ain't done nothin', Verna Lee."

"Are you sure? Think very hard. Is there anything you might have forgotten or that could have been taken the wrong way?"

Drusilla tilted her head, an indication of deep thought. Then she shook her head. "Not one thing."

Verna Lee sighed, released her grandmother and sat down

heavily beside Libby. "We have to call the police, Gran. It's the only way to find out what's going on."

Drusilla's lips tightened stubbornly. "I ain't goin' to no police."

Verna Lee spoke soothingly. "Libba Jane called her father. You won't be alone. We'll both be with you. I'm sure it's just a misunderstanding."

"I ain't goin' to no police, Verna Lee."

A knock sounded on the door. Verna Lee's hand moved to her throat. Her eyes went wild. "Dear God."

"Stop it, both of you," Libby ordered. "This is ridiculous. It can't be all that bad if Drusilla doesn't even remember." She crossed the room, moved the curtain aside and looked out the windowpane. "It's my father." She opened the door. "Hi, Daddy. What did you find out?"

Cole Delacourte stepped inside and closed the door behind him. He went right to Drusilla and took her hands in his. Her face went blank.

"What is it, Mr. Delacourte?"

"Tell me about the baby, Drusilla."

"What baby?"

"The one with missing parts."

Verna Lee gasped.

Drusilla shook her head and looked at the floor. "She was in a bad way, Mr. Delacourte. Only the little head was normal. The rest of her—"

"What did you do, Drusilla?"

Tears spilled over and dribbled down the woman's face. She looked at her granddaughter. "It was an act of mercy, Verna Lee."

Cole Delacourte's voice, warm, soothing, insistent, pierced the quiet. "Tell me, Drusilla."

"She was breathin'," the old woman sobbed. "She wouldn't stop breathin' so I put my hands against her throat and squeezed."

Libby caught Verna Lee's body as it sagged against her.

"Easy, Verna Lee. Easy now," she said soothingly, bracing her hip against the black woman's.

"Call the police, Libba Jane," her father said. "Tell them Drusilla is coming into the station and that I'll be representing her." His hand rested on Verna Lee's shoulder. "You go home with Libba Jane. Everything will be all right."

Verna Lee shook her head. "I'll be fine right here, Mr. Delacourte. Take care of Gran and bring her back here as soon as possible."

"I'll have her back by morning," he said.

Twenty

The air conditioner in the small EPA office didn't work as well at night after running all day. Libby turned off the computer, twisted her hair back and lifted it off the back of her neck. The blinking light on her message machine indicated two missed calls. She stared at the phone, decided to take a chance, picked it up and dialed Cliff's number. Incredibly, he answered. Tongue-tied at the sound of a human voice instead of a message machine, she hesitated.

"Who is this?" he asked.

"It's Libba," she said quickly. "Something isn't right, Cliff. I need to run it past you."

"What's on your mind?"

"I don't think PCBs are the culprit."

"Why not? Paint and steel manufacturers, companies producing farm products and home appliances, nearly every business that requires a smooth finish and a nonstick surface produces them."

"I know that, but levels have been seriously reduced, and they haven't been linked to the kinds of serious mutations evident here in the Tidewater. I think somewhere along the freshwater tributaries of the Rappahannock or in the shallow blue crab spawning grasses of the Patuxent something else is leaking, something far more serious."

There was a moment of silence on the other end of the phone. "Spit it out, Libba."

"I'm thinking it might be radiation."

"That's ridiculous," he said quickly. "The lab reports dispute that."

If only she had the authority to order in inspectors. Only Cliff could do that. She was already regretting her phone call. "I suppose you're right," she said. "It was just a thought."

"Get some rest, Libba Jane. You're working too hard."

"Good night, Cliff."

She looked at her watch. It was late. She'd lost track of time and missed dinner for the third time this week. One of the messages on the machine was probably her mother. She pressed the button. Two messages. She smiled when she heard Chloe's voice. "Grandma said to call. She wants to make sure you have something to eat because you're so-o-o skinny. I'm going to the movies in Salisbury with Granddad. We'll be home about eleven."

The next message gave her cause to sit up. "Libba, this is Russ. I've thought of something and I need your help. Call me."

She picked up the phone and dialed the old Hennessey number. The phone rang, once, twice, three times, four times. There was no answering machine. Libby replaced the receiver. Russ's house was on the way. She would stop by before returning home.

She'd left the car windows open. Sliding behind the wheel, she breathed the hot, muggy air that smelled of peaches and fish, hot tar and wet earth and sweet grass. Turning the key, she felt the engine engage and moved out on to the road. A hot wind lifted her hair. She was restless, on edge. Her mind returned to the last time she'd seen Russ, composed, loose-limbed, square-jawed, deceptively relaxed, blue eyes narrowed, faded jeans hugging his lean frame. He'd very diplomatically turned what could have become an argument. He was different, somehow, from the boy she remembered. She couldn't put her finger on it, but his new

maturity was attractive. She'd been unprepared for his bla-
tant appeal.

Libby had worshipped at his shrine since she was seven
years old, a shy, serious little girl, spoiled by adoring parents
who'd instilled in her that the worst possible fate was to be
unexceptional. Because she was her father's daughter, Libby
achieved. Because she was her mother's daughter, achieve-
ment came easily. Riding trophies and academic awards
adorned the walls of her bedroom. Piano was twice a week
at four, ballet and deportment at five-thirty, sketching and
watercolor on alternate Saturdays. When her regimen of lessons was over and the long daylight hours of spring and
summer loomed ahead, there was Russ.

With him she learned to laugh, to free her mind, to reach
for the pure, indulgent pleasure of feeling good. He made
her dizzy with a constant, rushing, room-spinning swirl of
light and color and laughter and passion. She'd trusted him,
loved him. And in spite of all that he'd given, she'd left
him.

It was after ten and the house was dark, but the front door
was open and country music played on the stereo.

Libby left the keys in her car and walked toward the
house. Above the roof she saw lightning streak unevenly
across the sky and counted the seconds. One, two, three,
four, five...a low rumble followed. The upstairs shutters
creaked and slammed together. By the time she reached the
porch, heavy, tubelike drops pelted down on her head. The
wind was strong, the rain warm. Libby, who'd seen a lifetime of storms, was drawn to the warm wetness of the downpour. She stood on the steps and lifted her face to the sky.
Instantly, she was drenched. Her blouse clung to her body
like a second skin.

Libby loved the rain. Her earliest memories included the
steady drum of a spring rain against her bedroom window.
It lulled her to sleep as warm milk never could. Nola Ruth

had refused to countenance the research claiming that wet
hair and clothing did not bring on a cold. She would not
allow her daughter to arrive at school soaked to the bone.
But later, when the last bell rang, signaling the end of the
day, Libby would dash from the schoolyard with Russ and
Mitch, delighting in the wetness that turned the potholes on
Main Street into small ponds. With her hair plastered to her
small skull and her face running with rain, she would take
off her shoes and socks and stomp and splash her way to
Hennessey House. There, Cora handed out towels and
served cinnamon chocolate and graham crackers to her waterlogged sons and Coleson Delacourte's pixie-faced daughter.

Later, at Shad Landing, when Libby was much older,
there was a night when rain came down in sheets and lightning crackled dangerously above the boat she and Russ had
taken out on the water. Terrified that their bobbing heads
would attract the hissing electricity, Libby pressed her palms
together and murmured Hail Marys while Russ calmly
rowed toward shore. When a zigzag streak of light hit the
bow, Libby screamed and began to breathe in the shallow
rasping way that all watermen knew and dreaded.

Russ took one look at her pinched white face, threw the
oars into the boat and pushed her down until she lay flat in
the hull. Then he lay down on top of her, covering her
completely, murmuring softly into her ear. The boat rocked
crazily, but Libby was warm and, soon, no longer afraid.
Her arms came around him and this time her trembling had
nothing to do with fear. His mouth tasted like clean wind
and warm rain, and for the rest of her life, when thunder-
heads appeared, Libby's breathing quickened and she would
remember.

She remembered now, as if it were yesterday. She felt the
sensual touch of warm water on slick skin, saw the smeared
edges of a crescent moon behind dark clouds. The lightning
was miles away. Libby stepped out of her shoes and dropped

them on the porch. Laughing, she lifted her arm to an imaginary partner and began swaying to the strains of a Garth Brooks refrain.

She hummed and circled the porch, losing track of time and inhibitions, making up her own version of the country singer's lilting ballad.

A square of light appeared in the distance and disappeared. She ignored it, her feet moving to the music. She twirled wildly, grabbed at the porch pillar to steady herself, and then she saw him.

He stood there quietly, watching her, heedless of the downpour soaking his shirt.

The music changed from Garth Brooks to Willie Nelson. She could feel his eyes on her, narrowed, probing. Her mind felt detached from her body. The rain pounded on the roof. Gutters ran, the sky crackled with light, and the hypnotic lyrics of a country music hit poured from the stereo speakers.

He walked toward her, unhurried, careful, feral, a lethal mix of grace and wildness. She watched the light play across his face, handsome, murderously so, highlighting the prominent bones, the square chin, throwing into shadow the hollow cheeks, the narrowed, all-seeing eyes, the beautiful, guarded mouth. She watched him come and she couldn't move. The lightning, the rain, the music and the dryness of long empty years held her there, waiting, wanting.

Russ climbed the porch steps, not quite trusting what he saw. Was she real? Or was this the familiar apparition he conjured up when his tortured nerves could no longer stand the mental images of the woman he ached to touch, the woman who should have been his, sharing another man's life?

He was close enough to see the blood pounding in her throat. She lifted her head and looked directly at him. Her eyes were dark, so dark the iris and pupil were one color. Her pull was strong. He reached for her and bent his head.

Libby lifted her mouth to meet his. Again, he tasted like warm rain and clean wind. Again, she was not afraid. Her lips softened and parted under his. Before sensation claimed her, she was conscious of a single thought. He had asked her, when he first came home, if he made her nervous. She had never stopped to consider it before, but now it seemed to Libby that everyone she had ever known made her nervous. Everyone, except Russ.

Her arms came up to circle his neck. He held her against him, lifting her to fit against his chest. Her heels came up off the floorboards. She'd forgotten how tall he was, tall and solid and warm. His hand, rotating against the base of her spine, urged her closer and closer still. Every nerve came to life. She made a small inarticulate sound and pressed herself into the vee of his legs as naturally as if she'd done so only yesterday.

Russ's breathing altered and stopped. He waited for a timeless moment, his lips clinging to the softness of hers, until he'd regained the edge of his control. Slowly, tentatively, his tongue traced the edges of her lips.

"What are we doing?" she whispered against his mouth.

"What we should have been doing for the last seventeen years."

She tilted her head, giving him greater access to her neck.

His nerves were raw. She was making him crazy, leaching the sanity from his brain. Dipping his head, he found the pulse at the base of her throat and sucked lightly. Her eyes closed and her head fell back as his mouth moved down her shoulder to the slope of her breast. He stayed there, breathing heavily, pressing down on the tempting fullness, remembering when he'd had the right to slide his hands under her blouse, lift the cups of her bra and feel the soft weight of her in his callused fisherman's palms.

Libby could feel the heat of his mouth through the clinging material of her blouse. She trembled.

"Easy, baby, easy now," he muttered, shifting her into

the saddle of his hips. He settled her against him, gritting his teeth, feeling the ache in his middle that had started when he first saw her dancing in the rain. He brushed his hand against her cheek. Her eyes were closed, the lashes dark half moons on her cheeks. Bending his head, he began to kiss her, deliberately at first, with unhurried skill and then, when the tip of her tongue touched his lower lip, with increasing intensity.

The strength of his arousal thrilled her. Refusing to think of the disaster she courted or how she would feel tomorrow, she slipped one hand inside his shirt, laying it flat against his smooth, water-slick chest. The other, she slid down between their tightly wedged bodies and cupped him.

He jerked and froze, holding her against him for agonizing seconds. Libby was aware of nothing but his deep, shuddering breaths, the incessant rain and the slamming of his heart against her ribs.

His hands tightened on her arms and he swore. "Damn you, Libba Delacourte. This time I'm not going away with a slap on the wrist."

She released her breath. She hadn't realized she'd been holding it, wondering if it was too late, terrified that he would change his mind. Shamelessly, she wanted him, wanted him to take her here in the middle of a driving rainstorm on the floorboards of the Hennessey porch. And why not? She was an adult and she was single. No one would be hurt. "I want you," she whispered. "Whatever happens tomorrow, I want you now. No regrets. I promise."

He believed her and it was enough, more than he'd hoped for. Slipping his arm under her knees, he lifted her against him and started for the door. Light streaked across the sky, illuminating the porch and the short hall leading to the kitchen. Pushing the door open with his foot, Russ carried her through the hall to the stairs.

Standing at the top of the landing in a knee-length

T-shirt, biting down on her thumbnail, was his daughter, Tess.

Libby's dreamlike trance was broken. For one horrified, humiliating moment she stared at the child. Then, succumbing to cowardice, she buried her face in Russ's shoulder. "Let's see you charm your way out of this one, Hennessey," she mumbled into his shirt.

Russ swore under his breath. Apparently, nightmares came dressed in T-shirts with tangled curls and doe-brown eyes. The drawbacks of parenthood had never been more clear. He cleared his throat. "You're up late, Tess. Is anything wrong?"

Tess's voice shook. "The storm woke me." She pointed a finger at Libby. "What's wrong with her?"

"The storm must have bothered her, too," he improvised. "She got soaked and stopped by to dry off."

A bubble of laughter rose in Libby's throat. Trust Russ to come up with a lie that was almost the truth.

"Is she sick?" Tess demanded.

"Nothing that won't fix itself by morning," Russ answered cheerfully.

"Why are you carrying her?"

"I'm taking her upstairs. Sometimes adults need some pampering."

Libby untangled her arms from around Russ's neck and kicked her legs from his grasp. "Actually, I think I'm okay now." She folded her arms against her chest. "A dry T-shirt and something warm to drink would be great."

"I'm sorry," he said quietly. "Bad timing."

Whose, Libby wondered, hers or Tess's?

He smiled. "How about some hot chocolate?"

"That sounds wonderful." Libby smiled at Russ's daughter. "How about you, Tess?"

"Yes, please."

Russ disappeared into the kitchen.

The girl walked slowly down the stairs until she stood even with Libby. "You're Chloe's mother, aren't you?"

"I'll admit to it," said Libby, "although sometimes I wonder if I should."

"She's different," observed Tess.

"She's a Californian," answered Libby. "That explains a lot."

"I like her," Tess said.

Libby looked, really looked, at this frail, ethereal child for the first time and her heart melted. "Would you do me a favor?"

Tess looked wary. "What kind of favor?"

"Would you tell her that?"

Tess looked horrified. "It's not something that would just come up in normal conversation."

Libby's smile faded. "I guess not."

Tess frowned, opened her mouth as if to say something, then closed it again without speaking.

Libby explained. "Chloe doesn't feel as if she fits in here. She wants to go home."

Tess's eyelashes fluttered. "Why can't she?"

"I want to stay here. This is my home."

"But it isn't hers. She wants to live with her dad."

"Did she tell you that?"

Tess nodded.

Libby's shoulders sagged. "I know."

"It might be better to let her go back," Tess advised.

Libby collected herself. This heart-to-heart with a peer of her daughter's wasn't appropriate. "Maybe you're right. Shall we see about that hot chocolate?"

Tess eyed Libby's shirt. "I think I should get you something else to wear. You're pretty wet." She eyed Libby's full breasts, clearly exposed under the soaking shirt. "I don't think anything I have would fit you. I'll check in Dad's closet."

She was back in a minute with a soft gray sweatshirt.

Libby excused herself and changed in the bathroom, leaving her dripping blouse hanging in the shower stall. Then she joined Russ and his daughter, taking a seat around the old oak table in the kitchen.

"This is nice, isn't it?" asked Russ. He appealed to Tess. "Wouldn't it be great if Chloe was here, too?"

Tess was sitting beside her father. The light from the overhead lamp shone down upon them. She rolled her eyes and looked across the table, giving Libby an unshadowed view of her face. Her eyes were brown, a deep velvety brown, without the slightest touch of hazel.

Libby looked from father to daughter and back again. *Blue eyes, brown, blue.* She looked down at her cup of hot chocolate and called up the memory of her last encounter with Tracy Wentworth. *Pale hair, clear gray eyes.* The genetic law so without exception that it was used as a model for decades of schoolchildren popped into her mind: *Two recessives can never, absolutely never, produce a dominant. Light-eyed parents do not produce dark-eyed children.* Once again her eyes moved from Tess to Russ, searching for the slightest resemblance. Then she went completely still.

"Libba." Her name on Russ's lips revived her. "I think it needs to be explained to them."

She looked dazed. "What?"

"The watermen. The problem needs to be explained to them in terms they understand. I think you should do it."

"Me?" Dismay clouded her features.

Russ nodded. "Who better?"

"I can think of a number of people."

"Think about it. These people know you. If you treat them like you're on their side, you won't be seen as the enemy, the one shutting them down." He leaned forward. "They'll have plenty of time on their hands and you said you needed help."

"What are you talking about?" Tess asked.

Russ spoke first. "Remember I told you there's a problem with the crabs?"

She nodded. "Everyone's talking about it."

"We need to find out why," Russ explained. "And we need to do it quickly or we can't fish."

"I need trained help, Russ," said Libby.

He shrugged impatiently. "What does it take to check out the waste systems of production plants? At least they'll know what they're looking for. C'mon, Libba Jane. Give them a chance."

"I'll think about it," she said reluctantly. "However, it's a big job and a lot more complicated than you think."

Russ winked at this daughter. "Think fast because I've called a meeting for tomorrow evening."

"You have four trawlers, Russ. How many people do you employ?"

"Twelve. But this concerns all the fishermen on the bay, not just me. We'll have the meeting in the library and we'll figure out how to get through this."

Libby stared at him, dismayed. She'd only just returned to Marshyhope Creek and still felt like a newcomer, insecure of her welcome. The last thing she wanted was to hold a town meeting under false pretenses. Still, Russ's request made sense. She really couldn't refuse. It wouldn't hurt to have everyone know the facts, if only she was sure of what the facts were. Searching for PCB leaks wasn't a bad idea. It certainly couldn't hurt, and maybe someone would uncover something more in the process. "All right," she said reluctantly. "I suppose it is a good idea to keep them busy. At least I can tell them about collecting their benefits."

Twenty-One

Nola Ruth Delacourte's dark eyes were fixed on her husband's face, their expression of horrified disapproval so palpable that he felt as if her hands were around his throat squeezing the air from his breathing passage. Sweat broke out on his brow. Carefully, he lifted his water glass to his lips and looked back at her steadily. They were in his study. He sat behind his desk. She faced him from her wheelchair.

Her voice was surprisingly clear. "How could you, Cole?"

"The case would have been mine, anyway."

"You're nearly retired."

"I'm pleased you recognize the operative word is *nearly*."

"Please don't do this."

Cole sighed, stood and walked around the desk. He knelt beside his wife. "She's an old woman, Nola Ruth. Who else is there? She's done a dreadful thing, but not maliciously. There's no one else to help her. Surely you don't want an old woman to spend her final years in a jail cell."

"She's a murderer," Nola Ruth said icily. "How can you represent someone who killed a child?"

"I'm an attorney. That's what I do. I represent all kinds of people. You know that."

"What she did was wrong."

Cole stroked his wife's hand. Nola Ruth had lovely hands, long-fingered and graceful with beautifully kept oval nails.

"That isn't the way it works, Nola Ruth. You're an intelligent woman. You know that."

She remained silent.

Cole didn't want to play his trump card. It wasn't necessary. He would represent Drusilla Washington no matter what reservations Nola Ruth had.

"You've involved Libba," his wife said petulantly. "I didn't want that."

"On the contrary. You confided in Libba. You had every intention of involving her on your terms. Only something else got in the way. She's bright, Nola Ruth. Did you think she would leave it alone? Her powers of observation are strong. She'll know everything before long. She's already drawn to Verna Lee."

Nola Ruth pulled her hand away. "I don't know what you're talking about."

Cole frowned. This conversation was unproductive. He had work to do and the evening was getting away from him. He rose, crossed the room to open the door and then returned to wheel Nola Ruth down the hall and into her room. "I'll tell Serena you're here."

"I don't want Serena," Nola Ruth said coldly. "I want Libba Jane."

Cole's patience never thinned. "I'll be sure she knows that when she gets in." He kissed his wife's cheek. "Good night, Nola."

She didn't answer and after a minute he left the room once again, returning to his study and the case before him. Drusilla was an old woman. Her age was in her favor. She was not a criminal nor had she been an activist, not even during the early civil rights years when nearly every black woman in domestic service was. Not a single complaint had ever been filed against her by those she'd served, and she'd served many, mostly the disenfranchised who knew by implication that Dr. Balieu would never receive them in his pristine office on the right side of Marshyhope Creek. She'd single-handedly raised her granddaughter, an educated woman who'd returned home to run her own small business. So much for character. Now, for her defense. Obviously premeditated murder wasn't a charge he needed to concern himself with. Drusilla had gone to the young sharecroppers' dwelling to deliver a baby, to bring forth life. Murder was the last thing on her mind. She was not a murderer, yet the coroner's report said the child was strangled. What then, were the circumstances that led her to such an action?

Cole picked up his pencil and notepad and jotted down the facts as he knew them: the child was horribly mutated, possibly even in pain. He struck that. Drusilla would not have known if the child was in pain. But she did know that the infant was obviously deformed. Drusilla, with years of midwifery behind her, knew it could not survive. Then why didn't she allow it to die naturally? Why had she taken matters into her own hands and orchestrated the time of death? Cole thought of various possibilities, both actual and those he could convince a jury to believe. More than likely Drusilla was afraid the child would live and two teenagers who survived hand-to-mouth picking crops would end up abandoning the child somewhere by the side of the road. A mercy killing. That would be Cole's defense. After all, it wasn't the young parents who'd questioned Drusilla's action. The plaintiff was the State of Maryland. Again he jotted down notes, questions he would ask the mother and her husband. With any luck they would be sympathetic witnesses. Perhaps Drusilla had prior knowledge of what they would do. Perhaps she'd seen something similar.

"Granddad?" Chloe's voice interrupted him. She stood in the doorway, unsure of her welcome. He set aside his notes, removed his glasses and beckoned her into the room. "What a wonderful excuse for a break," he said.

Relieved, Chloe curled up in a wing chair that swallowed her small form and regarded him seriously.

"Is this purely a social call or do you have something on

your mind?'' her grandfather asked. ''Because I refuse to
consider anything important unless I have a piece of Serena's cobbler with ice cream in front of me.''

Chloe grinned. ''You're on.''

He stood and reached for her hand, leading her down the
long hallway into the kitchen.

''So,'' he said, when they were seated across from each
other at the small table in the breakfast room, enormous
helpings of peach cobbler à la mode in front of them. ''Tell
me everything.''

Chloe nibbled at the edges of her cobbler. Her cheeks
were flushed. ''Skylar Taft said some mean things about
Bailey's mother.''

Cole knew he should say something, anything so that
Chloe would continue, but teenagers were particularly sensitive. ''Oh?'' was the best he could come up with.

Chloe nodded. ''They said she'd had a lot of boyfriends
and that she didn't even know who Bailey's father was.''

''I'm fairly sure that Lizzie Jones has never taken Skylar
into her confidence,'' Cole said dryly.

''So, it isn't true?''

Cole considered her question. ''Some of it may be true,
but certainly not all of it. I'm sure she knows who Bailey's
father is and, yes, she's probably had a lot of boyfriends.''

Chloe held her spoon over her plate and watched the
melted ice cream drip down into the pastry and peaches.
''She's sick.''

Cole nodded. ''I've heard.''

''Do you think it has anything to do with, you know—''
she hesitated and then continued ''—her lifestyle?''

Cole studied his granddaughter under lowered eyelids.
She was a small girl, slender and delicately muscled with
fine features, exotic blue eyes and flyaway silvery hair, an
ethereal child, fairylike. But she was much more than that.
She had a quick intelligence and a seeking mind, perhaps
even more than her mother had at the same age. He won-

dered, not for the first time, if he had done Libba a tremendous disservice by asking her to come home. His concern had been for his wife and, to a smaller extent, his daughter. But he had completely disregarded Chloe. Before he knew her, she had been Libba's daughter, a mere child whose needs and wants could be sacrificed according to the wishes of the adults around her. Now, with the living breathing Chloe before him, he saw his mistake. He loved her desperately and he was ashamed. The years rolled back, oblivious years, when he was caught up in righting the grievances of his generation at the expense of knowing his daughter. He collected himself. Chloe needed an answer, an honest one. "Are you suggesting that Lizzie might have AIDS?"

The blue eyes swam with tears. "She's so nice, Granddad. But she's really weak and she looks worse every time I see her."

"Have you ever actually seen anyone with AIDS, Chloe?"

"Not that I know of."

He spoke slowly, choosing the right words. "It's a relatively new disease here in America and almost always restricted to certain communities. Lizzie Jones's behavior has been completely different since she had Bailey and that was sixteen years ago. I believe that whatever she suffers from, it isn't AIDS."

"What do you think is the matter with her?"

Cole took the time to chew and swallow his last bite of cobbler. Then he looked at Chloe's barely touched bowl. "Are you going to eat that?" he asked.

She picked up her bowl and set it in front of him. "Have you ever heard of cholesterol, Granddad?"

"That's a California word, sugar. We don't worry about cholesterol down here in the South. If it isn't deep-fried, honey-basted or smothered in cream, we want no part of it. Look at me." He patted his stomach. "What do you think? Am I not just as lean as I was at twenty-six?"

"Well." Chloe looked dubious. Her sense of honesty warred with her desire to please this very beloved grandfather. "You look great for your age, but I've seen pictures when you were young and you were pretty thin, Granddad."

His eyes twinkled. "I suppose that's true. Don't tell your grandma."

Chloe laughed. "I won't."

"Are you feeling better?"

She thought a minute. "I guess so. Why doesn't she get help?"

"I don't know, Chloe. Have you asked Bailey?"

"He's prickly about that subject."

Cole nodded. "You would be, too, I expect. In that case it's best to leave it alone."

She sighed. "I don't have any choice."

Cole collected the dishes, rinsed and stacked them in the dishwasher. "Run in and say good-night to your grandma, Chloe. Little things mean a great deal to her."

Chloe knew her grandmother better than anyone suspected. "I will, Granddad. Good night."

Back in his study, Cole had lost his enthusiasm for his project. His mind was elsewhere, sullied with old regrets and a sense of unfinished business. What if he'd followed a different path? What if Nola Ruth Beauchamp had never sought him out that day at the beach? What if she'd walked right past and left him for a different future? His questions were pointless, of course. It couldn't have happened any differently, not unless he'd never seen her. The way her aunt kept her holed up in that house, it would have been entirely possible. But once he'd seen her, heard her speak and known her smile, Coleson Campion Delacourte was well and truly caught.

He'd courted her for six months, calling daily at her aunt's home. Her visit, which he learned was to be only for another month, turned into two and then three and then six.

Her father, after a discreet note from his sister, stopped asking when she would be returning to New Orleans.

When Cole asked her to marry him, he had the blessing of both families. Nola Ruth was eminently suitable. She was French, Catholic and well connected. Louisiana-born, she voted the way her state had traditionally voted in every election since 1876, straight down the line on the Democratic ticket. She was beautiful, intelligent and educated, the perfect future politician's wife. If she was somewhat reserved when they were alone together, he explained it away as embarrassment due to inexperience. A woman who moved and spoke and smiled like Nola Ruth, a woman whose sensuality was so pronounced the roof of a man's mouth went dry just speaking to her, had hidden depths crying out to be discovered.

Every day they were together Cole delighted in her conversation, reveled in the clarity of her mind, the richness of her imagination, the complexity of her vocabulary. She was never boring, a possibility inconceivable to him. They became inseparable, attending dinners, banquets and balls up and down the James River. Everything was possible in that bright, new, anything-was-possible American era. Cole and Nola Ruth, people would say, as if the names were only complete when spoken together. He couldn't imagine a life without her.

With utmost care, he'd selected a ring. A family heirloom wasn't acceptable for the hand of Nola Ruth Beauchamp. He wanted something more, something large and brilliant with hidden fire. Settling on a diamond solitaire of flawless color and clarity, he had it wrapped in silver paper and made reservations at Armand's, a favorite restaurant in Richmond. After a perfect dinner, he posed the question.

There was a moment of awkward silence before she refused him, politely but firmly, giving no explanation other than, *Marrying me wouldn't be in the best interests of a man with your future.* Cole was brokenhearted, but he was also a Southern gentleman. Swallowing hard, he assured her that he harbored no ill feelings and encouraged her to order dessert and coffee. If he wondered why she had postponed returning to her home state for six months longer than she'd intended, or why she had allowed him to monopolize all of her time with the end result being that every gossip columnist in the capital had predicted a June wedding, he remained silent on the subject. One did not embarrass a lady simply because her affections were not engaged.

Nola Ruth returned to New Orleans and Cole buried himself in his work. An interesting case had come across his desk. Oliver Wade, a Negro railroad worker, was suing the board of education of Laurel, Mississippi, on behalf of his daughter, Susan, for the right to attend an all-white elementary school close to her home. Companion suits had already been filed and won in Topeka, Kansas, Delaware, Virginia, Illinois and Washington, D.C. But Mississippi was the heart of the South, Ku Klux Klan country. It was a case destined for the Supreme Court. Cole could feel it in his bones and he wanted in at the ground level. He was a Southerner with a two-hundred-year-old pedigree, abolitionist roots, and a reputation as the finest up-and-coming young lawyer in Washington circles. With his law firm securely behind him, Cole drove down to Mississippi.

For a man who wanted to carve out a name for himself, it was a case made in heaven. Since the Civil Rights Acts of the last decade guaranteeing blacks the right to use public accommodations, all legislation by the Supreme Court had followed the indifferent attitude of the American public. *Plessy v. Ferguson,* a case heard before the Court in 1896, upheld the principle of separate but equal facilities, virtually legalizing segregation. With nothing to lose, Mr. Wade, middle class, black, defensive, was willing to test the system. With his entire future resting on the outcome, Cole Delacourte, wealthy, white, powerful, was eager to give it a try.

Thurgood Marshall, a brilliant young former NAACP attorney with grandiose ideas was head counsel. He was thrilled and more than a little relieved when Cole offered his services. The press went wild. Southern Lawyer Defends Negro's Right to Attend White Schools in Segregationist State. Delacourte Supports Integration. Southern Democrat Betrays His Roots.

Nola Ruth Beauchamp read the New Orlean's *Chronicle* while sipping her morning chocolate. The Supreme Court had agreed to review what she now called Coleson's Case. She read the article, word for word. They called him a hero in the North, a traitor in the South. Her father peering over her shoulder, caught a glimpse of the headline and shuddered. "You showed remarkable judgment over that one, my dear. He would not have done for you at all."

Nola Ruth was nineteen years old, a young woman of astute intelligence, remarkable charm and no marriage prospects in sight. Coleson Delacourte had a brilliant future. Nola Ruth had a sordid past, too much pride to hide it and too much integrity to lie. At the time he proposed, she thought it best to end the relationship. She'd cringed at the thought of destroying his regard for her and decided to take the painless way out, offering no explanation. But that was before *Wade v. Laurel, Mississippi*. A man who would risk his reputation and defy his heritage might just possibly be the kind of man who could weather the storm that could arise from rumors of a less-than-perfect wife.

Folding the paper, she passed it to her father and picked up the phone. "Carrie Jean?" she said pleasantly to the woman at the switchboard, "this is Nola Ruth Beauchamp. I want to send a telegram to Mr. Coleson Delacourte at the law offices of Hayes and Brackett in Washington, D.C. Can you call the office for me?" She waited. "That's fine, just as long as it gets there this morning." She laughed. "No, one line is all I need. Ask him if his proposal is still on the table. I'll be down to pay you later."

When she hung up and faced her father, his eyes were the cold gray of Arctic ice. "Are you mad?" he asked, aghast.

"No," she replied briefly and firmly. "I'm in love."

"You've said that before," he reminded her.

"The circumstances are different."

"I forbid it."

Her voice would have frozen the words in a better man's mouth. "We both seem to be repeating ourselves this morning."

Unwisely, her father brought up the subject he'd forever closed. "What will he do when you tell him about your previous indiscretion?"

She smiled and lifted her sweater from the back of her chair. "I have no idea, but when I find out I'll be sure to let you know."

She received her answer that very morning, a single word on yellow paper, *"Yes."*

The next afternoon she flew to Washington. Cole met her at the airport, taking her small white-gloved hands in his large ones. "I may not win this one, Nola. Will you be happy with a simple country lawyer?"

"That depends."

He frowned. It wasn't the answer he expected. "If you have doubts, I won't rush you," he said slowly. "It's a lifetime we're deciding here."

Her tears were already forming. She didn't deserve him. "You don't have to worry about me, darling. But there is something I have to tell you. If you decide you can't marry me, if you have any reservations at all, tell me now."

"That won't happen," he said firmly.

She laid her finger against his lips. "Just let me talk and don't interrupt."

"Where would you like to go?"

She thought a minute. "The Lincoln Memorial might be an appropriate place."

He threw back his head and laughed. "We were meant for each other, Nola Ruth. What are the odds of two Southerners choosing the Lincoln Memorial to exchange confidences?"

"A million to one," she replied promptly.

They climbed the sunlit steps leading to the massive statue of Abraham Lincoln. There, in the privacy of hushed darkness, she began. "I may not be capable of having children."

Cole expelled a sigh of relief. "Is that all? If you want children, we can adopt."

"It's not that simple."

He waited.

Nola Ruth bit her lip and forced out the words. "I had a baby, Cole, when I was seventeen years old. I gave her up."

He was stunned. "Why would you do such a thing? Wouldn't the father marry you?"

"He did marry me."

This was worse, much worse. Cole wasn't what anyone would call a practicing Catholic, but he would no more have changed his religion than he would deny his parentage. Nola Ruth would not be allowed to marry in the church. He looked at her downcast face. Tears welled up in her eyes. Cursing himself for his insensitivity, he led her into a darkened corner and pulled her into his arms. "Don't cry, darling. Just tell me. We'll get through it, no matter what."

And so she told him, leaving nothing out. She spoke of the intoxicating sexual pull that had drawn her down such a path. She described the illicit meetings, the mind-stealing power of their lovemaking, her family's disapproval, the makeshift wedding in the sleazy parlor of the justice of the peace in Nicholson, Mississippi, their humiliating discovery by her father, and the silent ride back to New Orleans. With her face pressed against his shoulder, her sobs muffled by the expensive wool of his coat, she told of the weeks that followed. Cold, lonely weeks spent in the isolation of her room, never once visited by either parent, boredom interrupted only by delivered meals, weeks where she waited for word from the man who'd promised to love her forever.

Finally, her father demanded her presence in the library. There, he told her that she would spend the rest of her confinement with her aunt Eugenie in Marshyhope Creek. She would spend the entire time inside the house so as not to embarrass her aunt. Arrangements had been made to take the child. She would return home when the ordeal was over. It had all happened according to plan, except for returning home. Not able to even think of going back to New Orleans, she'd stayed on in Marshyhope Creek and, later, met Cole.

When she finished, Cole's hands were clenched and his mouth was tight with rage. "Do you know what happened to the father of your child?" he asked.

She looked up at him, her eyes burning with intensity. "What do you think happens to a black man in the Deep South who has the effrontery to marry a white woman, Cole?"

When he spoke, his voice had a quality she had never heard before. "Nola," he said humbly, "if you'll have me, I promise to treat you with the utmost respect for the rest of our lives."

They were married the following week at St. Jude's, the small Catholic chapel in Frenchman's Cove. According to Father Raymond there was no impediment to a marriage in the church as long as Nola Ruth made a full confession. Her aunt Eugenie was the only attending member of the Beauchamp family. The Delacourtes were weak with relief. Despite Cole's notoriety, he had chosen well, a Southern woman of good family, from his own class and religion. They knew nothing, of course, of Nola's indiscretion.

Meanwhile, Cole's star burned brightly. He gained national approval for his role in *Wade v. Laurel, Mississippi*. Case after public case came his way. There wasn't a national newspaper or magazine that didn't carry his picture at least once a week. James Farmer, leader of the Congress of Racial Equality, requested his services, as did Floyd McKissick and a young minister named Jesse Jackson, who headed the Southern Christian Leadership Conference. His defense of civil rights leaders shook his popularity with those who would have preferred that he limit his practice to whites who could afford his services.

Public opinion did not concern Cole. He won cases, hundreds of them. That was enough, that and the interesting prospect of rising to Attorney General of the United States. Cole Delacourte was ambitious. If waiving his fees and if saving the skins of men with a cause was the price he had to pay, he would pay it.

Nola Ruth was the perfect wife. While she disagreed with his taking pro bono cases, in public she supported him unconditionally, never complaining of late nights or long, empty weekends when his work kept him in Washington, while she remained in Marshyhope Creek awaiting the birth of their eagerly anticipated first child.

Nola was a wonderful mother. The lessons she'd learned growing up in the Beauchamp household were put to good use. Years of silent disapproval and icy reprimands were thrown out the window. Libba was surrounded with all the glowing warmth and welcome stored inside Nola Ruth's sensitive heart.

Coleson Delacourte, Catholic, a generational Democrat, well-known attorney and civil rights advocate, was borne along on the tidal wave of change and opportunity that had begun in the early sixties, with a handsome, young, Catholic idealist who had occupied the Oval Office and promised a new beginning for America. For Cole, those years were a dream come true until that dream was shattered with dramatic and shuddering finality.

At first, the path of his career mirrored the dead president's policies. Cole believed that his successor would carry out Kennedy's plans. But Johnson couldn't get past Vietnam. His obsession for victory divided Congress and, eventually, the country. It put Cole and the man who would determine his future on opposite sides of the fence. Cole couldn't support Vietnam. It was a hopeless struggle and the death toll was terrifying.

Faces on the television screen haunted his sleep. They were boys' faces, mostly black, like the faces he'd grown up with. The South was unfairly represented in Vietnam. Injustice disturbed him, and this war, more than anything else, more than the accepted segregation still prevalent everywhere he looked, was unjust.

But Cole Delacourte was a powerful and popular political figure. The new president needed his endorsement for a second term. Cole thought long and hard but ultimately decided against it. He had his future to think about. His enemies would have a field day. Every liberal cause he'd supported, every controversial case he'd fought through the long and difficult sixties would have been for nothing. He wasn't naïve enough to believe that the schoolteacher from Texas would lose the election, but victory would have to come from someone else's endorsement. Johnson wouldn't be president forever, and when he stepped down Cole would still be a young man. There was time enough to return to Washington. Better to go home, spend time with his wife, watch his daughter grow.

Two days after his conversation with the president, the first letter came, typewritten on a manual machine with a faulty *"y."* Cole was more than a little shaken. Who could possibly have known about Nola Ruth's former psuedo-marriage? No demands accompanied the letter. He decided to ignore it. Three days later, another came. This time the words were handwritten, in block print, and accompanied with a photo of seventeen-year-old Nola Ruth Beauchamp standing beside a handsome, light-skinned black man, Anton Devereaux.

Cole stared curiously at the picture of his wife. He had never seen a photo of her as a young girl. When the Beauchamps refused to attend their wedding, Nola Ruth had written them off. She knew nothing of their lives and they knew nothing of hers, save what was written about her famous husband in the newspapers.

A candid photo rarely captured the essence of a person, but this one revealed something that captured Cole's interest. The young woman with the huge dark eyes and rounded cheeks was on the brink of laughter. She sparkled with a brimming, youthful vitality that Cole didn't recognize. His Nola was always pleasant and cultured and extremely accommodating, but she never sparkled.

He'd first noticed the lack in family pictures taken with Libba. Side by side, his two women were incredibly alike in figure and feature, but Libba glowed from within with a radiance that her mother couldn't compete with. The young woman whose hand clutched Anton Devereaux's arm so possessively had that same bright, inexplicable quality. Whatever had happened to Nola back in New Orleans had forever taken the luster from her face.

The next time, the letter came with explicit instructions. Endorse Lyndon Johnson's candidacy or the political career of Cole Delacourte was finished. Nola Ruth's annulment would become front-page news. The marriage alone would have posed no problem. The Catholic Church had assured Cole of that. It was his illusive nemesis's knowledge of her adopted child that swayed him. Blackmail was repugnant to Cole. Normally, he would have accepted the challenge, but this time there were others to consider. He couldn't forget Nola's face when she confessed her sordid tale all those years ago. And now there was Libba to consider as well.

After his less-than-enthusiastic public endorsement of the president who, in the end, decided against another term, Cole retired from politics and began his own practice in Marshyhope Creek. The golden years were over. He preferred small, noncontroversial cases, although he continued to take on needy clients. Slowly, he amassed a comfortable living. Life was good, but uninspired. There were moments of regret for the man he had been, the one who couldn't be bought. With them came the knowledge that Nola had been right from the beginning. A man with his future should not have married a woman with her past. Then he would look at her face, run his hands down the ivory-skinned length of her body, feel the blood-searing heat of his need and her answering passion, and know it could have turned out no other way.

Twenty-Two

Chloe turned around and looked over her shoulder into the mirror, adjusting the new denim skirt and sleeveless yellow top. Her hair was her own again, shiny straight and very blond. Last night she'd allowed her mother to trim off the black ends. Despite her protestations otherwise, she was nervous and more than a little concerned about making the right impression on her first day at school. At least she didn't have to walk in alone. Tess Hennessey was meeting her in front of the flagpole. Chloe wanted to go with Bailey, but he wasn't sure if he was going to show up at all.

The verdict was still out when it came to Bailey Jones. He fascinated and repelled her at the same time. She'd never known anyone who was allowed such freedom, and yet, in Bailey's case, it came with huge responsibilities. She definitely didn't want to trade places with him. His mother was dying and he could do nothing but make her as comfortable as possible and wait. It wasn't as if he was frightened about what would happen after she was gone. Bailey had been on his own for a long time.

"It's time, Chloe. You don't want to be late the first day," her mother called from the hallway.

Chloe slipped her feet into red mules, grabbed her backpack and ran downstairs. "I don't think I want to buy lunch today," she said. "I'll just grab an apple from the refrigerator."

Libby dug into her purse, producing three one dollar bills. "Take these, anyway. You might change your mind."

Chloe tucked them into her pocket. "Thanks, Mom."

Libby bit her lip. Her heart overflowed with love for this gamin-faced, difficult child. "Chloe, you've been a good sport about this, especially lately. If it doesn't work out for you, we'll figure something else out. Okay?"

Chloe nodded. "Okay. Let's go, Mom. We don't want to be late."

The green lawn surrounding the brick buildings of Marshyhope Creek's single high school milled with adolescents sporting bright new clothing, summer tans, tentative smiles and shoes not yet broken in. Boys and girls congregated in small groups segregated by race, laughing, talking loudly and animatedly gesturing. Libby's hand tightened on the steering wheel. What had she done? Had she been insane to think that Chloe, an outsider from California, could actually infiltrate one of these tightly knit groups and be accepted? Suddenly she felt ill. She turned to Chloe, words of apology forming on her lips.

Chloe stared out the window, eyes narrowed. Then her face lit with relief. "There's Tess, by the flagpole. You can let me out here."

"Are you sure, Chloe?" Libby whispered.

Chloe frowned at her mother. "Are you sick? You look really pale. Maybe you should go back home and lie down."

"I—I'm fine," stammered Libby. She leaned over to kiss Chloe's cheek. "Have a good day." She watched as more than a few heads turned to follow Chloe's progress across the courtyard. Resting her head against the window, she waited until Tess Hennessey and another dark-haired girl separated to include Chloe into their circle. Unable to stand the drama any longer, Libby pulled out onto the road and drove the rest of the way into town.

Perk's Open for Business sign hung in the window. Libby parked, grabbed her wallet and keys and walked inside. A bleary-eyed Verna Lee sat at the counter nursing a cup of coffee.

Libby sat down beside her. "What's new?" she asked.

Verna Lee threaded her fingers into her long curls and pulled them through. "This has been the longest week of my life. You probably already know they let my grandmother out on bail. Apparently they didn't think she was a flight risk."

"I should think not."

The black woman shook her head. "Don't be too sure. She's talking about going away, disappearing. She thinks she won't get a fair trial."

"Of course she will."

Verna Lee's yellow eyes flashed. "*You* know that, Libba Jane, and I know it, but we're talking about an old black woman who's lived through some tough times. It shouldn't surprise anyone to learn that my grandmother doesn't trust our judicial system."

"Does she have a choice? Where would she go?"

Verna Lee sagged against the counter and pressed her palm against her forehead. "I don't know."

"What about you? Do you trust the judicial system?"

Verna Lee's lower lip pursed. "To tell you the truth, Libba Jane, the only one I trust is your daddy."

"That's not a bad place to start. Drusilla's out on bail, isn't she?"

"For the time being. I just wish—"

Libby waited but the woman didn't finish. "What?" Libby prodded her gently.

Verna Lee shrugged. "It's nothing. It's just that I feel very much alone. Some people are never here when you need them." She laughed bitterly. "That says something, doesn't it?"

Privately, Libby agreed with her, but she kept thoughts of Cliff Jackson to herself. She slipped her arm around Verna Lee's shoulders. "How about dinner? It's Chloe's first day of school. She'll torture us with details about who wore what and who said this or that until you're so confused you won't be able to think about this for a while.''

"Dinner?" Verna Lee stared at her. "At your house?" She shook her head. "I don't think so, but thanks for the invitation."

"We could do lunch," Libby suggested.

"I stay open for lunch. It's my busiest time."

Libby shouldered her purse. "Suit yourself. It seems to me that you could use a friend."

Verna laid a placating hand on her arm. "I appreciate your offer, Libba Jane. Really I do. It's just not the right time. I'm sorry."

Libby studied the black woman. Verna Lee was lovely and scared and very proud. "Don't worry about it," she said. "Another time, maybe."

Verna Lee nodded. "Maybe."

Outside again, Libby looked at her watch. It wasn't even nine o'clock in the morning and a wet September heat had already blanketed the bay. Praying that the air-conditioning in the EPA office had kicked in, she drove down the street toward the dock. If all had gone as planned, Russ's meeting was scheduled for tonight.

She heard their voices before she stepped out on the street. His was low and measured. Hers, high, strident, close to hysterical. Both were obviously furious. Libby stepped into the fray. Russ was seated behind his desk. Tracy stood near the door.

"Good morning," Libby said brightly. She looked from Russ to Tracy, once more making a mental note of the woman's clear gray eyes. "Am I interrupting?"

"No," Russ said bluntly. "She was just leaving."

Two bright spots of color dotted Tracy's cheeks. Her eyes glittered. "Hello, Libba Jane. What do you think of a man who refuses to take financial responsibility for his own daughter?"

He cut her off. "Did you think of that one all by yourself, Tracy, or did you swim along the bottom with your mouth open?"

"I can't believe I ever thought you were a gentleman."

"I can't believe you would use Tess as leverage to get more money from me," he countered. "She's a child, not to be used for purposes of blackmail. Support has nothing to do with visitation. Besides, the issue has already been settled legally. Your own daddy couldn't get any more from me than you already do. If you need more money, get yourself a job."

"How can I work when I have Tess?" she snapped. "I'm a mother."

"So is Libba and she's worked since her daughter was born, along with the majority of the American work force, which you would know if you ever picked up a newspaper."

"Really?" The spots of color on Tracy's cheeks deepened. "Well, bully for Libba Jane and all the other superwomen in America." She picked up her purse. "I wasn't raised to work, Russ. You knew that when you married me."

"The circumstances are different. You're a single mother. You have one child and she's in school most of the day. I'm not asking you to leave a baby. Hell, I'm not even asking you to work if you don't want to, just live within your means like the rest of the world. You might *like* working, maybe find some purpose to your life, besides Tess. You might even meet someone and find some happiness. How are you gonna do that holed up in your daddy's big white house all day?"

"One venture into marriage was disaster enough for me," Tracy said primly. She nodded at Libby. "Good day, Libba Jane."

Libby waited until Tracy's steps died away on the boardwalk. Then she turned to Russ, her eyes wide and amused.

"My goodness. I had no idea she was such a drama queen. Her talents are wasted here in the Creek."

He laughed, pushed his chair away from the desk and walked around it to stand in front of her. "She always wants more money. Her daddy spoiled her. She's thirty-six years old with nothing to show for it except a useless college degree that's as untouched as the day she got it. She's smart enough, but her sense of entitlement makes it hard for her to associate money with working. She's undisciplined and mentally scattered, hardly employee material. Tess gives her an excuse to harass me."

Libby stared at him. "This can't be good for you, Russ. How's your blood pressure?"

"There isn't much I can do about it. She's got my daughter."

Libby folded her arms and looked at the floor.

"I know that look," he said. "What's on your mind?"

"It seems to me you can do a lot about it."

Russ frowned. "How?"

"Don't allow yourself to get so upset. You said you have a legal agreement. Stick to it. Stop arguing. Be logical and brief and mature. Don't allow the manipulation. When you feel yourself losing it, tell her you'll get back to her later."

He was silent for a long minute. Libby wondered if she'd gone too far.

Suddenly he smiled. "Where did you get to be so smart?"

She groaned. "I've spent my purgatory in the D.A.'s office in Ventura County watching lawyers mediate between angry parents."

"Good Lord. I'm sorry."

"That's behind me for the time being." She changed the subject. "I wanted to know how long the meeting will be tonight and if there's anything specific you want me to cover."

"Just be up front. Explain why there's a fishing moratorium and what you're looking for. You might give them some background on some of the side effects of PCBs in drinking water and fish. Allow about a half hour for your talk and then some time for questions. Anything less than that and they'll feel it wasn't worth the trip."

"I think I can manage that."

His face changed. "You're beautiful," he said unexpectedly. "I don't know if I've ever told you that, but you are. More so than when you were a kid."

"Thank you," she said.

"I'd like to kiss you, Libba," he said softly. "In fact, I'd like to do a whole lot more than that. Will you let me?"

He'd tossed her the ball. It was a new strategy for him. Libby had been perfectly willing to assume the subservient role, justifying her response by claiming he'd swept her off her feet. But he'd pulled the rug out from under her, forced her to step up to the plate and stand by her actions as an equal participant. She stared at him, lost in a quandary of surprise and indecision.

"What's the matter, Libba Jane? Cat got your tongue?"

She shook her head.

"Say something. I'm not gonna jump your bones unless you want me to."

"That's—" Her voice cracked. She cleared her throat and tried again. "That's just it."

"What, sweetheart?"

"What if I want it now and not later, or what if you do and then later don't?"

"You're confusing me."

She tried again. "What if one of us changes our mind and the other doesn't?"

"That's life, Libba Jane," he said gently. "No one knows how he's gonna think or feel in ten years. It's a crapshoot. You just do what you feel is right and see where the roll takes you."

"That philosophy didn't work for me before."

"For me, neither," Russ agreed. "But would you change it now that you have Chloe?"

"I'd change a lot of it."

"No, you wouldn't. If Eric Richards hadn't come into your life you wouldn't have that gorgeous blue-eyed spitfire of a daughter."

She almost said what she was thinking, but decided against it. She would not open the subject of blue eyes with Russ.

He reached out and took her hand, pulling her closer.

His throat was brown from working on the trawlers. He smelled like salt and soap and sun. This was better, much better. She wasn't comfortable being the initiator.

He bent his head. His lips touched her ear, his breath stirring the wisps of hair at her temple. "I asked you a question. What's your answer?"

She closed her eyes. "A kiss," she whispered. "A kiss would be nice. You always were a good—"

His mouth, warm and firm and assured, stopped her words. It wasn't a long kiss, but it was long enough for her to know the answer to the rest of his question. She wanted Russ Hennessey, more than she'd wanted him all those years ago when he'd first sweet-talked her out of her virginity. Her hands sifted through his hair. She twined her right leg around his left and pressed against him.

"Jeez, Libba Jane." His voice was air-filled, shaky. He held her away from him, searching her face. Her eyes were brown-black, the pupils and irises all one color. Her mouth was soft and kiss-swollen. He swore softly and dropped his hands. "You better mean this."

She stared back at him. "I need you to promise me something."

His eyes narrowed. "What's that?"

"If we do this, you can't do it with anyone else."

"What's that supposed to mean?"

"You heard me," she said calmly. "If we have sex, I want you to stop having it with anyone else."

"Are you accusing me of something, Libba Jane?"

"No."

"That's all? No explanation."

"Just say yes or no, Russ. It doesn't require anything beyond that. If you say yes, I'll believe you. If it's no, we can leave it at that."

"Negotiating terms is a hell of a way to begin a relationship."

"We're not beginning a relationship. We already have one, or we did," she amended. "We're discussing whether you're willing to be sexually faithful. This is a small town. We both have children. It can't be any other way for me."

"There won't be anyone else. If there was, I wouldn't be here with you."

"When you don't want me anymore or if you decide you want someone else, you have to tell me before it happens. I don't want to be made a fool of."

His voice gentled. "What happened to you, Libba?"

"I grew up. Fairy tales are for children."

"You didn't just grow up, honey. You've been emotionally beaten and you have the scars to prove it."

Libby didn't answer.

"Do you want to tell me about it, tomorrow, over dinner? I'll take you out for the best crab cakes on either side of the bay. And then we'll talk about telling our girls about us."

She wanted to, more than anything, if only for the look on his face when she told him that he was the one who'd done the beating. But she wouldn't. The damage had already been done and he couldn't take it back. "Dinner sounds great," she said, "but let's keep the conversation light."

"I'll pick you up at seven."

It was while driving back to her office that Libby had her

first serious doubts, and every one of them had Chloe's name on it. She sighed, summoning her stiffest resolve. Thirty-seven was too young to throw in the towel on the rest of her life. Chloe would have to adjust.

Twenty-Three

Cole Delacourte leaned back in his well-padded chair and fingered his notes. The courtroom in Salisbury where he'd practiced for more than three decades had changed enormously. Court reporters had replaced stenographers, typewriters had given way to computers, and an efficient air conditioner kept the rooms at a constant and comfortable sixty-eight degrees. A different type of attorney now walked the halls. She was usually female or black or both. Jurors lounged about in sandals and T-shirts, carrying laptops and cellular phones, and smoking was no longer allowed in the main building.

There was no doubt about it. Things had changed and not necessarily for the better. Cole missed the old days. There had been a grandeur to the bench that he could no longer find. It had disappeared along with the mildew when the new air conditioner was installed. He missed waking the heat-stunned jury with an eloquent opening. He missed the deference of his secretary and the way she would knock softly on his door every hour to ask if he would like his coffee or iced tea freshened. He missed the hum of portable fans set up in the four corners of the courtroom. He missed the grateful looks on the faces of the court when he asked for an early dismissal on account of the weather.

He should have retired. Others his age had. There were few lawyers in Maryland or Virginia who worked beyond the age of sixty-five. If he'd listened to Nola Ruth he wouldn't be sitting here now watching a mere child make her case against a woman older than he was who'd acted on her conscience and done society a favor.

The bailiff addressed the courtroom. "Please rise. Court is in session. Judge Quentin Wentworth presiding." Cole sighed, stood and helped Drusilla to her feet.

"What have you to say for yourself, Mrs. Washington?" the judge asked.

"Nuthin' much, suh. I ain' to blame for that chile's mizry."

"What about the bruises on the infant's neck?"

"I don' know nuthin' 'bout those."

The judge frowned. "Are the parents here?"

Cole stood. "Yes, Your Honor." He acknowledged a young black couple in the last row. The woman looked tired and confused. She clung tightly to her husband's hand.

"Are they pressing charges?"

"No, Your Honor," Cole assured him. "They have the utmost respect for Ms. Washington's midwifery, as does Dr. Balieu." He looked across the aisle at the assistant district attorney. "He is ready to be called as a witness."

"That won't be necessary." The mention of a respected friend and family doctor reassured the judge as Cole knew it would. Martin Balieu would never countenance murder, no matter what the circumstances.

The judge stood. "I'll read the transcripts in my office and render my decision. Court dismissed until tomorrow. Cole, if I could have a moment with you in my chambers."

Cole frowned. Now what? He rubbed the back of his neck and watched the courtroom empty. Picking up the envelope that contained his copy of the newly submitted pictorial evidence and several sworn statements, he said goodbye to Drusilla and her granddaughter, assuring them he would call later in the day. Then he walked back through the courtroom and down the hall into Judge Quentin Wentworth's chambers. He smiled at the secretary. "Mornin', Norma Rae."

"Good morning, Cole." She gestured toward the door. "Go right in. He's expecting you. I'll bring y'all some iced tea in a minute."

Immediately, Cole felt better. Quentin was old school. He wouldn't suffer a bright new administrative assistant who refused to bring him coffee.

Wentworth, a corpulent, red-faced man vain enough to part his hair on the side of his head and comb it over his balding dome, sat behind his desk. The shades were drawn and a fan hummed from the far corner. "C'mon in, Cole, and sit down." He pulled out a bottle of Jack Daniel's. "Care for a drink?"

Cole sat down and stretched his legs. "I wouldn't say no."

"You like it neat, if I remember."

Cole nodded.

"Don't worry about the Washington case," Wentworth said. He poured two glasses half full and set one in front of Cole. "I'm declaring the charges dropped."

Cole's eyebrows rose. "Why?"

"I would have thought it was obvious."

"Not to me."

"It's a high-profile case and not the kind we need to make the papers."

"I don't understand."

"How many anglers do you think we'll see if something like this gets out? How many small businesses will be ruined? Who'll want to buy fruit and vegetables from our farms and orchards?"

"What has that got to do with Drusilla Washington murdering a deformed baby?"

"C'mon, Cole. No one could tell where the deformities ended and the strangling began. Doc Balieu hasn't seen anything like it in all his years of practice. That's good enough for me."

Cole thought of Libba. "Maybe we need the exposure."

"Now I'm the one who doesn't understand."

"Maybe we should make this so big every environmental expert and every newspaper in the States sends someone here. For God's sake, Quentin, we live here. Our children and grandchildren live here. What if we're being poisoned?"

"That's ridiculous."

"Is it? You put everything together, same as I did."

"Now, Cole, this isn't one of your human rights violation cases. This is too damn dangerous for you to be terrifying people when it could amount to nothing."

"Wouldn't you rather be sure?"

"I am sure, Cole."

Cole Delacourte finished his drink and stood. "Thanks for the refreshment, Quentin. I'll be in touch."

"I'm dropping the case, Cole."

Cole nodded. "Mrs. Washington and her granddaughter will be relieved. I'll tell them right away."

He left the courtroom and walked down the tree-lined street to a renovated old brick building set back beneath shady poplars. He greeted the woman at the front desk and proceeded directly to his office. He sat down in his chair and sighed. In the old days, before Lily retired, there would have been ham and cheese on rye and a fresh cup of coffee on his desk. His new secretary was a different breed entirely. She'd frozen him silent the first time he'd asked her to order up a sandwich. That wasn't her job, she'd informed him. Maybe it wasn't. The funny thing was, more often than not, he'd ordered sandwiches for Lily when she stayed late. Poured her coffee, too. Yes, times had changed.

Settling back into his chair, he pulled out the pictures, trying to focus. He frowned, searched his pockets for his reading glasses and put them on.

The film was color, thirty-five millimeter, newly developed by the district attorney's office and sent over for his perusal. It was the first time he'd seen the pictures. Cole's eyes widened. Good God! He blinked, stared and blinked again. Just before his face paled and his stomach began to twist, there was the strangest feeling in his chest. Could this really be a human child? Had the attractive, dark-skinned woman sitting in the back of his courtyard actually given birth to this…this creature? Bile rose in his throat. He swallowed, reached for his water glass, only to find it empty. Hastily pushing back his chair he ran for the bathroom and heaved up the remains of his stomach. Shaking, he turned on the faucet and splashed cold water over his forehead and cheeks. Weakness washed over him. His legs buckled. He sat down on the toilet seat and dried his face.

Cole Delacourte had seen nearly every abomination there was to see in his three decades serving the public, but this one was different. This one involved a child whose mother had given birth less than two miles from his own front door. Terrifying thoughts flickered through his mind: the red globular masses on the baby's chest and abdomen, the high incidence of leukemia, the mutated crabs Libba Jane was so worried about. It could be coincidental, of course. Quentin could be right. There was no telling where a family of sharecroppers had been or whether the crabs were directly affected by something in the local waters. It could just as likely have been pesticides dumped into the bay much farther north where the farmers polluted the Susquehanna.

Chloe looked around the crowded lunchroom at the sea of unfamiliar faces hunched over trays at the long, banquet-style tables. It wasn't much different than it was at home, she thought, watching the cliques gather and settle in, trade jibes, conversation and gossip as they wolfed down whatever they could in the thirty minutes allotted for the noon break. Skylar Taft and her group of girls were in the center of the action. Already acknowledged as queen of the in-crowd, she held court at one of the noisier tables.

Tess caught Chloe's eye and beckoned to her. Chloe pretended not to see her. While she wouldn't have minded trading impressions of the morning with Tess, she couldn't stomach Skylar for lunch. She glanced around the room, her eyes lingering occasionally on a straight, dark-haired head, and then moving on when she saw that it wasn't Bailey. Where was he? He'd told her he might not make the first day, but she hadn't believed him. No one missed the first day of school.

Someone jostled her from behind. Tess's exasperated voice sounded above the din in the lunchroom. "I've been waving to you for five minutes. Didn't you see me?"

"I was looking for Bailey."

"Bailey Jones?" Tess drew back in horror. "Oh, Chloe," she wailed, "please don't."

"Don't what?"

"Bailey isn't a good person for you to be around, especially when no one knows you yet."

"I like him."

Tess's eyes widened.

"Not that way," Chloe assured her. "He's a friend. I wonder why he's missing the first day."

"Bailey comes and goes as he pleases," Tess explained. "You don't have to worry about him. He can take care of himself. Besides, he won't thank you for feeling sorry for him. Bailey Jones can be the meanest thing when he wants to be." She pronounced it *thang.* "I can't believe you like him." Her voice turned conciliatory. "C'mon, Chloe. I saved you a seat at Skylar's table. When people see you there, it won't matter who you're friends with. It'll be okay. You'll see."

Chloe relented and followed Tess, who picked her way around chairs and over backpacks through the crowded room to where Skylar sat with her friends. "Why is it *Skylar's* table?" she asked.

Tess shrugged impatiently. "Why are you always asking *why?* Some things just are. It's easier that way." She pasted a bright artificial smile on her face. "Hi, y'all. Look who I brought."

Skylar moved over. "Where have you been all morning?" she asked Chloe. "We looked for you at snack."

"I was working on my locker combination," replied Chloe. She was very aware of the glances in her direction. They were curious, considering glances, neither hostile nor friendly.

"Who's your partner?"

"Marsha Bradbury."

Skylar nodded. "Marsha's all right. She's a swimmer so you won't see much of her."

Chloe wasn't hungry. She looked at the clock. Three more hours before she could go home. It would be nine o'clock in the morning in California. She would be checking over her schedule with Sharon Simms and Casey Reilly, to see if they shared any classes. They would be planning whose house to go to after school and which clubs they would join. Chloe would be signing up for auditions for the fall play.

Her vision blurred. Horrified, she blinked back tears. She would not cry in front of Skylar Taft. They could pull out her fingernails and she wouldn't give them the satisfaction of a single tear.

Suddenly, for an instant, the room went silent. A single titter broke the stillness and then the hum of conversation continued. Confused, Chloe looked around. Her glance settled on the thin, ragged figure sauntering defiantly toward the cafeteria line. *Bailey.* Their eyes met and held. He looked terrible. Chloe's heart sank. She smiled tentatively and waved, but he turned away. She tried to stand, but Tess's hand pressed down hard on her knee.

"Don't do it, Chloe," she whispered. "He doesn't want you to say anything."

"I don't care," muttered Chloe, furious at both Tess and Bailey.

Tess looked her full in the face, her brown eyes dark with

worry. "If everyone starts talking about you and saying awful things, you'll care."

"He's my friend."

"That's why he ignored you. Think about it," Tess pleaded.

Chloe frowned. "You're not just saying this, are you? You're really worried about me."

"Incredibly worried."

"Why?"

Tess smiled shyly. "I like you. You're funny and interesting. I don't want you to hate it here. Bailey Jones isn't your only friend, Chloe."

"Wow," Chloe said, completely disarmed. "Thanks."

Tess sighed and bit into her apple. "Just don't do anything stupid."

Chloe looked at the clock again. Somehow, she would find Bailey and make him talk to her.

Later that afternoon, Cole found Libby and Chloe in the kitchen. "What a nice surprise," he said, kissing his daughter's cheek. "You haven't been home early all week."

Libby licked ice cream off the back of her spoon. "I wanted to see how Chloe's day went."

Cole poured himself a glass of iced tea and sat down at the table. "How did it go, Chloe?"

"Better than I expected," Chloe replied. "The teachers are okay and the kids are nice enough." She stood up to rinse her plate and stack it in the dishwasher. "I already have homework, so I guess I'll go upstairs and start on it."

Cole watched her leave. "She's a winner, Libba Jane. I'm sure you know that."

"Thanks, Daddy." Libby reached for a glass and held it under the faucet. "I really should be getting back. I have that meeting with the watermen tonight. I only stopped in for a minute to check on Chloe." She lifted the glass to her lips.

Instantly, Cole was on his feet, his face wild, his arm extended, moving faster than he'd moved in twenty years to knock it from her hand. The glass shattered into a thousand sparkling shards, covering the counters and kitchen sink.

"Daddy! What on earth—?" Libby's face was frozen into a horrified mask.

Her father lifted a shaking hand to his head and wet his lips. They tasted like steel wool. "Forgive me. I'm not myself. I think I'll lie down." He rested his hand on Libby's shoulder. "Use the bottled water for drinking, honey. You can never be too careful."

Libby's eyes were huge in her chalk-white face. She had never once seen her father lose control. It shook her to the core. "Are you all right, Daddy?" she whispered.

He nodded. "Run along now. I'm going to spend some time with your mother."

Libby backed out the door and walked slowly to her car. She rolled down the windows and started the engine. The sun beat down on the summer-baked earth and the humidity was so great it was hard to breathe. For the first time, the home where she was born had brought no respite. Something significant and unpleasant had happened. Her father was afraid. For Libby, who'd relied on his cool judgment for a good part of her life, the very idea was terrifying. She wanted nothing more than to put whatever distance she could between herself and the place where she had been.

She slowed down at the bridge, turned right and drove to the crest of the small hill, where she parked, climbed out of the car and looked down on the lawn of Hennessey House.

Russ, a football under his arm, was yelling at Tess, who stood across the lawn, poised to catch. "Hike," Russ yelled, lifting the football above his head. "No, not that way." He waved Tess in the opposite direction. "Left, left. That's it. Atta girl. Go for the pass." The pigskin sailed through the air, a perfect arc against the cerulean blue of the sky.

Tess ran backward and to the left, her arms raised in anticipation of the ball. It dropped into her grasp as smoothly as butter across a hot skillet. With a delighted chuckle, she charged across the lawn, running wildly, weaving first right and then left to avoid Russ's tackle. He caught her, of course, but not until she'd maneuvered her way down what would have been a good many yards on a real football field.

From her vantage point on the rise, Libby could hear the girl's shriek of glee and Russ's lower, deeper laugh. A lump rose in her throat. She ached for Chloe, filled with regret for her own troubled marriage and the broken home in which she'd raised her child. She wondered, once again, if she had done the right thing by moving back to Marshyhope Creek.

They were having such fun. Libby knew she should turn around and leave them to their bonding, but she started down the hill, anyway. Russ, caught in a tangle of legs and long hair, didn't see her until she was standing directly over him. Separating the curtain of hair that obstructed his vision, he looked up and grinned. ''We were just about to get a burger. Care to join us?''

''Where were you going?''

''To the drive-through. Tess wants a burger.''

Tess lifted her head from Russ's shoulder and rolled over to lie spread-eagled on the grass. ''You can bring Chloe if you want.''

Libby smiled. ''Who could refuse such an invitation? I'll call Chloe and see if she wants to come.'' Maybe they would have their dinner with the girls, after all.

Later, in the air-conditioned coolness of the Dairy Queen, between bites of her cheeseburger, Chloe eyed Russ dangling fries into his salted ketchup. ''What was my mother like as a little girl?'' she asked him.

Libby stopped chewing. ''What brought this on?''

Chloe shrugged. "You don't talk much about when you were small."

"I don't remember much," Libby replied. "Why don't you ask your grandparents?"

"Because they didn't know you like Russ did. You were friends from the beginning, right?"

"What do you want to know?" Russ cut in.

Chloe tilted her head to the side, considering the matter seriously. "Was she smart?"

"Very."

"Was she pretty?"

"Chloe," Libby protested.

"I know you were pretty, Mom," Chloe explained. "I've seen the pictures. I want to know whether people back then thought you were pretty." She looked at Russ. "Well?"

He nodded. "She was pretty."

Chloe threw down her French fry in disgust. "You're no help. Can't you give me more than that?"

"If you wanted a story, you should have told me," Russ answered agreeably, settling into the subject. "I just happen to remember the first time I ever really spoke to your mother. It was the morning after a rain and I was late getting out of bed. I was on my way when I heard the school bell ring. I started to run. When I got to within fifty yards of the playground, I saw her. I already knew she was a Delacourte from school. She was bending down, looking at something. When I got closer, I could see that she was picking up earthworms from the sidewalk and putting them back in the grass. She heard me coming and stood up. "You can't walk through here," she said, her face as fierce as she could make it. "I'm not through." When I got closer, I could see she'd been crying. There must have been a hundred squashed worms lying there on the ground."

"What did you do?" Tess asked breathless with anticipation.

Russ popped a fry into his mouth, chewed, sipped his

Coke and swallowed. "I laid my books down on the ground and helped her rescue the rest of those worms."

Chloe looked at her mother and then back at Russ. They were staring at each other in a way that made her uncomfortable. Russ's face was expressionless. Nothing she could make out there, but her mother's mouth was soft and her eyes were round and very bright. Chloe recognized that look and she didn't like it.

"Both of us had to miss recess and write fifty sentences about the importance of arriving at school on time," Russ finished.

Libby laughed and Chloe relaxed. Everything was all right. She must have imagined her mother's look. She was being overly sensitive.

They were down to the last runny spoonfuls of chocolate sundae when the door opened, framing Shelby Sloane's flame-red head. Immediately following her was Fletcher's balding blond one. He scanned the room and his face lit up when he spied Russ and Libby. "Hey, y'all! Got any room over there for two more?" Taking his wife by the arm, he pulled her across the floor.

"Evenin', Fletcher, Shelby." Russ extended his hand. Fletcher pumped it enthusiastically. "Pull up some chairs."

Chloe rolled her eyes. It was going to be one long dinner now that the Sloanes were here. She turned to her mother, prepared to raise her eyebrows in a signal they both knew, when she stopped, stunned, her disapproval forgotten.

Libby's mouth was no longer soft, and the slanted, angry pools leveled in her friend's direction bore no resemblance to her mother's eyes. Chloe glanced back at Shelby. What she saw confused her even more. From chest to forehead, Shelby's fair, freckled skin was stained a wine-dark, self-conscious red and she looked nervous. She hadn't said a word since entering the Dairy Queen, a circumstance every bit as unusual as her scarlet cheeks and the dagger looks exchanged by the two women.

"We don't really have time to visit," Libby said tightly. "Chloe has plans."

"Aw, c'mon, Libba Jane," Fletcher protested. "Just because you girls are in a spat shouldn't ruin a fine evenin'. Russ and I haven't had a chance to talk in a while."

Libby stood. "I really need to get Chloe back home."

Russ pushed back his chair and stood. "I'll drive the ladies home. We'll get together another time, Fletch. It was nice seeing you again."

"Libby." Shelby dug her fists into her waist. "I can't believe you're still mad at me. You know I'm harmless. I didn't mean anything. I never do."

"I don't want to discuss this now," Libby said coldly. "If you've forgotten my phone number, you know where I live." She turned away.

Shelby reached out and gripped her arm. "I've called every day this week. You always have an excuse. What do I have to do? Make an appointment?"

Russ broke in. "The girls and I will wait in the car while you ladies settle up."

"Maybe I should come with you," Fletcher suggested. "Never did want to interfere in a catfight."

"There isn't going to be any fight," Libby said. "I'm going home with Russ. Shelby and I will talk tomorrow."

"When?" Shelby asked.

Libby held the redhead's glance. Shelby's cheeks burned even darker, but she didn't flinch.

"Possibly during lunch. I may have some time then."

They drove home in air-conditioned silence. Tess sat in the car while Russ walked Libby and Chloe to the door.

With a hurried "thank you," Chloe raced inside the house to answer the ringing phone.

Russ chewed the inside of his lip, pondered the question that had bothered him since encountering Shelby and Fletch, and decided to go for it. "Maybe you shouldn't be so hard on Shelby."

"I beg your pardon?"

"It's not my pardon you should be begging. Your friend is miserable. Care to talk about it?"

"No."

"It doesn't have anything to do with me, does it?"

"No," Libby lied.

"Because if it does," he continued, "I'd have to wonder why it matters enough for you to risk a friendship that used to be almost as important to you as your family."

Libby opened the door and stepped inside. "Don't flatter yourself," she said coolly. "I'll change clothes and meet you in town for the meeting."

He turned back to the car. Something was bothering her. He couldn't tell if it had anything to do with Shelby's need to prowl. Not that he'd ever considered Shelby Chartier seriously, not even years ago when they both were single. He had Libba and she'd been enough for him. Hell, she'd have been enough for any man. Still was.

The problem was that he no longer had her. He didn't have anybody, and Shelby had made it plain that she was available and that she wanted him. She was aggressive and sexy as hell, but she was married to Fletcher. Russ made a point of staying away from married women. There was something unclean about sleeping with another man's wife.

He dropped Tess at home, backed out of the driveway, rolled the window down and reached for his cigarettes. Funny how pressure always brought the craving. He could feel it in his gut, the slight tension, the tightening, and then the old familiar pull that he couldn't seem to lick. He'd tried once or twice to quit and then he'd be hit with a job unlike any he'd done before and he'd be right back at it.

Back on the porch of Hennessey House, he stubbed out his third cigarette and looked at the house, at the wide expanse of lush green lawn and the quiet lapping of the bay against the shore.

He hadn't counted on the fishing ban. Although he wasn't

in danger of starving and Hennessey House was paid for long before, he couldn't last forever without an income. Damn his unholy luck. It wasn't with him in love or money. He thought of Mitch and was instantly ashamed. Unlike his brother, he was alive. He had a place to live and plenty of money in the bank. Now, if the tests from the lab were clear, he'd buy a bottle of the best champagne on the coast and celebrate.

Twenty-Four

Chloe looked at the sky and pedaled the bike furiously down the old pony path by the water. It wouldn't be dark for another hour or so, and with any luck, Bailey would drive her home. She refused to think about the possibility of his not being there. He'd scared her earlier in the school cafeteria. She could see it in his face. Something was terribly wrong, something much worse than the amused stares of his classmates.

She turned into the woods and prayed that the rutted, bumpy path wouldn't pop one of her tires. It was darker here in the shelter of the southern pine forest, the faint rays of a setting sun barely dappling the shadowed stillness. Only extreme worry would have coaxed Chloe into this dark place devoid of human company. She knew nothing about the woods, deliberately pushing aside thoughts of bugs and wild creatures. She concentrated on reaching Bailey's trailer, praying he would be there cooking up appetizing smells while Lizzie waited patiently on her bench outside. What did they do when the weather was bad for days?, she wondered. Bailey would paint in his shed, but Lizzie would be trapped inside the trailer, breathing the stale air of the single room. Chloe shuddered. Of all her senses, the least she would be willing to spare was her sight.

She had never come on her own like this, so late in the day, on a bike. She hadn't told anyone, either. "Please," she prayed, "just let me make it there. I'll figure out the rest later."

She coasted into the clearing, stopping the bike by dragging both feet on the ground, and sat back on the seat. She stared in dismay at the Jones's trailer. It was completely dark. No one was home. Yet, how was that possible? Lizzie never went anywhere. She looked around and sighed with relief. Bailey's truck was parked near the shed, nearly hidden by trees.

"Hello," she called out. "It's Chloe. Is anybody home?"

A bird circled in the sky above her head and two squirrels scampered across a tree branch.

"Bailey," she called again. "Where are you?"

Again, nothing but silence.

She climbed off the bike and propped it against the picnic table. It was too late to bicycle home. She would have to wait for Bailey. She sat down on Lizzie's bench and leaned back against the trailer. It shifted against her back as if someone had moved from one side to another. She jumped up and pounded on the door. "Bailey, it's Chloe. Answer the door."

"Go away."

She frowned. It was Bailey's voice, faint and raspy, but definitely his. She knocked again. "Open the door, Bailey. Something's wrong. I know it is."

"It's none of your business. Go away."

She tried another approach. "C'mon, Bailey. It's dark and I rode my bike. I don't know the way back."

"I can't help you. Go away."

Now she was really frightened. The Bailey she knew would never let her ride home through the dark. "Please, Bailey," she whimpered. "I'm scared. Where's Lizzie?"

She heard him curse and fumble with the lock. Finally the door opened. She took one look at his face, at the stubble on his chin, at his torn shirt, the scratch on his face and the bloodshot whites of his eyes, and stepped back. "What's the matter with you?" she whispered.

He shook his head. "Nothing."

"Where's your mother?"

He laughed wildly, insanely.

Chloe felt the blood pound in her left temple. Suddenly, it was very important to find Lizzie. "Where's your mother, Bailey?"

His hand snaked out and grabbed her wrist. "You want to know where my mother is?" He pulled her through the door. "I'll show you."

She stood quietly for a minute, waiting for her eyes to adjust to the dark room. She was terrified, but every instinct told her to remain quiet. Bailey wouldn't hurt her. Bailey was her friend.

Gradually, her vision returned. Everything looked in its place, neat counters, closets closed, dishes clean and drying in the sink. Lizzie Jones lay on a narrow cot beneath a light blanket, facing the wall.

"Is she sleeping?" Chloe whispered.

A ragged cry burst from Bailey's lips.

Chloe tiptoed to the bed and bent over the woman. She was very still. Too still. Tentatively, Chloe reached out and touched her cheek. It was cold. Chloe had never seen a dead person, but she knew without a doubt that Lizzie Jones was dead.

With her eyes swimming in tears, she turned back to the boy. "Oh, Bailey," she said, "I'm so sorry."

He fell against her, his sides heaving, his breathing harsh. Instinctively her arms wrapped around him and together they slid to the floor. He buried his face in her neck and sobbed while she soothed him with senseless words and silly, half-remembered songs and trite platitudes until her voice was raw and her legs cramped and the violent racking of his body settled into soft hiccups.

She knew she needed help, but Chloe had scanned the

walls and counters. There wasn't a phone in sight and Bailey was in no condition to drive his truck. She desperately wanted her mother or her grandfather and vowed never to go anywhere again without telling someone where she was going.

Libby decided on a knee-length skirt, pumps and a sleeveless linen blouse. A power suit in the midst of an unemployed town wouldn't be appreciated. She wore her shoulder-length hair parted on the side with the layers falling against her cheeks, again a simple, wholesome style that spoke of girl-next-store, I'm-on-your-side sympathies.

Russ met her at the library door. She was fifteen minutes early and already every seat was taken. Her audience was mostly made up of men, but there were a few women represented, evidence of progress along the Chesapeake. Someone had donated coffee. The rich smell of chicory wafted through the room.

Libby was nervous. It wasn't often that so much was at stake. People became emotional when it came to their livelihoods and rightly so. She hoped for understanding and some patience. More than that would be a gift.

She moved throughout the room, greeting familiar faces, making her way to the podium where a microphone had been set up. Russ had been thorough. Libby ignored the mike and cleared her throat. "Hi, everyone," she began. Her voice was low and well pitched and clear.

Immediately the room went silent.

"Thanks for coming out tonight. It's good to see you here. I hope what I have to say tonight is worthwhile." She'd decided against jokes. It wasn't the occasion and she wasn't good at pulling them off. She would offer them the facts, get straight to the point and let the chips fall where they may. "I'd like to talk about the ban on blue crab and oyster harvesting and shad fishing. I'll start by telling you worst and best case and what we can do if it comes to that.

Then we can talk about how to keep those of you fed and clothed with your bills paid until this is behind us.''

Russ stood in the back of the room, his stance casual, arms crossed, an expression of polite interest on his face. He was analyzing the mood of the room and at the same time watching Libba disarm the crowd. A pretty woman went a long way toward getting a hard-living man to accept the inevitable without grumbling. In fact, she was so pretty it was hard for him to concentrate on her words. He wondered if it was the same for every male in the room or if he was the only one she had this effect on. Willing himself to pay attention, he focused on the clock above her head and listened.

"Mercury poisoning is a problem," she said. "As you know, it isn't a new problem, but for the first time people are eating more fish than meat. One out of two people who eat swordfish, albacore and tuna have mercury levels that are higher than they should be to maintain good health. Pregnant women are particularly at risk because we know mercury moves from the placenta to the fetus almost immediately. This is considered to be a substantial risk, enough to make it illegal not to mount warnings near the fish markets of all grocery stores and on the menus of restaurants.''

"What if you're not pregnant?" someone asked.

"That goes for most of us," a man sitting near the door called out.

Several people laughed. Most didn't.

"Mercury poisoning causes heart attacks," she replied.

"Those are saltwater fish. What about shad and blue crab?''

"The Chesapeake is brackish. Our fish have trace amounts of mercury as well. But that isn't why you're here tonight. That's my introduction intended to ready you for something much more frightening. I'm not talking about rationing your intake of fish for mercury or parasites. I'm talking about PCBs, chemicals that smooth out surfaces and make nonstick coatings for appliances and paints and almost every other kind of equipment we use. They were outlawed twenty years ago, but because they're so important it couldn't be done collectively."

"No big words, Libba Jane." Fletcher Sloane's voice could be heard from the back of the room. "We're simple folk here."

"All at once," Libby amended. "Manufacturers are still allowed to make PCBs as long as they're disposed of properly, although they'll have to make less and less as time goes on."

Billy Dupree leaned forward in his chair. "So, what's so awful about PCBs?"

"Over time, enough time, they cause health problems," she said simply, "like cancer."

"What kind of cancer?" a woman asked.

"Specifically, they've been linked to ovarian and testicular cancer and to leukemia. In other words, people who take in enough PCBs become sterile or else they die."

The room went silent and then angry muttering swelled from the middle of the crowd. "What does all this have to do with us, Libba Jane?" the same woman's voice broke through.

"An entire generation of crabs have mutated," she explained, "which could indicate PCBs in the bay. It could also be something else. I'm not sure yet. The lab reports show nothing but what I've told you. And that isn't all. Animals, specifically wildcats and rodents, have also shown up with missing parts. That indicates seepage into the streams, ponds and freshwater creeks. From there, it's only a matter of time before the subterranean wells are affected."

"Sharecroppers and country people drink from those wells," said Fletcher Sloane.

Libby nodded. "Yes. I'm afraid so."

"What can we do?" he asked.

Others took up his question. "What can we do?"

She waited until it was quiet again, a straight, slender figure with an intense message. "Someone is leaking toxins into the bay. More than likely it's been happening for quite a while because, as I said, an entire generation of fish and animals has been affected. That doesn't happen overnight. The good news is whoever it is probably doesn't know he's doing it. That should make the situation easy to correct. What I need is information. I need you to go out into the surrounding areas and find every company that makes machinery or paint or building supplies—" she hesitated "—or anything else that looks odd. I need you to find out how their waste is disposed of and where. You won't be able to do it officially. You'll have to ask people you know. Maybe some of you can even get inside to see for yourselves."

She paused and her voice lowered. "I can't do this alone. It would take one person years to gather this kind of information, and by then the fishing industry on this side of the bay would be destroyed."

Russ was moved. It was a plea, a poignant one, made more so because she'd put it so that everyone in the room believed she was working for them.

"Now for the practical part." She bit her lip. "This isn't going to be easy for you. It's never easy for people with a lot of pride. Accepting handouts isn't your thing. What I propose is that the fleet owners give their employees Reduction in Force notices for lack of work. That allows workers to collect unemployment for up to six months. Here, in Maryland, that's two-thirds of your take-home salary. It's not the same as a handout because you'll be unofficially working for me, which is the same as working for the government. I believe that we'll have this under control in less than six months. It'll take some time to get things going again, but I think it can be done."

She looked around the room, making eye contact with nearly everyone there. "I don't know of any other way to fix this,'' she said softly. "I guess you could try to get other jobs and hope that I'll come across the problem on my own. Or you could take your boats farther and farther out into the bay. But there's a risk. I'm sure you've already figured it out. Marshyhope Creek is too small to have such high incidences of leukemia. People are being affected. We could wait for a task force to declare this an environmental hazard area. But no one likes to do that. It destroys tourism and real estate values and it could take years to recover. If anyone has a better idea, I'd like to hear it. It doesn't need to be tonight, but please come forward soon. I'm open to anything." She was silent for a long moment and then she smiled.

"Think about it," she said. "If you have no more questions, I'll say thanks for coming out tonight and please help yourself to coffee and a piece of cake."

They came up courteously, one by one, to shake her hand and tell her it was good to see her home again. She knew no one would offer an opinion. It was too soon and these were men slow to reach a decision. They would think and talk and think again, and not until the entire issue had been debated a thousand times would they take a side. She only hoped it wouldn't take too long.

Russ waited until they were alone. "You look worn out," he said. "How about coming home with me for a swig of Jack Daniel's and a view that'll make your heart drop?"

"I'll pass on the Jack Daniel's, but a glass of wine and the view would be nice."

"I've got that, too."

"You're on. I'll meet you there."

Libby walked up the steps of Hennessey House and went through the screen door just as she had a thousand times before. Russ was true to his word. A glass of clear, sparkling wine and a plate of crackers and cheese sat beside his Jack Daniel's on the back porch table. She picked up her wineglass and sank, gratefully, into a chair. "I'm glad that's over," she said.

He leaned against the railing, hands in his pockets, and looked at her thoughtfully. "You were great," he said, "a real natural in front of people. I'd forgotten that about you."

She shrugged. "So did I."

"I never really gave you credit for wanting the acting thing so badly. I thought it was a phase that would pass. I thought you'd marry me, we'd settle here and raise a houseful of kids."

"You mean like, every pretty girl wants to be an actress?"

He winced. "Something like that."

"You were right. It was a phase, a very short one."

"That's the reason you left, isn't it?"

She looked out across the dark water. "Partly."

"Why did you stay in L.A. all those years, after it was over?"

Libby wondered the very same thing. She sipped her wine and tried to explain. "I'm not sure I realized the dream was truly over for a long time. When I did, there was Chloe and I was in school. I had too much pride and didn't want to give my parents the satisfaction of knowing they were right. I'm not sure I wouldn't do it all over again."

He separated himself from the railing and walked toward her. "You broke my heart. Do you know that?"

"You're not entirely blameless."

He stopped, surprised, pulled out another chair and sat down facing her. "You've alluded to that before and I still don't know what you're talking about."

She drew a deep breath. She'd known this moment was coming. She'd rehearsed it for years, choreographing every expression, editing the words. It was time for opening night. "I found out about you and Shelby."

Russ could feel the blood in his cheeks. "Excuse me?"

"Shelby can be very distracting."

"If you're referring to that scene at the club, you're making more of it than it was."

"You don't have to defend yourself, Russ," Libby said softly. "Shelby's very persuasive. You're not the first man she's gone after with a vengeance. It's like a game with her. The harder you resist, the greater the challenge." She twisted a strand of hair around her finger. "I don't think you were much of a challenge, though, were you, in the beginning?"

Russ froze, his glass suspended in midair, and wondered if he was going insane. "What's your game, Libba Jane?"

Libby swallowed, promising herself that this time she would shelve her temper. She began calmly enough. "For all her faults, Shelby was my dearest friend and you were my boyfriend. Those relationships are sacrosanct. I had to choose, Russ, and I chose friendship."

He was beginning to get angry. "You're way off base. I've never been interested in Shelby."

"Really? What about when we were kids? Was I the first girl you ever slept with?"

"Why bring that up now?" he asked warily.

She kept her eyes on his face, forcing him to look at her. "You knew exactly what to do. There was no awkwardness, no fumbling, and you lasted a long time."

"Since when are you the expert on seventeen-year-old virgins?"

"Eric wasn't much older when I married him."

He whitened, surprised at the sudden twisting of his stomach. Libba had never directly alluded to the intimate aspects of her marriage. If he pretended hard enough, he could almost believe it never existed.

She didn't give him a chance to regroup. "It was Shelby, wasn't it?"

Russ twisted his glass in his hands. "Whatever I had with Shelby happened a long time ago, Libba, long before there was anything between you and me. Let it rest."

Her voice cracked with emotion. "There was never a time before you and me. I've known you since I was eight years old."

"It wasn't the same," he insisted. "I didn't think of you that way."

She was bitterly, blazingly angry, but only her eyes gave her away, her eyes and the words, clear and slow, that formed on her lips. "You're a liar, Russ Hennessey. You were sticking your tongue down my throat since I was fourteen years old. You would've done more too if I'd let you. Don't tell me your affair with Shelby was anything but complete and total betrayal. You cheated on me."

"Did she tell you that?"

"No. Mitch told me, the summer I met Eric Richards, the summer I *broke* your heart."

It was true, all of it, and he was guilty, although he never expected his own brother to betray him. *Why* no longer mattered. Mitch was gone and whatever motivation he had in those long-ago days when they were kids was gone with him.

There was no good rationalization for his lapse with Shelby twenty years ago in the peanut fields, except that he'd been sixteen years old with raging hormones and the girl he preferred wouldn't let him do more than run his hands up and down the front of her sweater. Not that he would have done anything more. There were two kinds of girls in Marshyhope Creek, those who put out and those you brought home to Sunday dinner. Shelby was the first kind and Libba, the second. He would no more have expected Cole Delacourte's daughter to drop her panties than he would have expected Shelby to wear any.

In the end, it hadn't mattered. He and Libba had fallen in love, the serious, forever, one-man-one-woman kind of love, and because Libba never did anything halfway, the panties and everything else had come off after all. None of which explained why she was madder about events that occurred in the distant past than she was about anything he'd done since.

He spoke quietly with no hope of immunity. "Like I said, it was a long time ago. People make mistakes. I made mistakes. We were kids. There was never anyone after you. What's the point of all this now?"

"I wanted you to know why I left and why I'll leave again if I have to and why I don't want to hear about your broken heart. You have no idea what you did to mine when I found out about you and my best friend."

"All right, Libba. I apologize. I'll do whatever you want."

Libby's eyes widened. She hadn't expected instant capitulation, not from Russ.

"There is one condition, though."

Of course. She should have known. Here it was, right from the horse's mouth. "What is it?"

"We play it out in the open, so that everyone knows about us, your daughter, mine, your parents, my ex-wife."

Color flooded her cheeks and chest. She'd grown up in a household where protocol was a way of life as natural as bees on honeysuckle and confession on Saturday. In her world, more specifically in Nola Ruth's world, there was no room for bypassing formalities.

She wet her lips. "How am I supposed to explain to my daughter and my parents that I'm sleeping with my old boyfriend?"

His expression was unreadable. He dumped the bourbon out over the railing, opened the cooler on the porch and pulled out a beer. Popping the lid, he threw the flap across the deck and into a trash can. "You'll think of something," he said. "You always were good with words."

The night was warm and the alcohol made it warmer. Libby poured herself another glass of wine. "I have a condition, too."

"What is it?"

"Shelby's on the prowl again. I don't want you encouraging her."

"The thought hadn't occurred to me."

"Like I said, she can be persuasive."

He lifted her chin. "Is that why you're mad at her, because you think there's something between us?"

When she didn't answer he laughed. "You're a fool, Libba Jane. The only times I've ever looked at anyone else is when you wouldn't have me." His voice lowered. "Stay with me tonight."

She shook her head. "I'll sleep with you, but waking up beside you is something different."

He frowned. "Explain that."

She held his gaze, her eyes shadowed and colorless in the moonlight. "This is about sex. I'm not interested in a relationship."

He looked incredulous. "You're kidding."

"No."

He moved close to her, his eyes narrow and serious. "Tell me why you're here if you don't want anything real."

"Lust," she said bluntly. "You're sexy and attractive and it's been a while."

A slow, amused smile crossed his face. "Shame on you, Libba Jane. You've changed. What would your mama say?"

"More than likely my mouth would be around a bar of soap."

He set the beer down on the deck and reached for her hands. "I don't believe you," he said softly, "and I can think of better uses for your mouth." Circling her palm with his thumb, he lifted her other hand and pressed his lips against the skin inside.

She couldn't seem to breathe properly. His mouth moved from her palm to the inside of her wrist, to the tip of her elbow. She leaned back and closed her eyes, content to wait for whatever came next.

Russ took his time, his lips moving from her shoulder to

her collarbone, settling for a time on the pulse in her throat. Finally, when she was all boneless heat, he found her mouth, holding her still while his tongue plundered and swept and teased until her arms wound around his neck and she pressed against him, urging his hands into places familiar and new.

One at a time he eased the buttons from their holes, pushing aside the white linen, exposing the lacy scrap that barely concealed her breasts. She was fuller than he remembered, with mature breasts and long, silky legs. He wanted to see her, all of her. He lifted his head. "Let's go upstairs."

She nodded. Leaving her blouse in the chair, she gave him her hand and followed him up the stairs and into the large front bedroom that had once been Beau and Cora Hennessey's.

The bed was high. He pulled her after him, and there, in a tangle of sheets, he played her, caressing and kissing and probing until she wound her legs around his thighs, cupped his cheeks and pulled him into her. She felt his body go rigid and tight, and for a long, timeless moment he didn't move. Burying her face in his neck, she tasted salt, smelled his scent, heard his harsh, shallow breathing. Finally, it began, the rhythmic moving, slow at first and then faster and still faster until, caught up in a swirl of desire and motion, she lost track of time and direction and space and gave herself up to the moment, to warm arms and hair-roughened legs and the warm, wet heat exploding inside of her.

Libba lay on the bed, her head pillowed on Russ's shoulder, marveling at the wasted years of her marriage, wondering why she'd waited so long to satisfy such a basic primal need. Russ slept beside her. She didn't want to analyze her feelings for Russ Hennessey. It was too early for that, and sex, she knew, tainted the truth, wrapped it in a rosy haze that faded all too quickly, like a room in the harsh light of early morning after a party.

She'd thought of Russ over the years and imagined him

married to someone else, someone after Tracy, an outsider, a stranger, a woman from somewhere other than Marshy-hope Creek. It could still happen and if it did, she would be prepared. She closed her eyes and imagined what the future Mrs. Russell Hennessey would look like. Red hair…no, that was too close to home. Blond would be better. Libby's mind wandered. A tall, athletic blonde with strong features and straight, even teeth. Russ noticed teeth. It was odd, really, his fetish for a woman's mouth. Most men noticed breasts, legs or hips. With Russ, it was teeth. It was one of the first things he'd noticed about her, way back in the third grade, the way her teeth, baking-soda white and much too large for her mouth, clung to her bottom lip when she laughed. For years after, he had remarked on her childish overbite and how she'd finally grown into her smile. Whoever Russ's future wife was, the woman would definitely need good teeth.

Libby was prepared to accept a stranger, a woman who even now walked and slept and ate and talked, a woman whose life existed somewhere else on the planet. What she couldn't accept was someone who'd shared the same child-hood, recalled the same memories, a woman who'd known Russ when he was a boy as Libby had known him. Those years were hers alone, the free, joy-filled, gilt-touched hours of a magical childhood. They were all she had of unfettered happiness and she wouldn't share them.

Carefully, she extricated herself from Russ's arms, pulled the covers over him and gathered her clothes. Downstairs she found her blouse, her purse and keys and quietly let herself out of the house. It was after midnight. The roads were dark and empty. Hopefully everyone would be asleep at home and she wouldn't be required to come up with an explanation, an absurdity for a thirty-seven-year-old woman, but still necessary.

The last thing she expected was her family home ablaze with lights and two police cars, red lights blinking, in the driveway.

Twenty-Five

Her first thought was for her mother. Libby raced up the front steps and through the long entry. She stopped abruptly at the living room. Two police officers stood talking with her father. Bailey Jones sat on the couch, his face pale as bleached bone, his eyes lifeless. Chloe was curled up with Nola Ruth in her wheelchair, her slight body tucked in beside her grandmother's.

"Libba Jane," her mother said, "thank God you're home."

Chloe separated herself from her grandmother and ran across the room into Libby's arms.

"What happened?" she asked.

"Bailey's mother died," sobbed Chloe.

That explained Bailey, but not the police and not Chloe. Bewildered, Libby looked at her mother.

"Chloe went to see Bailey on her bike," her mother said, her words startlingly clear. "Lizzie died inside that trailer. Bailey was with her when it happened. Together Chloe and the boy brought her body here in Bailey's truck. Chloe drove."

"Dear God," Libby gasped. She clutched Chloe fiercely. "How did you manage such a thing? Why didn't you call?"

"There's no phone."

Libby spoke to the boy on the couch. "Bailey, I'm so sorry."

He didn't answer.

Cole spoke to his daughter. "Tell Serena to make up a room for Bailey. He'll stay with us until other arrangements are made."

Libby nodded. Keeping Chloe with her, she climbed the stairs to the third floor and knocked on Serena's bedroom door.

The woman answered immediately, clucking with sympathy when Libby explained. "I knew something was wrong when those red lights kept flashing outside my window. That poor boy." She took Chloe into her arms. "There, there, sweetheart. You're a brave thing. You did exactly right. I don't know anyone else who would have been brave enough or smart enough to do such a thing."

Chloe managed a watery smile.

"I'll make up that room right away, Miss Libba. That boy could use a good dose of Verna Lee's valerian root. I'll see if Mr. Cole has any."

"If not, chamomile tea might be a good idea," suggested Libby. "Chloe might like some, too, if you can get either of them to swallow anything."

"I'll see to it. Just give me a minute to dress."

Libby walked Chloe into the bathroom, settled her on the edge of the tub and gently sponged her face and hands with a hot washcloth. She spoke gently, soothingly, until the child's trembling eased and then stopped altogether. Chloe yawned. "I'm tired," she said.

"I imagine so," replied her mother. She led Chloe to her room and pulled down the bedcovers.

"I'm not sure about school tomorrow, Mom."

"We'll worry about that in the morning."

"What about Bailey?"

"Serena will take care of him." Libby hesitated. "There isn't much we can do for Bailey right now," she said gently. "He's hurting and he'll have to work his way through the pain himself. The best thing you can do is give him space. Don't push, Chloe. It never works."

Chloe's eyes welled up. "He was so sad, Mom. You should have seen him cry. I've never seen anyone cry like that."

"She's all he had, sweetie. Not only has he lost his mother, he's all alone. That's hard for anyone, especially an eighteen-year-old boy."

"He has me."

Libby's heart sank. "He knows that," was all she said. She kissed both of Chloe's cheeks and her forehead. "Good night, love. I'll check on you in the morning."

When Libby returned to the living room, the scene had changed slightly. The police were gone and her father was sitting beside Bailey on the couch. She could hear the low, measured tones of his professional voice. The boy nodded.

Cole looked at his daughter. "I'll take Bailey into the kitchen for something to drink. I doubt if he'll eat anything. You and your mother will wait for the mortician. He should arrive shortly."

"God, Mama." Libby rubbed her temples. "How did we ever get into this?"

"I believe," said Nola Ruth slowly, "that involving ourselves with unsuitable people runs in our family, at least on the female side."

Libby lifted her head and stared at her mother, eyes blazing. "How dare you say that? You, of all people. Neither Chloe nor I have ever been involved with anyone as *unsuitable* as your Anton Devereaux." She spat the name from her lips, as if were a thing so repellant, so dirty, that she could no longer hold it inside of her.

Half of Nola Ruth's mouth smiled. "So, it finally comes out," she said softly. "I wondered when it would happen. You've been so cool, so accepting. I wondered whether or not there was any of my Libba Jane left."

"What are you talking about?"

"When you were a girl you had more life in you than a Thoroughbred fresh out of the starting gate. You smoldered with it, just like Chloe does. I think you brought her back here because you were afraid, Libba. She wants what you wanted and you're afraid she'll be hurt the way you were.''

''What's wrong with that?''

Nola Ruth, well into her reminiscences, ignored the question. ''Lord, you were a handful. I wanted a little girl who kept her Mary Janes shiny and her ribbons tied. Your favorite thing to do was wade through marshes looking for tree frogs. I'll never forget the time you came home with leeches stuck to every square inch of both legs.''

''I was eleven years old, Mama.''

''And remember when Tom Hadley planned to sell a portion of his groves to that private developer? You stood up at the town meeting and convinced everyone that condominiums and fast-food restaurants would be a disaster for Marshyhope Creek. It was the most eloquent speech I'd ever heard and you were sixteen years old. Even Tom had second thoughts, and when your granddaddy offered him a loan to make ends meet until the next harvest, he jumped at it. The land and the water were in your blood, Libba. They still are.''

''What has that got to do with anything?''

''Where's the life, honey? You haven't done any more than tell me *yes ma'am, no ma'am* since you got here— when you are here. Where were you all night, anyway?''

Libby looked at her mother but she didn't see her. She was remembering Russ's words: *''We play it out in the open, so that everyone knows about us, your daughter, mine, your parents, my ex-wife.''*

''I was with Russ Hennessey,'' she said deliberately.

Nola Ruth's expressive eyes warmed with pity and something else Libby didn't recognize. ''Oh, Libba, will you never learn?''

''Like you did?''

Nola Ruth leaned forward. ''Yes, like I did. I learned my lessons. I don't make the same mistake twice.''

"And I do?"

"Apparently so."

"I'm not going to marry him. Besides, what's wrong with Russ Hennessey?"

"For starters, he's divorced with a child, and if you think Tracy Wentworth will sit back and let you have Russ when she runs to him for every little thing, you've got another thing coming. If you must have a divorced man, why not look for one with an ex-wife who's remarried and whose children are grown?"

Libba stared at her mother in amazement. "I'm not looking and not everybody plans who they fall in love with, Mama. The most I hope for in my next husband, if there is a next one, is some compassion and a large dose of character."

"That's very nice, Libba Jane. What about practical matters like earning potential, security and no previous baggage?"

"When did you get to be so cold?"

"When did *you* get to be so naive?"

Libba shook her head and stood. "How did we get to this subject, anyway?"

"By asking that very question."

The doorbell interrupted them. Relieved, Libby left her mother in the living room and answered the door. A neat man in a black suit smiled at her. "I'm Harvey Madison. Sorry to disturb you at this hour, but Mr. Delacourte asked me to come out and remove Mrs. Jones."

"Of course." Libby stepped aside. "Please, come in. I'll call my father."

Cole was right behind her. "How are you, Harvey?"

"Fine, thanks, Mr. Delacourte."

"Come with me."

Libby watched the two men walk down the hall and into one of the downstairs bedrooms. She shuddered to think of Chloe and Bailey lifting Lizzie's lifeless body into the truck

and driving with it between them on the single bench seat.
Guilt assailed her. When her daughter was facing the crisis
of her young life, Libby had been with Russ. Chloe's where-
abouts had been the furthest thing from her mind.

Nola Ruth's New Orleans Catholicism raised its superstitious head. Chloe's experience was retribution, a warning
sign. Libby was a mother. She had no business finding pleasure in a man's bed, especially a man who wasn't her husband.

She walked slowly back into the living room. "It's late,
Mama," she said wearily. "I'll take you to your room."

"When will you be ready, Libba Jane?"

"For what?"

"For the rest of the truth."

Libby sighed. "There's more?"

"There's a great deal more."

Libby pushed her mother's wheelchair across the carpet
and down the hall into her bedroom. Maybe this was a mistake. Maybe she didn't belong here in this place where dark
secrets crept slowly to the surface, like parasites eating away
at stones and tree bark. She didn't want to learn that her
mother was human, and a less-than-perfect human at that.
Libby loved her mother, revered her opinions, respected her
decisions. A flawed mother didn't fit her image of what a
mother should be. Suddenly her eyelids felt heavy. "Will it
keep, Mama?" she asked. "I don't think I can take any
more tonight."

"It'll keep. It's kept for forty years now, but it has to be
said."

"Then another night won't matter."

Nola Ruth sounded tired, defeated. "It won't matter at
all, Libba Jane."

Libby settled her mother in her bed and closed the door
behind her. On her way up the stairs she met her father
coming down. He held her close for a minute and kissed

her cheek. For the first time he looked old and it frightened her. "Are you all right, Daddy?"

"I don't know what we're comin' to, Libba Jane."

"What do you mean?"

He smiled and instantly she was reassured. "Never mind, honey. How's Chloe?"

"She's sleeping now, but she's worried about Bailey."

"That girl's got good instincts. We should all be worried about him." He patted her shoulder. "That's all I'll say now. By the way, the charges against Drusilla Washington have been dropped. There are conditions, but she can live with them. I thought you'd want to know."

"Will there be an investigation?"

"Only if we can link the fetus's condition to the problems we're having in the bay. Is that possible?"

Libby frowned. She knew her father and it seemed as if his question was more than casual. "I'm not sure," she said slowly. "It could take years." She smiled tentatively. "Verna Lee must be pleased."

"Very pleased."

"And grateful, I hope."

He grinned. "Maybe I'll never have to pay for another latte again. Sleep well, Libba Jane."

She climbed the stairs to her bedroom, switched on the light and walked into the bathroom. Shedding her clothes, she poured bath gel into the tub, turned on the tap and sank into the soothing bubbles. The night had been a long one and her head reeled with half-finished thoughts. Foremost in her mind was the phone call she would make to Ventura County resigning from her former job. She was needed here in Marshyhope Creek, and after tonight's meeting she wouldn't desert the watermen who believed in her. The problem of Chloe was resolved, although Libby wished it had happened differently. She wouldn't leave Bailey Jones, not now when he had no one. And there was her mother. Nola Ruth was determined to make a full confession, and whether she wanted to or not, Libby had been appointed to hear it. She supposed it all needed to be said, that, and more. Libby had some questions of her own. Real peace would never be found without the answers.

She deliberately avoided all thoughts of Russ. Russ Hennessey had been deliberately relegated to the think-about-it-later part of her brain. She would admit there was chemistry. There had always been a powerful adult attraction between them. She thought, when she was younger, that the blind, absorbing, thick-tongued kind of love she felt for Russ was because he had been there for every significant first in her life. Later, she knew better. The magnetic pull she felt, that pulsing rise of tension and the slow, sweet anticipatory slide from wanting to absolute desire was because Russ was Russ, and the plain truth of it was, for her, there had never been anyone else with the same combination of unconscious charisma and personal charm. There still wasn't. He was quite capable of getting her to do just about anything he wanted, although he didn't know it and never would since she had no intention of giving him such an advantage by telling him.

All of which were very good reasons for not falling in love with him all over again. Loving Russ would be a disaster. She would be forever insecure, always jealous of other women, forever worried that he would leave her for someone else because she wasn't interesting enough or smart enough or good enough in bed. That had been her Rubicon once already. Images of Shelby and Russ, her best friend and her true love, had sent her on a downward trajectory of pain and rage and retribution that led her out of Marshyhope Creek and the tree-lined shoals of the Chesapeake to a place where it never rained enough to turn anything green and more days than not the horizon was smeared with a mustard-yellow haze. The fact that five years had passed by the time Mitch told her about Russ and Shelby and that the two had been no older than Chloe made no difference. The hurt was still bitter. She tried to resurrect it, testing the images. She felt nothing. She tried again. Still nothing.

She shrugged. There were far more important things to think about, such as how and when she would begin to provide a home for Chloe. She couldn't live with her parents forever. It wasn't healthy for Chloe to see her mother as a dependent and it wasn't what an adult would do.

As often happens when a sleep pattern is disturbed, Libby woke earlier than her usual time. The rest of the house was silent, shrouded in lowered shades and curtains pulled against the light. Soundlessly, she pulled on her shorts, a sleeveless T-shirt and running shoes. Then she tiptoed out the door and down the path toward the water line. There, she started her run.

A smoky blanket of mist settled over the wetlands, covering all but the spiky tips of the tall southern pine, colorless in the early gray morning. It was already warm. Libby breathed in the moist air flavored with smells of peach, salt, water and mineral-rich soil. She ran past the dock, across the flat, open road and out past the fields filled with sharecroppers bent in half, hoisting boxes filled with produce to their muscular, sweating shoulders. Road stands spilled multicolored fruit and vegetables and trucks hauling tomatoes, oranges, onions, coriander, cabbage and lettuce passed her by.

When the sun burned away the clouds, bringing the distinctive blue color to the bay water, she stopped, bent over, breathed deeply and checked her watch. It was only seven-thirty. She turned around and jog-walked home. Verna Lee's red car was in the driveway. Once again, Libby checked her watch. Why would she be here at eight in the morning? Fearing another unpleasant surprise, Libby slowed her steps to a crawl. She stopped at the door, drew a deep, steadying breath and opened it quietly. The house was silent. She frowned, stooped over to untie and step out of her tennis shoes, picked them up and walked down the hall.

Voices pierced the silence. She heard her mother's, slow and deliberate, coming from the sitting room. Then she heard Verna Lee's higher one. It was angry and insistent. Libby was both fascinated and repelled. She wanted to know more and at the same time she wanted no part of the truth she'd guessed for some time now. The fabric of what she had believed was a well-structured childhood had been rent from top to bottom until it bore no resemblance to the memory in her mind. The one constant of her life, her perception of her childhood, was being destroyed, and she wasn't sure how much more she could take. Electing to pass by the room quickly and hope she wasn't seen, Libby moved quickly past the door and started up the stairs.

"Libba Jane." Her name on her father's lips stopped her short.

Slowly, she turned around. He stood at the entrance to his study, his retreat where, except for Chloe, the women of the family never ventured.

"Good morning," she said softly.

"I'd like to speak with you when you have a chance."

She looked down at him, a vital, lucid man, even though he was nearing seventy. She swallowed. "I have time now, Daddy."

"It can wait until you've cleaned up."

She nodded and continued up the stairs, checking on Chloe on the way. She was sleeping soundly. Her cheeks were flushed from the heat, but her breathing was slow and even and she hadn't moved from the position she was in when she'd gone to bed last night.

Libby showered, washed her hair, changed into clean clothes and walked down the stairs to meet her father. Chloe slept on and the voices in the sitting room were muted, almost friendly.

She stepped into her father's study and closed the door. "What's going on in there?" she asked.

Cole marked his place in the book he was reading and looked up. "Your mother and Verna Lee have an issue that needs settling. I imagine they'll let us in on it when the time is right. What I have to tell you is much more serious."

Libby felt the cold fist of fear in the pit of her stomach. "Where's Bailey?"

"Bailey didn't do much sleeping," her father replied. "He wanted to go home as soon as possible. I dropped him off about thirty minutes ago. Now I'm not sure I did the right thing by letting him go."

"Why not?"

"Lizzie Jones was murdered by asphyxiation. The coroner says someone held a pillow over her head and smothered her."

Libby's hand flew to her mouth. "Dear God. Who?"

Suddenly, her father looked old and tired. "Bailey is the only suspect the police have."

Twenty-Six

"What are you going to do?" Libby asked. Her voice was hushed, shaken.

"If Bailey is charged, I'm going to represent that poor boy," her father answered.

"Why would he do such a thing?"

Cole Delacourte shook his head. "I won't know until I ask him. My guess is that his mother was suffering and they couldn't afford the medication to keep her pain free. She may have even asked him to do it. Lizzie Jones was wedded to that land. It's been in her family for generations. More than anything she wanted to leave it to her son."

"I can't imagine a mother doing such a thing. Surely she knew he would be blamed."

"Lizzie was a simple woman. Her mind wasn't whole. I doubt if she knew how sophisticated forensics has become."

Libby was cold for the first time since she drove her rental car out of the air-conditioned airport in Richmond into the wet heat of a Southern afternoon only two months ago. She rubbed her arms and began to walk back and forth across the room. "This is awful. We never should have come back here. Chloe will take this on. Clearing Bailey will become her special project. I know it will. She'll feel as if she has to rescue him. Oh, God, Daddy. What am I going to do?"

"Calm down, Libba Jane. Chloe will have to answer some questions. Although she's not directly involved with Bailey and his mother, she was probably the last person to see the two of them together. They trusted her. She'll be asked about their relationship.''

Libby stared at him, horrified. "She couldn't possibly be considered an accessory, could she?''

Cole smiled. "No, honey. No one would even consider it.''

Libby's heart pounded. Every instinct told her to take her daughter and run as far away from Marshyhope Creek as four wheels and a manual transmission would take her. "What will I tell her?''

"The truth, Libba Jane. Always fall back on the truth. If everyone would just follow that path, we wouldn't spend so much energy on trying to fix it later on.''

A soft knock interrupted them. Chloe's voice followed. "Mom, I need a note for school.''

Libby opened the door. "Come in, sweetheart. Are you sure you're up to going in today? Under the circumstances, it wouldn't hurt to stay home this time.''

Chloe stared at her mother in amazement. "You never let me stay home, not unless I'm throwing up.''

"I thought you might like to for once.''

Chloe shook her head. "It's the second day of school. Will you drive me?''

Libby smiled brightly. "Of course. Let me get my purse and I'll meet you out front.''

Chloe disappeared down the hall. Libby glanced at her father. "Wish me luck," she said softly.

"She can take it, Libba Jane. Give her some credit.''

"I don't want to tell her this minute.''

"I'd warn her about the rumors," Cole warned her. "News spreads fast in a small town. She'll hear it at school. Give her a heads-up so she's prepared. You want her to have the advantage, don't you?''

"I hadn't thought of that.''

"Would you like me to drive her to school?" her father asked.

Libby shook her head. "No. I'm her mother. I'll do it."

Cole smiled approvingly. "Good girl." He cleared his desk, reshelving his books and sweeping the pens into the top drawer. "Now, I think I'll look in on your mother and Verna Lee. My guess is the fireworks are over."

"Is it what I think it is?" Libby asked.

"You always were a clever child," said her father. "What gave it away?"

"Besides the fact that the resemblance is remarkable?"

He nodded. "I've always thought so. Usually no one looks past color. I'm surprised you did."

"All the years I grew up here, I missed it. It took a seventeen-year absence to see what was right in front of my nose."

"You aren't taking it too badly," her father observed.

"Don't think for a minute it isn't important to me, Daddy. I like Verna Lee, more now than I ever did when we were kids. It's what Mama did that's disturbing. I'm not sure why, but I feel as if she's betrayed us, somehow. As for my not becoming hysterical, there are more important things to worry about, like euthanasia, for instance."

"It's a tangled web we mortals weave," he said softly. "Don't take too much on yourself, Libba Jane. It'll work out the way it's supposed to. Meanwhile, I want you to do something for me."

"All right."

"Keep on this pesticide thing. There's more here than we know. If you have to go public, do it. I can't help thinking these two incidents, Drusilla Washington and Bailey Jones, are related."

"What are you saying?"

"Nothing yet."

Chloe poked her head in. "Are you coming?"

"Right now, honey. I'm on my way."

Chloe followed her mother into the front door of the high school attendance office. Her head felt light and distant, as if it was attached to someone else's body. She waited while her mother filled out the requisite papers and said something about the yellow one Chloe was to take around to the teachers whose classes she'd missed. She wondered what Bailey was doing and why he'd wanted to go back so soon to that horrible place where it had happened. He wouldn't be here today. She knew that. But maybe she could pave the way, somehow, and make it easier for him to come back.

She walked outside, waiting for Libby to say goodbye. Her mother was the goodbye queen. She couldn't just get it out with a simple two-syllable word. She had to drag it out, kiss one cheek and then the other, stroke her hair, touch her arm, hug her once and then again, all the while saying things like "Have a good day" and "Work hard and pay attention" or "I'll miss you" and always, always the proverbial "I love you."

Normally Chloe would have remained stoic, neither complaining nor condoning her mother's separation anxiety, but today, in light of Bailey's loss, she welcomed it, even going so far as to encircle Libby's waist and kiss her cheek.

She pulled away and saw that her mother's eyes had welled up. "Don't cry, Mom," she said, embarrassed. "I'll be all right."

"Chloe," Libby began. "There's something you should know."

"If I don't go now, I'll be late for another class."

"This is important." Libby pulled Chloe down on a bench outside the office. "Bailey may be in some trouble."

"That's an understatement."

"No, Chloe. I mean legal trouble."

"What kind of legal trouble?"

"Oh, God." Libby's hands twisted in her lap. "I didn't want to do this now. Can't we just go home? I don't want to leave you here, not after you hear this."

Chloe's temper flashed. "Just tell me."

Libby wet her lips and strove for a matter-of-fact tone. "Lizzie Jones was very ill, but she didn't die because of that. She suffocated, Chloe. The police think someone smothered her. There's a possibility that Bailey may be charged."

Chloe's mouth dropped. Her eyes were two blazing slits of blue in her pointed little face. "That's insane. Bailey *loved* his mother."

"He may have loved her so much that he did what she wanted him to. She was in terrible pain with no hope of recovery."

"He wouldn't do that. I know he wouldn't."

Libby looked down at her clenched hands. "Maybe he wouldn't."

"There's no *maybe* about it," Chloe insisted. "He wouldn't."

"Can we go home, Chloe? Others may know and say things. I don't want you to face that right now."

The girl shook her head. "No way."

Libby stared at her daughter. "I don't know what to say to you. I'm frustrated and yet I'm incredibly proud of you. You're the bravest person I know." Once more she kissed the smooth, young cheek. "Good luck, love. Call me if you need me. You aren't alone."

Chloe picked up her backpack and walked slowly up the steps into the student entrance of the brick building.

Libby watched until her daughter had disappeared behind the double glass doors. For the first time in years, she felt the urge to genuflect before a church altar and light a candle. She sat for a minute inside her car waiting for the air conditioner to kick in. Then she pulled out on to the road and made her way slowly into town. Work was what she needed. It would pass the time and keep her mind off of Chloe's ordeal.

On another day she would have stopped at Perks, but it was closed. Verna Lee was otherwise occupied. Libby pulled into the diagonal parking space in front of the EPA office beside Russ's Blazer. He sat in the front seat holding a cup of coffee and a sugary beignet.

She waved. He grinned and handed her a second cup of coffee and a beignet through the window. Her heart lifted. "Thanks," she said softly.

"What's going on?"

"You mean you don't know? I thought everyone would know."

He shook his head. "I fell asleep last night beside a beautiful woman. I woke up less than an hour ago and she was gone. I don't know about anything."

Libby blushed. "Lizzie Jones is dead."

Russ looked puzzled. "I didn't realize you were friends," he said carefully.

"Don't be ridiculous, Russ. You know we weren't friends. But Bailey and Chloe are and she was there when the police came."

"Whoa, Libba." He reached out, removed the coffee and beignet from her hands, set them on the roof of her car and drew her to him. "Slow down and tell me what happened."

Libby closed her eyes and rested her head against his chest. They were in the middle of Main Street at nine-thirty in the morning and she didn't care who saw them. Without embellishment of any kind, she told him, beginning with the police lights flashing in front of her family home, to her last conversation with Chloe. She finished with "And there's every possibility that Verna Lee Fontaine is my half sister."

He whistled softly. "Holy Christ, Libba Jane. No wonder your heart's fluttering like a shad caught in a net."

She laughed in spite of herself. "You certainly did stay Southern."

"Only for effect."

"What am I going to do?"

He lifted her chin and looked down into her face. She was smaller than she looked, a combination of long brown legs and thigh-skimming shorts. "How about if we go for a drive?"

She nodded. Sensing her mood, he dumped the food into the nearest trash receptacle, settled her into the Blazer and climbed into the driver's seat. Within minutes Marshyhope Creek was behind them. "Will you be hungry some time today?" he asked.

She shrugged. "I could eat, I suppose."

"If we took the ferry, we could be at Steamers by noon."

Libby hesitated. It was appealing, but there was Chloe to think of.

He read her mind. "We'll be home in plenty of time for you to pick up Chloe from school."

Suddenly the idea of Steamers' hush puppies wrapped in newsprint and eaten on a picnic table overlooking the bay sounded wonderful. It was like time rolling back before all the trouble. "All right," she said. "Let's go."

Russ grinned. "Good girl."

Steamers sported a new coat of paint, but otherwise it was exactly the same. The food was still limitless, dumped in piles in the middle of tables. The hush puppies were just as tasty and the corn as sweet. Libby bit into the last fried chicken leg, tossed the remains on the table and sat back with a contented sigh. "That was delicious. What a great idea."

"You're welcome."

"You never answered my question."

"I'm getting around to it. You asked me what you should do. A question like that requires some thought."

"And?"

"What comes to mind is that it isn't about you, not any of it, and you can't really do anything that will make a difference."

"Explain that, please."

He signaled the waitress for a refill on his iced tea. "Do you want another glass of wine?" he asked Libby.

She shook her head, waiting for him to resume his conversation.

"Chloe will have to tell what she knows whether you go back to California or stay here, and your father will represent Bailey. Both of those things will happen no matter how you feel about them. As for Verna Lee and your mother, that's their story. I'm not saying you don't have an interest, but they'll make their own peace or they won't." His voice gentled. "Relax, Libba Jane. Don't try to control the world. Things'll work out."

She didn't know whether it was his straightforward Hennessey logic or the mellowing effect of copious amounts of protein and the glass of wine she'd consumed with her lunch, but suddenly she felt better. She laughed out loud. "You're right. Have you learned a lot in the last seventeen years or was I just too blind and stupid to notice?"

"A little of both."

"You're different," she said bluntly.

"I hope so."

His answer surprised her. "Why is that?"

"I've been around awhile longer. Experience is worth something." He reached for his cigarettes, remembered he'd quit and drummed his fingers on the table.

She leaned forward. Her hair in the sunlight was a deep, rich brown. "Do you have demons?"

"Everyone has demons."

"What are yours?"

"Why do you want to know?"

"You seem so grounded," she replied slowly. "I want some of that."

"Why, Libba Jane," he teased her. "I thought I'd made it quite clear you could have it any time you wanted."

She sighed. "Don't make this into a game. I'm serious. If I'm prying, just tell me it's none of my business."

His eyes narrowed. Against the backdrop of the water they were a thin line of glittering blue. "I thought it was fairly obvious that my worst demon is my ex-wife and the power she continues to wield over me because of Tess.'' He laughed bitterly. ''I had no idea I'd care about a child like this. The funny thing is, I wanted a boy. I was disappointed when it turned out she was a girl. Now I wouldn't have it any other way.''

''That isn't unusual, Russ. Statistically, most men, and women, too, want their first child to be a boy.''

He reached across the wooden table and linked her fingers with his. ''You're pretty good with those statistics.''

''Occupational hazard.''

''Let me ask you this. What are the chances of two blue-eyed people producing a brown-eyed child?''

She looked out across the bay, unable to meet his gaze.

''Answer me, Libba Jane.''

''You know the answer to that, Russ. We both took first-year biology.''

He sighed. ''Any chance for error?''

She shook her head. ''No.''

''I didn't think so.''

''Why ask me this now? You've had years to ask questions.''

He was silent for a long time. Finally he spoke. ''Mitch died of leukemia. Mutations are occurring all over the bay. We've got an unusual number of birth defects in a town this size. I've checked it out.''

There was something he wasn't telling her. She could feel it.

''I've been to a urologist.''

She waited, heart pounding, wanting to help and yet not wanting to hear.

''My sperm have no motility. I can't father a child outside of a test tube. It's quite a common phenomenon for Vietnam vets in the sixties and seventies who were exposed to Agent Orange. Tess isn't my daughter, Libba. I don't know whose daughter she is and now I wonder if it matters. Not that I don't want to murder Tracy. All those years of child support, making me feel guilty because I wasn't here and the kid isn't even mine.''

Libby gripped his hand. ''Don't jump to conclusions, Russ. There are other possibilities.''

''What are you suggesting?''

''Maybe Tracy went to a sperm bank.''

''Why would she do that? We were only married two years.''

''Maybe there was something wrong with her and she didn't tell you. Maybe there was a reason for her to choose genetic selection. I have no idea. The point is, you already know it doesn't matter. If you suspected this from the beginning you should have done something earlier. Now it's too late. Tess is your daughter. You love her and she loves you. She has no other father. The courts see it that way, too. They won't order a DNA test after a child is eighteen months old. Emotional bonding is more important than a shared gene pool. You know that.''

Some of the tension left his shoulders. ''You're right. There's no point in confronting Tracy. She'd use it against me with Tess. The part that galls me the most is that I can't even tell her I know. She has the satisfaction of believing she's pulled something over on me.''

Libby shook her head. ''I doubt it. If it were me, I wouldn't be thinking that way, not after all this time. I'd be thinking you and I share a daughter, that's all.''

Russ looked at her, a creamy-skinned woman with whiskey-brown eyes. If it had been her, they wouldn't be having this conversation at all. ''Let's take the day off tomorrow and go to the beach,'' he said.

''We're taking a day off today,'' she reminded him.

''Tomorrow will be better. We'll take the boat and go over to the island like we used to.''

Libby hesitated. It was terribly appealing, but there was so much work to do.

"Your watermen wouldn't approve if they knew I was slacking off while they're working."

"Write off the day if it makes you feel better."

"I'm not independently wealthy, Russ."

"Don't tell me your daddy makes you pay rent, because I wouldn't believe it."

"All right," she said recklessly. "Maybe, to make it legitimate, we could do a little investigating on the way."

"We could," he agreed easily. "Shall I pack a lunch or will you?"

"I'll do it if you pay today."

"You're on."

Twenty-Seven

Chloe was very subdued that evening and Nola Ruth said nothing at all. Dinner was strained, nearly without conversation, even though Libby and her father tried valiantly to maintain a semblance of normalcy. Eventually, Chloe excused herself to finish her homework, Cole disappeared into his study, and Libby wheeled Nola Ruth into the den to watch the news.

"Would you like me to stay here with you, Mama?" Libby asked. Nola Ruth looked at her for the first time that evening. "We should probably talk sometime soon, Libba Jane, but not tonight. I'm exhausted."

Libby nodded.

"Do you have plans for tomorrow?"

Libby drew a deep breath. "Actually, I do. I'm going to the beach with Russ Hennessey."

"Don't you have to work?" asked her mother.

"I'm taking a break."

There was a silence and then a cool "I hope you know what you're doing, Libba." Nola Ruth's Louisiana accent was very pronounced, a sign that she was troubled.

Libby frowned and lowered her voice. "I never realized that you disliked Russ as much as you do."

"It isn't Russ that I disapprove of." Nola Ruth pronounced her words carefully. "I just wish you would involve yourself with someone other than the Hennesseys."

"No one else is breaking down my door."

"Don't be ridiculous. You've always had your sights in Russ Hennessey's direction. I guess nothing's changed. I just don't want any more of my family hurt."

"What are you talking about?"

"It isn't just you anymore. There's Chloe to consider. If she attaches herself to Russ, she'll be hurt all the more if it doesn't work out."

"What makes you think it won't?"

Nola Ruth dismissed her question. "I won't argue with you. Just don't get so mule-headed that you can't see what's plain to everybody else."

Libby was speechless. Never, in her entire adult life, had her mother been less subtle. The lovely Southern charm so characteristic of Nola Ruth was bluntly, unpleasantly absent. "What are you talking about?"

"There's a stubborn streak in you, Libba Jane. Not too many women would run off and, except for a few brief visits when Chloe was little, stay away for seventeen years. You certainly have your share of pride and that isn't a compliment."

"Really?" Libby said sweetly. "It sounds like it's exactly what you did except that I didn't give birth to and give up a daughter."

The good side of Nola Ruth's mouth turned up. "It's like I said, honey. I know what I'm talking about. Don't make my mistakes."

"Why didn't you come after me, Mama? If you wanted me home so badly, why didn't you say so?"

"You mean I should have come charging into town, dragged you home and had Eric Richards murdered?" Nola Ruth shook her head. "No thank you. That would have been history repeating itself. I didn't want that."

"Good night, Mama."

Nola Ruth stared silently at the television.

Tonight, Libby didn't want company, but it was too early to go to bed. She walked into the kitchen where Serena was washing the dinner dishes. "Can I help you with anything?" she asked.

The black woman looked up. "It looks like rain. You could take down the laundry from the line."

Libby picked up the basket in the laundry room and headed out back. A hot wind laced with the smell of damp earth lifted the hair from her shoulders and rustled the tree branches framing the house. Rain was minutes away. Quickly she gathered armfuls of stiff, sweet-smelling clothes, dropping the clothespins efficiently into the bag hanging on the line. She piled the last shirt into her basket when the first drops fell. Lifting the clothes basket, she ran for the porch, barely making the shelter before the sky opened up in earnest. She left the basket for Serena and went upstairs to check on Chloe. She'd fallen asleep with the light on. Libby removed the book from under her daughter's cheek, pulled the sheet over her and turned out the light.

It rained most of the night, a warm, thick, frog-strangling rain that forced vehicles off the road and kept everyone indoors, leaving behind a haze that colored the water and sky an indistinguishable blue-gray.

It was just past dawn the following morning. The boat's wake was a shock of white in the unending grayness. Libby looked behind her at the disappearing dock. She broke the silence. "Where are we going?"

"To Assateague Island."

Libby sat up. "That's a day trip, Russ. I didn't tell anyone we'd be gone that long."

"We'll be back by six. You can call from the boat."

"I can hardly wait to explain that to my mother," she mumbled under her breath.

Russ grinned. "I don't have a hearing problem, Libby."

"What you have is a lot of nerve."

He shrugged. "I wanted to get you alone."

She maneuvered her way to the front of the boat and sat down next to him. "Any particular reason?"

His arm circled her waist. "More than one. We'll have to wait for the fog to burn off first." He pressed his lips to her bare shoulder. "You smell good. It's the same smell you had when you were a kid. What's it called?"

"Mimosa."

"Don't ever change it."

She turned to answer and never did. Her breath caught and the words left her, all her concentration on the man by her side. He faced the bay, his profile outlined against the brightening sky. Black lashes, unfairly long for a man, swept upward, framing steel-blue eyes. The lean, angular features of youth had firmed into scooped-out cheeks and jutting bones and a narrow, slightly beaked nose. Black hair fell across his forehead and curled at his neck, and his skin was dark from long days spent in the sun. He was handsome, in a masculine, undomesticated way, but it wasn't just his features or even the startling warmth of his smile that gave him his appeal. It was the way he carried himself, the implied strength in his lean, ropy body, the loose-hipped, predatory way he moved, the arch of his eyebrow, the tightening of his jaw, the sudden narrowing of his eyes. There was no one like him. There never had been, not even Mitch, and he and Russ had been as alike as two people could possibly be. She'd been insane to think that Eric Richards could fill the gap.

Russ turned his head. "You're awfully quiet. What are you thinking about?"

"You."

"Come to any conclusions?"

She tangled her fingers in the hair at the back of his neck. "Do you know that you're still beautiful?"

To her delight, he reddened. Russ never could take a compliment. "Thank you, ma'am, but I brought you out here to show you something that really is beautiful.'' He pointed toward the shoreline. ''Look.''

The sun had burned off the haze and the water was a pure gunmetal gray against the green marsh grass. Here, at the tip of the bay, pine forests grew down to the sand and only the hardiest survived. The less resilient succumbed to the salt, their white-encrusted roots face-up on the sandy shoreline, a testament to their struggle for survival. Libby felt the roll of the boat and saw the white foam of another wake cut across the inlet. The water was rich with life. Fish leaped from the depths. Insects skimmed across the surface, and black, biting flies feasted on overheated human flesh and salty blood.

In the distance, clammers, sunburned and bent over, harvested sandbars with their rakes. On the pilings, snowy egrets, brown terns, blue herons and gulls waited patiently for the humans to depart, intent on their share of leftovers from the oyster beds. The steady lapping of the water soothed Libby's spirits. Comfortably cool, she leaned against Russ's shoulder. ''You love it here, don't you?''

''Yes,'' he said simply. ''So do you. I can't believe you spent so much time in California.''

''California's nice.''

''But it isn't home.''

''No.''

He waited, giving her time to gather her thoughts.

''Out here on the water it's an angler's paradise,'' she said at last, ''and it's green, so green it's an assault to the eyes. I'd forgotten all about the green. It's not something I thought about until I came back, green trees, green grass, green corn, every imaginable shade of green.'' She looked up at the sky. ''The heat does it. The heat and rain produces a country that God most likely modeled after heaven.''

He kept silent, afraid to break the mood. She had never talked like this to him before. She sounded almost poetic.

"They don't have graveyards west of the Mississippi River," she announced.

He laughed. "Of course they do."

Libby shook his head. "Not real graveyards. Westerners hide their dead behind stone walls and wrought-iron gates. Not seeing the headstones is a way of denying age. Death won't come if you aren't reminded of it. Yuppies fight aging. It's a veritable youth culture out there in California."

"Were you surprised at the changes when you came home?"

"I wasn't thrilled to see that every fast-food chain in America had discovered the Chesapeake. Who needs another hamburger stand?"

"Chloe wouldn't agree with you."

Libby laughed. "I wouldn't expect her to. It's called the price of progress."

Several hours later, Assateague Island, Virginia's famous wildlife preserve, materialized in the distance. The forest looked black against the white sand beach. Russ increased his speed and within minutes had pulled up close to the deserted shore. He dropped the anchor, picked up the lunch basket and held out his hand. "Let's go."

Libby stepped out of her shorts, adjusted her bathing suit and slipped into the water. She took Russ's hand and followed him to the beach, splashing through the warm water.

"Shade or sun?" he asked when they had reached the deserted sand.

She looked speculatively at his skin. "You're dark enough to stand a little sun, I think, and it'll keep the bugs away."

He dropped the basket where he stood and pulled her down beside him. "What'll you have?" He rummaged through the food she'd packed. "If you aren't hungry yet, we've got beer, iced tea and lemonade."

"I'm hungry, all right," she said, resting her hand on his shoulder.

Startled, he turned around, blue eyes wary, assessing the look on her face. What he saw surprised and delighted him. "Why, Libba Jane, I do believe you are hungry, but not for food."

Her voice was husky, sensual. "You always were a fast learner."

Russ stood and held out his hand. "Let's move to the trees."

"Why?"

"I'll fry out here. My cheeks are whiter than a baby's butt, or haven't you noticed?"

Libby pulled the elastic out of her hair and shook it over her face to hide the wave of red creeping up from her chest. Suddenly she was off the ground, cradled in Russ's arms. He walked toward the trees.

"After all this time, I can still embarrass you," he murmured. "It's amazing."

She locked her arms around his neck. "What's so amazing about it?"

"We've known each other since we were kids. I'm surprised that anything I could do would still make you self-conscious."

"I think you like it," she said. "For some reason it gives you pleasure to unsettle me. It always has."

He set her down in the shade. She faced him, hands on her hips. "Am I right?"

His glance took in every detail of her trim, rounded figure. It always surprised him to realize how small she really was. From a distance she seemed taller. She was right. When they were kids, he had worked at shaking her poise. It made her softer, more vulnerable, and it made him feel stronger. Now it seemed childish. That air of calm reserve she wrapped around herself was nothing more than a shield against pain. He'd learned that just recently. It was important that she know it, too.

"There's only one way I want to unsettle you now, Libba," he said softly. "Will you let me?"

Her mouth went dry and she nodded. He stepped closer and slid his hands up her arms. Then he bent his head to her lips, moving against them until they parted.

Her skin was smooth and hot and the feel of her tongue in his mouth was driving him insane. He broke the kiss, breathing heavily, and pulled her against him. Her body molded bonelessly to his and the sensation of soft breast and taut nipple against his chest altered his breath. He wanted her and he didn't want to wait.

His hands shook as he pulled down the straps of her bathing suit, sliding it down over her hips. She kicked it away and then moved back to him. He lifted her chin, holding her gaze while his hands sought the fullness of each breast, the dip of her waist, the smooth skin of her bottom and, finally, the heat between her thighs. When he kissed her again, it wasn't slow and sweet like the first time, it rocked her with its need and she answered it with her own, her mouth and fingers playing over tight skin, lean planes and sharp angles, tasting moist, salty skin, teasing earlobes and pulse points and pebbled nipples, her palms seeking out the pleasure spots only she knew how to find, moving beneath the waistband of his trunks, touching the fullness of him, lightly, teasingly, until he gasped and gripped her wrist painfully.

"Stop," he rasped in a voice that was low and winded as if he'd run a great distance.

His heart pounded against her chest. She waited, clinging to his shoulders. Seconds passed. She lifted passion-dark eyes to his face. His mouth was tight and careful and very close to hers.

"The hell with it." He lowered her to the sand, his head and the width of his shoulders blocking out the canopy of trees. "There's no reason to wait."

She laughed and pulled him close. His lips opened over hers. Libby no longer felt the heat, the flies, the scrape of sand against her shoulder. There was nothing but this man, the sensation of lean, strong hands on her breasts and the heat radiating from the pit of her stomach to every nerve ending in her body.

They came together on the warm, salty sand of Assateague Island, hands clinging, hearts pounding, blood running, in as desperate and fierce and sensual a mating as that of the Spanish stallions credited with populating the island.

When he could breathe normally again, Russ opened his eyes. Libba was asleep. Her hair, a mess of sand and salt, cushioned her head. Wine-dark lashes rested against her cheeks and her skin was gold from a combination of sun and Beauchamp genes. Russ ran his finger over the slope of her shoulder. She had beautiful skin, clear and poreless, warm and dark, skin made to absorb the rays of the merciless Chesapeake sun.

He leaned over and pressed his lips to hers. He felt her response. Slowly her eyes opened. When he took his mouth away, she smiled.

"Now I am hungry," she said, "for food. But first I want to swim." She stood, a fluid, graceful motion of loose sand and naked, golden skin. "Are you coming?"

"In a minute. You go first."

"Too tired?" she teased him, lifting her arm to flip her hair over her shoulder.

"Not exactly," he hedged, his eyes on the shape of her breasts.

She laughed and turned her back to walk toward the water.

Russ looked down at his lap. Fatigue was hardly his problem. He wondered if she realized that she hadn't a stitch on, and then he wondered why he was embarrassed to have her see that he wanted her all over again.

After he regained sufficient control to join her in the water, the day passed too quickly. They swam to the sandbar, scooped up clams and ate them raw. Hiking around the half-mile loop that made up the bird sanctuary, they spotted Canada geese, blue herons and terns lining the inlet. In the distance, nearly out of sight, the famous Chincoteague ponies, their stomachs rounded from marsh grass, grazed in the shadows.

Sated with sun and sand and food, Libby lay beside Russ, whose eyes were closed. She'd nearly drifted off to sleep when he spoke.

"You never told me when you changed direction."

"How do you mean?"

"You wanted to be an actress. You're a long way from that."

She opened one eye. "It started with a volunteer assignment on Catalina Island. Have you ever heard of it?"

"It's one of the Channels, isn't it?"

"Yes. Chloe went to camp and I earned a few units. We were sent there because a necropsy on a bald eagle revealed that the bird was riddled with DDT, two hundred and twelve parts per million in its brain, to be specific. That's a larger amount than any found in the wild for thirty years. After that, I was hooked. It was so much more important than anything else."

Russ frowned. "DDT was banned twenty-five years ago. No one uses it."

"That's the point. An investigation showed that the entire food chain around the islands, from benthic worms and kelp bass to gulls, falcons and eagles are still lethally contaminated."

"How can that be?"

"Apparently, from 1947 to 1971, Barnaby Chemical Corporation flushed DDT-contaminated waste into Los Angeles County sewers that empty into the ocean. The deposit covers thirty miles of coastal shelf. Everyone thought it would go away in time. But it didn't. We know now that ecological problems will occur for another century because DDT is slowly leaking to the surface from the ocean floor. Most of the animals are surviving, but because of the poison accumulated in their bodies, their offspring die. None of the fifty bald eagles introduced to Catalina Island since 1980 have been able to reproduce. Their eggs contain ten times more DDT than the amount that causes fatal shell thinning. We're talking about complete reproductive failure.''

A strange tingling began at the base of his spine.

"Because DDT is soluble in fat, it doesn't break down or become diluted. It binds to silt on the ocean floor and converts to a chemical that is equally toxic. It clings to bottom sediment where shrimp, worms and fish burrow down, stir it up and store it in their fat.'' Her face was very close, very intense. "This is the terrifying part. Each step up the food chain, the concentration in an animal's fat roughly doubles. Two parts per million in a worm magnifies to four parts in a fish that eats the worm and eight parts in a bird that eats the fish. At the top of the food chain, predators absorb the biggest doses, predators like eagles and falcons and seals.''

"And people,'' Russ said grimly. "People who eat fish caught in Pacific waters.''

Libby nodded. "People who eat contaminated fish caught in areas around San Pedro face an elevated cancer risk, a sharply elevated risk.''

"Is that what's happening here?'' he asked.

She shook her head.

"I don't think so. I'm not sure what is happening here, only something's not adding up. The reports from the lab don't indicate enough toxins in the water to be dangerous at all, and yet there's a fishing alert, crabs have mutated and people are dying of leukemia. It doesn't make sense, and Cliff Jackson is deliberately stonewalling me. I don't know what to do.''

Russ sat up. "Is the Barnaby company being prosecuted?''

"There was a lawsuit pending.''

"What happened?"

"A judge threw it out. He said the statute of limitations had passed."

"Christ."

Libby nodded. "Exactly."

"Whoever is contaminating the bay is in trouble. It won't be easy to stop them. It might even be dangerous."

"I've thought of that, but I can't start a riot based on speculation. I need test results and so far I don't have them."

"When you asked for help at the meeting, you didn't mention that."

She stared straight ahead. "No."

"Why not? People's lives could be at risk."

She wiped the sand off her hands, her thighs and her knees, anything to keep from looking at him. Even now, after all this time, it was painful to know he disapproved of something she'd done. "I don't think you understand the gravity of the situation," she began slowly. "The food chain is compromised. Women are giving birth to babies with horrible deformities." She lifted her eyes to his face. "Sterility and cancer are on the rise. People are dying. *All* of our lives are at risk. Just because no one is pointing a shotgun doesn't mean the end result isn't the same. Do you really think those men don't know they need to be careful?"

She was right. It was a hell of a situation. "How difficult is it to find out what's going on here?"

"About as difficult as finding a needle in a haystack."

"In other words, it's not gonna happen."

"It could," Libby hedged, "if we're lucky or if someone responsible is honest and puts two and two together."

"It doesn't sound good."

She shook her head.

"What are our options?"

She pulled a sandwich from the basket, unwrapped it and handed it to him. Then she took one for herself. "If Cliff won't push to make this a red flag with the EPA, I'm going over his head. But I can't continue here indefinitely and allow my daughter to be poisoned."

"Does that mean you'll leave the rest of us to fend for ourselves?"

"Of course not," she said, stung that he would suggest such a thing. "I'm not giving up. The situation here needs to be exposed. I'm going to make a full report and recommendation, but as a newly hired staff member I don't have a lot of credibility. Our current administration doesn't consider environmental concerns a priority."

"What about the press?"

"That's a possibility. People should be informed. If this becomes public enough we'll find the source of contamination. But that doesn't mean it's over. An ecosystem takes time to reestablish itself and it isn't cheap. Valdez, Alaska, is still recovering after twelve years. Once the people of this area have the facts, they're on their own. Decisions about relocating or taking extra precautions are individual matters."

"So, you're leaving."

She sighed. "I didn't say that for sure, Russ. It's a possibility, but only if Cliff stonewalls me."

He bit into his sandwich. "Are you scared?"

"Terrified."

He reached for her hand. "Be terrified with me."

She swallowed. "All right."

"Promise?"

"Promise."

Twenty-Eight

Chloe stood by the snack machine and pretended to look at the various choices sitting isolated in their refrigerated cubicles. She didn't feel like eating. She would probably never feel like eating again. There were two kinds of people, she decided. One kind ate more when they were nervous and the other couldn't eat at all. She was the other kind. Her stomach was twisted into tight, angry knots and the thought of anything sliding down her throat brought on an immediate gagging reflex.

Where was Bailey? She had seen his truck in the parking lot, but there was no sign of him. It was lunchtime. The benches under the trees were filling up with brown-baggers and the line for the cafeteria was lengthening by the minute.

"Hi, Chloe." Tess Hennessey had materialized beside her. "Are you buying today?"

Chloe shook her head. "I'm not hungry."

Tess shifted her books into her other arm and nodded toward the cafeteria. "Sit with us, anyway."

Slowly, keeping her eye out for Bailey, Chloe followed Tess into the air-conditioned cafeteria. She slid onto the bench, leaving room for Tess to follow.

As usual, Skylar Taft was holding court. "Hey, Chloe. We missed you this morning."

"I came late," Chloe mumbled.

"How come?"

"I was tired. My mom let me sleep."

Skylar leaned forward, her shiny dark hair swinging against her cheeks. "Is it true?"

"What?"

"That you were with Bailey Jones in his trailer just minutes after he killed his mother?"

Chloe reared back. Her cheeks were the color of bleached bone. She opened her mouth to speak, but the words wouldn't come.

Tess spoke for her. "Skylar Taft. What an awful thing to say."

Skylar shrugged. "All I did was ask if Chloe was there."

All eyes were on Chloe. She cleared her throat. "Bailey didn't kill his mother," she said clearly. "Lizzie Jones was sick."

"My dad said he smothered her. He got word of it from the sheriff."

"Stop it, Skylar. You know those are only rumors." Under the table, Tess squeezed Chloe's hand.

"Chloe can tell me to stop," said Skylar. "She doesn't need you to speak for her."

Suddenly Chloe was angry. "Stop asking stupid questions, Skylar. I don't know what you're talking about."

Suddenly the room went quiet. Chloe closed her eyes and prayed for the impossible. Then, slowly, like a film in slow motion, she turned toward the door. Bailey Jones, in a frayed shirt and faded jeans, stood at the entrance. For a fraction of a second, he hesitated and then walked toward the serving line. Chloe's heart plummeted. *Why had he come?*

All eyes followed Bailey as he picked up a tray and took his turn through the line. The hush was absolute. Chloe could hear the clock ticking on the wall. Coins in the register clinked as the cashier made change. Time slowed. The hole in her stomach burned. Her eyes blurred. She wished herself a million miles away. Her mother was right. Why hadn't she stayed home today?

Suddenly, a whistle pierced the quiet. Then a voice called out, "How's your mama, Bailey?"

Chloe cringed. She looked at Bailey. The line of his jaw was tight and hard and his skin was stained a dark, passionate red. He walked with his tray to a table half filled with students and sat down. Within seconds, the table was quickly and silently evacuated. Bailey picked up his fork and began to eat.

A serious drumming began in Chloe's ears. She picked up her books.

Tess's hand snaked out and clutched her arm. "Don't Chloe," she whispered.

Chloe pulled her arm away, and under the regard of a roomful of hostile eyes, walked across the room to sit beside Bailey.

He didn't look up.

She pitched her voice at a slightly lower-than-normal level. "How are you?"

"How do you think?"

"That bad?"

He nodded.

Voices around them had started up again.

"Have you heard what they're saying?" she asked.

"I heard."

"What are you going to do?"

Bailey looked at her. "Nothing I can do."

Chloe swallowed. "Bailey, I—"

"Go away, Chloe. It's only gonna get worse for you."

"Why did you come here?" she asked. "You had to know what would happen."

He looked at her and the rage in his black eyes was a palpable thing. She swallowed and forced herself to keep eye contact.

"I couldn't stay there," he said, his voice so low she barely heard him. "I had to do something normal, be where people are."

She didn't hear him. Her eyes were fixed on the door. Two men in police uniforms stood at the entrance. They'd taken up positions at the door, steely-eyed, hands on their belts. One stayed behind. The other walked deliberately toward Bailey.

Chloe struggled for air. *Run away,* her mind screamed. She said nothing.

The policeman stopped behind Bailey. "Stand up, kid," he said.

Bailey stood and started to turn. He was pushed forward. His arms were pulled back and cuffs slapped on his wrists.

"Bailey Jones, you're under arrest," the man began. "You have the right to remain silent. Anything you say may be held against you in a court of law."

Bailey said nothing.

Tears streaked down Chloe's cheeks. "No," she said out loud. "No."

"Go home, Chloe," Bailey muttered. "Go home now."

Unable to muster enough strength to stand, she buried her head in her arms. She did not want to watch Bailey being taken away in handcuffs.

Minutes passed. She felt a small hand on her shoulder.

"It'll be all right, Chloe," Tess said. "C'mon. Let's go."

"I don't think I can," Chloe mumbled into the crook of her arm.

Tess's breath was warm against her ear. "Don't cry. Just stand up and walk out of here with me now."

Somehow, Chloe managed to collect her belongings. Keeping her eyes on Tess's back, she followed her out of the building, across the cool, shaded grass and out to the sidewalk leading into town. Two blocks later, Tess was still walking.

Chloe caught up with her. "Where are we going?"

"I don't know," Tess confessed. "Maybe my dad is in his office."

"I don't think so," Chloe said. "He took my mom to the beach on some island."

Tess slowed her pace. "Oh."

"I don't care anymore," Chloe said. "Not after everything else. Do you?"

"You mean about them being together?" Tess shook her head. "It doesn't bother me. I don't remember my parents being married and I like your mom. It's just that my mom's insane. It's going to bother her and she'll figure out a way to make everything worse." She waved her hand. "Never mind. That isn't important now. We have to figure out what to do."

"Do you realize that we're ditching school?"

Tess nodded. "It was that or be emotionally stoned to death."

Chloe stared at her, pleasantly surprised. Tess Hennessey had insights she never would have imagined. It suddenly occurred to her that the mousy, brown-eyed girl she'd dismissed as shallow and boring had a spine of steel. Suddenly she was ashamed. "Thanks, Tess. I really appreciate your standing up for me the way you did."

"You're welcome." Shock had loosened Tess's reticent tongue. "I didn't only do it for you. I did it for Bailey, too. They persecute him for no reason. I can't stand Skylar Taft. I can't imagine why I have anything to do with her, except that there wasn't anyone else until you came along. She controls everybody."

"Where are we going?" Chloe asked.

"I don't know," Tess confessed. "We can't go to my house. My mom will be furious."

"Mine would understand, I think," said Chloe, "but she's not home."

"What about your grandparents?"

Chloe shook her head. "My grandma's not doing very well and my granddad has enough on his plate right now."

Suddenly she brightened. "I know. We'll go to Verna Lee's."

Tess frowned. "Why would we go there?"

"She's a friend of Bailey's and she's my friend, too. She'll let us hang out there for a while."

Tess stopped and turned to Chloe. "We're going to have to tell them, you know. It's just that I'd rather wait for my dad. He's more rational."

Chloe nodded. "My mom isn't always rational, but we didn't do anything wrong."

"We left school in the middle of the day without permission," Tess reminded her. "My mom is going to flip out and my grandpa will be even worse."

"Why did you do it?"

Tess shrugged. "I knew I had to do something. I mean, you were just sitting there all alone. What are friends for?"

Chloe's heart was full. She felt like crying. "I don't know, Tess," she said softly. "I'm beginning to think I never had one until you."

Perks was empty. Verna Lee, dressed in a bright yellow sarong skirt and peasant blouse, was cleaning the counter. She smiled when she saw Chloe. "Hi, sweetie. Did school let out early today?"

Chloe flopped down on to one of the soft couches. "It's a long story." She glanced at Tess. "This is Tess Hennessey."

"I know Tess," said Verna Lee. "Her daddy talks about her all the time. Make yourself at home, honey."

Tess sat down beside Chloe, leaned her head back against the pillowed back and moaned. "This feels so good."

Verna Lee filled two large glasses with apple juice and set them down in front of the girls. She sat down on the couch facing them and crossed her legs. "Tell me what's going on," she said.

"Bailey was arrested," Chloe said.

"It was at school, in front of everybody," Tess added. "They're saying he killed his mother."

"Holy shi—Moses." Verna Lee's yellow eyes took up half her face. "That can't be right."

"It is." Chloe sat up. "It happened like this." She proceeded to explain the events of the last forty-eight hours, beginning with her strange foreboding the day she'd bicycled to see Bailey and ending with Tess leading her out of the cafeteria and toward Main Street.

Verna Lee's voice shook. "That poor boy. Have you told your grandfather about this, Chloe? If anyone can help, he can."

"He already knows. He's the one who told my mother."

"Does he know what happened at school?"

Chloe shook her head. "We came straight here."

A smile hovered at the corners of Verna Lee's mouth. "I'm flattered that you would come here first. It's a wonderful compliment. But your grandfather needs to know what happened." She stood. "C'mon. I'll drive you home."

"What about Tess?" Chloe asked.

"I'm coming with you," Tess said quickly. "Your mom and my dad will be home at the same time. I can wait at your house and he can take me home."

Verna Lee knew Tracy Wentworth by reputation and said nothing.

The trip from Assateague Island was filled with comfortable silence. Libby was tired and Russ concentrated on motoring the boat back to the Cove. It was nearly six o'clock when they arrived. Without a word, Libby jumped out on to the dock to secure the line to a piling. Russ turned off the motor and checked the ropes, turning to see if she would wait for him. She stopped at the end of the dock and leaned against the railing. He caught up with her and took her hand. "It's been a great day."

"If only we didn't have to face my mother."

Russ frowned. "Is there a problem with your mother?"

"I'm beginning to think there has always been a problem with my mother, only I didn't know it."

"I thought girls got along with their mothers."

"That's because you had no sisters."

Their banter was light and superficial the rest of the way home. Libby felt good, not excited or euphoric, but a contented kind of good that relaxed her muscles and brought a smile to her lips.

Russ turned down the long driveway. The sun was directly in front of the windshield. At first Libby didn't see the red car parked in front of the house. When she did, it was too late to hide her reaction. "This is ridiculous," she exploded. "Why doesn't she just move in?"

Russ frowned. "That's Verna Lee's coupe. What's going on, Libba?"

"I'm tired of the lies and secrets. Why don't they just come out with it?"

"With what?"

"The truth."

"You leaked some of it the other day."

"I can't say anything else. Not yet."

He shrugged, turned off the engine and walked around the car to open the door. "Shall we brave them together?"

"I'd appreciate it very much."

The front door opened and Tess ran down the steps into her father's arms. "Where have you been? I've been waiting for hours," she cried.

"Waiting for what? Where's your mother?"

Tess pulled away. "She's really mad at me, Daddy. I left school early. I guess you could say I ditched, but I couldn't help it. Chloe was in really bad shape and I was the only one who could help."

Panic rose in Libby's throat. "Where is Chloe?"

Chloe appeared at the door. "I'm here, Mom."

"Thank God." Libby ran up the porch steps and threw her arms around her daughter.

"Bailey was arrested at school." Chloe's lip quivered. "I couldn't—" She stopped, unable to continue.

"Chloe was sitting with him," Tess continued. "Everybody's saying he murdered his mother. Chloe couldn't go back to class, Daddy."

"Of course not," Libby said quickly, tightening her arms protectively around Chloe. "Why didn't you go to the office and ask to come home?"

"My mother wouldn't have understood," Tess said.

"I knew you weren't home," Chloe added. "We went to Verna Lee's and she brought us home. Granddad is with Bailey, wherever that is."

Libby leaned against a pillar and chewed on her lip. She was an unfit parent. Somewhere along the way she'd missed out on acquiring the skills that every other mother naturally assimilated. It wasn't through lack of trying. Where had she gone wrong? Her own upbringing had been sane enough. Nola Ruth made it all look so easy. Even Shelby was a good mother. Her red-haired, green-eyed friend managed her twins with a scattered, down-home consistency that left no doubt in their minds when she meant business. Of course Shelby had Fletcher, a man who had adored his tiny scraps of humanity from the moment they drew their first breath. Nola Ruth had Cole and Shelby had Fletch. Libby had been alone since the moment the obstetrician pronounced her child a girl. She hadn't wanted it that way, but Eric hadn't been interested in parenting.

She gave herself a mental shake. That was water under the bridge. "C'mon, everybody. Let's go inside. We're home now. Russ can call Tess's mother and explain and we can get something to eat. Everything will be all right."

"Verna Lee fixed us dinner," Chloe said.

Libby frowned. "Where's Serena?"

"It's her night off."

Could her guilt be any worse?

Apparently Russ could read her mind. His voice, smooth and warm and slightly amused, came from behind her in the hallway. "Easy does it, Libba. You're allowed a day off now and then. No one could have predicted this."

Verna Lee came out of the kitchen. She slung her purse over her shoulder. "I'll be leaving now," she said quietly. "I never intended to stay this long, but Cole left and your mother—" She paused. "She's sleeping now. I didn't tell her much. You can do that."

"Thank you for everything you did today."

Verna Lee waved away her words. "Don't think twice about it. I like Chloe. I've liked her since the first day I met her. I'd have liked her even if she wasn't your daughter. She's unusual. You've done a fine job, Libba Jane." She looked embarrassed. "That was a mouthful. I'll be going now before I say any more."

Chloe waited for the door to close behind Verna Lee. "What was that all about?"

Tess spoke up. "I think she just gave you a compliment."

Over Chloe's head, Russ's eyes met Libby's. "You know where the phone is," she said. "The girls and I will wait in the living room."

Ten minutes later, white-lipped and monosyllabic, Russ returned. "Get in the car, Tess. I'll take you home."

"Is everything all right?" Libby asked.

"Fine," he said tersely. "I'll tell you about it later."

"Is Mama really mad?" Tess asked anxiously.

Russ attempted a smile. "You know the answer to that, Tess. You knew it when you took off today without telling anyone. You have to face the music." His voice gentled. "But don't worry, you won't face it alone. I won't let her beat you."

"She doesn't do that."

"Not physically, anyway."

Tess stood. "Bye, Chloe. I'll see you tomorrow."

Chloe nodded.

Libby walked them to the car. "What's going on?" she asked when Tess was safely in the car.

Russ shook his head. "I'll handle it. Thanks for the day."

"You haven't done anything wrong," she reminded him. "It's not your fault that Tess left school and came here. She has to know that."

"You're assuming Tracy thinks logically." He took her hand and kissed her briefly on the lips. "Don't worry so much. We've all got our problems. I'll handle my ex-wife."

She watched them drive away until there was nothing left but a swirl of dust in the distance.

Inside the house, Chloe lingered on the stairs. "What's going to happen to Bailey?"

"I don't know," Libby said honestly. "Granddad will do everything he can." She hesitated. "Did Bailey ever talk about his mother's illness?"

The girl shrugged. "Not specifically. I asked him about it once. She was blind, you know, and in pain. It hurt him to see her like that. She wouldn't sell her land. She wanted it for Bailey."

None of it sounded promising. Once again Libby had a sudden urge to go to church. She hadn't stepped inside one for years, but the hold of her religion was still strong. It was just as impossible to be an ex-Catholic as it was to be an ex-daughter or an ex-female, although she'd read about people who'd tried. Right now the pull was strong. She felt vulnerable, out of control, desperately in need of something more powerful and competent than herself.

She felt sandy and sticky. "I need a shower. We can go for a drive later, if you want," she suggested. "Maybe we could find some ice cream in Salisbury."

Chloe shook her head. "I'm tired. I'm going to bed early."

Libby slung her arm around Chloe's slim shoulders and together they walked upstairs.

Despite the purifier she knew her father had installed, she showered quickly, keeping her head down and the seam of her lips tightly shut. Slightly ashamed of her phobia, she turned off the water and toweled herself dry. Wrapping the terry cloth around her head, she wiped the mirror with her hand and stared at her reflection, critically examining her body. Not perfect by any means, but not bad. Libby had only recently been obsessed with appearances, not like Shelby who bemoaned every new wrinkle and suffered agonies over some future date when she imagined walking across the street and hard hats continued about their business instead of turning to whistle in appreciation. Hers was a milder obsession. She had a sense of time marching on and leaving her behind less, somehow, than she'd been before.

She cupped her breasts and tightened her stomach muscles. Finally, concave again, and not only because of her regular morning runs. Anxiety was the best diet in the world. Only contented women who had their lives in order with nothing to hide had meat on their bones. She wanted to be one of them, round-faced, comfortable women who carried a sweetness within them, women who were long past relationship worries.

Libby sighed. If only Chloe wasn't traumatized. That was more than enough to ask for. If they could get through this, and if Chloe still wanted to go home, she would make her happy and take her back.

Meanwhile, there was Russ. He had a slow hand and an easy touch and a way of making her heart pump and her blood sing. For Libby, the dry spell was over. The strength of her desire shook her. He would no more than move his hand across her skin and she was lost in that swirling whirlpool of heat and color and longing that rocked her senses and stripped her of the inhibitions collected over a lifetime. She knew every intimate crevice of his body, the taste of his skin, the sound of his breathing, the pulse beat in his temples. Each time, with the trembling anticipation of the first time, she waited for the moment when it would all begin again and the slow, careful, seductive touch of his hands and mouth and tongue would change the woman that was Libby Delacourte, Eric Richards's cold and uninspired wife, into a sensuous, flame-lit addict of the flesh.

What would it be like to begin again with Russ, somewhere far away from Marshyhope Creek and Nola Ruth, from Bailey Jones and Tracy Wentworth, somewhere safe and suburban and normal, where people and animals could drink from the taps and swim in the lakes and fish in the streams? Maybe he would come back to California with her.

She sighed. There was no going back. There would always be Tracy because there was Tess, and for Libby, right now, there was Chloe and Nola Ruth.

Twenty-Nine

Cole Delacourte wrote out his signature, tore off the check and handed it to the officer at the desk. Then he turned to the boy standing silently beside him. "C'mon, son," he said gently. "We're going home."

Bailey's eyes flickered for an instant and then went blank again. Without speaking, he followed Cole out to the car.

Cole slid in behind the wheel and backed out of the parking lot. "How serious are you about finishing school, Bailey?"

The boy blinked in surprise. "Serious enough," he replied.

"Do you intend to go on to college?"

Bailey shrugged. "I'd like to go to art school."

Cole nodded. "Have you looked into whether or not you need a high school diploma?"

"No, sir."

"My guess is you do." Cole was silent for a minute. "What do you think about a home teacher until we sort this thing out?"

"I don't want to put you to any trouble or expense."

"Don't worry about that. The school district will pick up the cost. It's simply a matter of turning in your work once a week to a teacher who makes up assignments for you and helps out when you have questions. How does that sound?"

"It sounds good enough."

"Your hearing is set for next week, son. I'd like you to

tell me exactly what happened. You'll need to tell me the truth. Don't leave anything out. Do you understand?''

Bailey stared out the window, his face white and drawn.

"You'll stay with us until this is over," Cole continued. "It'll give you some time to think things through. No one will bother you." He glanced over at the boy. "Is that all right?"

"It's fine."

Cole decided he'd gotten enough response for a short ride home and they managed the rest of the drive in silence.

Chloe was sitting on the front steps when they pulled into the driveway. She stood, biting her lip until Bailey stopped beside her.

"Hi," he said.

She smiled. "Hi. How are you?"

He considered her question. "I've been better."

"Do you want to take a walk?"

Her grandfather stepped in. "Not now, Chloe. Bailey needs a break."

Reluctantly, she turned and walked beside them up the steps. "Are you going to school tomorrow?"

Bailey shook his head. "I'll be doing my schoolwork here for a while."

She looked at her grandfather. "I don't suppose I could do that, too?" she asked.

"I don't think so, honey," answered Cole.

Crestfallen, she nodded. "It was worth a try." She brightened. "But at least you'll be staying here." She thought a minute. "What about your studio? How will you paint?"

"I don't know. I haven't thought about it."

"If you give me a list of what you need," Cole said, "I'll send someone over to get it."

For the first time since Cole had seen him, Bailey smiled.

Russ cut the engine, threw the anchor over the side, pulled out a cigarette and struck a match. Bending his head, he lit the unfiltered end and inhaled deeply.

Libby sighed and pulled on a pair of latex gloves. "When are you going to give those up?"

His eyebrows rose. "We're here, in illegal waters, attempting to measure radioactivity near the Patuxent River Naval Air Station and you're worried about my lungs?" He shook his head. "If anyone spots us, we're in some serious trouble."

"There has to be an explanation for the side effects present in the ecosystem," she explained. "The PCB content in the water isn't enough for the fish advisory imposed on the watermen. It isn't enough for the elevated BOD levels in the water and it certainly isn't enough for genetic mutations in the animal population. Manufacturing here in the Tidewater is strictly regulated, which makes leaking of contaminants for any length of time impossible. There's something funny going on and I can't help but think it's going on legally under the auspices of the government. There's nothing left to do but this."

Russ held her gaze for a long minute. Then he nodded. "Go for it. I'll keep an eye out."

Without a word, she pulled a small box from her bag, flipped a switch, adjusted a dial and leaned over the side of the boat, submerging the instrument.

Russ's stomach tightened. He couldn't remember when the bay had been more silent. Seconds passed. Then he heard it, a tick-ticking that resounded like a time bomb in his ears.

Libby sat up quickly, wiped down the box with a paper towel, stripped off her gloves and reached for her notebook.

"What is it?" he asked, striving for calm.

"The radioactivity in the water is beyond acceptable levels."

"How beyond?"

"Way beyond. There's activity up and down the bay, but it's stronger here than anywhere." Her hands shook. "I think we've found the source."

His eyes focused on the embankment, the barbed wire and the sign above it that read Patuxent River Naval Air Station, Trespassing Prohibited.

"What do we do now?"

"We talk to an expert," she said.

Dr. Susan Saunders, manager of the university lab in Annapolis and a former classmate of Russ's, welcomed them warmly. "How can I help you?"

"I need to ask you a few questions," Libby said.

Susan grinned. "As long as we can eat at the same time. I'm starving."

"Let's go," said Russ.

Over hamburgers and large glasses of milk in a local coffee shop, Libby posed her question. "Tell me about the Patuxent River Naval Air Station."

"Anything specific?" Susan asked around bites of her burger.

"I have water samples from all over the bay, Shad Landing, Holland Sound, Crisfield, Toddville, the Nanticoke River, Nancy's Point, Hooper Island and Cedar Point. All have levels of radiation exposure that are unacceptable. The highest levels recorded are near the air station. I'd like to know what kinds of hazardous waste are stored there."

Susan frowned. "The usual, plant sludge, cesspool wastes, sewage treatment sludge, spent oil absorbents, pesticides, you name it."

"What about nuclear waste?" Russ asked.

Susan shook her head. "I don't think so. If there is any nuclear waste at the air station it would most likely be low level, you know, protective clothing, lab equipment, nothing serious. We have natural uranium. You know as well as I do it exists in seawater."

"What would you say if I told you the local waters are showing high levels of uranium and cobalt 60?" asked Libby.

"That's impossible," Susan said flatly. "You're talking about waste from nuclear reactors, glass logs, even plutonium."

"Do we know for certain that radioactive nuclear fuel isn't being stored there?"

"No, but it's highly unlikely."

Libby leaned forward. "More than 200,000 tons of spent fuel has a home somewhere, Sue. The Atomic Energy Commission claims there will be 450,000 tons by the middle of the century. Does anyone know for sure that Patuxent isn't being used for such a purpose?"

Susan pushed her food away. "Good lord, Libby. Do you have any idea what you're suggesting?"

"Do you want to see the samples and the Geiger counter readings?"

"I certainly do, and the sooner the better."

Russ slid out of the booth. "I'll get the check."

Cole Delacourte carried a plate of ham sandwiches, two glasses and a pitcher of lemonade out to the back lawn. Bailey Jones sat at the picnic table overlooking the Chesapeake, a still, solitary figure, his face dark and expressionless beneath the shadowed umbrella. Cole set the plate on the table and poured the lemonade.

"I've got to prepare your case, son," he said, coming right to the point. "It's time you told me what happened."

Bailey stared at him. "Pardon?"

"I want you to tell me what happened with your mama, Bailey, and I want the truth. No surprises, son. Do you understand? As long as you tell the truth we have a chance."

Bailey waved his hand at the bay. "It's beautiful here."

"Yes." Cole looked out over what was his. "It is, isn't it?"

"Mama and I lived our whole lives in a room no bigger than that bathroom you're letting me use upstairs."

Cole kept silent.

"They wanted her to give that up, too."

"Who wanted her to give what up?"

"They did."

"Who?" Cole persisted.

"The developers who wanted her land. They wanted the last little bit of her and she wouldn't give it to 'em. She said she'd rather die."

"Did you kill her?"

Bailey gazed out over the glittering blue water. "Yes, sir. I suppose you could say that."

Cole hesitated. He didn't want to put words into the boy's mouth and yet he wanted the whole story. "Did she ask you to help her die, Bailey? Was it her idea?"

Bailey didn't answer. "Do you know," he said instead, "that she never ate in a restaurant?" His voice shook. "She didn't know about things that most people know about. She never had credit or a bank account or an ATM card. It was like we lived in another world different from everyone else. She liked me to read her the newspaper, every bit of it, from beginning to end, except for sports. She didn't care about sports. I wanted to buy her a television. We had one once, but it broke down." He shrugged. "We could have bought another, I suppose. The ADF check came every month. I guess it wasn't important enough to us. She couldn't see it and I didn't care either way."

Cole tried another approach. "Tell me what happened that day from the beginning."

"What day?"

"The day she asked you to help her die."

Bailey thought a minute, his dark eyes opaque and distant. "I can't remember the exact day. It started a long time ago."

Cole frowned. "She asked you more than once?"

Bailey stared out over the sun-steeped water. "I lost count

of the times she asked me. It started when the pain got bad. Doc Balieu saw her in the beginning, but after a while we didn't have the money for the prescriptions she needed. Finally, she wouldn't go anymore. She said it didn't help.''

"How long ago was that?"

"A year ago, maybe longer."

"Your mother was in pain for more than a year and no one would help her?" Cole was incredulous.

"She could have had Medicaid, but she would've had to sell the land." Bailey's mouth twisted. "They won't give you anything unless you have nothing left. She wouldn't do that."

"Did you tell Dr. Balieu what was happening?"

"Yes, sir."

Cole willed himself to remain calm. "Do you remember when she first said that she wanted to die?"

"It was after we got the results of the new cancer. She said she didn't want to go through the radiation again. She wanted to die at home, with dignity. That was when she asked me to do it."

"What did you say?"

"I said I couldn't. We argued. I told her it wasn't fair to me, that I'd get in trouble."

Cole waited.

"She asked me if I thought what was happening to her was fair. I said it wasn't, but I still couldn't do it." Bailey's temper flared and he clenched his hands. "She was my mother."

"Easy, son. Take it easy now." Cole poured a glass of lemonade and set it in front of the boy. "Settle down and have something to drink. We don't have to go through this all at once."

But once he'd started, Bailey seemed to want to finish. "She stopped for a piece," he continued, "but then the pain would come back and when I'd ask her what I could do, she'd say it again." Tears flowed unchecked down the brown cheeks. "It got worse and worse. Bourbon helped, and marijuana. But after a while she had to be drugged all the time. I got to a point where I couldn't leave her, she was so bad off." He shrugged and scrubbed his eyes. "Then I decided to do it."

"Good Lord." Cole couldn't help himself.

"I took her to Shad Landing and we ate barbecue outside." Bailey smiled, remembering. "She liked it. Then we drove to the point and looked out over the wildlife sanctuary. She couldn't see it, but I described what it looked like. She liked that, too. After dark, we went home." He swallowed. "I poured her a glass of bourbon, all the way to the top. She drank it down. I thought she'd gone to sleep. I held the pillow down over her face. She struggled some, but not much. And then she was gone."

"They found your skin under her nails. Why didn't you stop when she struggled?"

"We talked about it," Bailey said. "She told me not to."

Cole Delacourte had practiced law for forty years, and he was quite sure in all that time that he had never heard anything quite like Bailey Jones's confession. He was also quite sure he had never taken on so complicated a case. There was no doubt that the boy was guilty of the act of homicide, but was it justifiable? Cole believed it was. It helped that the trial would be held south of the Mason-Dixon Line where the average man drove a pickup and quite often that pickup had a gun rack in the back, complete with a rifle or two. Would it be enough? He had no idea how a jury would react to the idea of a boy playing God with the life of his own mother.

Susan Saunders leaned against the building, one leg propping her up. Her hands shook as she lit a cigarette, inhaled and blew out a stream of smoke. "If those samples come from as far east as Marshyhope Creek Bay, we've got a real problem.''

"There are ways of dealing with this," Libby replied. "Have you heard of uranium eaters, organic phosphorus? When combined with uranium it forms an insoluble material.''

Susan snorted. "That's very experimental. The problem with phosphorus is that the same property that allows it to travel through soil also keeps it from sticking to anything.''

"That's where microorganisms come in. When you combine genetically mutated phosphorus it would combine with uranium.''

"First, you've got to get the powers that be to admit we've got a problem.''

"Why would that be an issue? I'll show it to them, just like I did with you.''

"Don't be ridiculous, Libba Jane. Do you really think no one else knows what we've got down here? They're keeping it quiet. Why do you think the EPA lab keeps telling you there's nothing wrong with the water? Cliff Jackson worked here before you took over. Do you think he never ran tests?''

Libby frowned. "What I can't understand is all the secrecy. People should know what they're dealing with.''

"Because it's expensive," Russ said. "Because people will file lawsuits against the government. Why do you think the military refused to admit that soldiers in Vietnam were endangered due to exposure from Agent Orange? In terms of money, the ramifications are enormous.''

Libby shook her head. "People are using contaminated water. It has to come out.''

Susan ground out her cigarette. "Do me a favor, you two. Please don't involve me. I have a family, and quite frankly, I'm scared." She pushed herself away from the wall. "It might be better if you ran your tests in the government lab from now on.''

"We don't want to cause any trouble for you, Susan," said Russ. "Libba will take her samples to the designated lab. But we're going to challenge the results if they come up clean, and if there's a problem, we may need your help."

Libby slung her bag over her shoulder. "We all have families, Susan. I'm just as scared as you are."

Susan Saunders nodded. "Good luck."

"Thanks."

Hand in hand, Russ and Libby walked back to his car. "It looks like you did it, Libba Jane," he said.

She looked at him and bit her lip. "Do you think Cliff knows and covered it up?"

"I've known Cliff Jackson for a long time. He's a decent guy. If he's kept this thing quiet, it's for a reason. You need to check that out first before jumping to any conclusions. It's possible something's already being done and it hasn't gone public."

"He's not always available to answer my calls."

"I'll handle Cliff," Russ said grimly.

"What are you going to do?"

"Scare the pants off him."

Thirty

"Hello, Libba Jane." Cliff Jackson's big linebacker's shoulders filled the doorway. His face was somber, unsmiling.

She lifted her eyes from the computer screen. "Well, well, well, if it isn't the ghost of Marshyhope Creek."

"I'm sorry I haven't been all that available," he began.

"No, Cliff. You haven't been available at all. That's it. Period. You've been deliberately avoiding me and I know why."

"It isn't how it looks."

"Isn't it? I have the samples and I have your reports and I have mine." With one foot, she pushed her swivel chair away from the desk and crossed her arms against her chest. "Tell me how it is."

He sighed and looked around. "May I sit down?"

"You *may* sit down, but you can't. There's only one chair and I'm in it."

"You aren't gonna make this easy on me, are you, Libba?"

"No."

"All right." He propped himself against the wall. "The reason I'm here is to explain why your request to visit the air station has been denied."

"I already know why it's been denied. Tell me something new."

"First of all, you need to know this is under control. We

discovered the leakage a year ago and immediately took action."

She frowned. "What are we dealing with?"

"Intermediate-level waste, metal fuel cans that originally contained the uranium fuel for nuclear power stations. It's usually stored at the place of production, but in this case, the landfills were already filled to capacity. The spent fuel, which this is, is stored in water-filled cooling pools. Patuxent was one of them. After twenty years or so, leakage isn't uncommon."

"My God, Cliff. How could you not tell anyone? People are being poisoned."

"Hold on, Libba. Several investigations and cleanups are already complete. We've run an engineering and cost analysis and we'll be removing the rest of the waste by the end of next year. All the damage has already been done and it's because of what's gone on before. There's no cover-up involved."

"Why the secrecy?"

"To avoid panic and, to be honest, to avoid lawsuits."

"People have a right to know they're drinking contaminated water. People whose lives have been affected have the right to compensation."

"What do you want me to do, put an ad in the paper?"

"That's exactly what I want you to do. Explain it just the way you did to me. Tell it like it is, that we can expect high levels of cancer and possible birth defects because of what happened here twenty years ago. Tell these people why they can't eat the fish from these waters for a long time to come."

"It's a year or two, not a long time."

"It's a very long time in the life of a person whose income comes from the bay. Young people, especially those who will have children some time in the future, should have all the facts."

"You're making this more than it is. There's no conclusive evidence that anything that's happened in this area was caused by nuclear contamination.''

"You're turning a blind eye, Cliff. Bailey Jones is on trial for the murder of his mother. It was a mercy killing. The woman had inoperable cancer. She was in terrible pain and they couldn't afford medication.''

"Lizzie Jones had other problems, Libba. We don't know what factors contributed to her illness.''

"What about Drusilla Washington? Can you be so cold-blooded when it comes to Verna Lee's grandmother?''

He looked puzzled. "What about Drusilla?''

"You mean Verna Lee never told you?''

He shook his head.

"She strangled to death a hideously deformed newborn, the child of sharecroppers. Again, another mercy killing. My father represented her. The charges were dropped.''

"Why didn't Verna Lee tell me?''

"Maybe she knows more than you give her credit for,'' Libby snapped.

"Since when have you become an expert on Verna Lee?''

"You might say we have a lot in common.''

Cliff shook his head. "You've changed, Libba Jane.''

"Why did you hire me, Cliff? Surely you knew I would figure this out.''

"I didn't think you'd figure it out so quickly,'' he admitted. "You'd been away from the industry for a long time. You were inexperienced. I assumed it would take a while for you to come to any conclusions, and when it all came out as planned, there would be someone the community trusted already in place. Actually, your coming home was incredibly fortuitous.''

"You set me up.''

"Give me a break, Libba Jane,'' he protested. "I simply didn't give you all the information. I wasn't sure of your reaction.''

"Tell me what's really going on here,'' she demanded.

"You're an environmentalist. How can you sweep this under the rug? What are you thinking?"

He hesitated. She could see the sweat beading his brow.

"I'm up for a promotion, Libba Jane," he said at last. "Surely you know how hard it's been for me to get where I am. Whistle-blowing could ruin my career."

She didn't trust herself to speak for a long, charged minute. Finally she stood. "I have the name of a reporter, an environmentalist, who would love to tell this story. I've just been reading her latest article. If you don't want to use her, find someone else, but do it quickly, or I will." She hesitated. "I'm not the only one who knows about this. I told Russ and Verna Lee."

His face darkened. "Are you suggesting that you might be in danger because I'm a thug?"

"No. Of course not. You're just an evasive liar who's pulled the wool over the eyes of an entire population of people. Pardon me if I got the two confused."

Libby tied the laces of her tennis shoes and stretched out her legs, first one and then the other. A run before dinner would calm her nerves and her temper. Despite Russ's assurances that most companies had money built in to weather emergencies, she was still rattled over her findings and worried about the future of the marine industry around the bay and the watermen who depended on regular fishing for their livelihood.

She had run less than a mile when she heard the car behind her. Making her way to the side of the road she kept running, expecting the driver to pass. When he didn't, she looked back over her shoulder.

Shelby Sloane's red head and bare shoulders peeked over the dashboard of a late-model SUV. Fletcher couldn't be doing too badly if Shelby drove a car like that. Libby stopped and waited for Shelby to pull up beside her.

"I need to talk to you, Libba Jane," she said.

"So, talk."

"Please get into the car, honey. We can't have a conversation with me shoutin' out my window."

Sighing, Libby stopped and leaned against the car door. "What do you want, Shelby?"

"I need you not to be mad at me anymore. Fletcher's mad at me and the girls only speak to me when they have to and now you're mad at me, too, over something that happened twenty years ago."

"It didn't happen for me twenty years ago."

"It did, too, Libba. You found out about me and Russ the same summer you ran off with Eric. That was seventeen years ago, and if you ask me, seventeen years is long enough to get over a grudge. You're madder now than you were then. Why is that?"

The dam of hurt inside Libby's head exploded. She turned on Shelby. "Because you haven't changed," she said furiously, "not in all this time. Because then I was shell-shocked, now I'm not and everything's come back. Because you were my best friend. That's supposed to mean something. And because *you* never told me. I left everything I loved because of what the two of you did."

Shelby stopped the car, turned off the engine and set the brake. Then she turned to Libby, green eyes wide and wise. "No, you didn't, Libba Jane. You left because you didn't want to stay here. You were made for better things than living here in Marshyhope Creek, the wife of a waterman. So was Russ. If you hadn't left, neither of you would have gone on to what you were supposed to do and that's a fact. Stop lookin' at me that way. You know it's true."

"I can't trust you."

"Of course you can. I never messed around with your boyfriend. Everything we did was before the two of you were together. We were kids. Why can't you see that?"

Libby shook her head. "I don't know. It still makes me mad."

Shelby threw up her hands. "Lordy, you've got it bad, Libba Jane. Why not just marry the man and put us all out of our misery?"

"I don't know if I can trust him, either."

"Well, here's one truth, sugar. I wouldn't have Russ Hennessey on a silver platter, not with that ex-wife of his. She's never gonna let go. You should know that if you're serious about him. He blew it when he settled down with her. That was your fault, too, you know."

Libby sighed. "All right, Shelby. You've made your point. I need to finish my run and go home."

Shelby's forehead wrinkled. "Are you ever gonna forgive me, Libba Jane? Are we still friends?"

Libby sighed. "Yes, Shelby. We're still friends."

"Well, thank God. I didn't have to grovel nearly as much as I thought I would."

"Don't press your luck."

"See ya, honey."

Libby watched her drive away. Shelby was who she was, a generous, impulsive woman with the mind of a fifteen-year-old and a heart as big and warm as a sunspot. There was no point in holding her accountable for what couldn't be changed. Love was measured by a different standard for different people. She thought of her father and Nola Ruth. Some things had to be put aside. Libby began to run.

Chloe looked around the dinner table. "Where's Bailey?"

"He decided to eat in his room tonight," her grandfather answered.

"Why?"

Cole Delacourte waited a moment before answering. "It's hard for him, Chloe. He's grieving for his mama. Sometimes he needs to be alone."

Chloe considered the possibility of Bailey preferring his own company to that of her family's and decided her grandfather was probably right. Still, Bailey's decision must have been sudden because Serena hadn't removed his place setting.

Her grandmother wasn't eating. She seemed preoccupied, and more than once, Chloe caught her looking at the entrance to the dining room. "Is everything all right, Gran?" she asked.

Nola Ruth turned her head so that the unaffected side of her face was toward her family. She spoke slowly, deliberately. "I thought we would have a guest for dinner, but apparently I was mistaken."

Libby picked up her water glass. "Who did you ask, Mama?"

Nola Ruth swallowed and nodded to her husband at the other end of the table. "Verna Lee Fontaine."

Libby's eyes widened.

"I didn't know you were friends," said Chloe.

"We aren't friends, Chloe. It's a great deal more than that," said her grandmother.

Chloe looked at one grandparent and then the other. Her mother was strangely silent. "I don't understand."

Nola Ruth shook her head. "Cole, I don't think—"

"It's a long story, Chloe," said her grandfather. "Maybe, when your grandmother is up to it, she can tell you about it."

The doorbell, muted by the thick drapes and solid walls of the dining room, sounded in the distance. Libby, in the middle of buttering her roll, froze. Minutes passed.

Serena entered the room. "Miss Libba has a visitor," she said quietly.

Libby frowned and looked at her mother. Nola Ruth was particular about her meals. She did not like them interrupted. "Who is it, Serena?"

The black woman hesitated.

"It's all right, Serena." Libby folded her napkin and left it beside her plate. "I'll be right there." She looked around at her family. "Keep eating, please. It probably has something to do with the job. I'll take care of whoever it is and send him away."

Nola Ruth's lips tightened in disapproval. "Tell him we eat at six-thirty, Libba Jane."

Libby nodded. She really needed to find a place to live for Chloe and herself. "Yes, Mama."

"It's your ex-husband," Serena whispered after she closed the door to the dining room. "He's in the parlor. I told him you were at dinner. He said he'd wait. I'm sorry, Miss Libba."

Libby's stomach dropped. *Eric.* What could he possibly want that couldn't be taken care of by telephone? "Thanks, Serena," she managed. "It's all right."

She waited a full minute, composing her features and mentally preparing her mind for what she knew would be an unpleasant encounter. Then she opened the door.

He stood looking out the window, his back to her. "Hello, Eric," she said calmly.

He turned, his face rigid with anger. "What in the hell is going on with my daughter?"

Her eyebrows rose. "You flew three thousand miles to ask a question? We have telephones."

His face reddened. "Just answer it."

"A woman has died," Libby said without embellishment. "Chloe may be called as a witness. We're not sure yet."

Eric swore feelingly.

"Spare me, Eric. What do you really want?"

"I want my daughter to come home with me."

Libby folded her arms. "I don't believe you."

He walked past her and stopped at the door. "I won't make a scene and insist on seeing Chloe now, but my lawyer will contact you. The venue will be California. Meanwhile you can reach me at the Roanoke Lodge in Salisbury."

"She can't go anywhere yet, Eric. Surely you can see

that. It isn't what I want. You can't imagine that I would be willing to traumatize Chloe in any way.''

She was conscious of his eyes moving over her face, assessing her words, gauging her integrity. "Please. Come and have dinner with us. Talk to my father. He's representing the boy involved.''

She saw some of the tension leave his body. "Please," she repeated. "Come in and sit down.''

"All right, Libby. I'll sit down to dinner with you, but only for Chloe's sake. I still can't believe you brought her back here. She belongs in California.''

She wouldn't allow him to provoke her, not now, not when Chloe needed them both. "I'll tell Serena you'll be staying," she said smoothly, and led him out of the parlor and down the long hall to the dining room.

Once again the doorbell rang. Libby waved Serena away and answered it herself.

Verna Lee smiled tentatively. "Hello, Libba Jane. Sorry I'm late. I had some trouble with last-minute lingerers at the shop.''

Libby's sense of the ridiculous overflowed. First Eric and now Verna Lee. One big happy family. "Come in," she said to the striking, elegantly dressed black woman. "Have you met my ex-husband, Verna Lee?''

"I don't think—''

Libby cut her off. "Of course not. Verna Lee, this is Eric." Then she threw caution to the four winds. "Eric, this is Chloe's aunt, my mother's eldest daughter, Verna Lee Fontaine.''

She had to give him credit. Eric was a better actor than she thought. Not a single eyelash flickered in surprise.

"It's a pleasure to meet you, Verna Lee. I always thought Elizabeth was an only child.''

Verna Lee's lips turned up in amusement. "She thought so, too. I imagine I was something of a shock to Libba Jane.''

Libby laughed. "I'm recovering quickly, and speaking of shock, why don't we go into the dining room and let everyone know the two of you are here."

Verna Lee's tawny head bent close to Libby's. "Am I interrupting something?" she whispered.

Libby shook her head and threw open the door to the dining room. "On the contrary. You're going to make it all palatable. Look, everyone," she called out. "Look who I've brought."

"Dad." Chloe jumped up, ran to her father and threw her arms around him. "You didn't tell me you were coming."

"Shooting wrapped up sooner than I expected," he explained. "I hope I'm not intruding."

Nola Ruth's beautiful manners asserted themselves. "Of course not, Eric. We're happy you and Verna Lee could make it. Please sit down, both of you. Serena will set another place."

"How long are you staying?" Chloe asked her father.

"I'm not sure yet." Eric looked at Cole. "I have a few questions for your grandfather. How are you, Mr. Delacourte? It's been a long time."

Cole's eyes twinkled. "Call me Cole."

Chloe frowned. "What kind of questions, Dad?"

"They can wait until after dinner." Eric smiled brightly and looked around the table. "So. How is everybody?"

Nola Ruth's words were slightly slurred, but her accent was the same, rich and deep and very Southern. "Why, Eric, you still have that lovely smile. How nice of you to ask. We've been just fine, haven't we, Libba Jane?"

"Yes, Mama." Libby's eyes met Verna Lee's. "We're all just fine."

"Do you have a place to stay, Eric?" asked Cole.

"I'm staying in Salisbury."

"That's all right, then." Cole did not volunteer a spare bedroom. "I'll bring you up-to-date on the case Chloe is involved in after dinner. Meanwhile, I assume you've met everyone.''

Eric's eyebrows rose slightly. ''Libby introduced me to your—'' he paused ''—your stepdaughter on the way in.''

Chloe choked. ''What did you say?''

Verna Lee picked up her fork. ''He's talking about me, Chloe,'' she said as naturally as if she'd asked someone to pass the salt. ''I was adopted as a baby and I've been looking for my birth mother for a long time. It turns out she's your grandmother. Your mother and I are half sisters. I guess that makes me your aunt. I hope you can stand it,'' she teased.

Chloe glowed. ''I knew I liked you right from the beginning. It's probably because we're related. I could feel it.''

''I don't know about that,'' Verna Lee hedged. ''People don't always get along with their relatives, but I'm pleased that you're pleased.''

Libby released her breath. The revelation that Verna Lee was part of the family had gone much better than expected. The absurdity of her thinking followed immediately. Why wouldn't it have gone well? The only person unaware of the relationship was Chloe and she was a child of the twenty-first century, where racial boundaries virtually did not exist. Libby discounted Eric completely. His opinion simply didn't matter.

''How long are you staying, Eric?'' Cole asked.

''I hadn't planned on it at all. I want to take Chloe home with me.''

Cole swallowed the last of his wine. ''That's understandable,'' he agreed, ''but not practical. Chloe will be called as a witness. You'll have to bring her back several times between now and the trial date.''

''When is that?''

''It's scheduled for six weeks from tomorrow.''

Chloe's indignant voice interrupted. ''I'm not going anywhere. Bailey needs me. I'm the only friend he's got. I can't go home yet.''

Eric frowned. ''You've been telling me you want to come home since you got here.''

''Things have changed,'' said Chloe flatly. ''I'm not leaving.''

A ghost of a smile hovered at the edges of Cole's mouth. He'd realized long ago that he would learn much more if others did the talking.

Thirty-One

The courtroom was filled to capacity. It seemed to Cole that every reporter in the state had shown up, first on his doorstep when the story broke weeks ago and now here. Jury selection had been remarkably quick. He could find no fault with the nine women, three men and two alternates filling the jury box. Apparently, neither could the prosecution. Once again, Quentin Wentworth was presiding. Cole didn't think Bailey would slide through the cracks as easily as Drusilla Washington had. At least the boy looked presentable. Libba and Chloe had taken him shopping in Salisbury. He wore a severe dark suit with a white shirt and maroon tie. Even his shoes had been shined properly.

The bailiff called the courtroom to attention. "All rise for the Honorable Quentin Wentworth."

The judge strode into the room and took his place at the front of the court. He did not look out over the courtroom but busied himself with the papers in front of him.

"Please be seated," droned the bailiff.

"Mr. Delacourte," the judge began, "are you ready to present your case?"

"I am, Your Honor."

Wentworth looked over his glasses at the prosecuting attorney. "Are you ready, Miss Cameron?"

"Yes, Your Honor," the assistant district attorney replied.

"The prosecution will present opening arguments."

Cynthia Cameron, a striking brunette whose leggy beauty was a stigma to rise above in the conservative Tidewater community, leaped to the challenge. "Ladies and gentlemen of the jury, we are gathered here today to right a wrong, to prove beyond a reasonable doubt that this young man, Bailey Jones—" she pointed with her finger "—did cold-bloodedly plot and carry out the premeditated murder of his mother, Lizzie Jones, for the purpose of acquiring her considerable estate. On the evening of September 8, Mr. Jones smothered his mother with a pillow as she slept. Her subsequent struggle was to no avail, ladies and gentlemen." Miss Cameron's voice dropped dramatically. "Bailey Jones, showing no mercy, held the pillow over her face until her struggles stopped and she was dead."

Judge Wentworth nodded at Cole. "Mr. Delacourte, it's your turn."

"Thank you, Your Honor." Cole rose and looked at the jury box, making eye contact with every juror. He shook his head. "Where is the justice, ladies and gentlemen? Where is the justice that allows a woman to suffer debilitating pain, enough to beg her only son to do her one last favor and put her out of her misery? Where is the justice that sentences an eighteen-year-old boy to watch his mother slowly and painfully die, day after day with no relief? How many of us, ladies and gentlemen of the jury, could watch a loved one suffer and, for months and months, refuse her last request? Bailey Jones loved his mother, so much that he risked his own freedom to bring her peace. I ask you, is that wrong? I hope not. I hope we all are loved to the degree that Lizzie Jones was loved by her only son. God help us, because I can truthfully say, not a one of us, not a single person on either side of Marshyhope Creek, cared as much about Lizzie Jones when she was alive as we now care how she died.

"The defense will show that Bailey didn't cause his mother's death. Lizzie Jones was already dying, consumed by a cancer that began years ago, a cancer that required treatment she couldn't afford, not unless she gave up the only thing she had of any value, her land. Lizzie had a hard life. We all know that. She didn't give Bailey much in the way of material things. But she knew he would have the land. That knowledge kept her alive, through unbearable pain, up until the end when she could take no more of it. We will prove, ladies and gentlemen, that Bailey was a devoted son who could no more refuse his dying mother's last request than he could stop the tide from rising.''

Two weeks passed before Chloe was called as a witness. Wearing a simple pale blue cotton dress, she looked very young and frightened and wonderfully earnest as she took her seat in the witness box. From across the room, her eyes met her mother's. Libby swallowed and smiled. Where in the hell was Eric?

Reassured, Chloe held up her hand and was sworn in.

Her grandfather approached the box. "Chloe, tell the court how you came to know Bailey Jones."

Chloe relaxed. This she could do. "I met him in July when I first moved to Marshyhope Creek. He gave me a ride into town."

"And after that?"

"I ran into the woods after an argument with my mother. He found me and invited me home for dinner. I met his mother. She was blind and very nice. Bailey told me she was sick. He cooked dinner. Then he showed me his paintings. You should see his paintings. They're beautiful. Then he drove me home."

"Can you explain your impression of the relationship between Bailey and his mother?"

Chloe nodded. "Bailey loved his mom and she loved him."

"At any time did you observe anything in Bailey's behavior that would lead you to believe he could be violent?"

"No."

"Tell the court about your last visit to Bailey's home."

Chloe watched Russ whisper something into her mother's ear. Libby's mouth was tight with worry.

"Bailey came to school that day," she said.

"What day, Chloe?"

"The day it all happened."

"Let the record show that the witness refers to September 8."

"So recorded."

Cole smiled at this granddaughter. "Go on, Chloe."

"I knew something was wrong. He looked sad and worried. I didn't see him any more that day so I went to visit him after school. At first it was really quiet. I thought no one was home, but then I heard something inside the trailer. I called out and Bailey opened the door." She swallowed and her lip quivered.

Cole waited. "Take your time, honey."

Chloe nodded. "Lizzie was on the bed. At first I thought she was sleeping, but I felt her. She was so cold. I knew she was dead."

Libby couldn't breathe. She fought back brimming tears and clutched Russ's hand.

Cole's voice was very gentle. "What happened then, Chloe?"

"Bailey cried," she said to the hushed courtroom. "He fell down on the floor and cried so hard I thought he would be sick. I think he cried for hours. Then we carried Lizzie into his truck and I drove home."

"Thank you, Chloe. No more questions."

A full minute passed before Judge Wentworth spoke. He cleared his throat. "You may step down for now, Chloe. The court will recess for twenty minutes."

Russ brought two cups of coffee back to the table in the cafeteria where Libby waited. She accepted one gratefully. "Thanks."

"How are you doing?" he asked.

"I'll be much better after the day is over. I don't know why this is so stressful for me. I'm sorry."

"There's nothing to be sorry about. Your daughter is sitting in front of a room full of people. She's nervous, and in about fifteen minutes, the prosecuting attorney is going to try to twist her words into something she didn't mean. It would be strange if you weren't nervous."

Libby groaned. "If only they would have allowed her to come out here with us during the break." Her eyes flashed. "She was looking around for Eric. Damn him. Why does he always disappoint her?"

"Easy, Libba. Planes are late and cars break down. Give the guy the benefit of the doubt."

She stared at him in astonishment. "Give him the benefit of the doubt? He doesn't deserve it. He could have flown in yesterday. That's what parents do. They don't take chances."

She was holding together by the edge of her nerves. "Sorry," he said soothingly. "I stand corrected."

"It's my fault. I didn't mean to bark at you."

He dismissed her apology. "You've got a lot on your mind." He looked at the clock on the wall. "It's time to go back in."

She nodded and opened her mouth to agree, but the words didn't come. Instead she looked at him, really looked at him. It was as if a screen had rolled back and she could see clearly into the window. She saw a man, reasonable and kind, a man with character and conscience, an adult. And he was here for no other reason than to show support for her and for Chloe. Her heart swelled. "Thank you," she whispered.

He grinned. "My pleasure."

Back in the courtroom, after everyone was settled and the jurors had taken their seats, Chloe was escorted in by the bailiff.

Judge Wentworth spoke to her. "If you agree to abide by your former oath, we don't have to swear you in again. Is that all right with you, Chloe? Speak clearly, now."

"Yes."

Wentworth nodded at the prosecutor. "You may cross-examine, Miss Cameron."

Vulturelike in her black suit, Cynthia Cameron swooped down on the girl. "Chloe, you do understand the meaning of *premeditated,* don't you?"

Cole Delacourte rose. "Objection."

"Sustained. Please explain the term, Miss Cameron. The witness is sixteen years old."

"Certainly, Your Honor." She turned to look at the jury while she addressed Chloe. "*Premeditated* means planned ahead of time." She turned back to the girl. "Did Bailey Jones ever mention that he planned to kill his mother in cold blood?"

"Objection, Your Honor."

"Sustained. Please dispense with the editorials, Miss Cameron."

"Yes, Your Honor."

"Chloe, did Bailey talk to you about his mother?"

"Yes," answered Chloe.

"What did he tell you about her?"

"He said she was sick and they couldn't afford the medicine."

"How did you feel when he told you that?"

"It didn't seem right. I asked him if there were any places that would take people who couldn't afford to pay."

"What did he tell you?"

"He said his mother had land, but she wouldn't sell. She wanted him to have it and only a few places would take people who can't pay."

"Did Bailey ever tell you how much the land is worth?"

"No."

"Did you ever see him or hear him express anger toward his mother?"

"No. Not really."

"Explain *not really*."

"He was frustrated because she needed help and she wouldn't sell her land."

Cynthia Cameron looked at the ground, her hands clasped in front of her. "What are Bailey's plans now that his mother is dead?"

Cole rose. "Objection, Your Honor."

"Sustained. Rephrase the question, Counselor."

"Very well, Your Honor. Has Bailey ever shared with you what he plans to do now that his mother is gone?"

Chloe thought a minute. "Bailey wants to be an artist. He wants to leave Marshyhope Creek and go to art school."

"He can certainly do that now that nothing's holding him back, can't he?"

"Objection," Cole called out.

"Strike that from the record," the judge ordered. "Miss Cameron, I won't warn you again."

She flashed a contrite smile. "Sorry, Your Honor. No further questions."

"You may step down, Chloe," said the judge.

Chloe glanced at her grandfather and then walked past her mother and out the double doors. Libby and Russ followed her.

"Have you seen Dad?" she asked immediately.

Libby shook her head. "Obviously he's been held up." She changed the subject. "Are you hungry?"

"No." She gestured toward the courtroom. "What will happen next?"

"More witnesses will be called," Libby explained. "Both lawyers will ask questions and then the jury will decide which side is more credible."

"Will Bailey go to jail?" Chloe asked, as if the possibility had only just occurred to her.

Libby hesitated. Before she could speak, Russ cut in. "I doubt that very much, Chloe. Bailey is eighteen years old. He's never been in legal trouble before and he's lived under stressful conditions for a long time. I can't imagine the jury will see it any differently."

"What *will* happen to him?"

"I don't know, honey. We'll have to wait and see. Maybe someone will step forward and take care of him."

"Bailey doesn't need anyone to take care of him," Chloe said scornfully.

"Probably not," Russ agreed.

She looked at her mother. "Can he stay with us?"

Libby worked to conceal her dismay. "Oh, honey. That's a lot to ask. Your grandmother isn't well. Granddad has enough to do with all of us."

"He won't be any trouble," Chloe insisted. "He isn't any trouble now. I'm going to ask Granddad."

"Chloe." A voice called from down the hall.

Chloe turned toward the sound and her face lit up. "Dad, I knew you'd come."

"I'm sorry I'm late," he said when he'd closed the gap between them. "The traffic was terrible."

"In Salisbury?" Libby was incredulous.

"I came from Richmond," he explained. "There was construction on the bridge."

Libby turned to Russ and attended to the briefest possible of introductions. "Russ, this is Chloe's father, Eric Richards. Eric, this is Russ Hennessey."

Eric nodded pleasantly. Neither one extended a hand.

"Well, I'm glad you and Chloe didn't have to go through this alone." He smiled at his daughter. "How did it go in there?"

Chloe shrugged. "Okay, I guess."

"Is your part finished, for good?"

"My father estimated the length of the trial to be about

one month. I'm not sure whether or not Chloe will be called again. Probably not,'' Libby guessed.

Eric took Chloe's hand. ''How about coming home with me, Chloe? I think you could use a break and see some of your old friends.''

''That sounds nice,'' she said dutifully.

''How about it?''

''When I know what's going to happen to Bailey,'' she said. ''Then I'll come.''

Eric sighed. ''All right, Chloe. I'll get a room in Salisbury and we'll wait this out. Are you going to school?''

''Of course she is.'' Libby was furious. ''Today was an exception.''

Russ squeezed her shoulder. ''I'm for getting a bite to eat. How about you, Chloe?''

Chloe looked at her mother and then at her father. ''That sounds good,'' she said dubiously.

''I'd like to speak with you privately, Eric,'' Libby said. ''Why don't you take Chloe to lunch, drop her off at school and meet me at the house later?''

Chloe brightened. ''Thanks, Mom.''

''Don't mention it. See you later.''

Russ waited until they'd left the building. ''What are you going to do?''

''What can I do?'' she said bitterly. ''He waltzes in and offers Chloe what she wants, knowing that I won't just send her away.''

''What do you mean?''

She wouldn't look at him. ''I'll have to go back to California. I can't just give up my daughter.''

''You and I need to talk, Libba Jane.''

''Not now, Russ. I've got enough on my plate.''

''Now,'' he said firmly.

Instinct told her not to argue. Silently, reluctantly, she walked beside him out of the courthouse, down the steps and into a small diner at the end of the block.

He ordered coffee and a sandwich. She wasn't hungry. He didn't press her to eat. "What is it, Russ?" she asked, unable to bear the silence any longer.

His eyes were level on her face. "It's been one long hot summer since we got together again, Libba Jane. We've been dancing around this issue since the beginning. Now I've got to know. What are your intentions?"

"I beg your pardon?"

"You heard me and you know what I'm talking about. I've waited my whole life for you. Hell, I've made world-class mistakes because of you. I've handed you my heart and you've carved it up pretty well. Now it's time. I've got to know if there's any point to all of this. I'm thirty-seven years old. That's on the edge of late for starting over. I'd like someone to care if I come home or not. I'd like to raise a family. We're good together, Libba. What do you say?"

"Is this a proposal?"

"Yes."

Suddenly she was angry. "That's not fair. You're making me choose between you and my daughter. What if I made you the same offer? What if I asked you to choose between staying here with Tess or coming with me to California?"

"Are you making me an offer?"

She wadded up her napkin, threw it on the table and slid out of the booth. "Damn you, Russ Hennessey," she said, and stalked out of the diner.

Thirty-Two

Cynthia Cameron was even more striking in a pair of skin-hugging jeans and a sleeveless white blouse tied at her waist. The white emphasized her tanned arms and the blue of her eyes. Her long, dark hair was pulled back into a ponytail and gold hoop earrings hung from her ears. She stood in the doorway of the EPA office and waited for Libby to hang up the phone.

"I'm looking for Elizabeth Delacourte," she said.

Libby stood. "You've found her."

Cynthia smiled a dazzling white-toothed smile. "You've got quite a family."

"Thank you," Libby said smoothly. "What can I do for you?"

"I'm Cynthia Cameron and I'm prosecuting the case your father is defending."

Libby waited.

"I'd like to ask you a few questions."

Libby's eyebrows rose. "I'm not involved in this case, Miss Cameron. I can't imagine how I'd be of any use to you."

"Call me Cynthia. I'd like to know more about the water contamination in this area of the bay."

"In that case, let's go next door to Perks. As you can see, I'm short on chairs."

The two women chatted easily as they walked to the coffee shop. Verna Lee was behind the counter. She smiled at Libby. "How's everything going?" she asked.

"It could be better. We'll have to talk soon." She gestured to the woman beside her. "This is Cynthia Cameron, the prosecutor for Bailey's case. Cynthia, this is my sister, Verna Lee Fontaine. She brews a mean cup of coffee."

"How do you do, Verna Lee?" Cynthia looked at Libby. "Like I said, you've got quite a family."

"Two iced teas, Verna Lee." Libby pointed to a spot in the back. "We'll take that table."

"Coming right up," said Verna Lee.

"Tell me about leakage into the subterranean wells," Cynthia said when they were seated.

"We don't know for a fact that there is leakage," Libby replied carefully.

"The front pages of every local newspaper in the area say there is."

"You know better than to believe everything you read in a newspaper."

Verna Lee brought over two tall glasses of amber liquid. "Anything else?" she asked.

"No, thanks," replied Libby, "unless you have more of those brownies you had last week. I'd like to bring some home for Chloe."

"I'll wrap them for you," she said, and walked away.

Cynthia picked up her straw and stirred her tea thoughtfully. "Tell me what you do know for a fact."

"We know the air station was a sight for intermediate-level nuclear waste and that some of the containers leaked into the bay water. A cleanup was requested and implemented even though it was not reported to the community."

"Why not?"

Libby shrugged. "Fear of reprisal, lawsuits, you name it. Why are you interested?"

"I'm trying to link Lizzie Jones's cancer with water contamination."

"Why?"

"Is there a link?" the woman persisted.

"Possibly," Libby admitted, "but it hasn't been proved, not yet, anyway."

"Will you testify that there is a possibility?"

Libby stared at her incredulously. "Are you serious? And help you devalue that boy's land so that his mother died for nothing? I don't think so. You don't need my help. It won't make a difference to the case."

"What if I subpoena you?"

Libby's smile froze. Her warm feelings toward the prosecutor disappeared instantly. "You don't want a hostile witness, Miss Cameron. I'm not stupid and my father is the best trial lawyer this side of the Chesapeake. You may get what I have to say stricken from the record, but the jury will hear it. The facts are that we have water contamination here in the bay and that a few people, a *few,* Miss Cameron, have come down with serious illnesses. Why, we can't be sure. Many have not been affected at all. The government is doing its job to clean up the pollution. Those of us who live here would like that issue to stay out of this trial for obvious reasons."

Cynthia Cameron stood and threw two dollars down on the table. "Thanks for your time, Ms. Delacourte."

Verna Lee watched her walk out. She made her way to where Libby sat. "That one doesn't look happy."

Libby sighed. "No. I can't blame her. She's going to lose that case."

"Let's hope so. No one around here wants to see Bailey in any trouble."

"It's odd, isn't it? Lizzie was a pariah when she was alive. Now it's all turned around."

"Life doesn't always run smoothly."

"Tell me about it," Libby groaned.

"What's up?"

"Eric wants to take Chloe back to California and I think she'll go with him. Russ wants me to stay here."

"That is a problem," Verna Lee agreed. "What are you going to do?"

"If Chloe decides to go back, I'll have to go with her." She looked at her watch. "I've got to get back to work."

"What do *you* want, Libba?"

"What do I want? Why, I want—" She stopped, unable to find the words. "I don't know what I want," she said at last.

Verna Lee smiled. "When you figure it out, you'll know what to do."

At the door Libby hesitated. "Verna Lee?"

"Yes?"

"We've never really talked."

"Do you want to?"

"I think so."

"When you know for sure, tell me."

Libby laughed. "I know for sure."

"You name the time and place."

"Maybe we should all talk, you and Mama and me."

Verna Lee smiled. "You need to talk to your mama, Libba Jane. Nola Ruth and I have buried our demons. I think we're fine where we are."

"Where is that, Verna Lee?"

"Maybe we should discuss that when we have our talk."

Once again Libby laughed. "All right. I can take a hint. Why don't we get together tomorrow night?"

"Are you sure that's a good time? Your daddy's case should wrap up soon. If the jury comes up with a verdict, you might not want company."

"You're not company," Libby said firmly. "You're family. Come for supper."

Verna Lee's smile was full and warm. "I'll be there."

Normally, Cole wouldn't have called Bailey to the witness stand. But somewhere around the second day of the trial he decided the boy's testimony was his best defense. Attired once again in the dark suit, with a fresh haircut and glossy shoes, he looked more than presentable.

After he was sworn in, Cole approached the witness stand. "Bailey, will you tell us what happened the night of September 8?"

The boy's voice, choked, well pitched and sincere, carried to all corners of the courtroom. "Yes, sir." Not a sound could be heard in the courtroom. "Only it didn't start on September 8. My mother went to the doctor for the first time nearly two years ago. She had pain in her back and her legs. At first Dr. Balieu said it was arthritis and to take aspirin. But it got worse so he tested her blood. He said she had leukemia and needed chemotherapy." He stopped and drew several deep breaths.

"What happened then?"

"It was expensive. We didn't have insurance. She sold off a piece of land to get the money. That's when the developers started coming around. They wanted the whole thing, but she wouldn't sell. She said it was all she had to leave me." Again he stopped, unable to continue.

Cole waited until the boy was in control again. His voice was very gentle. "What happened after the chemotherapy?"

"She seemed better for a while. We thought it would be okay. But then it came back. I wanted her to go for more treatment but she wouldn't. She said we could sell everything off and if it still didn't work we'd be broke and she'd still be dying."

"How did you feel about that?"

"I used the computers at school. There were plenty of cases where the first round of chemo didn't work, but later ones did. I wanted her to go for more."

"Did you tell her how you felt?"

Bailey nodded. "All the time. We argued about it, but she wouldn't listen. Finally, the pain got so bad she talked about killing herself. I wouldn't hear it." His voice shook but it was clear. "I told her to stop talking like that. I took all the knives in the house and hid them in my truck. Finally she did stop. Then she refused to take any medication, even the pills Doc Balieu gave her as samples. The pain got so bad she would cry for hours. Then she would beg me to help her die."

Cole Delacourte looked at the jury. Every eye was focused on Bailey. "For how long did she beg you to do this?"

"Every day."

"For how long a period?"

"Six months."

"Are you saying that for *six months* your mother was in dreadful pain and she asked you to help her die every day?"

"Yes, sir."

"What did you say to her?"

"I told her I couldn't do it. I told her I'd be in terrible trouble. She said if I loved her I'd do it anyway." His voice lowered. "Finally, I did."

Cole gripped the boy's shoulder. "Are you all right, Bailey? Would you like to take a few minutes?"

"I'm all right, sir."

"Very well. Tell us about the night you decided to go through with it."

"I took her to Shad Landing and we ate barbecue outside." Bailey smiled, remembering. "She liked it. She'd never been to a restaurant. Then we drove to the point and looked out over the wildlife sanctuary while I described it to her. She liked that, too. After dark, we went home." He swallowed. "I poured her a glass of bourbon, all the way to the top. She drank it down. I thought she'd gone to sleep. Then I held the pillow down over her face. She struggled some, but not much. It didn't take long."

"Did you ever think that she might have changed her mind while she was struggling?"

"We talked about that. She knew she would struggle. She said it was every animal's instinct to fight for breath. She told me not to falter in my resolve because she knew what she asked me to do was for the best."

"Thank you, Bailey," said Cole. "I have no more questions."

Cynthia Cameron, hands palmed in a prayerful position, slowly approached the witness box. "How much is your land worth, Bailey?"

"I don't know, ma'am."

"Really? You never discussed with your mother how much money she was sitting on?"

"No."

"I'll tell you. Your mama left you nearly two million dollars of prime Maryland pine acreage."

Bailey gasped and whitened.

"Do you know how much another series of chemotherapy treatments would have cost, Bailey?"

He shook his head.

"Answer the question verbally for the court reporter, please."

"No."

"About ten thousand dollars."

He looked bewildered.

"Do you think anyone needs two million dollars, Bailey?"

He didn't answer.

She pressed him. "Do you think you could have spared ten thousand dollars to give your mother another chance at survival given that you still would've had $1,990,000 in land equity?"

He didn't answer.

Cynthia Cameron turned to the jury. "Cat got your tongue, Bailey?"

Cole stood. "Objection."

"Duly noted," she said quickly. "I withdraw the question. In fact, I have only one more question to ask the defendant. If you had to do it over again, knowing what you know now, would you still take your mother's life or would you give her a chance to survive if it meant reducing your inheritance by less than half a percent?''

Bailey sat completely still, his face frozen in misery.

''Answer the question, Bailey.''

''No,'' he whispered.

Cynthia Cameron shook her head. ''No more questions, Your Honor.''

Cole Delacourte's voice resounded throughout the room. ''I'd like to cross-examine, Your Honor.''

''Do so.''

''Bailey, did your mother ever discuss finances with you?''

''No, sir.''

''Did you have any notion of the value of your land?''

''No.''

''Did you believe your mother when she told you she would rather die than part with any more of her land?''

''Yes.''

''No further questions, Your Honor.''

Judge Wentworth pounded his gavel. ''The court will recess for lunch. We'll resume at one-thirty for closing arguments if there are no more witnesses.''

Cole Delacourte spoke of nothing but inconsequentials as he drove Bailey home that evening. The jury had been excused for the day. There was nothing left to do but wait for the verdict. He knew this might very well be the boy's last night of freedom. Murder in Maryland was not taken lightly, and an eighteen-year-old boy could be sentenced to the men's penitentiary. That was worst case. Cole did not expect worst case, but he was prepared for it. Cynthia Cameron was a worthy opponent. She had done her homework. He had no idea what the outcome would be.

* * *

The morning dawned crisp and clear. The Indian summer was over and fall had settled in overnight. The trees were ablaze with color. Energy hummed in the air and the smells of burning leaves and smoking fireplaces wafted through the small waterfront towns.

Bailey, dressed in his dark suit, sat on the front porch. Chloe, who insisted on being in court to hear the verdict, sat with him. Neither one wanted breakfast. Even Serena, who believed food was the panacea for all ills, didn't press them.

Shortly after ten o'clock the phone rang. Cole walked outside. "The jury has reached a verdict," he said. "It's time to go."

Somberly, as if they were heading for a funeral, the boy and girl climbed into the back seat of the car. Cole drove and Libby sat beside him. No one said a word until they reached the courthouse.

Cole turned and spoke to Bailey. "If it doesn't turn out for us, it isn't the end, son. We can always appeal."

Bailey nodded.

Libby was close to tears. She had no idea how Chloe was managing. Her daughter's eyes were dry and her small hand gripped Bailey's. She walked purposely beside him.

Russ was already inside. Tess sat beside him. Libby and Chloe took their seats in the next row. Again the courtroom was filled to capacity and again Eric was nowhere to be seen. The jury filed in. The bailiff announced the arrival of the judge. Everyone stood and then sat down again.

"Has the jury reached a verdict?" the judge asked.

The foreman rose. "We have, Your Honor." He passed the verdict to the judge, who read it and passed it back. "Please proceed," he ordered.

"We find the defendant, Bailey Jones, not guilty of murder in the first degree."

Chloe cried out and sagged against her mother. Libby clutched her fiercely and blinked back tears.

"Thank God," Russ said under his breath. Tess clapped her hands.

Libby watched her father shake Bailey's hand and then pull him into his arms. For the second time in the long, harrowing saga of Lizzie Jones, the boy lost control. The tears broke and he wept against the older man's shoulder.

Cynthia Cameron walked across the aisle and patted Bailey's shoulder. Libby saw that her eyes were very bright. Perhaps the prosecutor was human after all.

"I'm taking Bailey to lunch at the Crab Pot," Cole said. "You're all invited."

"There won't be any crab on the menu," Libby warned him.

"We'll order burgers. Are you coming?"

Libby laughed and looked at Russ.

"You bet," he said.

Thirty-Three

Verna Lee sat on the couch in the sitting room. Libby sat opposite in the wing chair. Steaming cups of spiced cider sat on the coffee table between them. "When did you know for sure who I was?" Verna Lee asked.

Libby tilted her head and considered the question carefully. "I think I knew from the minute Mama told me she had a daughter with a black man. It all came together for me. You resemble her, you know."

"So do you."

"I know, but in a different way, because you and I don't look anything alike."

Verna Lee acknowledged it was so. "How did it make you feel?"

"Do you really want to know?"

"Of course."

Libby sighed. Why did people do that? she wondered. Why did they ask for truth when they didn't really want it at all? She had no delusions about truth. It was powerful enough to destroy relationships. The problem was, once someone asked for honesty, there was no way around it but dishonesty and that was unacceptable. "I felt betrayed," she said simply. "I couldn't believe it. I didn't want to believe it."

Verna Lee nodded. "I can understand that."

Libby leaned forward in her chair. "It had nothing to do with you. But it was horrifying to learn that my mother had kept such a secret for forty years. It was as if everything I'd known was a lie.''

"I would have reacted that way, too.''

Libby was dying to ask what went on between her mother and Verna Lee when the air was finally cleared between them, but she allowed that the two of them deserved some privacy. After all, she'd had Nola Ruth all her life while Verna Lee had grown up without a mother. "When did you find out about Nola Ruth?" Libby asked.

"Drusilla told me on my twenty-first birthday. She was having problems with her heart and she didn't want to die without telling me the truth." She smiled. "I was terribly resentful of you. You had everything I wanted. But I got over it. You weren't to blame. I settled for hating Nola Ruth instead. Then I got over that, too. Eventually, I just wanted to know her. I never expected to have a relationship with you. I'm so glad you came home. I mean that."

There was no doubting her sincerity. "You've been a godsend to Chloe."

"What will happen now, Libba Jane? Are you taking Chloe back to California?"

Libby chewed her bottom lip. "It looks that way."

Verna Lee hesitated and then she spoke. "Will you listen to some advice?"

"All right."

"Chloe wants to go home to check things out, to see if she really belongs here or there. She's like a college student who goes home the first weekend after moving into the dorms to reassure herself that home is the same, and then her parents don't see her again until summer. If you go with her now, she'll have no options, and worst of all, you'll hate it. You came back here because you wanted to be here, not there. Why not send her back to her father to get her bearings? She may very well come back to Marshyhope Creek on her own. If she doesn't and if you can't stand having her gone, you can always go back later." Her voice softened.

"Don't go, Libba Jane. You have a dozen reasons for staying, and I'm not talking about Russ Hennessey, although he's certainly one of the possibilities. Your parents are here and they aren't getting any younger. I'm here and I'd really like to know you better. Marshyhope Creek needs you. This whole water thing would never have been exposed without you. Even Shelby Sloane needs you. She's become a real human being since you came back to town."

Libby laughed. "Shelby's harmless."

"Will you think about it, Libba Jane?"

"I suppose so." Libby was confused. Verna Lee's arguments made sense, but Chloe was sixteen years old. How would she feel about her mother sending her home alone?

Verna Lee stretched and stood. "It's been nice, but it's late. I've got an early day tomorrow. Don't bother walking me to the door and try not to agonize too much."

"There's something else I've been meaning to ask you."

"Go ahead."

"It's about Cliff," Libby said. "We didn't part on the best of terms. I was disappointed in him." She hesitated. "I don't think he's a bad person, Verna Lee, but he's not in your league."

Verna Lee shrugged. "I'm used to involvements with men who aren't in my league. That's why I'm single."

"Seriously. Is it over between you two?"

Verna Lee hesitated. "I wouldn't say it's over, exactly. But it has gone as far as it's going to go. Cliff knows that. We're fine the way we are."

Libby sighed with relief. "I was hoping he wouldn't be my brother-in-law."

Verna Lee laughed. "No chance of that. Good night, Libba Jane."

"Good night, Verna Lee."

Libby walked into the kitchen to rinse her cup. The porch light was on, the door was slightly ajar and she heard voices outside. Peering through the window, she saw Bailey and her daughter sitting on the top step. Chloe was talking.

"Aren't you scared to be completely on your own?"

Bailey's laugh was without humor. "Nothin'll ever scare me again."

"You know what I mean?"

"I won't be alone. Your granddad helped me find a room. It's near the art institute. If only I get accepted," he added.

"You'll get accepted," she assured him. "You'll be a famous artist and I'll say I knew you before you were discovered."

Bailey cleared his throat. "I won't forget you, Chloe. Meeting you has been the best thing that's ever happened to me. I don't know what I would have done without you and your family."

"Thank you," the girl said simply.

Libby smiled. She could learn something from her daughter about accepting compliments.

"Have you decided what you're doing?" Bailey asked.

Chloe nodded. "I'm going back to California."

"What about your mom?"

"I don't know," Chloe said slowly. "She'll probably come with me."

"You sound like you don't want her to?"

"I'd feel better if I thought she wanted to go, but I know she doesn't. It's hard wanting something so badly and knowing that if you get it, someone else will be miserable."

"Tell her."

"I will, but it won't matter. She won't let me go back by myself."

"What about Tess? I thought she was a good friend of yours."

"She is a good friend." Chloe sighed. "Everything is so complicated."

Libby tiptoed out of the kitchen and up the stairs to her room. She'd heard enough and she had a great deal to think about.

* * *

Russ threw the football in a perfect arc toward his daughter. Tess assumed the stance he'd taught her and caught it easily. Instead of throwing it back, she cradled it under her arm and walked across the lawn to meet her father.

"What's going on, honey?" he asked.

"Your heart's not in throwing a football, Daddy," she said. "You tell me what's going on."

Russ looked at the sky and then at the ground. "Want to go for a walk?"

She nodded and fell into step beside him.

They walked in silence for several minutes. Tess spoke first. "Does it have anything to do with Ms. Delacourte?"

Rush looked surprised. "Does it show?"

"You've been so happy lately," Tess said. "For a long time you weren't and now you are. It wasn't hard to figure out why. She's a nice lady. I like her."

"It doesn't matter," Russ said. "She's leaving with Chloe."

"Did you ask her to stay?"

Russ laid his hand on his daughter's head and ruffled her hair. She'd grown so tall. "I did, but Chloe wants to go home."

"Did you tell her you'd go with her?"

Russ looked surprised. "I hadn't considered it."

Tess stopped. "Why not?"

Russ kept walking. "I can't just pick up and move all the time, Tess. For one thing, you're here and my job is here. I'm tired of missing out on your life and I have to make a living." He refrained from explaining that a good part of his living he paid to her mother.

"What if I came to stay with you every summer?"

This time Russ stopped and turned back to look at Tess. "Would you do that, every summer and all long vacations?"

"I think I'd have to split the holidays, Daddy. It wouldn't

be fair otherwise, but I know I could come for Christmas or Easter and definitely all summer.''

Russ's mood was light. ''That puts a whole new spin on things,'' he said. ''But there's the fleet, and what if your mother won't agree? She hasn't exactly been accommodating.''

Tess shrugged. ''I don't see a whole lot of fishing going on right now, and Mom will agree if I tell her I want it that way. I didn't know you before, so it wasn't as important to me.'' Tess laughed. ''I don't think she's wild about having me around all the time.''

Russ laughed. ''You do have a mind of your own, Tess Hennessey. I like it. But I imagine your mama doesn't know what's come over you.''

''Well, will you?''

''Will I what?''

''Tell Ms. Delacourte you'll go with her.''

Russ's smile faded. ''There's more to it, Tess. Libba and I have known each other for a long time. She left me once before. It's possible she doesn't feel about me the way I do about her.''

''Have you asked her?''

''No,'' he said, exasperated. ''I don't think I should be discussing my love life with my fifteen-year-old daughter.''

Tess shook back her hair, handed the football back to her dad and stuck her hands in her pockets. ''It's your funeral, Daddy. You can do what you want, but I'd tell her.'' She blew him a kiss. ''I see Mom's car out in front. I have to go home.'' She ran toward the road. ''Call me,'' she shouted over her shoulder.

Chloe leaned on her elbow and picked at the threads of her comforter. Her silvery hair, longer now but still silky fine, fell across one shoulder. She looked up at Libby through her eyelashes. ''What are you saying, Mom?''

Libby caught her lower lip between her teeth. *Get a grip on yourself, Libba Jane.* She smiled bracingly. "I'm not going back to California with you."

Chloe frowned. "Why not?"

"I don't want to," Libby said. It felt good to say it. "I've spent seventeen years in California. That's long enough to know I prefer it here. I like small-town life. I like living close by my family. I like my job. I'm doing what I went to school for."

"And you like Russ Hennessey," Chloe finished for her.

Libby didn't miss the bitterness in her daughter's voice. "I thought you liked Russ," she said.

"I do." Chloe's chin quivered. "But I like Dad more."

"Oh, honey." Libby gathered her child in her arms, marveling at the slim, delicate bones and the long length of her. Where was the chubby-cheeked baby she remembered? "I'm so sorry it turned out this way for you. But your dad and I are finished. You're the only good thing that ever came out of that marriage and there won't be any going back."

"Are you going to marry Russ?"

"I haven't even come close to thinking about that. But if it happens, you'll be the first to know."

"If you aren't, why are you staying?"

"I told you why." There was more, but Libby wasn't talking. She knew Eric Richards better than her child did. She had given the matter a good deal of thought. Verna Lee had hit the nail dead center. If she took up residence in California, Eric would rely on her more and more until he assumed the same role he always had. Chloe's reason for going back would no longer exist and Libby would be stuck in the same place she'd been before she'd left six months before. "I'll be here whenever you want to visit. How about summers and vacations?"

"I like summers in California. This place is too hot."

Libby gently eased the golden head back on the pillow. "We'll work something out," she promised.

The living room was dark except for the glow of the fire and the lamp Nola Ruth used for reading. Libby watched her mother mark her place in the book with her finger before she looked up. "Is the child in bed?" she asked.

"Yes."

"Did you tell her you were staying?"

Libby rubbed her arms against the chill. "I told her."

"It's hard to lose a child," her mother remarked, "no matter what the circumstances."

Libby faced the fire. The heat was soothing. "I'm not losing Chloe, Mama. She's going to be with her father. I can see her whenever I want."

"There is that," her mother agreed. "Still, it'll be harder for you than for her."

"She won't be gone long."

Nola Ruth was quiet for a long time. Finally, she spoke. "Is there something you wanted, Libba Jane?"

"There is one thing."

"What is it?"

"When did giving up Verna Lee start to bother you? When did it become so unbearable that you had to make it right?"

Nola Ruth put her book aside. "Those are two questions, really. The first one is easy. It bothered me my whole life. I swore I'd make it up somehow, but it wouldn't be enough. I didn't know it then, but nothing would ever be enough to make up for what I did. As for your second question, I think it was after the stroke, when I first woke up. I knew I had to tell everyone who mattered what happened. I couldn't leave without righting a terrible wrong." She looked at her daughter. "I love Verna Lee. She's my child, just as you are, but I don't know her. I'll never know her the way I know you."

Libby rubbed her arms. "You didn't call me when I was in California, not once. Daddy did all the calling. Why is that, Mama? Didn't you miss me?"

Nola Ruth's good eye widened. "Good Lord, what have I done? You have no idea how hard it was for me not to reach for that phone time after time and *demand* that you come home. I didn't want to be like my father. I wanted you to come when you were ready. Now—" She lifted her hands and let them drop. "Now it's nearly too late and it no longer matters why you're here, just that you are. I won't be here for too much longer, Libba Jane. The doctor says I'm in a holding pattern, but that strokes repeat themselves fairly quickly. I'm so delighted and so grateful to spend the last of my life with you and with Chloe. Never doubt that, honey. Never doubt that I missed you terribly."

Unshed tears burned the insides of Libby's eyelids. *She knew. Somehow her mother knew what she was feeling.* Libby knelt down, buried her face in her mother's lap and closed her eyes.

Nola Ruth stroked her daughter's smooth head. "There, there, child," she murmured. "Go ahead and cry. It's all right, honey. Mama's little girl can't always take on the world by herself. Mama's right here."

Cole Delacourte, on the way to wheel his wife into her downstairs bedroom, stopped at the entrance to the living room. After assessing what he thought was a long-overdue meeting of the minds between his wife and his daughter, he backed out of the room and walked away. Now, if Nola Ruth's life was cut short, she would go without regret.

Fall was Libby's favorite season. Cold, crisp days and the final piercing brightness of sunlit afternoons before the chill gray of winter set in revived her spirits. Early in the morning when the boats moored out of the docks, frost lay on lawns and latticed windows, freezing bottled milk and shriveling the last vegetable pickings in summer gardens. Wools, smelling of mothballs and cedar, came out of closets, and rosy-cheeked children blew smoky breaths at one another with renewed energy, the indolence of summer gone for another year. It was a time for apple cider, hot cocoa and wood smoke, for Christmas shopping in Salisbury and wild duck on restaurant menus.

Chloe had been gone nearly three weeks. She talked to Libby on the phone every evening and planned to be back in Marshyhope Creek for Thanksgiving. Gradually, like marsh grass struggling to sprout through mud-thick ponds in search of sunlight, Libby began to adjust to life without her daughter. It was Russ she missed. He had disappeared after the trial, leaving Hennessey House closed and shuttered. She was hurt that he hadn't said goodbye or told her where he was going, but she couldn't really blame him, not after their last conversation.

Slowly, the fish count was rising in the bay. Watermen reported activity around the oyster beds, but Libby was skeptical. Oysters weren't like shad or blue gill. They needed time to reproduce, generations of time. Still, there was enough work to keep food on the table for most who depended on the water for a living. Once again, there were fall vegetables for sale at the farmers' market. Libby's favorite haunt was Drusilla Washington's booth. She had never seen vegetables like Drusilla's harvest. Golden squash and orange russets, huge tomatoes and the tenderest purple string beans she'd ever tasted. She brought home boxes of produce, stirring them into soups and stews, steaming and flavoring them the way Serena taught her. Even Nola Ruth, whose appetite was waning, was tempted by plates piled high with tender-crisp greens and salads filled with beets, cucumbers, scallions and mushrooms.

''The earth is forgivin', Miz Libba,'' said Drusilla. ''Jus' look at these here greens. One season later and they come back jus' as fresh and healthy as befo'.''

"Too bad it's not the same for people," Libby muttered.

Drusilla rolled her eyes and laughed, a deep rumbling sound that came from her belly. "Ya got some learnin' to do, Miz Libba. People is jus' like the soil. Ya got to give it some help now and then, tha's all, jus' like ya got to help people. Patience helps, too. The Lord wants us ta have patience."

"I've never been very good at that," Libby admitted.

The black woman's dark eyes gleamed like points of fire between the wrinkled folds of flesh. "Well now, seems ta me that knowin' what you need to work on is the first step."

Libby stuffed her bag into her bicycle basket and pedaled toward home, taking the short cut along the creek. For the first time since Bailey's trial she felt her spirits lift. Leaves brushed her cheeks and insects swarmed in airy circles around her head. She hadn't taken this route in years. Laughter bubbled up inside of her and spilled out. She would give Serena a night off and make spaghetti for dinner.

Her father sat in a chair on the porch. Someone was with him. Libby couldn't see who it was until he stepped out from behind a pillar and waved.

Life wasn't fair, was her first thought. Where was it written that a woman should hope and wait and want only one man for twenty long years? She brought the bike to a stop, swallowed and smiled brilliantly. "Hello, Russ. It's been quite a while. Are you staying for dinner?"

He hesitated. "I'd like to, if it's no trouble. Otherwise, I could take y'all out."

"It's no trouble." She stepped around him and walked through the door. "I'll start now."

Cole Delacourte looked thoughtfully after his daughter. There was something in her face that hadn't been there in a long time. The serenity she'd worked so long to achieve was gone, replaced by a wariness completely unlike the calm poise with which she faced the world. That wasn't exactly right, either. He couldn't describe it, he who was so good with words.

At dinner, around the banter of polite conversation, he watched her surreptitiously. A memory danced on the edge of his consciousness. She looked younger than usual and her eyes were very bright. Her responses were spontaneous and teasing and she smiled frequently. He was struck by the softness of her. Libba always seemed so competent, so sure of herself. *Soft* was a word he never used when describing his daughter. His memory sharpened and focused. Awareness dawned. She looked like Nola Ruth, but not the Nola Ruth who was now confined to her bedroom. It was the woman he'd first met that Libba resembled.

Tactfully, he excused himself as soon as dinner was over. "Since Serena's off, I'll do the dishes and look in on your mother," he said. "You two stay here and talk."

Libby looked up in surprise. "That's all right, Daddy. I'll do them."

Russ stood. "Libba and I will do them."

Silently, she rinsed plates and handed them to Russ. Just as silently, he stacked them neatly in the dishwasher and waited for the next one. After the last piece of silverware was put away and the counters wiped down, he spoke. "Is this a standoff, Libba Jane? Aren't you going to talk to me at all?"

She dried her hands and folded the dish towel. "You haven't said anything, either."

"Do you want to know why I'm back?"

She turned around and leaned against the counter, facing him, taking in the dark, archangel beauty of his face. "I assumed you had some time between trips and came to see Tess."

He grimaced. "I suppose I deserve that."

Libby frowned. "You aren't making sense, Russ. Has anything changed?"

"I read your article in the *Washington Post,*" he said softly. "You've done a good job here. I'm proud of you."

"Thank you." She smiled and his breathing altered. There was nothing in the world like Libba's smile. It had haunted his dreams for twenty years.

"All right," she said, laughing. "What brings you back to Marshyhope Creek? I thought you were done with us for good."

"You brought me back," he said softly.

"Oh?" She crossed her arms, wary once again.

Warning signals went off in Russ's brain, but he'd thought a long time and driven a long way to have her hear what he had to say. "There isn't anyone better than you," he began, and stopped. He couldn't even articulate. No one messed him up like Libba.

"And just exactly where did you research that very interesting opinion?" she asked calmly.

"Damn it, Libba, I can't even think when you're around." He searched his pockets for his cigarettes and remembered he left them on the porch. "Don't go away. I'll be right back."

Her heart pounded painfully in her chest. She reached for the chamomile tea, poured hot water into a cup and waited for it to steep. The sweet, golden liquid always soothed her. She dimmed the lights and sat down at the kitchen table to think. Her life was settled again. If there was no passion, there was contentment and stability, not a terrible compromise for a woman.

Libby believed in windows of opportunity. There was a window for learning to speak, for crawling, for becoming fluent in a foreign language, for balancing a hula hoop around your middle. Once the window closed, the opportunity was still possible but never as easily attained.

She looked down at the liquid in her cup. Slowly, she stood and walked out of the kitchen, down the hall to the glassed-in porch where she knew Russ would be smoking his cigarette.

He looked uneasy. The corners of her mouth turned up.

"Listen, Libba—"

She cut him off. "Nice night. We don't see too many of these this time of year."

He stared at her. "I know that. I grew up here, or don't you remember?"

"You haven't exactly been around on a regular basis," she retorted.

"I had to settle a few things in D.C. I thought you were going back to California with Chloe."

"No." She wrapped her arms around the pillar behind her and struggled to control her voice. "Do you still blame me for the way your life turned out?"

Russ looked out the window. "I don't blame you for anything. The problem—" He stopped and started again. "*My* problem is I love you and I can't seem to work things out between us. It's almost as if we've been hexed by that old voodoo woman at the market." He turned around. "You've changed and I don't know how to handle it. You're so damned bossy and independent I can't imagine you wanting to hook up with anybody at all, especially me. All I want, all I've ever wanted is to be with you, but honestly, Libba, I don't know if I can take it. You don't give an inch, and the truth is, I think you're a lot smarter than I'll ever be."

Libba was suddenly very tired of the misunderstanding between them. Someday she would tell him about those years in California, the years that would explain the changes in her, but not now, not when so much more stood between them. Slipping off her shoes, she walked across the porch to where he stood and slid her palms slowly up his chest. "You were saying?"

He pressed his lips against her throat. "You better not be

changing your mind," he muttered, "or this time I swear I'll wring your neck."

Bending his head, he nearly found her mouth when she pulled away, out of reach, his cigarettes in her hand.

"You can come in," she said in a breathy voice, "or you can go home. But the power's off at your house and we don't allow smoking in ours."

His laugh was warm and easy like the air around them. "What if I get the urge in the middle of the night?"

A smile started in her eyes and moved to her mouth. "It's been a long time, Russ Hennessey, and this is a big old house, but I'm sure you can still find your way to my room."

"What will I find in it, Libba?"

"A bossy, independent woman."

Russ hooked his fingers through the belt loops of her jeans and considered her answer.

Seconds passed. Libby held her breath.

"I'm open-minded," she heard him say. "I suppose I can take independent. I don't know about bossy, though."

Her heart pounded. "Maybe I could work on that."

Again, Russ said nothing for slow, agonizing seconds while he thought. Someday he would tell her about his years with Tracy, emasculating years when nothing he touched was his own. He would tell her why he needed words like *always* and *forever*. But not now, not when she was starting to let him in. She wasn't the Libba Delacourte of his youth. She was more than that, a careful, confident woman, a woman who knew her own mind, a woman who would take some getting used to.

He took the cigarettes from her hand and threw them on the table. Then he swung her into his arms. This was as good a time as any to start.